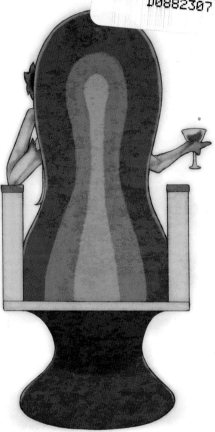

FUJINO OMORI

ILLUSTRATION BY
SUZUHITO YASUDA

© Suzuhito Yasuda

IS IT WRONG TO TRY TO PICK UP GIRLS IN A DUNGEON?

VOLUME 8

FUJINO OMORI

ILLUSTRATION BY SUZUHITO YASUDA

YEN ON

NEW YORK

IS IT WRONG TO TRY TO PICK UP GIRLS IN A DUNGEON?, Volume 8
FUJINO OMORI

Translation by Andrew Gaippe
Cover art by Suzuhito Yasuda

This book is a work of fiction. Names, characters, places, and incidents are the product of the author's imagination or are used fictitiously. Any resemblance to actual events, locales, or persons, living or dead, is coincidental.

DUNGEON NI DEAI WO MOTOMERU NO WA MACHIGATTEIRUDAROUKA vol. 8
Copyright © 2015 Fujino Omori
Illustrations copyright © 2015 Suzuhito Yasuda
All rights reserved.
Original Japanese edition published in 2015 by SB Creative Corp.
This English edition is published by arrangement with SB Creative Corp.,
Tokyo, in care of Tuttle-Mori Agency, Inc., Tokyo.

English translation © 2017 by Yen Press, LLC

Yen On
1290 Avenue of the Americas
New York, NY 10104

Visit us at yenpress.com
facebook.com/yenpress
twitter.com/yenpress
yenpress.tumblr.com
instagram.com/yenpress

First Yen On Edition: April 2017

Yen On is an imprint of Yen Press, LLC.
The Yen On name and logo are trademarks of Yen Press, LLC.

The publisher is not responsible for websites
(or their content) that are not owned by the publisher.

Library of Congress Cataloging-in-Publication Data
Names: Ōmori, Fujino, author. | Yasuda, Suzuhito, illustrator.
Title: Is it wrong to try to pick up girls in a dungeon? / Fujino Omori ; illustrated by Suzuhito Yasuda.
Other titles: Danjon ni deai o motomeru nowa machigatte iru darōka. English.
Description: New York : Yen ON, 2015– | Series: Is it wrong to try to pick up girls in a dungeon? ; 8
Identifiers: LCCN 2015029144 | ISBN 9780316339155 (v. 1 : pbk.) |
ISBN 9780316340144 (v. 2 : pbk.) | ISBN 9780316340151 (v. 3 : pbk.) |
ISBN 9780316340168 (v. 4 : pbk.) | ISBN 9780316314794 (v. 5 : pbk.) |
ISBN 9780316394161 (v. 6 : pbk.) | ISBN 9780316394178 (v. 7 : pbk.) |
ISBN 9780316394185 (v. 8 : pbk)
Subjects: | CYAC: Fantasy. | BISAC: FICTION / Fantasy / General. | FICTION / Science Fiction / Adventure.
Classification: LCC PZ7.1.O54 Du 2015 | DDC [Fic]—dc23
LC record available at http://lccn.loc.gov/2015029144

ISBNs: 978-0-316-39418-5 (paperback)
978-0-316-39423-9 (ebook)

13 5 7 9 10 8 6 4 2

LSC-C

Printed in the United States of America

VOLUME 8

FUJINO OMORI
ILLUSTRATION BY SUZUHITO YASUDA

BELL CRANELL

The hero of the story, who came to Orario (dreaming of meeting a beautiful heroine in the Dungeon) on the advice of his grandfather. He belongs to *Hestia Familia* and is still getting used to his job as an adventurer.

HESTIA

A being from the heavenly world of Tenkai, she is far beyond all mortals living on the lower world of Gekai. The head of Bell's *Hestia Familia*, she is absolutely head over heels in love with him!

AIZ WALLENSTEIN

Known as the Sword Princess Kenki, her combination of feminine beauty and incredible strength makes her Orario's best-known female adventurer. Bell idolizes her. Currently Level 6, she belongs to *Loki Familia*.

LILLILUKA ERDE

A girl belonging to a race of pygmy humanoids known as prums, she plays the role of supporter in Bell's battle party. A member of *Soma Familia*, she's much more powerful than she looks.

WELF CROZZO

A smith who fights alongside Bell as a member of his party, he forged Bell's light armor (Pyonkichi MK-V). Belongs to *Hestia Familia*.

MIKOTO YAMATO

A girl from the Far East. She feels indebted to Bell after receiving his forgiveness. Former member of *Takemikazuchi Familia* who now belongs to *Hestia Familia*.

HARUHIME SANJOUNO

A fox-person (renart) from the Far East who met Bell in Orario's Pleasure Quarter. Belongs to *Hestia Familia*.

EINA TULLE

A Dungeon adviser and a receptionist for the organization in charge of regulating the Dungeon, the Guild. She has bought armor for Bell in the past, and she looks after him even now.

CHARACTER & STORY

The Labyrinth City Orario——A large metropolis that sits over an expansive network of underground tunnels and caverns known as the "Dungeon." Bell Cranell came in hopes of realizing his dreams, joining *Hestia Familia* in the process. After being saved by the Sword Princess Aiz Wallenstein, he became infatuated with her and vowed to grow stronger. As he ventured into the Dungeon, he fought fierce battles beside the supporter Lilly, the smith Welf, and the Far East girl Mikoto, before the renart Haruhime joined their familia as well. It's another peaceful day for their home Orario. Even if the Kingdom of Rakia tries to march on the Labyrinth City…

TSUBAKI COLLBRANDE

A half-dwarf smith, she belongs to *Hephaistos Familia*. Currently at Level 5, Tsubaki is a terror on the battlefield.

BETE LOGA

A member of a race of animal people known as werewolves. He laughed at Bell's inexperience one night at The Benevolent Mistress. However, he recognized the boy's potential after witnessing Bell's battle with a Minotaur.

FINN DEIMNE

Known for his cool head, he is the commander of *Loki Familia*.

OTTAR

An extremely powerful member of *Freya Familia*.

SYR FLOVER

A waitress at The Benevolent Mistress. She established a friendly relationship with Bell after an unexpected meeting.

MIACH

The head of *Miach Familia*, a group focused on the production and sale of items.

HERMES

The head of *Hermes Familia*. A charming god who excels at toeing the line on all sides of an argument, he is always in the know. Is he keeping tabs on Bell for someone…?

TAKEMIKAZUCHI

The head of *Takemikazuchi Familia*.

CHIGUSA HITACHI

Another member of *Takemikazuchi Familia*.

MARIUS VICTRIX RAKIA

The crown prince of the Kingdom of Rakia, second-in-command of *Ares Familia* as well as Ares's right-hand man.

HEPHAISTOS

Welf's former goddess and the head of *Hephaistos Familia*. She has loose ties with Hestia dating back to their time in Tenkai.

LOKI

She leads Orario's most powerful familia and has a mysterious western accent. Loki is particularly fond of Aiz.

RIVERIA LJOS ALF

High elf and vice commander of the most prominent familia in Orario, *Loki Familia*.

FREYA

Goddess at the head of *Freya Familia*. Her stunning allure is strong enough to enchant the gods themselves. She is a true "Goddess of Beauty."

ALLEN FROMEL

A cat person who belongs to *Freya Familia*.

LYU LEON

An elf and former adventurer of extraordinary skill, she currently works as a bartender and waitress at The Benevolent Mistress.

NAHZA ERSUISU

The sole member of *Miach Familia*. She gets extremely jealous of other women who approach her god.

ASFI AL ANDROMEDA

A very gifted creator of magical items. She belongs to *Hermes Familia*.

OUKA KASHIMA

The captain of *Takemikazuchi Familia*.

ARES

The ruler of the Kingdom of Rakia (aka *Ares Familia*). He wields power equal to that of the king.

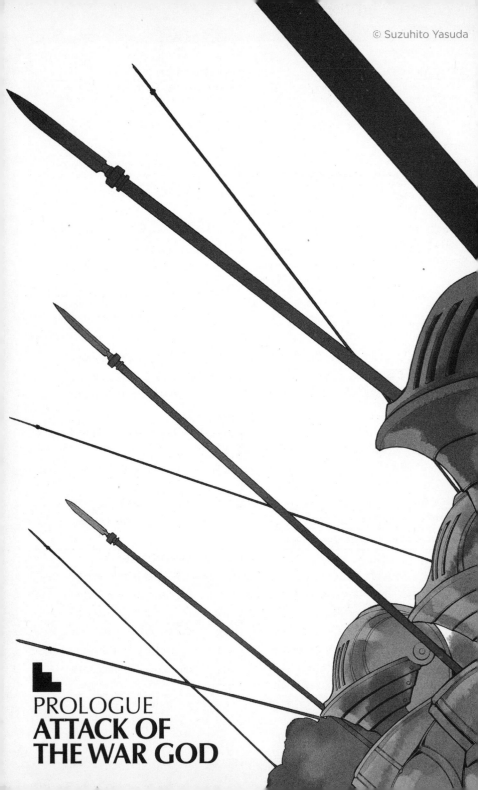

© Suzuhito Yasuda

PROLOGUE
**ATTACK OF
THE WAR GOD**

—The Kingdom of Rakia's army is advancing.

That news spread like wildfire through neighboring nations.

Warriors clad in thick metal plates, as well as thousands of armored horses, traveled beneath partly cloudy skies, ranks of spearheads glinting. Many merchants and travelers caught a glimpse of them in long columns as they passed beyond the outer limits of their territory.

The Kingdom of Rakia.

A monarchy that was situated on the western side of the main continent. It was said that at least 600,000 people currently lived under its rule. A large castle loomed at the center of its largest settlement, complete with its own castle town surrounding it. Lush and green, Rakia possessed a great deal of fertile land but very little culture, its people living under constant martial law.

Everything went according to their king's wishes, which were one and the same as their only god's divine will.

Ares, the God of War. He sat at the very top of Rakia and controlled every part of the country.

Ultimately, the Kingdom of Rakia was actually much like the many other familias but on a completely different scale of size and complexity, operating as its own country.

Every Rakian soldier had been blessed with Ares's Falna. The subjects of Rakia who were tasked with running the industries of the kingdom were the equivalent of noncombatant members of other familias. Being the one and only deity, Ares had chosen its king—the leader of the familia—throughout the country's history.

A familia that started with Ares and only a handful of followers had overcome many struggles to become its own country and now stood as a powerful nation with a rich history.

Due to their god's love for war, the Kingdom of Rakia had been the aggressor in many wars over the centuries. But the idea that this conflict was caused by Ares's warmongering was solely the opinion of the other nations watching these events from the outside.

The advancing troops numbered around 30,000.

This army was once called invincible when armed with a certain type of magic sword, and now their target lay even farther to the west, on the periphery of the continent. A city that held the world's only Dungeon and had therefore come to be known as the "Center of the World": Orario.

High walls and a white tower that looked tall enough to pierce the heavens appeared on the horizon. The heavy footsteps of fully armored warriors drew ever closer. The plate armor that encompassed their bodies was decorated with an extravagant, larger-than-life emblem as crimson-red flags rippled in the air.

It wasn't long before the army advancing straight west entered the lands surrounding the city.

Rakia's army arrived unannounced on their doorstep, but inside the city itself—.

"You won't believe your eyes! An entire dodobass for only two thousand valis! That's right, two thousand valis!"

"From weapon repairs to custom orders, we do it all!"

"Would someone please join my familiaaaaaaaaaaa?!"

"Excuse me, young elf maiden. I see you're an adventurer. Please accept this potion as a gift from me. It would be tragic for your beautiful face to be burdened with a scar."

"Th-thank you…!"

"Miach's making girls fall for him without realizing it again…!"

""""It's Miach, what do you expect?""""

—Nothing was different.

No citizen of Orario showed even the slightest concern. The sky over the city was bright and clear, as opposed to the dark clouds approaching from the east.

Amid their normally busy days, there was one thought that they all shared during the time before Rakia's arrival:

Ahh, it's happening again...

While the citizens were going about their daily lives inside the city walls, yells echoing from outside the wall signaled that the battle had begun.

The cries of horses were thunderous.

But that sound was drowned out almost immediately by thousands of hooves slamming into the dirt as they charged across the plains.

The open grassy field expanded thirty kirlos east of Orario. Thousands of red flags whipped about in the air as the soldiers carrying them raced forward.

It's said that knights are the roses of the battlefield. Armed with lances and shining armor, mounted on horses as heavily armored as their riders, the knights charged forward, trampling everything in their path. The tips of their weapons thrust forward, their formation could carve a path through any battlefield.

A wall of silver lances raced across the plain, the weapons glistening in the sunlight.

It was a sight that would make any foot soldier on the same battlefield weak in the knees. But—this particular unit of cavalry was shaking in terror.

The color drained from their faces beneath their helmets.

Every set of eyes was wide open and locked on the single dwarf who stood in their path. Every muscle in his stout figure bulged beneath layers of thick armor. A cape hung from his shoulders.

His helmet sat low over his eyes. An incredibly large battle-ax rested on his shoulder, just waiting for action.

The dwarf swung the ax into position the moment echoes of the horses' hooves reached his ears. Then, as soon as the cavalrymen came within ten meders of his position, he charged out to meet them head-on.

Holding the ax out to his right, the dwarf tensed every muscle in his body to bring it forward.

"Ngahhh!"

A moment later, the "invincible cavalry" was launched skyward.

"GAHHHHHHHHHHHHHHHHHHHHHHHHHHHHHHHHHHHHH!"

Airborne knights and horses dotted the horizon. The unbelievable spectacle could be seen from all around the open plain.

Tears fell from the knights' eyes as their helmets and pieces of their armor fell away from their bodies in midair. What's worse, the expressions on their now-exposed faces revealed they knew full well this was going to happen. Screams of agony filled the air as they fell to the ground, crashing down one by one next to their horses and scraps of broken metal.

The next wave of knights halted their charge in the face of the thrashing, but the group farther back didn't notice in time and plowed straight into them. Both the second and third ranks of knights fell off from their mounts into stunned disarray.

The dwarf—*Loki Familia*'s Gareth Landrock—watched the opposing soldiers fall over one another and sighed to himself.

"Dammit, Finn…pushin' this job on me."

Two more companies of knights arrived on the battlefield but hadn't learned from their allies' mistake. Gareth didn't even bother to sigh again as he lifted his battle-ax back onto his shoulder. The new arrivals charged in, only to meet the same fate. Once again, the bodies of horses and people alike decorated the skyline, their tears sparkling in their wake.

Orario's top-tier adventurer Gareth Landrock.

Having reached Level 6, his prowess and skill with an ax were known the world over.

Facing him in battle were companies of mostly Level 1 knights from the Kingdom of Rakia. Their captains might have been Level 2 but no higher.

In terms of experience in strength, tactics, techniques, and the difference in Level, Gareth was too powerful for them to overcome.

The Knights of Rakia now knew exactly how reckless their attack had been.

—The days when overwhelming numbers could win in war, especially in battles between people, were coming to an end.

In the current Divine Era, "quality over quantity" reigned supreme.

The presence of one incredibly strong individual—a warrior who carried the Blessing of a deity—had the ability to turn the tide of any battle. It had been said that a small group of warriors with a leveled-up Status could take on hundreds, even thousands of enemy troops and come out victorious.

Should a Blessed person's Status reach Level 6 in today's world, they would be on par with, or even exceed, the ferocious monsters that had rampaged through the world during the Ancient Times.

In other words, this dwarf—at least in the eyes of Rakia's Knights—was no different from a dragon in the days of old.

It was also true that an army that lacked a hero could never hope to slay a dragon.

The battle that unfolded was not much different from what happened to those armies in stories of heroes or fairy tales: The lone dwarf mowed down the hapless knights with little resistance. There was no way for the mounted soldiers to continue the battle.

"Tione, sound the gong. The retreating battalion is a feint. Circle around so that it's trapped between friendly forces."

"You got it!"

"Also, that hill over there…There's a squad of magic users firing on top of it. Tiona, tell *Ganesha Familia* to surround and take them out without being seen."

"Sure, sure…Delivering messages is such a drag."

Screams of pain reached all corners of the battlefield, even to the clearing a good distance away from the nightmarish scene unfolding at the hands of Gareth Landrock.

The prum Finn Deimne, field general of *Loki Familia*, had a spear in his grasp as he kept a keen eye on several unfolding battles from well behind the front lines. He was quick to issue orders.

Orario had no choice but to meet Rakia's invading army of 30,000 on the battlefield. The Guild had issued a mission—a sweeping order for specific familias residing in the city to stop the Rakian advance before it reached the city wall.

Their enemy had chosen to overwhelm them with numbers from the start. Therefore, this makeshift alliance of Orario's forces had chosen Finn as its commander. As someone who was in charge of the familia that led the way in clearing the Dungeon, someone who possessed the insight and ingenuity to deal with unexpected Irregular monsters and who was famous for his leadership skills, Finn was ideal for the position on this battlefield. Even now, he was analyzing enemy movements and guiding the flow of battle.

"General, some familias aren't listening to us...especially *Freya Familia*."

"Our forces are just a loosely bound coalition of many smaller groups, but we don't have to be the most efficient of shepherds. Just give them a direction and let them be. I highly doubt *Freya Familia* is worth worrying about."

"Finn, there are reports that more enemy reinforcements are arriving from the east. What are your orders?"

"Hmm...I'm a bit more concerned about the forest to the north. Riveria, I hate to ask you, but would you take Aiz and that group up in that direction? It's probably the main army."

The prum issued orders to his slightly dejected subordinate and a high elf magic user. A quick lick of his right thumb let Finn predict what was about to happen next and provided clues to the enemy's strategy.

Many different familias, not just *Loki Familia*, were busy engaging Rakia's forces on several different fronts around the battlefield. Orario's adventurers were making quick work of their opponents. It was as if the mythical Hydra were standing in the clearing, with each of its many heads working independently as Orario's Alliance tore through Rakia's advancing ranks.

"How very boring…"

"Yeah, an' there's so much waitin' for me to do back home…"

Farther back from Finn's command station, the gods and goddesses of the summoned familias watched from the top of a hill as the battle unfolded.

A tent and chair had been prepared for each of them. Sitting beneath the most elaborate canvas and drinking wine in her equally fancy chair was Freya. Meanwhile, Loki sat cross-legged in her own chair under the next tent over. Both of them watched the incredibly one-sided battle while complaining that they had nothing to do.

"It was over the moment they mounted their horses, don't you agree?"

"The kiddos with higher Statuses are still faster anyway. Don't know if they're tryin' to look cool or somethin', but it's like tellin' everyone their Statuses have a lot of growin' left to do."

There wasn't even a hint of tension among the deities sitting under the tents. Their thoughts on this battle were similar to their followers'.

The only other beings around the gods and goddesses were a few members serving as a private guard. The flags of each familia waved in the breeze next to the tents of their god. *Loki Familia*'s and *Freya Familia*'s flags—which also had a strong presence on the battlefield and among the adventurers—particularly stood out. The sight of Loki's Trickster and Freya's Warrior Maiden emblems sent waves of fear through Rakia's soldiers.

As a result, the soldiers' coordinated movements became sluggish as their will to fight vanished. Even their charges lacked enthusiasm. The very presence of those symbols dealt a serious blow to the invading army's morale.

"Puttin' it another way, us not bein' here would put a li'l more pep in their step…Haa! Havin' the title of 'best' is such a pain in the ass."

"It's too late to complain now."

Loki leaned back in her chair with her arms crossed behind her head. Freya watched her out of the corner of her eye, chuckling to herself.

"Oh, and by the way…Did you hear there hasn't been one casualty among Rakia's forces? How is that possible?"

"Ain't got much choice, not with all the merchants tellin' 'em not to kill their payday."

Loki sounded vaguely annoyed while answering Freya's question.

Looking out across the plain and hearing the pandemonium of shrieks and groans, it was obvious that Orario's adventurers had been striking with the blunt edges of their weapons.

"That and I don't want the kiddos in my familia dirtyin' their hands with this pretend 'war.'"

"That's true as well."

Loki fought back a yawn as the two goddesses made light of the farce unfolding before them.

"Ares, ya idiot, don't attack an opponent ya know you can't beat. You're gonna lose a lot more than ya bargained for," mumbled the vermilion-haired goddess as her line of sight moved from battle to battle.

"Hey there, fine soldier! If you buy right now, a potion brewed right here in Orario can be yours for just a thousand valis!"

Injured soldiers were carried into Rakia's forward camp one after another, and *business was booming.*

Countless tents had been raised in straight rows. The cries of the injured were relentless as they lay on their backs in shade the tents provided. At the same time, noncombatant demi-humans and deities were strutting around the camp.

Orario's mercantile familias saw an amazing business opportunity and swooped in to sell their wares.

"Doesn't that hurt? Isn't the pain unbearable? Don't you want to heal that wound right away?"

"Y-yes, I do…"

"Excellent! Let's make a deal!"

A few of Orario's deities stood over the badly wounded soldiers, smiling and dangling potions for sale just out of the soldiers' reach.

Indeed, these deities were selling not only to their own forces but to enemy troops as well. Their entrepreneurial spirits knew no bounds. They'd found a market and were going to take advantage of it.

"No one can fight with a broken weapon! Come and buy a new one!"

"I'll accept a trade!"

"Ba-ha-ha-ha-ha-ha! How do you like that, Miach? My goods are selling like there's no tomorrow! Looks like I win this one, too, wouldn't you say, Amid?"

"No, Lord Dian Cecht. Lord Miach and his familia are not here."

"What was that?! Chickened out, eh, Mi-aaaaaaaaaaaach?"

Weapons, armor, and even magic swords changed hands.

It was all a simple case of supply and demand, and the fact that Orario hadn't taken the slightest bit of damage meant that demand was overwhelming. Merchants were champing at the bit. Orario's adventurers had completely destroyed Rakia's supply lines and means of communication; these soldiers had no choice but to buy. The commanding officers could not go against the will of their god Ares, and so they cried rivers of tears watching a fortune disappear.

"Tsk, no real men anywhere...All the good ones must be commanding officers."

"Aisha! There're some really hunky knights a few rows over! It's time to feast!"

"W-wait right there, Samira! Right behind you!"

A few of the prostitutes from the Pleasure District had also come to the camp. Not belonging to any familia, the "free" beauties also came to conduct business. They offered services to some of the warriors, but as soon as the fearsome Amazons found a knight who met their standards, they "devoured" him on the spot. Every so often the wails of pleasure would break through the continuous moans of pain and despair.

With nothing to keep them in check, what was once Rakia's camp for the assault on Orario had become little more than a playground for the economic ambitions of the city's citizens and deities.

"A-a report from the front! Battalions one through five have been wiped out, and our front lines are retreating in an all-out rout across the board. The enemy seems to have predicted all our strategic ploys, as each one ended in failure…"

"C-curse theeeeeem…!!"

—A god sitting under a tent at the very rear of Rakia's forces clenched his fist in anger.

With golden hair as thick as a lion's mane, the deity was clad in stark red armor. His masculine and robust features would rival those of a male God of Beauty, the epitome of manliness.

He was none other than the instigator of this war, the true leader of the Kingdom of Rakia—and the familia's god: Ares.

He ground his teeth together as he listened to the messenger's report, his immaculate face warping into a frown.

"The forward camp has been overrun by Orario's greedy scum! Swindled by Amazonian prostitutes, our soldiers' morals have been thrown to the wayside…Morale is at an all-time low!!"

"Orario————! How cowardly, to use such underhanded tactics!!"

Ares's face flushed so red that it matched his armor. If Loki were there, she would be quick to hit him with a one-liner such as, "Ya think we'd do somethin' like that, blockhead?" Just the thought of it filled Ares with even more rage.

The god himself would call it his innate urge to fight, but the people around him would refer to it as recklessness.

Other deities described him as having 100 percent muscle between the ears. The young man currently at his side took one look at his god's infuriated state and let out a big sigh. His shoulders dropped as he shook his head from side to side, obviously tired of seeing it.

This was the god of the military, otherwise known as the God of War: Ares.

He might have been a god of battle, but he did not control victory.

An air of defeat had already filled the tent of commanding

officers. All of them fell silent. Only Ares's cries of rage echoed into the distance.

"Are you sure there's no scheme you want to put into motion?"

As a particular god was roaring in frustration...

A white cape danced in the breeze on top of Orario's city wall far from the battlefield, as the beautiful young woman Asfi, leader of *Hermes Familia*, asked her god a question.

Her god was leaning against the chest-high guard wall and watching a pillar of smoke, most likely the result of Magic, rise in the distance. He didn't move as he answered.

"Even if I did find a way to *introduce* Bell to Ares..."

The breeze ruffled Hermes's orange hair as his delicate smile thinned. He had to hold down his traveler's hat to keep it from being blown off his head.

"That's not to say doing so wouldn't make for a great show...but I'm a bit scared of how Lady Freya would react, for obvious reasons."

"...Has there been any communication from her or her familia since then?"

"Why, no. But that's the scariest thing. Her silence is her way of warning me that there won't be a next time."

The frenzy after the incident that took place in the Pleasure Quarter was starting to die down. However, that didn't mean the dandy god could do anything he wanted for just a little entertainment when it came to *Freya Familia*. Hermes closed his mouth and turned to his follower.

"The annihilation of a familia is no laughing matter," said Asfi with a stern glare.

"I know," responded Hermes with a shrug.

"I had a few words with the Guild and made sure that there's no way the Mission will come knocking at Hestia's door. Those children have been wrapped up in one incident after another recently; it's time they had a chance to relax and live a little."

Leaning with his back against the guard wall, Hermes looked up into the clear blue sky.

*   *   *

"K-Kenki?!"

"It's the Sword Princess!!"

"RUN AWAAAAAAAAAAAAAAAAAAAAAAAAAAAAY!!"

It was on the northern edge of the plain where the battle was taking place. A female knight had appeared in the line of sight of a small force staging an ambush at the perimeter of the forest. In that moment, every single one of the ambushers lost their will to fight.

Their commander yelled at the top of his lungs, trying to rally his troops, but it was in vain. The foot soldiers threw down their weapons and ran back into the forest as fast as their legs could carry them.

"That was to be expected."

"Dammit, Aiz, that's why we told you to stay in the back of the formation. Now we gotta go round them up. Gahh…"

"…"

Aiz stood ready for a fight, sword in hand. But her shoulders sank and her mouth shut tight as soon as she heard the words of Riveria and the werewolf Bete.

With golden eyes and blond hair, Aiz stood out like a sore thumb and was easily identifiable even in a large battle. Rakia's soldiers feared the girl who had once slain a floor boss in the Dungeon by herself. Aiz watched them disappear into the forest with an aloof expression on her face but was actually feeling a little depressed.

"Aiz, do not stand idle. Pursue. We cannot allow any harm to come to the surrounding villages."

"…Yes."

"Let's get this over with and head back to Orario. Being out here is a waste of time."

Riveria and Bete led the other members of *Loki Familia* and charged into the forest. Aiz joined them in chasing the panicked figures darting through the trees.

Directly to the southwest, a white tower tall enough to pierce the heavens stood as it normally did on any other day.

*   *   *

This attack by Rakian forces would become known as "The Sixth Orario Invasion."

Life went on as normal for the citizens of the Labyrinth City in spite of this war being drawn out longer than usual. Several small, unnoticed stories unfolded between deities and their followers.

CHAPTER **1** LOVE SONG TO A GOD OF MARTIAL ARTS

"So, here's where you were, Mikoto."

She saw it in a dream.

The air was cool on her skin as she sat on the roots of the withering tree.

Her younger self hugged her knees to her chest beneath its shade. That's when she knew it was not a dream but a memory.

"What's wrong? Are you hungry?"

The young Mikoto buried her face in her knees. She didn't look up even though Takemikazuchi—looking exactly as he did nowadays, with the exact same loops of hair hanging on either side of his face like bobbed ponytails—was calling out to her.

They were in her hometown in the Far East, behind the shrine in which they used to live. Their voices hung in the air.

"…Lord Takemikazuchi."

The little girl's voice came out from between her knees; she still refused to look up.

Takemikazuchi leaned down in front of her, patiently waiting until she opened her mouth once again.

"Why don't I have a mommy or daddy…?"

Because I'm an orphan.

The current Mikoto could answer that question right away.

Disasters, plagues, and monsters.

It wasn't all that uncommon for children in the Far East to lose their parents and be left all alone. Actually, Mikoto was one of the lucky ones, since she had been taken in by a shrine where gods like Takemikazuchi resided.

—They had taken her to see a lively town festival.

—Or perhaps it had been a port with ships in dry dock; maybe the big city.

She had been among friends like Ouka and Chigusa along with

the gods and goddesses, but all Mikoto saw at that time were parents playing with happy children. It left her with a feeling of desolation, and she couldn't take it anymore.

"…The mother and father who gave birth to you, Mikoto, left you in our care and went on a journey to the great beyond."

"Will I…ever see them again…?"

"Well…They might not return to this world while you are still alive."

It might be tens, hundreds of years before her parents' souls were reborn.

Mikoto had been too young to understand the full meaning of Takemikazuchi's words at the time. The only thing she clearly understood was she would never see them again. She squeezed her legs even closer to her body.

"Are you lonely?"

The young Mikoto couldn't move her head up and down or left and right.

She only tightened her grip on her arms, fingers digging deep into her skin as if she was desperately trying to keep something contained within that threatened to overflow.

Takemikazuchi kneeled next to the girl as her body began to shake.

Suddenly, he lifted her high into the air as if she were light as a feather.

Mikoto raised her face, surprised by the sudden burst of light coming in from under her arms. She looked at the deity beneath her.

"Mikoto, become my daughter."

Takemikazuchi's smiling face was reflected in the girl's wide, tearful eyes.

"Huh…?"

"Someday I shall bestow you with my Falna. Once that is done, we will share a bond of blood like a true family——a familia."

"Family…familia."

His words didn't just sound sweet, they provided warmth to a girl whose soul was filled with nothing but pain.

It was because she could see a tenderness in Takemikazuchi's eyes that was reserved for a parent beholding their child. He continued to hold her high above his head like a proud father would for his daughter.

"Pain dwells in spirit, and spirit dwells in the body—that's my theory. So I will teach you so many martial arts that your body and spirit won't have time to feel loneliness. Be at ease, Mikoto, and be ready," said Takemikazuchi to the stunned young Mikoto. Then, he smiled at her with childlike innocence. "Mikoto, what did you want to do with your mother and father?"

He then told her to speak from her heart with the same tenderness in his eyes.

"I...I wanted a piggyback ride from Daddy."

"I'll do that right now. Anything else?"

"S-sleeping next to one another in the futon at night so that we don't get lonely."

"Okay, tonight we shall. Is there anything else?"

"I wanted to eat *konpeitou*, that candy we saw in the city the other day!"

"A-all right. Leave it to me."

An earnest request for high-quality, colorful sweets brought a smile to Takemikazuchi's face.

Despite their shrine being incredibly poor, Takemikazuchi would bring her, Ouka, Chigusa, and the other children into the city and fulfill his promise only days later.

Child and deity, dressed in little more than rags, exchanged looks of affection and endearment.

"But it's okay if you'd rather be in Tsukuyomi's familia if you don't want to be in mine—"

"I want yours, Lord Takemikazuchi!!"

Young Mikoto's loud voice interrupted the deity.

Her little cheeks blushing pink, she kept her dark-violet gaze fixed directly on him.

"...Okay then."

Takemikazuchi blinked a few times before he finally smiled at her. He set the young girl back on the ground and ruffled her hair.

Mikoto squeezed her eyes tight as his fingers tickled. One last tear ran down her cheek.

She then climbed up on his back and the two of them went to rejoin Ouka, Chigusa, and the others who had been searching for her. Both the god and the girl smiled as their friends came to meet them.

From that day on, Takemikazuchi became her father, and Mikoto was surrounded with love.

And at some point, her love for him became something a little bit more special.

" "
...

Mikoto slowly opened her eyes.

Beams of soft light coming through the window and chirping birds outside let her know that night had come to an end.

She stared at the ceiling above, feeling light with nostalgia because of the dream. It didn't take long for her to realize that she was smiling, too.

As even more memories flowed forward to fill her mind, she started to climb out of her futon. *Zzz. Zzz. Zzz.*

The sound of someone else still sleeping reached her ears.

Looking to the side, she saw a renart girl—Haruhime—sleeping on her back in a futon next to hers.

Mikoto's lips once again softly curled up into another smile. The events surrounding *Ishtar Familia* had caused many trials and tribulations, but it was thanks to them that she had been reunited with her childhood friend from the Far East. Careful not to wake her up, Mikoto brushed a few stray golden hairs out of the sleeping girl's eyes and softly stroked her fox ears.

They were in a room of *Hestia Familia*'s home, the Hearthstone Manor.

Mikoto and Haruhime, both entering the familia by Conversion, had been given two rooms to themselves on the third floor.

There was no bed in this room, and the abundance of items from the Far East clashed with the continent style and design of the architecture. An open-frame closet stood in the corner with many colorful kimonos and Far East–style battle cloths draped across it.

Leaving her dream behind, Mikoto's attention shifted from the familiar shrine she once called home to the place she lived in now.

She took another look at the sleeping face of the girl she'd been fortunate enough to reunite with after all these years, before returning her gaze to the window that grew brighter by the moment.

"…On with the day!"

She stretched in the early morning light.

"Lady Haruhime, may I ask you to set the table?"

"Y-yes, of course!"

Delicious smells wafted their way through the manor's dining room.

Mikoto, with her long black hair tied back and an apron tight around her waist, was hard at work in the kitchen right next door. Several fishes were cooking over an open flame as she stirred a pot with a wooden spoon.

The clangs and crackles of her breakfast preparation mixed with the *tap, tap, tap* of Haruhime's feet as she busily traipsed back and forth between the kitchen and the dining room with food and utensils in her arms.

"Lady Haruhime, you need not push yourself so hard…"

"Oh, no, no. I have been accepted as a member of this familia. Please allow me to do this much, Miss Mikoto."

Haruhime was currently wearing a maid's outfit rather than her usual kimono.

Lilly had been wanting a housekeeper of some kind, and Haru-hime was quick to volunteer—"Please give me a job to do!"—the moment she arrived.

Born into nobility and having spent five years living in a brothel, she had very little experience with cleaning or serving others. However, she was quite eager to learn, and she now wore a black blouse with a white apron, her fluffy golden tail swishing her skirt back and forth. Mikoto was glad to have her help.

Orario's Alliance and the forces of the Kingdom of Rakia were clashing at this very moment.

Hestia Familia had not been summoned to the front because they didn't have enough members to qualify. Therefore, today was a peaceful day like any other.

"Whoa, that smells good…"

"So today was Mikoto's turn? That's why it's good."

"Ah, Sir Bell, Lady Hestia. Good morning."

Mikoto sampled her soup as she greeted the human boy and the goddess poking their heads in the doorway.

All members of *Hestia Familia* took turns preparing food each day. As long as nothing drastic had happened, typically two or three people, including their goddess, would prepare the dining room for a meal.

Some type of grilled meat or other flame-roasted "manly food" was typically on the menu on days Welf was in charge. Lilly, however, would find ways to put food on the table while saving as much money as possible. Everyone's specialties and personalities came through in their cooking, but it was only on days that Mikoto prepared the food that the entire familia unanimously agreed it was delicious.

She had developed her skills from a young age alongside Chigusa and the other girls at the shrine, turning whatever ingredients she could find into something palatable. Her combination of seriousness and skill came together to create dishes that even Hestia, obsessed as she was with Jyaga Maru Kun potato puffs, couldn't help but enjoy.

"Um, Miss Mikoto, the brown soup in this pot...What is it?"

"It's called *miso* soup."

Bell peeked over the rim of the pot as Mikoto happily answered.

It was a traditional soup from her homeland that combined fish stock with a spice called *miso*. Normally, Mikoto prepared meals using bread and ingredients easily found in Orario to match her allies' tastes. However, she thought it might be fun to make *miso* soup for the first time in a while after finding the spice at a marketplace a few days before.

She explained it was a specialty of her homeland, a taste she grew up with. Then she gave them both a spoonful of the mysterious "brown soup." Bell and Hestia looked back up, appearing pleasantly surprised.

"The flavor is...I don't know, relaxing."

"Yeah, this isn't half bad. So, this is what children from your hometown would call soul food?"

Mikoto couldn't be happier that her friends could enjoy flavors from her homeland.

Bell and Hestia smiled, continuing to shower her with compliments.

"Miss Mikoto, you're a really good cook."

"Yep, some guy's going to be really lucky to have you as his bride."

Then, all the color vanished from Mikoto's face the moment Hestia uttered those words.

"B-bride?!"

The ghostly white was quickly replaced by burning red as the girl shook her hands and fiercely denied everything.

"Wh-what could you possibly mean, Lady Hestia?! I'm still too immature to even be considered worthy of becoming a bride——Ah-ha-ha-ha-ha-ha-ha!"

"Miss Mikoto, the knife! The knife!"

"That's dangerous!"

Beet-red and laughing, Mikoto completely forgot about the sharp utensil still in her clutches as she vigorously waved off Hestia's words.

Hestia and Bell panicked and desperately tried to ward off her inadvertent attack.

The morning excitement and breakfast came to a close.

Hestia left to go to her part-time job while the others finished cleaning up. Mikoto put away the last dishes and went to join her allies already gathered in the living room.

"H-here you are…" Haruhime's hands visibly shook as she cautiously placed a cup of tea in front of Bell. He forced a smile as she sat down at the table and their morning meeting began.

"Today, Lilly would like to discuss whether or not to bring Miss Haruhime with us into the Dungeon…"

Lilly took charge of the proceedings as all eyes around the table turned to the renart sitting next to Mikoto.

Still wearing her maid outfit, Haruhime curled her golden tail nervously behind her.

"To be frank, Lilly would like her to join us under any conditions. The incredible strength her Magic provides us doesn't need to be explained."

"But Lady Lilly, we can ill afford to have the effects of Lady Haruhime's Magic be revealed to others…"

"Of course. But even so, Miss Haruhime's presence will be a valuable asset to our party. Each one of us will be safer for it. As long as steps are taken to limit and conceal the casting of her Magic, Lilly is in favor of bringing Miss Haruhime into the Dungeon."

Haruhime's Magic, *Uchide no Kozuchi*, instantly boosted the target's Level.

While she couldn't cast it on herself, the ability to make another adventurer level up for a period of time was very rare. This renart sorcery had nearly cost her her life at the hands of *Ishtar Familia* as a central piece of their plot. Should word of her Magic spread, it was almost a certainty that many would try to recruit her to assist in their own dark ambitions.

But at the same time, a jewel that never sees the light of day is doomed to collect dust. Lilly's argument was sound. As long as they were careful, the advantages of having her in the party were too great to be ignored. Lilly's opinion carried considerable weight because she had become the "brain" of the familia.

The men in the room listened to Lilly and Mikoto's argument—Bell wasn't sure whose side to take; Welf decided on a more forward approach and asked Haruhime directly.

"What did you do when you were with Ishtar? Did they ever take you into the Dungeon?"

"I was among them, participating in routine activities as well as the occasional venture deep into the Dungeon...However, I was either forced to ride with the cargo or completely protected during battle..."

"..."

"I have never faced a monster in combat..."

With the exception of Magic, all the Basic Abilities in her Status were below that of the group's supporter, Lilly. Since she never had to fend for herself, Haruhime couldn't be counted on to hold her ground when push came to shove. No one questioned that she could be a liability in battle.

Haruhime couldn't say anything in her defense and stared down at the table. Welf and Lilly looked upon the renart girl with pity.

"...So what's the call? Have her hold down the fort while we're gone?"

Welf suggested to have Haruhime stay inside the manor, like a real maid would.

Mikoto looked to Bell almost out of reflex.

Though imperfect, he was the leader, and Mikoto wanted to know the feelings of the boy who had once risked everything to save her friend.

"...I made a promise to Aisha. I don't know what the best decision is right now, but whether we take Miss Haruhime into the Dungeon or not...I will...protect her."

He started to blush as his words trailed off toward the end, but his position was clear.

Haruhime also turned a shade of pink as Bell fell silent. Lilly, however, was not amused. As for Mikoto, her expression grew brighter by the moment.

The white-haired human boy couldn't look at anyone, his eyes shifting between the floor and ceiling. Welf grinned at him and gave him a brotherly slap on the back. It wasn't long before all eyes returned to Haruhime.

It was up to her to make the final decision.

"...I shall accompany you. I, Haruhime, would like to become an asset to the battle party."

A few heavy moments passed before the girl spoke up and made her wishes known.

She looked at Mikoto and Bell, determination radiating from her green eyes.

"B-because I am...a member of this familia."

Her gaze fell back to the table as all confidence left her voice.

Bell, Welf, and Lilly exchanged glances and smiles before looking back at their newest ally, who was anxiously fidgeting next to the living room table. Her golden fox tail never came to a rest as her cheeks turned a slightly darker shade of pink. Even Mikoto was smiling from ear to ear and said nothing against the consensus.

A five-person battle party.

Haruhime Sanjouno had joined the team as a supporter and sorcerer.

The howls of monsters pierced the darkness that dominated the caves far belowground.

Ash-colored rocks and boulders lined the cave walls. Several bats flew high overhead, vicious wormlike creatures bored their way through the rocky walls, and the strong roars of liger fangs filled the air—adventurers called out to one another as they made their way through the monster-filled hallway.

"Weapons and armor all good to go?"

"No problems here!"

"Ready for combat!"

Bell's and Mikoto's blades whistled through the air as they prepared to engage the oncoming beasts and answered Welf's call.

The High Smith had repaired and renovated Bell's armor, now in its fifth incarnation. The blend of gold and white metals maintained its luster even in the dim light. Light armor was designed to protect the wearer without hindering their speed or agility, and it did just that as Bell unleashed a flurry of knife attacks on the closest beast. Mikoto was quick to finish it off with a thrust from her secondary weapon, a long spear. It broke through the liger fang's thick fur like tissue paper. The beast's dying howl echoed through the cave.

The fifteenth floor of the Dungeon.

The party, with Haruhime among its ranks, had gone straight into the labyrinth after the meeting that morning at their home.

Leaning heavily on Bell's second-tier adventurer Status and Welf's freshly forged weapons and armor, they quickly and efficiently plowed through the upper levels and arrived at one they had yet to completely conquer: the fifteenth floor.

Haruhime, obviously overwhelmed, stayed close to Lilly as she provided support to the front lines with her handheld bow gun. Meanwhile, the other three members fought tirelessly to keep the never-ending slew of monsters at bay.

"—Minotaurs will appear soon!"

"Incoming howl! Li'l E, cover your ears!"

Mikoto detected the arrival of more monsters on the battlefield thanks to her detection skill, Yatano Black Crow. Welf finished off the dungeon worm with his greatsword as he shouted a warning to the back of the formation.

The front line, consisting of Bell and Welf, and the middle support, Mikoto, charged forward to push back the line of monsters as the looming, two-meder-tall silhouettes of Minotaurs appeared deeper down the cave. Just as Welf had warned, the new arrivals reared back and unleashed a torrent of sound through their throats.

"UooOOOOOOOOOOOOOOOOOOOOOOOOOOOOOOOOOO
OOOOOOOOOOO!!"

The Minotaur's howl, a menacing sound that awakened the instinct of fear in weaker creatures and froze them in their tracks, blasted through the hallway.

Lilly was quick to shield her ears as well as Haruhime's to protect them from the howl. As Level 1 adventurers, the girls would have difficulty withstanding its effects. Welf, on the other hand, shrugged it off with a grin.

He used the strength of his powerful spiritual "container" to overcome the auditory attack and joined Bell and Mikoto in the counteroffensive.

"—Using the Magic Sword!"

Lilly had recovered from the howl's effects and saw Bell engage the Minotaurs. She realized that even more monsters were moments away from joining the battle, so she shouted a warning to her allies. The others glanced back over their shoulders in time to see Lilly pull a dagger-length scarlet blade from her oversize backpack. Bell, Welf, and Mikoto immediately darted out of its path.

A quick slash of the sparkling dagger sent a massive fireball hurtling through the battlefield.

"——————————————————————!"

The blast of fiery destruction wiped out every monster in its path.

Even the Minotaurs, whose skin was known to be naturally resistant to fire, were laid to waste along with their monster kin as every one of them was erased from the charred rocky hallway.

"Li'l E, don't be so quick to use that thing! It's only for emergencies—relying on it's not going to help us in the long run!"

"The situation was emergency enough! The Dungeon is unpredictable; only reacting to changes is too late!"

"T-take it easy, okay? Welf, Lilly?"

"P-please, both of you—using such loud voices now will only lure more monsters…Ohh."

"It is exactly as Lady Haruhime says. Calm yourselves."

The battle over, an argument started among the still-sizzling remains of their opponents. The source of Welf's anger was Lilly's haste to use the dagger-length Crozzo Magic Sword.

Welf had forged it and placed it in her care so that the back part of the formation could protect itself, or for an ace in the hole should disaster strike. This particular one might be weaker than the one he had used in the battle against the Black Goliath or the ones he had forged for the War Game, but it was still on par with the destructive power of many high-level magic users.

"Don't depend on the Magic Sword—you'll become weaker for it. We would have been fine on our own just now!" he angrily shouted at the prum.

Lilly responded by insisting that casual guesswork could be fatal in the Dungeon.

"It's better to ensure safety before being overrun." She wasn't changing her stance. The Dungeon was not known for its leniency, so she stated with the utmost confidence that it was better not to take chances.

Both views were correct. There was nothing wrong with what they said.

Both Welf and Lilly were thinking in terms of what was best for the party.

Bell and Mikoto could only smile weakly in response, and Haruhime timidly tried to play the mediator between them.

After getting the situation under control, everyone turned their attention to the task at hand.

"So this is a drop item, that's a magic stone…"

"That's correct. Drop items will go into Lilly's backpack, so please collect the magic stones, Miss Haruhime—be sure not to drop any."

"Y-yes!"

Haruhime listened to Lilly's instructions as she made her way through the ashes of the Magic Sword's charred victims and collected the loot left behind.

She was dressed in a Far Eastern–style battle cloth that resembled a priestess's garb, the same one she'd worn while with *Ishtar Familia*—forced on her by Aisha—and was equipped with a tubular backpack. She also wore a cloak of salamander wool, the same as her allies.

Lilly had declared that she would train the genuine noncombatant "into a full-blown supporter" for their battle party. Haruhime had bowed over and over, saying, "I devote myself to your teachings," and accepted her new role without question. A sort of master-and-apprentice bond had formed between them.

Mikoto and the others acknowledged this new development with a soft grin and continued pressing forward through the Dungeon, cutting down all monsters in their path.

"We've made good progress through the fifteenth floor and at a very good pace."

"That should be expected, with Mr. Bell's Level and the balance of our battle party."

"Miss Eina—er, my adviser gave us permission to go down to the eighteenth floor as long as nothing major happens."

Lilly and Bell responded to Mikoto's remark, nodding as they walked.

Lilly continued with a comment that the front of their formation was nearly perfect. "This party's weakness is the lack of power at the back where Lilly is. To be blunt, the two don't match. To fix that, Lilly would like to add a strong healer."

"And a magic user wouldn't hurt," added Welf nonchalantly, almost as if warning Lilly against using the Magic Sword again.

"Lilly's aware," she responded with a twitch in the corner of her mouth.

"What about Miss Lyu from that bar? She has great command of healing magic as well, yes? And the magic she used during the battle on the eighteenth floor was most impressive…Would she be willing to join our party?"

"No, I doubt it…A-and Mia is really scary."

Bell smiled but turned down Lilly's suggestion. Asking Lyu—an ex-adventurer who worked as a waitress at The Benevolent Mistress—to join them would probably anger the owner, Mia. The thought of her enraged face sent a cold chill down Bell's spine, so he responded with a flat no.

Their current formation consisted of Bell and Welf on the front line, Haruhime and Lilly at the back, and Mikoto filling an all-around supporting role at the center. The five of them made their way deeper into the Dungeon, all senses on high alert as they passed through the dim, rocky hallways.

While it was true for Lilly as well, a direct hit from a monster on the inexperienced Level 1 Haruhime would spell disaster. Thanks to Mikoto's Yatano Black Crow, they were able to detect approaching monsters and respond appropriately to defend her.

"After a little more exploration, Lilly recommends we return to the fourteenth floor. As discussed, it would be a good time to find the deserted corner of the Dungeon and test out Miss Haruhime's Magic one by one."

"Agreed. We wouldn't want to be confused experiencing it for the first time during a tense battle...Lady Haruhime, is that okay?"

"Yes. That would be fine."

"Hey, Bell, you've used it before, right? What's it like?"

"Well, um...There was a big flash, and I felt stronger, and I could move faster..."

Mikoto was quick to assist all her allies as the group fell into formation and continued traveling through the Dungeon.

It was almost dusk by the time Mikoto and the others returned to the surface.

After stopping to trade their loot for money at Babel Tower's Exchange, they made their way into Central Park, which was already filled with other adventurers heading out of the Dungeon. While they were excitedly talking and making their way to the bars or back to Guild headquarters, *Hestia Familia* chose to instead go straight home.

"Oh, you have returned."

"Lord Takemikazuchi!"

A deity with a bobbed hairstyle was waiting to greet them as soon as they passed through the iron gate and main entryway.

Takemikazuchi smiled at them. Mikoto was so happy to see him that she walked right up to the deity with a smile on her face large enough to rival his own.

"Sorry, Lord Takemikazuchi...Asking you to stay here while we were out."

"Think nothing of it, Bell Cranell. My own children took the day off from Dungeon prowling and kept me company."

Through Hestia, Bell had asked *Takemikazuchi Familia* to stay at their home while they were out today.

Unlike the hidden room under the old church that Bell and Hestia once shared, or the shack of a building where *Takemikazuchi Familia* resided, *Hestia Familia* now possessed a prime piece of real estate and the status of a middle-class familia. If all members and their goddess were to leave their home completely empty, there was a very real danger of burglars breaking in to steal items or information. The situation had changed from when they were far less known and recognizable.

That was why they'd asked a friendly familia to step in and keep watch while they were out. They had also asked the same from *Miach Familia*, and this situation would continue for the foreseeable future. Every member of *Hestia Familia* was extremely grateful to their house sitters, especially since they were doing it for free.

"Like I said, pay it no mind. We are helping each other. Each of us took full advantage of the bathing facilities as collateral," said the deity. "Rest assured, they were thoroughly cleaned afterward." The whole group shared a laugh.

"Thank you very much," said the group of adventurers one last time.

The two familias planned on sharing a large meal later that evening, so Bell and his allies returned to their rooms to remove their armor.

"Excuse me, Lord Takemikazuchi...Please take this."

Telling Haruhime, who shared a room with her, that she'd catch up in a moment, Mikoto went to speak with Takemikazuchi by herself. She held out a small bag full of something heavy.

Each of them had received their share of the money earned in the Dungeon that day; this was Mikoto's portion.

"Please send this to support the shrine."

The reason that Takemikazuchi and his familia had traveled to Orario in the first place was to raise money for the shrine in their homeland.

Mikoto pleaded with him to send the money to the shrine that had raised her, but the deity shook his head.

"Surely this is the money you earned fighting alongside Bell Cranell and his company. Don't use it for us; use it for your allies."

Going into the Dungeon required a lot of preparation, including weapon repairs and a small mountain of items.

Takemikazuchi urged Mikoto to use this money to benefit her battle party.

"B-but I'm the only one doing nothing to assist the shrine..."

Mikoto tried to insist again that Takemikazuchi take the money, but...

"Mikoto, you stand here now as a member of *Hestia Familia*."

"...!"

Those words put an abrupt end to her argument.

There was no way for her to refute such an obvious truth. Putting her current allies at risk for the benefit of former compatriots went against logic.

After all, she had joined *Hestia Familia* to repay a debt to Bell.

Even still, I...

Memories of that morning's dream floated to the front of her mind.

The moment that Takemikazuchi asked her to become his daughter. The connection by blood of a shared family; the word *familia*.

She had no regrets becoming a member of Hestia's family. She was proud to be one of Bell's allies and happily fought at his side. It was thanks to her new family that Haruhime was still alive.

But deep down—she didn't want to forget that she had once been a part of Takemikazuchi's family. She looked at the floor as all these thoughts ran through her head.

"...Mikoto, do you remember the day I asked you to become my daughter?"

"!"

Mikoto looked up in surprise. He had used the exact phrase from her memory.

Takemikazuchi stood before her, eyebrows sinking as he broke into an endearing smile—a tender, fatherly smile.

"The first ichor a child receives never completely disappears, even if they go through Conversion. Just as Hestia can sense you through the Blessing she bestowed, I, too, can feel every breath you take."

"..."

"You will always be my daughter, my family. I will never forget that. So please, don't make that face."

He read her feelings like a book. Stepping forward, the deity gently stroked her hair. The girl turned bright red in the blink of an eye.

His hand felt smaller than she remembered; she'd grown a lot since then. However, it still possessed the same warmth as it did all those years ago.

Takemikazuchi didn't notice the degree to which the girl was blushing as he ran his fingers through her silky black hair and lightly chuckled to himself.

"I am happy you still care about the well-being of the shrine. But you should know that Chigusa and Ouka reached Level Two during the skirmishes with *Ishtar Familia*. We're doing fine; there's no need to worry."

Takemikazuchi then reminded her that both familias would work together in the Dungeon when their schedules would allow it, and that was enough.

"Have faith."

Mikoto turned her face up to make eye contact with the deity. She gave him a firm nod.

"Good," said the god as he removed his hand from her head, then turned to walk away. Takemikazuchi casually said he would go call the others for dinner and went down the main hallway. Mikoto watched him leave until he completely disappeared from sight.

...*Now that I'm separated from his familia, I...*

The time apart had renewed her feelings of affection for him, she thought to herself, cheeks still bright pink.

Her heart thumped wildly in her chest. She squeezed the collar of her battle cloth in an attempt to get her pulse under control, but each beat thundered through her entire body.

"...Um, Mikoto?"

"———Uwah!"

A soft voice from behind nearly made Mikoto jump out of her skin.

Regaining her balance and spinning around, she spotted Chigusa standing behind her.

"Lady Chigusa! How long have you been there?"

"Umm, sorry...Quite a while."

Chigusa's bangs normally hid her eyes from sight, but right now they parted in such a way that Mikoto could see the girl's right eye and the pink on her cheeks. She knew immediately her friend had seen everything.

She'd seen how Takemikazuchi had refused her donation, how red she'd turned at the deity's touch, how she'd looked at him when he walked away—everything.

Even though Chigusa knew of her feelings for their god, Mikoto wanted nothing more than to dig a hole and bury herself right then and there.

"I really am sorry. Didn't want to interrupt something..."

"I beg you, Lady Chigusa, not another word!"

Mikoto was normally very serious and straightforward, but the dormant feelings of a young maiden came storming to the forefront, causing her to yell at the top of her lungs.

She squeezed her head between her hands, ears burning red in shame. The two girls had been close from a young age; there was very little they didn't know about each other. However, embarrassing situations were still embarrassing even in front of one of your best friends.

Chigusa looked remorseful and gave Mikoto a few minutes to regain her bearings before revealing why she was looking for her in the first place.

"So, it's a little late, but Ouka and the rest of us are planning to do our usual celebration for Lord Takemikazuchi..."

The normally shy Chigusa could talk about anything with Mikoto. Her words were smooth and clear as she informed her friend about the plan in the works.

"We'd like to invite Haruhime and prepare a present for him... What will you do?"

The change in topic finally pulled Mikoto away from her feelings of shame.

There was a glint of determination in her eyes.

Two days had passed since dinner with *Takemikazuchi Familia*.

Mikoto, who wanted some time off after a day in the Dungeon, made her way onto Orario's streets under the clear morning skies.

Bell and Welf were with her.

"So why are we here...?"

"My apologies to the both of you...but please lend me your assistance for today's shopping!!"

Welf mumbled as the group made their way through a street lined with many different vibrant shops that branched off North Main Street.

Mikoto put her hands together and bowed many times, asking the two who had to give up time in the Dungeon and the forge to join her. Bell forced a smile and asked a question.

"Well, um, you said we were going shopping, so what do you want to buy?"

"The truth is...Ouka and the others have been planning a celebration for Lord Takemikazuchi these past few days..."

Mikoto told Bell and Welf more about the celebration that Chigusa had brought to her attention.

Before they came to Orario, the children of the shrine did something special for the gods and goddesses on the anniversary of their arrival on Earth—similar to a birthday party for the deities. However, due to the War Game and the events involving Haruhime, they'd forgotten to do something for Takemikazuchi this year on the actual date just a few days prior.

Mikoto wanted to do the same thing that her childhood friends were planning to do: give their god presents to commemorate the special day.

"I have always put a lot of thought and sincerity into my gifts, but there was never enough money for something truly great. This being my second year in Orario, and having a decent income, I would like to give him a proper gift."

"I get that…but why are *we* here?"

"Oh yes! I would like your opinions as men, just like him, to find something that would make Lord Takemikazuchi happy…!"

Mikoto leaned in close to Welf as she answered his question.

The celebration was planned for tomorrow.

"Please lend me your assistance…!"

"That's…easier said than done."

"I, um, well…I'd really like to help."

Mikoto bowed even lower in front of the two young men. Welf scratched the back of his head at the same time Bell was scratching his chin. Neither of them looked up to the task.

Both of them were thinking the same thing. Basically, they didn't think their advice would be of any use.

When it came to the Dungeon or a forge, Bell and Welf were very knowledgeable. However, neither had much interest in anything else. If asked what most men enjoyed doing or wanted as a gift, both would struggle to come up with an answer.

"But, you know, you've known Lord Takemikazuchi a lot longer than we have. Wouldn't your ideas be better than whatever we come up with?"

"Y-yes, but…!"

"Hee-hee-hee…As long as we're here, we might as well have a look around."

Mikoto couldn't deny the truth in Welf's words and momentarily lost confidence. Bell smiled awkwardly at the look of shock on the girl's face and suggested the three of them see what the shopping area had to offer.

North Main Street ran along the side of Orario's first district. Shops that tailored to every race of demi-human stood out the most in the shopping area, but there were plenty of smaller stores and street stalls that sold handmade goods and other interesting items. Mikoto, being as serious and thorough as she usually was, took her time at each place and examined every item for sale one by one before moving on to the next shop. Just like Bell, she had lived in modest poverty until very recently and wasn't used to having so many options. She drifted left and right like an overwhelmed country girl in the big city for the first time.

Bell and Welf exchanged concerned glances as they followed close behind.

The sun was in the middle of the sky before they knew it. The three humans decided to take a break in the shade of a tall building after making one complete circuit of the shopping area.

"Miss Mikoto, did you see anything promising?"

"I-I don't know…"

"Oi."

Mikoto answered Bell's question honestly, only to receive a verbal jab from Welf.

An apologetic expression played over her face as she twiddled her thumbs, unsure how to proceed.

"In that case, what kind of presents did you used to give him?"

"While in the Far East, I collected pretty shells, acorns, and seeds to make necklaces and other little things…"

That information didn't do much to solve Mikoto's quandary.

Chigusa had told her that all of them were going to prepare individual gifts for Takemikazuchi this year, but she had no idea choosing one would be so difficult...She sat there, racking her brain, when Bell's eyes suddenly lit up. He turned to her and said:

"What about food? Is that an option?"

"Eh?"

"Miss Mikoto, you're a really good cook. So why not make something delicious for the party...? Just an idea."

He must've remembered the *miso* soup he had the other morning and made the suggestion. Mikoto gave it some thought.

"...Thinking back, there was never much food at the celebrations back at the shrine..."

At the very least, they had never made anything all that fancy.

Welf could see the gears turning in Mikoto's head while standing off to her side. "Why don't we try something along that line?" he proposed. "It's a party, after all. How about a cake?"

"Cake..."

Her lips involuntarily traced his words.

It wasn't Far Eastern, but Mikoto had a general idea—a soft and fluffy dough was baked in an oven and then decorated with cream and fruit...She had a feeling she had seen many examples of it when she attended the banquet that was hosted by Apollo.

It made more and more sense the more she thought about it. That was it.

"I will try...I will make a cake."

Welf and Bell thought it was a good idea and agreed.

Mikoto apologized for the hours of walking gone to waste and tried to figure out where to go from here.

"I'm sure you want to make it yourself, but can you?" Welf asked.

"I've never done it before, so I can't say with any certainty... But probably, if I have a recipe and taste one myself first," Mikoto replied.

"The Benevolent Mistress sells cake...Think they'd give us a recipe if we asked?" Bell said.

Although The Benevolent Mistress served as a watering hole for adventurers in the evening, it operated as a café during the day for the average townspeople. Bell had eaten cake there before and did his best to explain. Mikoto listened to every word and decided to visit The Benevolent Mistress where Syr, Lyu, and many other waitresses worked.

It was a little past noon.

Mikoto led the group to West Main Street and into The Benevolent Mistress.

Lyu was there to meet them at the door, and they explained the situation. Bell was in the middle of negotiating when the cat people Ahnya and Chloe, as well as the rest of the girls on staff, detected the presence of a juicy love story in the air and gathered around with grins on their faces. They agreed to help after teasing Mikoto into another blushing fit. Mia came in and added, "As long as you're eatin' lunch, I can look the other way, sure," and granted her permission. The cat-people cooks working in the kitchen wrote down the recipe and gave it to Mikoto.

After listening to Ahnya and the other waitresses complain about Syr being absent from work yet again, the three adventurers left The Benevolent Mistress.

"Well, we definitely got what we came for and then some…but do you think you can take it from here?"

"Yes, thank you so much, Sir Welf, Sir Bell."

"I'm glad we could help."

Recipe in hand and itching to get started, Mikoto said a quick thank-you to the two young men as they made their way back home.

She was carrying a box that contained a whole cake. Mia had been rather insistent that they buy the entire thing. They had eaten a few pieces while at the café, but now that they had the finished product and the recipe, Mikoto couldn't help but feel confident.

Lips curled up, she felt as though she was one step closer to her goal.

"Oh…"

"Something up, Bell?"

"Isn't that…Lord Takemikazuchi?"

They were in the middle of a side street when Bell suddenly stopped walking. Welf asked him what was wrong and he pointed farther down the road.

Mikoto turned to have a look, and sure enough, Takemikazuchi was standing not too far away.

He stopped a goddess with honey-colored hair who happened to be passing by.

"Oi, Demeter. You look pale. Are you feeling all right?"

"...Oh my, I must be a little under the weather and didn't realize it."

"Why are you acting so unconcerned? Come now, show me your face."

—With that, he wrapped his arm around her shoulders and pressed his cheek against hers without warning.

"You don't seem...to have a fever."

"Oh my my my...Y-you can't, Takemikazuchi. This kind of thing is for someone important, not just someone on the street."

"Don't be stupid, I'm concerned *because* it's you."

"..."

"I remember well who it was that brought fresh fruit and vegetables when my children were starving. We are forever in your debt."

"...Haaa! This is why you and Miach shouldn't be allowed to talk to women."

A small exchange of words with Takemikazuchi was enough to make Demeter blush.

The goddess certainly didn't look angry when she stepped away from him and walked off.

"..."

"M-Miss Mikoto?"

"H-hey."

Concerned, Bell and Welf glanced at Mikoto and tried to get her attention, but the girl pretended she couldn't hear them.

"L-Lord Takemikazuchi! Thank you so much for saving us from those perverted gods the other day!"

"Please, please accept this."

"Hold on, don't you think this is a bit much for such a small favor?"
Two human girls ran up to Takemikazuchi not a moment later.

They appeared to be average citizens who didn't belong to any familia. Both of them held out small bags of cookies, their cheeks bright pink. The deity tried to play off his good deed as common sense, laughing as he stepped closer to them and accepted their gift.

Then came the final blow. He gently stroked their hair, and both girls' faces turned beet red.

"......"

Squish! The box containing the cake twisted in Mikoto's grip after she watched the events from beginning to end.

"Geh!"

"Oi! Hel-looo?"

Shivers of fright jolted up Bell's and Welf's spines as the girl's fingers crumpled the container even further. But once again, she didn't acknowledge them.

From there, the physical contact between Takemikazuchi and other women on the street only continued to increase.

Sometimes the girls initiated, sometimes he did. Young or old, race or divinity made no difference, every interaction involved a certain degree of skinship. All the women reacted very innocently, turning various shades of red and smiling back at him. The worst part about all this was that it appeared Takemikazuchi had no idea what he was doing, nor did he notice their reactions.

Mikoto watched everything from the shadows. New women arrived when the previous ones finally stepped away from him, almost as if he was showing off how popular he was with the opposite gender.

"......"

"Miss Mikoto? Miss Mikoto!"

"Hey, say something—anything!"

Mikoto stood there like a statue, bangs covering her eyes as she looked at the stone pavement beneath her feet.

The shiver of fright from before became a torrent of terror as Bell and Welf witnessed a miasma of dark energy rise from the girl's shoulders. Their unusually high-pitched voices echoed through the side street.

She didn't say a word. However, the aura forming around her body became stronger with each passing moment.

"Lord Takemikazuchi!"

"Well, if it isn't Haruhime."

—Then.

"At last, I made them right! Please have one!"

"*Andango*...Let's see, let's see...Hmm?"

Takemikazuchi reached out to take one of the sweet dumplings from the tray in Haruhime's arms when he noticed something else. His hand went to her chin instead.

"Haruhime, you already ate a few, didn't you?"

"Whaaa?!"

"There are some big crumbs on your lips...My word, child. Now hold still."

He pinched the large crumb on her lip between his thumb and forefinger—and ate it.

"Yes, very sweet."

"Lord Takemikazuchi...Doing such a thing to me..."

"They're delicious, Haruhime. I'm sure they'll be most pleased... But yes, I have a feeling you will make a wonderful bride."

"Eh?!...Do you...do you really believe so?"

"Indeed. You have a good nature and an industrious spirit. That's exactly what I would want in a bride if I weren't a god. Ha-ha-ha!"

Snap!

Mikoto definitely heard something break deep inside her.

Step, step, step. She didn't look up, but her feet carried her forward. She couldn't even hear Bell and Welf yelling behind her. She was on her way to where the blushing Haruhime, both hands pressed to her cheeks in embarrassment, stood beside the airheaded deity laughing next to her.

"Mikoto?"

"Miss Mikoto?"

The two of them noticed her approach as she came to a stop.

Still silent and engulfed in an aura, Mikoto ripped the lid off the warped container in her arms with a loud *SHHK*.

"Oh? What's that…?"

Takemikazuchi tilted his head to the side in an attempt to see what was in the container. Mikoto finally turned to face him, her lips trembling.

"——Lord Takemikazuchi…"

Her head snapped up as she raised the container high into the air and screamed with all her rage:

"*Lord Takemikazuchi, you brainless man-whore!*"

"Bu-UOHH?!"

The whole cake hit him square in the face, splattering everywhere.

"Lord Takemikazuchi?!"

Mikoto jumped away from him as Haruhime's scream echoed through the street.

That was closely followed by the dull thuds of cake hitting the pavement at his feet.

"Little Mikoto, nice one!!" "Good work!" "Consider me officially a fan of the Eternal Shadow!!" A shower of applause and cheers came from other deities who happened to be hiding in the shadows, but she didn't hear any of it.

Mikoto turned her back on the stone-faced Takemikazuchi and ran away.

"The hell was that?!"

"Why did you do that?!"

Welf and Bell had caught up with Mikoto after her mad dash through the streets of Orario, and they yelled at her in unison.

All the running had given her a moment to get the fire burning in her heart under control. However, her eyes were filled with regret as she swayed back and forth on the spot.

"I-I'm sorry…My body took over and I just did it…"

"What you 'just did' was hit a god in the face with a whole cake!"

"It's blasphemous! Downright profane!"

Mikoto appeared to shrink under the strength of Welf's and Bell's loud voices.

She knew she should do as they said and reflect on the seriousness of her actions, but even still, the heat emanating from her heart was making her arms and legs shake.

"It was a grave error—my devotion is insufficient…But my body wouldn't listen to me…!"

"…"

"The only option left for me was to splatter something on Lord Takemikazuchi's face…! It is my fault for being unable to control the urge. I am completely, utterly worthless!"

"…"

"Oh, I could kick myself!"

She dropped to her hands and knees and repeatedly slammed her clenched fist into the surface of the stone road.

Bell and Welf looked on, unsure what to say. "What's that, what's that?" came the voices of passing demi-humans on the street, trying to figure out what was going on in the middle of the road. Many sets of eyes were glued onto the girl on the verge of losing her mind.

Mikoto had caught glimpses of Takemikazuchi's social interactions with other women while they were living at the shrine in the Far East. However, there weren't many people around, since the shrine was rather isolated, so she never saw enough to make her completely lose herself in the moment.

Things were different in Orario. More people meant more chances to make new connections. Now the only thought in Mikoto's mind was that while she was working hard in the Dungeon, Takemikazuchi was walking around the city doing *that*…and it was tearing her apart from the inside.

She was angry with herself, realizing that her anger was stemming from the lack of virtue in Takemikazuchi's words and actions, as well as her own jealousy. That only added fuel to the fire because she had thought she was more accepting.

Embarrassment was setting in; tears welled in her eyes.

"Umm, eh...Miss Mikoto?"

"What are you going to do?"

Bell tried to gently get her attention, but Welf took a more direct approach with the girl who'd slammed a cake into the face of a god.

Mikoto's watery eyes lifted from the pavement as she climbed to her feet on wobbly legs.

"Make a cake, as planned...and apologize."

Her voice was weak and dejected, as if it might cut out at any moment. But she was able to answer the question.

There was no choice but to apologize to Takemikazuchi. However, she didn't know how she'd react, almost scared of what she might say when she saw him again. A storm of complicated emotions raged within her as she took her first crestfallen step toward home.

Thump, thump. Bell and Welf looked on with worried eyes as she made her way through the backstreets by herself.

The sun sank behind the mountains in the western sky.

As adventurers started emerging from a long day's work in the Dungeon, dusk fell over a house in a run-down area in one of Orario's western blocks.

A good distance away from the main street, the house was prevented from getting direct sunlight by the surrounding buildings. This house also sold healing items, but very few people passed by. One familia's emblem, a basic outline of the human body, hung outside, serving as a billboard, with the words BLUE PHARMACY spelled out in the common language known as Koine. This was the home of *Miach Familia.*

A party of adventurers made its way through the small maze of shelves inside the store, looking for this familia's signature product, the double potion. Finding it, they made their way to a young female chienthrope standing behind a long counter. "Thank you..." she said with a wave as they left the store. A moment later, two young ladies made their way through the double wooden doors at the entrance.

Carrying weapons and dressed for combat, the two adventurers called out to Nahza, the chienthrope.

"We're back, home from the Dungeon."

"W-we're home…"

One with short hair, the other with long. One set of eyes sharp and focused, the other lazy and wandering. Side by side, they made an interesting pair. The one with short hair clearly announced her presence while the one with long hair made only a half-hearted greeting.

Nahza, who always looked drowsy with her eyes half open, smiled and greeted the two young women as they came inside.

"Welcome back, Daphne, Cassandra…"

The two women, Daphne and Cassandra—both third-tier adventurers and former members of *Apollo Familia*—walked through the store all the way up to the counter and put a sack of coins onto it.

"Here. Today's Dungeon earnings. We already took what we need for preparations."

"Sorry for the trouble—thanks…"

"N-no, no. We're in the same familia, after all…"

Nahza took the money from Daphne and expressed her gratitude. Cassandra's long hair swayed back and forth as she spoke.

Nahza, who until recently was *Miach Familia*'s only member, happily swished her tail.

"Bell becoming famous in the War Game was great advertising… More and more customers come in every day thanks to him, so I'm so glad to have you here to help."

Nahza smiled, took two flasks filled with juice out from under the counter, and handed them to the two women.

"Are you sure our familia was the best choice…? We have quite a bit of debt."

"After hearing that ridiculous figure of two hundred million valis, all other debts seem cute by comparison."

Click, click. Nahza's artificial right arm, an airgetlám, made mechanical sounds as she moved. Daphne took a swig of the juice and shrugged with a distant look in her eyes.

Both Daphne and Cassandra had gone to *Hestia Familia*'s first recruiting event in hopes of joining but had reconsidered after the bombshell of the familia's 200-million-valis debt was revealed. So the two young adventurers thought better of it and traveled a long, winding road that eventually led to *Miach Familia*'s doorstep. Having already gone through Conversion, they now officially had Miach as their god, and Nahza a friend and ally.

Cassandra had had her heart set on joining *Hestia Familia*, so she was still a bit disappointed by the outcome.

"Plus, Lord Miach is a great god. With a deity like that at the helm, we had nothing to lose by joining."

"While I'm glad to hear that…don't fall for him."

"As if I would."

"Heh-heh-heh…"

After a quick exchange of playful banter, "By the way…" said Daphne as she looked beyond Nahza and farther behind the counter. "What's going on in there?"

Through an open door, she could see two deities sitting on either side of a table in the guest room. One was a handsome man with long marine-blue hair tied behind his neck—Miach, the god of Nahza, Daphne, and Cassandra's familia. He wore an ash-gray robe that had seen better days, a sign of their financial straits, but his face could easily be confused for that of someone of noble birth.

The other one wore his black hair in two bobbed ponytails on either side of his head—the dignified deity Takemikazuchi.

"The most pointless meeting in history…"

On that slightly irritated note, Nahza left Daphne and Cassandra in charge of the shop and walked toward the kitchen.

The two gods continued their conversation in the guest room, ignoring the sounds of Nahza making her way through the building that served as both their home and their store.

"—That is what happened today."

Takemikazuchi finished recounting that afternoon's events involving Mikoto.

After taking a cake to the face, the befuddled deity had sought the advice of a mutual friend of Hestia's and fellow god living in poverty.

His problem: He couldn't figure out why Mikoto was angry.

"…"

Miach listened intently to the story from beginning to end without interrupting. Then he closed his eyes, took a deep breath, and sighed.

Opening his eyes, he looked directly at the deity who couldn't figure out the cause of his follower's outburst and said:

"—I haven't the slightest idea."

"I know, right?"

THUD! A dull echo came from the other side of the open door. Daphne and Cassandra, who'd overheard the conversation, each slammed their heads into the closest wooden pillar at the same time.

The two deities looked around for a moment, slightly confused. Cassandra massaged the side of her throbbing head as Daphne muttered, "How dense are they…?" They might be gods, but Miach's and Takemikazuchi's lack of sensitivity was giving them headaches.

"This is why Lady Hestia's followers get frustrated…"

"Nahza?"

Carrying on a plate two cups of tea she had prepared in the kitchen, Nahza made her way into the guest room.

She ignored the look on Miach's face and placed one cup in front of each of them.

"I feel sorry for her…for Mikoto."

"Oh…?"

"If you truly don't understand…I won't tell you to be careful, but…"

Takemikazuchi's shoulders shifted uncomfortably under Nahza's gaze.

At the same time, Miach felt that the chienthrope was including him in this as well when Nahza glanced in his direction. "What's wrong?" he asked. She didn't respond, only sighed in front of her god. When she was done, Nahza once again made eye contact with Takemikazuchi.

"Think it through carefully, and please accept whatever you may discover..."

Takemikazuchi remained motionless as the mortal's words rang in his ears. Then he folded his arms across his chest a few moments later.

Steam rose from the cup of tea in front of him on the table, and the deity's meek face reflected in its surface.

The day of Takemikazuchi's celebration had arrived.

Mikoto started baking the cake in the manor's kitchen early that morning.

She had made a few attempts yesterday after returning home, but none of them turned out as planned. She'd even asked Welf and Bell to sample her creations, and each spent the rest of the evening not far from a lavatory. Gloom started to set in, but she was quick to slap her cheeks with both hands and tell herself to focus.

She forced the events of yesterday out of her head and concentrated entirely on the task at hand.

"Excuse the intrusion, Miss Mikoto...About my meeting with Lord Takemikazuchi yesterday, I, um..."

"It's not a problem, Lady Haruhime. I don't mind at all."

"That's not what I meant...Mikoto, that was—"

"I said I don't mind!"

Mikoto didn't even look at Haruhime as she walked into the kitchen, focused entirely on the dough in her hands.

Haruhime wasn't sure how to respond to Mikoto's harsh tone and stood there with an apologetic look on her face. The renart left the kitchen a moment later.

Hestia and Lilly saw the brief conversation from a distance and were very confused until Bell brought them up to speed. Their

puzzled expressions quickly turned to frustration at Takemikazuchi, but they remained quiet and decided to stay out of it.

Mikoto chased all stray thoughts out of her mind by following The
Benevolent Mistress's cake recipe as closely as possible. First came
baking the dough in a metal pot, normally used for rice, over an
open flame, and then gathering all the sweets and fruit...And then
an impressive cake was complete.

Decorated with many types of berries, no one would have guessed
the continent-style cake had been made by someone from the Far
East.

"It's done, but..."

She stood in front of her masterpiece, but now all those stray
thoughts were coming back.

There was nothing else left to do. Mikoto lingered in the kitchen
until the sky started to turn dark. The time of the celebration was
upon her, so she put the cake, plate and all, into a box and got ready.

Leaving the manor, she made her way through Orario's twisting
streets toward *Takemikazuchi Familia*'s home while carefully holding the box in her arms.

Magic-stone lamps flicked on as the sky grew even darker, echoing the state of her mind. Many different feelings pulled at her all
the way until she reached her destination.

The old, run-down community housing she used to call home
was located on a narrow street in the northwest part of the city.
Right now, Takemikazuchi and the remaining five members of
his familia lived here. Light was flooding out of the living room
windows—perhaps the festivities were already under way?

"Forgive the intrusion..." said Mikoto as she opened the door and
made her way inside with an expression of uncertainty on her face.
Staying true to Far Eastern traditions, she removed her shoes. She
was a bit unnerved by the fact that no one came out to greet her.
Nevertheless, she walked through the entranceway and down a narrow hall.

Arriving at the door that led to the living room, she came to a
stop, took a deep breath, and slid it open.

A heartbeat later, *pop!*

"—Eh?"

A pleasant sound erupted from above her head, and long, multicolored ribbons and confetti fell around her like snow before she knew what was happening. Real flower petals fell past her shoulders. She could only stand there, struggling to take in the vibrant display.

"About time you came."

"Welcome, Mikoto."

Her friends greeted her with applause and kind words.

Ouka, Chigusa, the other three members of *Takemikazuchi Familia*, and even Haruhime were chuckling to themselves at Mikoto's look of shock. They had managed to re-create a Far Eastern *kusudama*—an origami ball stuffed with whatever the maker wanted and that could break open with a pull of a cord—and hung it on the ceiling.

The room was decorated with magic-stone lamps of many different colors and artificial flowers on the walls. There was also a small mountain of food sprawled out on the table. The Jyaga Maru Kun especially stood out.

Greeted as if she was the star of the day, Mikoto stood with the cake in her arms, more confused than ever.

"What...what is the meaning of this...? Today is Lord Takemikazuchi's day, is it not...?"

"Of course, that is true...but the main reason we gathered here today was to give you a proper send-off."

Mikoto looked at each of her childhood friends in turn until a smiling Ouka let her in on the secret.

She might be gone for only a year, but they had been planning to have a going-away party for Mikoto since she went to *Hestia Familia*.

They wanted it to be a surprise, so they disguised the event as Lord Takemikazuchi's yearly celebration and even got Haruhime involved.

Mikoto's jaw dropped the moment the cat was out of the bag. She looked at each of them once again.

"Haruhime lent her assistance to prepare this food…Said she wanted to help celebrate our reunion, too."

"…I also wanted to commemorate Miss Mikoto's departure."

Ouka did his best to contain a chuckle as Haruhime smiled at Mikoto like a blooming flower next to him.

One look at the dumplings sitting on the table, and Mikoto finally connected the dots as to why she had met with Takemikazuchi the day before.

"It was Lord Takemikazuchi who suggested we throw you a going-away party."

A wave of nervous energy passed through Mikoto as soon as Chigusa said those words.

Her friends stepped aside to make a path as Takemikazuchi came forward.

So many emotions assailed her heart at once that Mikoto couldn't move, much less say anything. The deity came to a stop right in front of her and gently placed his hand on top of her head.

"Ahh…My apologies for yesterday."

A small smile appeared on his lips at the look of shock on the girl's face. Takemikazuchi's expression softened and his shoulders sank.

"To be honest, I'm still unsure what I did to deserve such a reaction…but in the end, I did something that upset you, didn't I?"

"…!"

"Even back in the Far East, I often did things that upset you."

"Th-that isn't so!"

Mikoto came back to herself when Takemikazuchi started to apologize, and she vigorously shook her head.

"It's me, it's all my fault! My fault that I was upset with you, my fault that I felt anger…That I was jealous!!"

Her episode had caused Takemikazuchi distress, bringing even more shame and guilt into the storm of emotions swirling within her.

Tears began to pour out of her eyes, her face a light shade of red as she explained that she had no right to feel upset, angry, or jealous.

But she lacked the courage to tell him what was really going on in her heart. She felt she didn't have the right to do that, either.

"No, not your fault. Because I am your god, and also your father."

Mikoto's gaze was fixed on the floor, but Takemikazuchi's words made her eyes open wide.

"If there's something you want to say, say it. I will accept anything and everything. That's what families are for, is it not?"

Then he smiled and added that it was the only way for him to notice things.

Slowly, very slowly, Mikoto raised her head. Cheeks getting darker by the moment, her lips parted and closed over and over without any sounds coming out. Even though she was separated from the familia, they cared enough about her to organize a going-away party. They were still her family, and knowing that warmed her heart.

Accept what she had to say—would he really?

If it was true, she wanted him to. To not only accept but respond.

She wanted to hear what he would have to say about going beyond their relationship as father and daughter, as a family.

She wanted to know the true thoughts of the god she had put through so much trouble over the years.

Lips trembling, Mikoto's ears turned bright red as her heartbeat pounded audibly.

Chigusa, Ouka, and the other members of the familia realized what that meant and waited for Takemikazuchi's next words with bated breath.

Mikoto kicked her pride to the side and built up as much courage as she could muster.

"Lord Takemikazuchi, I—!!"

"Mikoto, I have a gift for you. Wait right here."

There was a hint of self-satisfaction in his voice as Takemikazuchi turned away from her and walked to the corner of the room, oblivious to Mikoto's once-in-a-lifetime level of determination.

Mikoto froze, a dark-red statue in front of the doorway. Ouka and the others stared at their god, disappointed by his horrible sense of timing.

A fresh torrent of tears made its way down Mikoto's cheeks.

Oblivious to the glares of dismay, Takemikazuchi returned to her with a gratified smile on his face and held his gift out to her.

"A going-away present."

"Eh...?"

A small sword the length of a dagger was in his outstretched right hand.

He held another one in his left hand, but a different color.

"...Male and female, a matching pair of swords."

Mikoto's voice trembled.

"That's right," Takemikazuchi responded with a satisfied nod.

"I used money earned at my part-time job without involving the familia...and, yes, a loan as well."

Astonishment overtook Mikoto's face with that admission.

Ouka and Chigusa didn't know about it, either. They were just as shocked as Mikoto.

"I heard that Hestia went into debt to acquire a knife for Bell Cranell. I'm not trying to compete with her, but I figured I should be able to do something on that level as well...I don't consider a loan to be appealing, but I..."

He closed his eyes toward the end, stumbling over his words. A faint blush appeared on Takemikazuchi's face.

Meanwhile, Mikoto gazed at the small swords in the god's hands as he admitted his rivalry with the young goddess.

One black, one white. Shaped like *katana*, even their sheaths were well-designed and high quality.

Goibniu Familia's signature was carved into each; both were custom made.

Mikoto's dark velvet eyes began to tremble and moisten.

"...Something for my beautiful daughter, a little token."

The smile she gave him broke what was left of the dam, sending more tears than ever streaming down her face.

Takemikazuchi hesitated for a moment, forcing a smile in front of the tearful girl. He took a step forward and bent his knees so that his eyes were level with Mikoto's.

"The male is Tenka, the female Chizan...I give this one to you now, and I'll carry the other."

With the box in her arms, Mikoto couldn't take the blade from him, so Takemikazuchi slid the dagger-size black sword—the female, Chizan—into the sash around her waist.

After making sure it was secure, he looked into Mikoto's still leaking eyes.

"And the other one shall be yours on the day you come back to us," he said. "So make sure you come back."

Showing her the white blade, Tenka, Takemikazuchi smiled once again.

"I will wait as long as I must, Mikoto."

More tears flowed as Mikoto closed her eyes.

A pleasant, warm feeling swelled within her heart and grew to envelop her entire body. Eyes still closed, she smiled back at him.

She envisioned the moment when the two blades would be reunited.

That would be the day she would reveal her true feelings, the ones she couldn't say this night.

She would become someone worthy of carrying both blades.

Next time, for sure, she would speak her mind.

"—Yes!! Please wait for me!"

Cheeks slick with her tears, genuine joy appeared in her expression.

She exchanged smiles with Takemikazuchi, face-to-face.

Chigusa, Ouka, Haruhime, and the rest of the group that surrounded the two couldn't help but follow suit.

"Um, this...this is a cake...so, Lord Takemikazuchi, everyone together..."

"Oh, thanks, Mikoto! Now then, all of you—let's dig in!"

""Yes!"" came their voices in unison.

Takemikazuchi took the box from the still-sobbing Mikoto as the room came alive. The men couldn't wait another moment and were around the table in the blink of an eye, hands outstretched.

Chigusa, Haruhime, and the other girls gathered around Mikoto.

All of them exchanged hugs, smiles, and pats on the back. The star of the evening wiped the tears away with her arm and smiled back at her friends.

Light from the magic-stone lamps outside came in through the living room windows.

It was just like back at the shrine. Their small home overflowed with laughter.

Warm sunlight shone down through clear blue skies.

Early signs of summer had arrived in Orario. A blade flashed in the sunlight from overhead as it whistled through the air.

Hestia Familia's home, the manor's garden.

Mikoto was by herself, shedding droplets of sweat as she practiced combat techniques among the lush green of the lawn, shrubbery, and trees.

Spinning, tumbling, and slashing like a ninja, she held Takemika-zuchi's gift Chizan tight in her grasp.

"My opinion of Lord Takemikazuchi has improved…a little…"

Bell and Welf watched Mikoto's training from the shade of a nearby hallway. Nahza spoke up next to them.

She had come to the manor to deliver the items that *Hestia Familia* had ordered. Hearing about what had transpired yesterday seemed to put her in a good mood. Even her tail swished back and forth with more enthusiasm than usual.

"Was a bit worried for a while there. Can't help but feel like we're missing something important, though," Welf remarked as he stood with his hand against a wooden pillar.

"But Miss Mikoto's back on good terms with Lord Takemika-zuchi. She certainly looks happy…" Bell, right next to him, wore a cheerful smile.

Every so often, Mikoto would stop practicing, admire the blade in her hand, and grin.

She looked to be in very high spirits. Bell and Welf watched her and shared a lighthearted, wry smile. On the other hand, Nahza narrowed her eyes at the girl. While she admired Takemikazuchi for preparing a weapon for Mikoto on his own, there was another concern.

"But, you know..."

Slowly but surely, the corner of her mouth tilted up.

"...he does *things like that* all the time like it's nothing. I think that's why people call him insensitive."

Dividing a male and female pair of blades between god and follower like Takemikazuchi just did.

The female blade to the woman, and the male blade to the man.

It was almost like—

"——An engagement ring. Deities tend to call it a 'proposal.'"

"...Well, yeah."

"Ah, ha-ha-ha-ha..."

Welf rubbed his neck with his free hand. An empty laugh escaped Bell's mouth before he could repress it.

It was easy to get the wrong idea as the recipient of something close to a marriage proposal. All three observers were thinking the same thing.

"Everyone! Why don't you join me in training if you have time—?"

Mikoto stopped her practice swings, turned to face the onlookers, and waved.

With the female half of the pair firmly in her grasp, a smile as clear as the sky above bloomed on her face.

© Suzuhito Yasuda

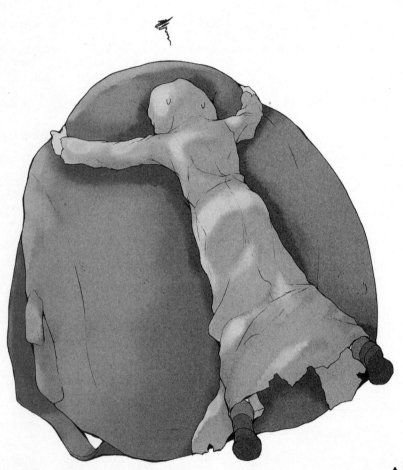

◢ CHAPTER 2 **THE PRUM'S PROPOSAL**

Fifty kirlos due east from Orario.

While life was going on as usual behind the city wall far away, the Alliance was still busy dealing with Rakia's army.

"Gahh, I'm soooo bored. Fiiiinn. End this already, will yaaaa."

The battle had begun five days ago.

Loki Familia had built their base of operations in a clearing in the middle of the plain. There they had a commanding view, from the harsh Alb mountain range all the way to the edges of the Deep Forest Seoro. While *Loki Familia*'s flag flew high above their heads, they kept a close eye on enemy movements.

A goddess lazily sprawled out over several chairs lined up side by side underneath the largest tent inside the base. Finn, meanwhile, leaned over a large map stretched across a table. He smiled dryly to himself.

"I would like nothing more than to do just that…"

Alone with his goddess inside the tent, Finn studied the locations of different pieces on top of the map.

"Their movements seem half-hearted, far too indecisive."

"What's that supposed to mean?"

"They cause enough commotion to get our attention but never truly go on the offensive…Even their generals, equal to our second-tier adventurers, refuse to show their faces. Their forces take one step forward and then three steps back. Our allies are being spread too thin chasing them down. We can't keep this up."

If Rakia had one advantage over the alliance of powerful adventurers, it was numbers.

It went without saying that many large familias resided within Orario, but none had the manpower to match that of an entire country. It might have been the era of quality over quantity, but overwhelming an opponent with numbers was still a viable strategy.

Even if the Orario familias committed their forces to eliminating all the small battalions that were cutting off Orario's trade and crippling its economy, they would inevitably end up chasing the enemy too far, stretching their already thin lines to the breaking point.

"So the main army's hidin' somewhere, and the guys we're fightin' now are just distractions?"

"That can't be completely ruled out, but..."

Finn begrudgingly answered Loki, who hadn't shown the slightest interest in, nor bothered to remember, any incoming information since the start of the war. That was when another member of *Loki Familia* ran into the base and entered the tent.

"General, I have confirmation."

"Good work, Raul. What's the latest from Port Meren?"

"Everything seems normal. There were no sightings of a fleet or even suspicious ships, from Lolog Lake up to the cliffs."

Finn listened to his subordinate's report and turned to face the map. His hands went to the west side of Orario, opposite to their base's location on the map, and he removed all the stones from the lake, all the way up the coastline.

"So there's no possibility of an incursion by sea..."

Loki got out of her makeshift chair bed and joined Raul beside the map. They could see that Finn had marked the location of the first battle and indicated the current location of Rakia's many battalions with red pieces. The troops that Finn had sent in pursuit were marked blue.

"It appears our enemy wants to draw out this war...They want to spread Orario's forces as thin as possible, chip away at our supplies and morale, then finish the bulk of the fighting outside the city."

"Ahhh, got it. So that's what's goin' on."

Loki smirked as Finn worked out Rakia's strategy piece by piece and arrived at their final goal.

The prum general had a little chuckle at the range of expressions that passed over his god's face.

"Let's return to the city for the time being. Whatever the enemy is after, it's there."

"Music to my ears!" Loki jubilantly clapped her hands, rejoicing in her newfound freedom.

"Raul, we're withdrawing. Spread the word to all units. Leave our flags in place. Rakia can't know we're gone."

"A-are you sure, General...? If we just abandon the front..."

"We have a good reason to return to the city. I doubt the Guild will complain."

Finn ignored his subordinate's shocked expression and started packing up his belongings.

"*Freya Familia* can take care of the rest."

"Hee-hee-hee! She can't say no to the Guild 'cause of everything that happened with Ishtar. That airheaded vixen got slapped with a mighty high penalty. They can take care of all the dirty work!"

Loki couldn't have looked more pleased, since a certain Goddess of Beauty would have no choice but to obey the Guild's orders. She could unload all the boring jobs onto that goddess's familia. A small group of messengers rushed out of the base to deliver the orders to field commanders. *Loki Familia* was in full retreat a little less than an hour later.

"Any powerful familias still left in Orario?"

"Hmm...Of the big ones...there's probably only Phai-Phai's kids."

"*Hephaistos Familia*? That's perfect. I'll have them help out as well."

After going over a few more things with Loki, Finn left to oversee the final stages of their withdrawal.

Much like during the expedition into the Dungeon, the familia's lower-ranking members quickly disassembled the base, packed it into cargo boxes, and carried it all away effortlessly. The only difference was that, this time, it was under a clear blue sky. They set their sights on the white tower rising up above to the west.

"General! Need something to drink? Or maybe some food? I just caught a wild boar! Should I roast some for you?"

"Oh, um, I'm going to have to decline, Tione. If you do start a fire, make sure there's no smoke."

"Will dooo!"

With bronze, wheat-colored skin and long black hair, the Amazon Tione Hyrute wore minimalist battle gear that barely covered her lush bosom and smooth skin. Finn gave his Amazonian field commander a vacant smile as she made another pass at him.

Tiona shot a look that screamed, *"Again?!"* at her older twin sister, Tione, who made no attempt to hide her intentions. This was a common occurrence in *Loki Familia*, so Aiz and the other members were used to it and took care not to get involved.

Finn waited out the storm until someone else got Tione's attention and she left.

"Finn, what are your plans after our return?"

"Okay to wait fer new orders at home?"

After Tione left, the elf Riveria and the dwarf Gareth came up to talk to him.

Finn turned to face the other two leaders of *Loki Familia* and opened his mouth to speak.

"I'll issue orders in advance, so could I have a little time off, Riveria, Gareth?"

"Oh?"

"Well, that's new. Got somethin' that needs takin' care of?"

Riveria and Gareth cast dubious glances at the prum, but he just smiled back at them.

"I've thought about looking into something for a while now…"

Finn's eyes, blue as the surface of a lake, narrowed as he looked at Orario's massive city walls off in the distance.

"There's one other 'mission' that's had no progress at all, despite the fact that I'm an adventurer, and I'll be checking it out."

"Hellooo. Lilly's here—."

The prum opened a door that didn't fit properly in its frame and entered a small house.

The sun was just barely visible on the eastern horizon.

Oversize backpack strapped to her shoulders, she paid the

pawnshop the Gnome Trader a visit. Passing through the messy living space behind the main showroom, she quickly spotted the owner of the establishment; he was barely awake and sipping hot water from a cup like a groggy child.

Glug, glug, glug. She could hear the water making its way past his white beard and between his lips.

"Oh, if it isn't Lilly…Mornin'."

"Good morning. But please wash up and sit up straight before drinking hot water. Lilly won't be here for long."

Without his usual red cap, the gnome's bald head was completely visible. "Sure, sure," he responded, mumbling to himself as he climbed out of his chair. Lilly set down her backpack and started preparing the store for business while the owner washed his face.

Lilly had lived here at the Gnome Trader until *Hestia Familia* acquired a new home in the War Game.

Her situation with *Soma Familia* had come to a head two months ago, and she had needed a place to stay. She was familiar with this shop from the days when she frequently stole items from other adventurers and sold them for money. On that particular day, however, she had arrived at the shop and said, "Please let Lilly live here in exchange for work." The owner had never seen her real face, but she'd placed all her faith in him as a person.

"Cinder Ella," Lilly's Magic, granted her the ability to change her physical appearance at will, and that was the first time she'd let him see what she looked like. "You're in luck; I've been wanting another set of hands around here," he'd said, and hired her on the spot. She'd been coming to check on him early every morning and help out around the store before going into the Dungeon, then again before going home each night—as a way of repaying her debt of gratitude—ever since.

"I feel a bit guilty with you comin' in every day like this even when your familia's grown so much."

"Don't worry about Lilly—worry about your health first, Mr. Bom. Lilly can't take care of everything if you collapse from overwork like last time."

"Don't know what I would've done without you. This geezer's not worthy."

The shop owner's name was Bom Cornwall.

The fairy races weren't known for individuality, but he had a vibrant personality. His superb dexterity and eyesight made him right at home in Orario. When Lilly had asked him why he chose to live in the city rather than out in nature, he'd simply replied, "This geezer is the worst of the worst when it comes to fairies."

He made his living by appraising items that came into the shop, buying them for as cheap as possible, and selling them for profit.

"This breakfast was prepared at Lilly's home this morning—make sure to eat everything. Also, the lamp in the storage room was broken, so Lilly replaced the magic stone. The stock of jewels in the safe is running low, so it might be a good idea to put more in."

"Ah, ahhh, thanks..."

Slightly intimidated by Lilly's efficiency, the gnome put on his signature red cap. Bald head hidden, his round eyes gazed up at the girl who stood a head higher than he.

"Off to the Dungeon again today?"

"Yes. We should reach the sixteenth floor today! As you know, Lilly's familia has been on a roll!"

A beaming smile appeared on her face as she spoke. Thinking of her friendly and dependable allies, she added, "Lilly will do her best not to hold them back!"

She did a few more things around the shop before taking a glance at the clock. It was time for her to meet Bell and her other allies at their usual spot at the base of Babel Tower.

"Mr. Bom, please don't forget to eat the food Lilly brought."

"I won't, I won't. Have a good day."

"Good-bye until tonight!" She responded with a smile still in place and waved as she went out the door.

"...She can smile like that now, huh."

The owner mumbled to himself, eyes on the door that Lilly had passed through.

Without the abilities they possessed in the Ancient Times, gnomes had fallen to the bottom ranks of the fairies, but he was still a member of a race that was considered closest to the gods themselves.

Lilly thought that her secret past was still hidden, but his eyes saw through her disguises.

An air of nostalgia filled his gaze. The white hairs of his beard ruffled as a happy smile grew on his lips.

The moon hung high above *Hestia Familia*'s home, Hearthstone Manor.

Back from the Dungeon, everyone had finished eating dinner together. Now they were taking turns going to Hestia's room to receive a Status update.

They had agreed that checking their Statuses should happen on a weekly basis, like this night. Unless one of them had special circumstances, Hestia would take a look at their Falna one at a time on the scheduled day.

It was Lilly's turn. She was a bit nervous to see how much her own excelia would be reduced, now that Haruhime had joined the familia, and exposed her back.

"All done."

Sitting topless in a chair, Lilly pulled her shirt back over her head as Hestia wrote down her updated Status on a piece of paper.

Lilly looked at the details that her goddess had translated into Koine, the common language of Orario.

Lilliluka Erde

Level One

Strength: I 81 Defense: H 123 -> 124 Dexterity: G 232 -> 236

Agility: F 383 -> 388 Magic: E 402 -> 404

(Magic)

"Cinder Ella"

• **Shape-shifting Magic**

- Target will take the envisioned shape at the time of the spell. Will fail without clear image.
- Imitation is recommended.
- Trigger Spell: "Your scars are mine. My scars are mine."
- Release Spell: "Stroke of midnight's bell."

(Skill)

"Artel Assist"
- Activates automatically when weight carried exceeds a certain level.
- Amount of assistance is proportional to weight carried.

"...Haaaaah..."

A long, slow breath of disappointment escaped Lilly's lips.

One look at the growth of her Basic Abilities was disheartening.

Lilly never thought that half a year's worth of excelia would be enough to level up, but...

There had been a six-month period when, as a member of *Soma Familia*, Lilly had never received a Status update due to circumstances within that group.

After undergoing Conversion to participate in the War Game, she'd finally received one. Although her expectations were low, her half year's worth of excelia unfortunately didn't amount to all that much. Her Basic Ability levels still placed her among the lower ranks of lower-class adventurers. Every Status update since had been similar to this one.

It didn't make sense for a low-level Status to improve by leaps and bounds in only six months.

"Supporter, I understand your frustration, but..."

"Lilly understands; she is a supporter. It's common knowledge that a supporter's Status improves at the slowest rate."

In fact, Lilly had become a supporter in the first place because she didn't do well as an adventurer. Growing at a slow pace certainly didn't help.

Her response was rather cold toward Hestia, who had pricked her own finger so she could use the ichor for Lilly. She turned her back to the sympathetic goddess and left the room.

She arrived at the living room after walking through the first-floor hallway.

Welf and her other allies were gathered in a happy circle, excitedly discussing and comparing the Statuses written on the papers in their hands.

Her arrival signaled that it was Bell's turn for an update; he was the last. Lilly thought about joining the circle as soon as Bell left, but…she caught a glimpse of the reflection of her back in the window and came to a stop.

Her usual robe was hanging in her room. The shirt she had on now was for relaxing in. Part of her lower back wasn't covered, and she could see some of the black hieroglyphs that made up her Status.

Seeing it in plain sight made her eyebrows sink into a stern expression.

"I've been curious for a while…"

She joined the circle in the living room as soon as she saw Bell and Hestia return from his completed Status update, and she was quick to bring up what was on her mind.

"Why are our Statuses visible?"

"Ah, I was wondering about that, too."

"I-I as well…I felt it strange that Lady Hestia made no attempt to conceal it."

"I was certain it was a policy in this familia…Did I assume too much?"

"Huh…? There's a way to hide Statuses?!"

Lilly's question got an immediate response from Welf, Mikoto, and Haruhime, each of whom had once belonged to another familia. Hestia was stunned—Bell also gave a surprised "Eh?!"—so Lilly explained that there was a way for gods to "lock" a Status.

It was a technique that deities used to keep the hieroglyphs on their children's backs invisible to the naked eye. This "lock" made sure that the valuable information contained in a Status was protected against prying eyes.

Hephaistos, Takemikazuchi, Ishtar, and even the good-for-nothing Soma knew how to use this Status-hiding technique. Hestia, who had only recently come to Gekai, was absolutely floored by this information.

"So that's why...I've never seen Statuses on any of the Amazons walking around the city...I always thought they used body paint."

"N-now that you mention it, Miss Eina said I should always 'lock up' so others couldn't see my Status...I guess she wasn't talking about locking the home's doors after all..."

"I'll, uh, ask Hephaistos or someone next time I see one of them..."

The others in the room softly shook their heads, while Bell's and Hestia's minds had been blown by such common sense. That's when Lilly finally joined the circle.

"Would it be okay if Lilly saw everyone's Statuses?"

"Sure, no prob."

"Of course."

"This is mine."

With Lilly asking politely, Welf, Mikoto, and Haruhime each passed their papers over to her.

Welf Crozzo

Level Two

Strength: I 67 -> 70 Defense: I 50 -> 53 Dexterity: I 78 -> 82
Agility: I 36 -> 38 Magic: I 57 -> 61
Forge: I

Mikoto Yamato

Level Two

Strength: H 133 -> 134 Defense: H 129 -> 130 Dexterity: H 178 ->
181 Agility: H162 -> 167 Magic: I 84
Immunity: I

Haruhime Sanjouno

Level One

Strength: I 8 -> 9 Defense: I 32 Dexterity: I 15 Agility: I 23 -> 26

Magic: E 403 -> 405

Okay, so this is normal...

Seeing that her level of growth was par for the course, she passed her own sheet around the circle.

Once everyone had seen Lilly's, all eyes fell on the boy who came in last.

Feeling the pressure from being the center of attention, Bell became flustered.

Scratching his head with his left hand, he didn't put up a fuss and slid his own paper into the center of the circle.

Bell Cranell

Level Three

Strength: F 377 -> 391 Defense: F 389 -> 396 Dexterity: F 377 -> 392 Agility: D 583 -> 594 Magic: F 352 -> 360 Luck: H

Immunity: I

«««« »»»»»
...

No one could say a word as they stared at Bell's Status. His Basic Abilities had improved by over fifty points. Of course, Bell was at a higher Level. Still, he had improved more than any of them.

Something strange was going on.

They were fighting in the same Dungeon against the same monsters. True, he'd delivered more blows during combat and probably had a higher kill count, but nowhere near enough to explain such a disparity in growth.

Each of them had thought it a bit mysterious whenever the topic of Bell's unusually fast growth came up, and today they were united in their curiosity.

"Seriously, what is going on with you?"

"B-beats me…"

Welf held the piece of paper in his hand and pressed the issue. Judging by the white-haired boy's reaction, though, he really had no idea.

Questioned about his unusual growth speed by so many other people at once, Bell was clearly uncomfortable because he didn't have an answer for them.

"Lilly thinks it's less Mr. Bell's natural talent and more some kind of special power at work…"

Making sure that Welf and Bell couldn't hear, Lilly quietly whispered to Mikoto, Haruhime, and Hestia, looking at them out of the corner of her eyes.

The young goddess closed her eyes and whistled like a child desperately trying to keep a secret. A bead of sweat rolled down her cheek.

Lilly rolled her eyes at Hestia before making brief eye contact with every other member of the familia—except Bell.

Her intent was simple: Today, we find out the truth.

"It's getting pretty late. Anyone done for the day should hop in the tub."

Welf made the first move.

He rolled his shoulders and neck, stretching as he turned to face the boy, and said, "Bell, why don't you head in first?"

"I, um, already took a shower at Babel…"

"But I already prepared the bath tonight. It would be a waste not to enjoy it, Sir Bell."

Mikoto's words made Bell feel a twinge of guilt.

Hestia stepped in to try and protect him, but Lilly's sharp glare stopped her in her tracks.

"B-but is it really okay for me to go first? Everyone's worked so hard…If it would go to waste, why not join me, Welf?"

"I got stuff to do in the forge."

"I must prepare ingredients for tomorrow's breakfast."

"I-I, um, that is…My tail requires grooming!"

Welf's and Mikoto's excuses rolled off their tongues, almost as if they had planned them. Without missing a beat, each left the circle and started toward their destinations. On the other hand, the renart was forced to improvise. As soon as she came up with something, Haruhime turned away from the circle while holding her tail awkwardly in both hands, pulling out loose hairs.

"Lilly has something to discuss with Lady Hestia."

"Eek…" came the goddess's voice, clearly intimidated by Lilly's half-eyed stare.

Everyone plainly told Bell to go ahead. "Well, in that case…" he said as he turned on his heel and left the living room.

Everyone came back to the circle the moment the boy disappeared, and they surrounded their goddess.

"Now then, Lady Hestia, if you know anything about Mr. Bell's 'growth,' please say it. Today we want the truth."

Hestia was speechless as Lilly stepped into the leadership role and began questioning her.

Her head on a swivel, the goddess searched in every direction, only to see she was completely surrounded. Even more beads of sweat rolled down her face until she finally gave in. Taking a deep breath, she made a long sigh.

"I suppose it makes no sense to hide things from members of the same familia…Fine, I'll tell you." She was quick to add, "But it doesn't leave this room, got it?" before revealing the secrets of Bell's "growth"—although it pained her to do so.

That's when Lilly and the others learned about the boy's Skill.

"Liaris…Freese…?"

Lilly's soft, stunned voice echoed Hestia's explanation about Bell's Skill, Liaris Freese.

Everyone was understandably shocked by a Rare Skill that could influence the rate of an adventurer's growth. But even more so, the finer details of the Skill left them speechless.

—Rapid growth.

—Continued desire results in continued growth.

—Stronger desire results in stronger growth.

The Skill was directly influenced by the feelings lurking within the boy's heart.

Those feelings—his feelings for Aiz—had become the driving force behind his unbelievably fast ascension to the upper ranks of adventurers.

"So basically him falling head over heels for that Sword Princess makes him grow stronger like there's no tomorrow?"

"Head over heels...?! W-well, I guess that's true..."

"The one...in Master Bell's heart..."

Welf was confirming that he understood Liaris Freese correctly after Hestia fell silent. Meanwhile, Haruhime and Lilly couldn't hide how jarred they were by the revelation.

Bell Cranell was more than just interested in Aiz Wallenstein.

That fact took all the wind out of their sails.

There was a reason he was trying so hard. I knew that, but...

Even when she first met him, Lilly knew there had to be something behind his motivation to work so hard in the Dungeon, that there was some goal.

However, to think that his goal had been to catch up to that famous woman, the Kenki...

Considering his age, it wasn't all that strange for him to harbor affection for someone of the opposite gender, but...knowing about how he and Aiz had met, with her saving him from a Minotaur, was making Lilly's chestnut-colored eyes tremble.

"D-does Sir Bell know of this? Have you told him nothing?"

"That boy couldn't keep a secret to save his life. If anyone pressed him for information about his Rare Skill, soon everyone would know. In this case, it's better to keep them in the dark...And it's not like he'd ever say it's all thanks to being lovey-dovey for Wallensomething!"

Mikoto and Hestia's conversation passed right through her ears.

It was as though her spirit was disconnected from her body. All sorts of thoughts and emotions coursed through her heart, but her arms and legs stayed unnaturally still. Her heart was ripping through her modest chest.

Lilly took an unsteady breath and said the words she just couldn't keep down. "L-Lady Hestia, c-can you accept…this?" Even as she stuttered, she questioned her goddess.

She knew that Hestia had feelings for Bell that went beyond a deity's love for her children. Would she allow this situation to continue? That was her question.

"…Bell himself said he wanted to get stronger. He made his decision. I couldn't bring myself to stop him once I saw how badly he wanted it."

She couldn't douse her child's determination. Lilly was taken aback by Hestia's words.

"But that doesn't mean I'll let her have him! Never, not in a million years! One of these days he'll notice me; I'll *make* him notice me…!!" Hestia clenched her fist, trembling.

Their goddess's public declaration made Welf and the others lean away out of reflex. At the same time, Lilly looked over at Haruhime.

The renart could feel her clinging gaze. Haruhime, dressed in her usual kimono, avoided making eye contact, glancing left and right before finally down at the floor.

She brought her hands together above the billowing fabric around her chest.

"I-I have lived as a courtesan…I have no right to pursue romance with Master Bell."

"…"

"…B-but as his concubine—no, as a one-night stand, surely even one such as I…!"

"HEY, HEY, HEY!"

The former courtesan's face turned red as she unwittingly loosed a bombshell into the circle. The goddess rose up, thundering with all her might.

"M-my deepest apologies!" Haruhime squealed, hiding her head behind both her arms.

"Did you actually think I'd let that slide?!" continued Hestia, her booming voice echoing throughout the room.

While Hestia and Haruhime's banter went on for some time, Lilly was isolated in her own little world.

Bell had someone special.

She had never seriously thought that there was a chance she could be by his side, but the shocking news still cut deep. Lilly was speechless that the boy's feelings were strong enough to create a Skill. She could only stand there, listless.

Lilly returned to her room shortly after that evening's events, completely forgetting to take a bath. She collapsed onto her bed right away but stayed wide awake, unable to sleep.

She stared at the ceiling of her room, her brain working at full speed. Her heart would twinge every time she closed her eyes. Even rolling over into a more comfortable position did nothing but make the sound of her rustling sheets hang in the air of her spacious room. Other than that, the room was silent.

Time crawled by as her thoughts clashed with the emotions in her heart. At long last, she climbed out of bed.

The darkness of night was coming to an end. Lilly left her room without a wink of sleep in the very early hours of morning.

"Laughable…"

Robe draped over her usual clothes, she closed the door behind her and berated herself with a tired expression.

She scolded herself over and over for getting worked up about something so trivial as she walked through the long hallway.

All members of her familia had rooms on the third floor.

There were times when Welf would spend the night cooped up in the forge, but for the most part, all of them slept up there.

Hestia's room was the first one at the top of the central staircase, then came Mikoto and Haruhime's double room. Welf's room was a few doors down from there…and finally Bell's. Lilly's feet came to a stop for a moment outside his door, but she thought better of it and decided to get a drink in the kitchen.

The first hints of sunrise were beginning to seep through the windows as Lilly lethargically made her way through the hallway... *Whoosh! Whoosh!*

The sound of something sharp slicing through the air came from a window above the garden outside.

"!"

She quickened her pace and followed the sound all the way to the window.

She could barely see over the windowsill when she stood on tiptoe. Once she looked down—a white-haired boy appeared.

She panicked and quickly ducked down to hide herself, even though she knew it wasn't necessary. A few moments passed before she ventured another peek.

Her eyes peered over the windowsill once again, and she saw Bell's violet and scarlet blades carving arcs through the air. He was practicing by himself.

Whoosh! His knives sliced through the air, trailing streaks of light and producing the sounds that had lured her to the window.

...Is he...fighting someone?

The boy launched his body, twisting and jumping at a furious pace all around the expansive garden. Every move flung droplets of sweat off his body. Lilly could tell he was visualizing an opponent and fighting as hard as he could.

That, and that his invisible opponent was terrifyingly strong.

Lilly had had many opportunities to watch adventurers at work up close and personal. Her insight as a supporter told her all this.

The boy was already a second-tier adventurer, and yet he couldn't keep up with the opponent in his head.

Ahh...He lost.

The boy came to a sudden, unnatural stop.

With his knives in an awkward position, almost like he was trying to block an oncoming attack, his upper body was leaning backward as though there was a sword against his throat. He held that position for a few moments before he let out a "Gah!" and finally took a breath, crouching down.

Hands on his knees and a small river of sweat flowing down his face, Bell's shoulders rose and fell as he tried to catch his breath.

"…"

Bell's white hair stuck to his wet cheeks and his shirt was soaked through. Lilly could tell that the boy had been practicing for a long time before she showed up. She continued to watch in silence.

Who was he fighting just now? Aiz? He'd been getting up this early to train every day to catch up with her? There was no one to answer her questions. Lilly stood there like a statue, forgetting to breathe while pondering.

The boy stood back up and started practicing once again.

The intensity of his strikes showed her the level of his devotion, in a very blunt and direct way. The longer Lilly watched him, the more thoughts began to stir in the back of her mind.

Turmoil, uncertainty, anguish, and a host of other feelings mixed together. She could practically hear them breaking her apart from the inside.

That day, everyone met in the morning to go into the Dungeon, as usual.

Having cleared the fifteenth floor the other day, they decided to go on to the sixteenth. The familia was on a roll and progressing at a good pace. The rest of the group was in high spirits, but a dark cloud was roiling inside the one wearing an oversize backpack, and it showed.

"…Lilly, are you okay?"

"!?"

Before she knew it, Bell had dropped back to the middle of their formation when he noticed she was hunched over and dragging her feet. He watched Lilly with clear concern.

"You look really tired…Are you sick?"

"L-Lilly's feeling fine, Mr. Bell! Lilly didn't get much sleep last night, but see? It's nothing to worry about!"

She forced a smile, putting on a well-rehearsed show. It was a skill she had developed during her time as a thief, a smile that could put someone at ease. Now she employed it to convince Bell nothing was wrong. It seemed that Bell was not convinced, but the appearance of monsters cut the conversation short, and they prepared to attack.

That was too close! What am I doing?! Lilly scolded herself again.

They were in the Dungeon. Even the smallest lapse in concentration put her and her party in mortal danger. Keeping a careful eye on the flow of battle between her allies and the monsters, Lilly focused on her breathing to keep her mind clear.

That's right. Lilly is Mr. Bell's...supporter.

But knowing the person whom Bell adored the most had shaken her to the core. Lilly was starting to wonder what Bell thought of her.

A support specialist. The object of unmasked contempt. A simple laborer for other adventurers.

Lilly's individual abilities did nothing to help the party. She didn't have the strength to put herself on the front lines to defend Bell, like Welf and Mikoto. Never mind standing beside him, she could not even follow from behind.

During her time as a thief, the adventurers she stole from had always called her "useless," with demeaning grins. All those memories were coming back. On the surface, her iron will let her put on the mask of the ever-dependable supporter. But underneath, Lilly's emotions were in chaos.

"..."

The Crozzo Magic Sword clenched tightly in her grip, Lilly was ready to unleash its power at any moment. Glancing to her side, she saw Haruhime nervously twitching while watching Bell and the others fight.

Haruhime held the same position as she did, working as a supporter. The big difference was that she could use a powerful spell.

Level Boost. A type of Magic that brought out amazing strength and speed from any adventurer it was cast on. With that spell at her beck and call, she could do more as a supporter to directly assist the party. Haruhime was worth far more than Lilly.

Not to mention that the renart was gorgeous.

Her bushy, golden fox tail and long, silky hair aside, Haruhime possessed soft, delicate features that Lilly could never compete with. Even the aura of purity that surrounded her might give the Sword Princess, Aiz Wallenstein, a run for her money.

And her breasts were…impressive.

When Miss Haruhime…

If she gained more experience, would Lilly be deemed unnecessary? Would she lose her place before she ran into the obstacle of Aiz Wallenstein?

Before that happens, should I…stop training Haruhime as a supporter? Or should I follow through as a teacher?

That's when Lilly realized where her train of thought was taking her—and vigorously shook her head.

"Lady Lilly?"

"…It's…nothing."

Haruhime had taken her eyes off the battle and was now focused on her. Lilly barely managed a perfunctory reply.

Why am I so shallow?! She felt sick to her stomach.

Calling herself horrible names, Lilly fell even deeper into the darkness.

Compared to the other women around Bell—she was nowhere near as pretty as Hestia, Eina, Syr, or Haruhime.

Her heart was unclean. She was so desperate to look good in front of others. She wasn't right for Bell, a pure, naive child who knew nothing of the real world.

In the end, this pain, all it really is…

That's right. To put it bluntly, Lilly had an inferiority complex. She couldn't compare with the girl whose beauty was in the league of goddesses and could make Bell blush just by talking to him.

She was beautiful, strong, refined. Many adventurers, not just Bell, idolized Aiz Wallenstein. Lilly could never win against her even if heaven and earth happened to switch places. Knowing this caused her pain. An inferiority complex told her she would lose at every turn. Her adversary was a flower in bloom at the top of a mountain—the place where Bell was always looking. She would never enter his line of sight.

Lilly could never become Bell's one and only.

That burning truth had kept her awake through the night and brought her to the brink of despair. Tormented by her jealousy and thrown for a loop by her emotions, she was disappointed in herself.

"..."

The battle had ended, so Lilly and Haruhime set to work on collecting the magic stones and drop items from the monsters slain by Bell and the others. She picked up a magic stone from the floor of the dark Dungeon. The reflection of her small face on its surface made her heart cringe.

"In that case, is it safe to assume you made it to floor sixteen today?"

"Yes. We still don't have a good grasp on the layout, but we can hold our own against the monsters without too much trouble."

I arrived at the Guild before dark. The blue sky's still visible outside the windows as I talk with my adviser, Miss Eina.

Our party came back to the surface and visited the Exchange at Babel before we went our separate ways. I'm sure they're back at home by now. But I decided to come here on my own and give a report on how everything went.

There were two reasons why we came back a little bit earlier than usual. The first was that we had collected an unusually high amount of loot in the Dungeon. Lilly's and Haruhime's backpacks were filled to the point of overflowing, so it would've been difficult to bring any more back to the surface.

And the second...was that Lilly didn't seem like herself.

"I couldn't be happier to hear you're making progress. Just don't push too hard, okay?"

"I'll be careful, Miss Eina."

She really seems glad to hear that we were staying safe despite all our progress in the Dungeon. Her short brown hair sways back and forth around her pointy elf ears as she smiles back at me.

We finish discussing everything at the counter rather than going to the consultation box, so we say our good-byes, and I turn toward the exit.

"Lilly…I wonder what happened."

It wasn't just in the Dungeon, either. Lilly hasn't been her usual self since breakfast, now that I think about it. She put up a strong front all day, and it's making me worry.

I cross the Guild's white marble lobby as I continue to think about my companions.

"——Bell Cranell."

"Huh?"

Someone calling my name snaps me out of my train of thought, right as I'm about to leave Guild Headquarters.

It sounds like a boy about my age, maybe a little younger. I spin around to find him—and my eyes shoot open as soon as I see the person standing behind me.

Light golden hair and a small stature.

With a face like his and a body that size, he could pass for a kid, but nothing about his appearance matches the mature aura emanating from him. No, this is definitely a top-tier adventurer.

Words leave me the moment I make eye contact with the prum.

"Finn Deimne…?!"

I can't hide my surprise that the leader of *Loki Familia* is calling out to me.

"Sorry to stop you like this. I'm not here to cause trouble, so please try to relax."

Finn smiles, completely calm. Meanwhile, I'm stiff as a board and can't stop shaking.

But there's something soothing about Finn's smile. It loosens me up a little bit, but I'm still in awe of this top-class adventurer who stands at the very peak of Orario, basically above the clouds. Trembling, I finally respond.

"Umm, wh-what can I do for you…?"

"Why so nervous? We met during the Minotaur battle, back on the eighteenth floor, so this isn't the first time, yes? I've been waiting for a chance to talk with you properly. Unfortunately, contacting you in

the usual way would cause a few inconvenient misunderstandings…
Sorry, but I had no choice but to wait for you here."

Hestia Familia's gained some notice almost overnight thanks
to the War Game. Finn explains to me that our quick rise to fame
caught a lot of attention, so knocking on our front door was out of
the question, no matter how much he wanted to say hello. Doing so
as a member of *Loki Familia* would have led to many troublesome
misunderstandings, so Finn was trying to be low-key.

"Actually, I snuck away from my subordinates," he adds. It's only
then that I realize many girls have gathered around us. He's the center of attention.

"He's so small!" "What a cutie!" "So cool!" Their voices echo
throughout the busy Guild lobby. He forces a smile and looks up at me.

"I have a bit of *a favor* to ask. If you're not busy, I'd like to sit and
talk with you for a while. What do you say?"

Of course, I have no reason to say no.

Finn and I leave Guild Headquarters and take a series of backstreets to reach a café called Wish in Orario's southwest district.

"A young elf magic user told me about this place," Finn says as he
leads me through a series of repeating narrow passageways to the
front door.

This is actually my second time here. Lord Hermes brought
Mikoto and me here not too long ago, but I haven't been back since.
I follow Finn inside, and we take seats on opposite sides of a table in
the quiet café.

"As this is a secret meeting between the highest-ranking members
of two familias, I would like to request we keep what is said confi-
dential. Agreed?"

"Y-yes…!"

We're the only ones in here, with the exception of the café owner,
an elf behind the counter. Being all alone with such an amazing
adventurer would make anyone nervous. Finn takes a sip of the tea
he ordered, ignoring all my anxious fidgeting. He casually starts the
conversation.

"For starters, I would like to congratulate you on your victory in the War Game. I watched the whole thing, and I must say I was impressed. Also, congratulations on the formation of your familia."

"Th-thank you!"

My body takes over, and I involuntarily bow the moment I hear his sincere praise.

This prum hero just complimented me...I think this is a serious honor. Even being singled out to talk face-to-face with one of the most famous adventurers in Orario doesn't feel real.

Finn smiles and watches me with his clear blue eyes. My heart is trying to leap out of my chest with nervousness, but I'm also really happy.

"Not to change the subject, but has anything strange happened recently?"

"Strange?"

"It's peaceful inside the wall, but it might be a good idea to keep your eyes peeled...Recently, it feels like there's going to be trouble," Finn says with his mouth behind the cup in his hands.

I tilt my head, wondering what he means by that. A hint of some kind, maybe? Is he referring to the recent trouble with Rakia...*Ares Familia*'s attack?

Well, I know that their army is basically a large group of low-level adventurers, and they've been fighting against several of Orario's familias for the past few days.

Wait, wasn't *Loki Familia* participating in the Guild's mission? Weren't they ordered to fight Rakia...? Is it okay for their leader to be here right now?

"That's enough small talk; let me get to the point." Finn changes the subject just as my thoughts start coming to a head.

"I would like you to introduce me to your supporter, a prum with chestnut eyes."

"......Huh?"

It takes a few long moments for me to comprehend that. But once I do, it hits me like a ton of bricks.

My supporter—he wants to meet her and is asking me to set it up. The unexpected request leaves me breathless.

But Finn isn't done. He goes even further.

"Well, I should be more direct. As a member of her race, I would like to offer her my hand in marriage." ·

The ton of bricks just exploded.

"—E-EHHHHHHHHHHHHHHHHHHHHHHHHHHHHHHH?!"

I jump out of my chair, almost sending it toppling to the floor.

This is no joke. My shocked voice is still echoing inside the empty café, but Finn just looks dead serious. This is by far the biggest surprise of today.

Lilly—is going to get a proposal?!

"Wh-what…what are you saying…?!"

"First off, I would like you to calm down. Then, I would like you to understand that this is not some spur-of-the-moment proposition."

I'm on the verge of losing my mind, but Finn is absolutely calm, never stirring from his chair and asking me to relax. Those serene, incredibly blue eyes lock onto mine. Gulping down the air in my throat, I manage to regain a semblance of composure.

The elf at the back of the counter looks through his glasses as he wipes off a just-cleaned goblet at the other end of the room. Meanwhile, I sink back into my chair. I try to listen to what Finn has to say.

"For starters, you might be wondering why I would make such a proposal to a member of my race who belongs to a different familia…But first I must ask: Bell Cranell, do you know of the goddess Phiana?"

The goddess Phiana…I've heard of her.

She's a *fictional* goddess who many prums believed in.

There once was a group of strong and proud prum knights in the Ancient Times who worshipped her.

Maybe it was because of their small size and gentle appearance, but prums were generally considered to have the least amount of potential, compared to other races like humans and demi-humans.

In truth, very few prums at all have become world famous in the thousands of years of their history.

The exception was that group of knights. Accomplishing one heroic act after another, they became known as "Spears of the Battlefield." Their glory became the pride of the prum race and also inspired deep faith in Phiana.

They were so acclaimed that even I've read about the exploits of those brave men and women in many of the *Tales of Heroes*.

—However, once the Ancient Times ended and the Divine Era began, faith in Phiana dried up in the blink of an eye.

It was all because the goddess revered by the entire prum race was not among the deities who descended to the mortal world, Gekai. Prums everywhere lost their confidence in their faith, and their lives completely fell apart. It was a decisive blow their race hasn't recovered from even today…or so I hear.

I lightly nod at Finn, and he cuts right to the chase.

"Prums need a light they can call their own. A new hope that can fill the role that faith in Phiana once held."

"…And that would be?"

"Just as you're thinking. I came to Orario to live as an adventurer so I could become that hope for my people and bring them together. I wanted my name to be legendary, so other prums could have someone to aspire to."

Finn's ambition—no, his magnificent cause—leaves me speechless.

He's fighting to change the fortunes of an entire race, carrying the future of all prums on his small shoulders. He arrived at the gates of Orario with the goal of becoming so famous that his very name would inspire his kin around the world.

And now he's a top-tier adventurer—a member of the highest echelons of the Labyrinth City, at Level 6.

In Orario—a place that's called the center of the world.

People of other races like me, even the gods and goddesses, know his name. I'd be surprised if someone didn't. I'm sure that stories of Finn's bravery and heroics have spread around the world and have already become a source of pride for prums everywhere.

"However—it can't stop there."

Finn strengthens his tone even though I can't string any words together to respond.

"One moment of glory is insufficient to build a future for my people. The light of hope must continue to be cast on prums for years to come."

Finn declares that his people would not know lasting prosperity if they had no hope. He doesn't try to pad his thoughts but instead speaks clearly and directly.

"Frankly, the light needs to be passed to the next generation. And the best way to do that would be to have an heir with my blood in their veins."

"…!!"

"A Half won't do. The pride of our race must be a pure-blooded prum."

Someone has to carry the torch and return their race to glory—it's necessary to pass on the genes of a prum given the title of "Braver" to the next generation and beyond. Finn insists that those descendants have a completely prum lineage.

All the races of demi-humans can reproduce only with themselves.

While it goes without saying that spirits like fairies can't have any offspring at all, elves, dwarves, and animal people cannot have children with one another. The exceptions would be humans, who can interbreed with demi-humans, and Amazons, who will always give birth to a female offspring of their own race.

So of course, marrying an Amazon is out of the question, as is having a human give birth to his heir—a half-prum would face tremendous difficulty being recognized as the savior of all prums.

Finn says that for the sake of his future child, he must marry another full-blooded prum.

"A-and you want…?"

"Indeed. I would like to take that girl as my bride and for her to bear my children."

So that's why. My face grows hot as the words flow out of his mouth.

—He's going to ask Lilly to bear his children.

My cheeks are absolutely burning. The scale of this "favor" has gone way beyond what I was expecting, on so many levels. I feel so awkward as shock and surprise swirl in my head, turning my ears red as well.

But Finn is completely the opposite. There isn't even a stutter in his voice, and that intense look in his eye is starting to make me desperate to find something to say, anything.

"But she's, um, not in your familia. People in different familias can't get married, right...?"

That's one of the things that makes being in a familia complicated. I brought it up to see how Finn answers.

He simply says, "That's not a problem. I have Loki's permission. Well, I should. I agreed to join her familia under two conditions: one, that I have her cooperation in assisting my people; and two, that she not get in my way."

Apparently, Finn was the first member of *Loki Familia*, and that's how the negotiation played out.

It was an even trade-off for Loki and her first follower.

She secured someone who had great potential for her familia, and he received the goddess's resources for his own needs.

Even now, the conditions of their agreement are still in effect.

"Of course, I care deeply for my familia. It's grown so much since the beginning, and I feel it's my duty to protect them."

To think a group as fearsome as *Loki Familia* had such humble beginnings. I consider that for a little bit, but he just shrugs and tells me to not get the wrong idea.

He looks so young, yet he carries all the responsibility of the leader with a smile on his face. I can tell he's speaking the truth.

"One other thing I'd like to make clear: Even if I do have Loki's permission, I can't allow this personal matter to make life difficult for my familia. Should your supporter, Lilliluka Erde, refuse, or should Goddess Hestia object to my proposal, I won't pursue her any further." Finn is being clear to avoid starting any problems between our familias. Then he smiles dryly and adds one more thing. "And

I'm not as young as I used to be. I can't urge someone into an engagement anymore."

"Huh…Um, I-I don't want to be rude, but…may I ask your age?"

"Over forty by now, I suppose."

"F-forty…?!"

"What? Don't tell me you don't know about the side effects of having a Status?"

Finn looks back at me with that incredibly youthful face and starts to explain, while clearly enjoying my surprise. He details how high-level adventurers gain the ability to slow the aging process.

Basically, a stronger spirit container doesn't wear down with age, and in fact has a greater longevity than most. The effect increases every time a person levels up.

When it comes to eternal life, with the exception of the creator of the Philosopher's Stone, mortals have yet to unlock the key to perpetual youth and true immortality. Instead, over the past thousand years, the repeated leveling up of many adventurers has displayed the possibility of conquering the aging process to the world, or so Finn says.

…If Lady Hestia were here, she'd probably say, "Leveling up brings a mortal closer to godhood."

We gain more abilities the higher we ascend. In other words, the closer we get to the eternally youthful gods and goddesses, the more we resemble them in various ways…That's not too hard to wrap my mind around.

Although, actually getting to where deities stand is probably impossible.

Finn ends his explanation by saying that I shouldn't assume anything about a high-level adventurer based on their appearance. "We got off topic a little bit there, but…if you don't have any objections, I would like your help in meeting her."

Since circumstances prevented him from talking to Hestia or Lilly directly, he needed to make his approach through me. Now that he's said his piece, he states his intentions one last time.

My head is still a swirling mess, but I'm calm enough to fight through it and gather my thoughts.

I wasn't able to ask much yet because I was shaking too hard. Regaining control from sheer willpower, I manage to ask a very important question:

"Why...are you interested in Lilly?"

A simple question. There are so many prums in the world, so why did he choose Lilly? I don't have the guts to say it, but even at his age, a top-tier adventurer like Finn could have anyone he wanted. All he had to do was make himself available, and he'd have more attention than he could handle.

And I don't think this is a case of love at first sight.

He's been so calm and collected ever since we arrived. There's been no wavering in his voice. It's—I don't know...Finn doesn't seem head over heels for her, and there's no heat or excitement. It's more like the calm of someone watching from the sidelines.

Finn closes his eyes when I ask. Then his deep-blue irises appear from behind his eyelids as he looks directly at me.

"How long ago was it, maybe two months? The day you defeated that Minotaur on the ninth floor."

The battle against a Minotaur that wielded a greatsword; the day of my first level-up. I fought that monster with everything I had. It just so happened that Finn, Aiz, and the rest of *Loki Familia* were in the middle of one of their expeditions and witnessed the fight.

Lilly was the one who'd led them to me in a desperate attempt to find help.

"She was so determined to save your life that she ignored her own injuries and threw away her pride in order to convince us to help you. Seeing her do all that...It made quite an impression on me."

Finn places his left hand on his heart as if to say that's how he truly feels. "She's not strong by any standards, but she showed enough bravery to rival anyone." He narrows his eyes for emphasis on that word. "It's true that I want a partner, but not just any partner. Right now, what my people need is bravery...I'm looking for someone who possesses this forgotten weapon of the prums to join my cause."

Prums are considered to be the weakest of all the races.

They lack the physical capabilities of humans, they don't possess the magical prowess of elves or the physical strength of dwarves, they haven't developed the combat expertise of the Amazons, nor do they have the enhanced senses of animal people.

The one weapon that the race shorter than all the others did possess—was bravery.

Like the prum knights of the Ancient Times, they possessed the courage to face enemies much larger than themselves in those days from long ago. Unfortunately, that one and only advantage had disappeared with the passage of time.

And that is how Finn is planning to restore his people to their rightful place in the world: by drawing out the courage they all have buried within them. His partner needs to be someone worthy of standing next to the man the gods had named "Braver." Someone who had a great deal of courage and could pass it on to his future child.

"So then Lilly..."

So that was the reason he wanted Lilly.

He recognized her courage because, rather than running away, she chose to try to save me. Finn had been moved by seeing her covered in blood and tears, calling out to Aiz and the other members of *Loki Familia* for help.

"B-but...if that's the case, wouldn't anyone who meets your standard be...?"

"Yes. You're absolutely right."

I had to remind myself to breathe before pressing further. He didn't try to deny anything and simply nodded.

Finn doesn't have any special feelings for Lilly herself.

"If they are worthy, and are at least a decent person, then I probably would offer my hand in marriage to anyone. The idea of having multiple partners doesn't sound half bad."

—My eyes fly open.

A sharp jolt shoots through my chest.

Gulp. That sounded a lot louder than I thought it would.

Open to the idea of having multiple partners...So, in other words...

A man's dream, the one Gramps would always talk about, the pinnacle of manliness, a man's romance…

"…A harem?"

Exactly what I fantasized about in my foolish, slightly younger days…

I can't help but tremble as I look at the prum hero facing me across the table. My lips won't stay still as I try to speak to him.

"I-I hear that's nothing but trouble…"

I wait with bated breath for his next words. And then he says:

"I'm completely serious."

Completely serious…

Looking at his bright, unclouded eyes, I realize the depth of his determination and resolve.

Finn possesses the courage to do whatever it takes to fulfill his mission without a second thought. A sudden rush of respect and admiration, one man to another, overwhelms me. I'd prostrate myself at his feet right now if there wasn't a table in the way.

"…But of course, I wouldn't actually do that." Finn looks me in the eye and flashes a quick grin. Adding that he wouldn't be able to help those who depend on him if he tried to maintain multiple partners, he smiles wryly to himself and closes one eye.

"I hold the rank of general now. I can't afford to give my subordinates the wrong idea."

"Ah…G-good point…"

I force myself to laugh and nod.

I feel so stupid for randomly thinking of this guy as a god among men for a moment.

"…I left all that behind me when I chose this path. I've dedicated my life to serving my people."

He sits up straight and falls silent for a moment, his face calm once again.

He sounds like a young teenager, but his voice is steady and clear. Each word resonates in my ears.

"As I stated before, if she or Goddess Hestia rejects my offer, then that's where this ends. On the other hand, should my offer be accepted, I will take it seriously and want to devote myself to building a strong bond with her."

All I can do is listen to him. Finn's face brightens with a smile. "She will live happily, that I can promise. Would you tell her all that I told you today, in my place?"

With that, he drinks the last of the tea in his cup. Getting to his feet, Finn withdraws a piece of paper from inside his vest and places it on the table. "Unfortunately, I only have time tomorrow." He says a few more words and leaves me sitting alone with the piece of paper, a location written on it.

He pays the entire bill and waves at me one last time before leaving the café.

"..."

—If she has an answer for me, tell her to go there tomorrow.

—If she doesn't want to answer, that's perfectly fine. I'll be there all day either way.

I take another look at the piece of paper. Directions are written in Koine, in really nice handwriting, along with a map to a meeting place. I look up at the ceiling after staring at the sheet for a few moments. I haven't moved from my chair, still leaning all the way back into it.

Honestly, I don't want to do this.

But I owe Finn, and Aiz, and really all of *Loki Familia* for everything they've done to help me. How would they react if I don't follow through with this?

At the very least, I owe it to him to give Lilly the message. I feel like it's my duty.

…What if…

What if Lilly accepts his offer after hearing what he has to say…? What'll I do?

This labyrinth I'm stuck in doesn't have an exit. I stay in the chair, staring at the ceiling for I don't know how long, trying to find an answer.

Lilly was still struggling even as everyone gathered to eat dinner together.

She acted like everything was normal, participating in conversation like usual. She sealed away the heavy feelings in her heart to keep the mood light around the table, even smiling and laughing along with everyone else.

Mikoto and Haruhime were in charge of preparing dinner tonight, and they received many compliments before they were soon deep in their own conversation, enjoying each other's company. Welf was busy chowing down and didn't try to engage Lilly in conversation. Hestia, however, could tell something was wrong. Her deep-blue eyes would occasionally glance in Lilly's direction, but the goddess said nothing and joined Mikoto's conversation like she normally did.

Bell looked anxious, and she noticed him looking in her direction more than once, but she pretended as if she hadn't.

Dinner ended soon after. Lilly didn't go to the living room, and instead started heading back to her own.

"Um, Lilly…do you have a minute?"

"!"

She was just about to go up the stairs in the main hallway when she heard Bell's voice behind her.

A small jolt ran through her body as she froze in place. All the uneasiness and emotions that had been building since last night came to a head. She was extra conscious of the young boy at the moment.

"Wh-what is it, Mr. Bell?" Lilly responded in a jumpy, forced voice. She turned to see that Bell seemed embarrassed.

"There's, um, something I need to tell you…"

Since she wasn't sure of her own feelings, she probably should have refused him. But he asked so nicely that she made an awkward nod and the two of them went to an unused room on the second floor. Going inside, they turned on a magic-stone lamp.

Then—

"An offer of marriage for Lilly…?"

"Y-yeah…"

Lilly opened her chestnut-colored eyes as far as they would go. Bell had told her about an offer of marriage from another prum. Earlier that evening, Finn Deimne had asked Bell directly to arrange an in-person meeting with Lilly.

With a stunned stare, Lilly looked up from the sheet of paper Bell handed to her. The boy trembled as he nodded to confirm.

Why would the Braver be interested in her? That was the first question to pop into her head, but it didn't stay there for long.

There was something more important. Lilly clenched her lips together and looked at her feet.

As expected, in Mr. Bell's eyes, Lilly is nothing more than...

The fact that Bell had delivered this proposal of marriage sent her into a tailspin. The fact that Bell offered another man's proposal to Lilly, instead of his own, gave sharp claws to the emotions coursing through her heart. She had already been dealing with the Aiz incident from last night, and now this. Her gaze didn't move from the floor.

Bell took one look at the girl, hunched over and trying to hide her reaction, and knew that his words had made her upset. Starting to panic, he quickly tried again.

"Y-you don't have to answer if you don't want to! Finn said he didn't want to force anything, so I can go tell him you're not interested...!"

She understood Bell's position. Lilly knew the boy could never turn down a request. Especially if said request came from Finn, the head of *Loki Familia*. Considering what they had done for him, Bell would never reject them.

But...

She didn't want to hear it.

She didn't want to hear that news from Bell. The pain tearing through her at that very moment was all because *he* delivered the message. That thought alone filled her mind.

Presenting another man's proposal showed Lilly exactly where she stood with him.

Bell thought of her as an ally, a member of the familia. If he loved her, it was as family, not in a romantic way.

Her eyes quivered. The pain, the anguish, and the loss in her heart forced tears to well up in her eyes. All the feelings crammed into her chest were about to burst. She had not heard anything he had been saying.

Lilly didn't look up as she forced words through her trembling lips, somehow making it past the storm of emotions swirling within her.

"Your thoughts, Mr. Bell…?"

She wanted to know his opinion about the offer and how he would respond depending on her answer.

The night sky was barely visible through the slightly open curtains covering the windows. The room's magic-stone lamp illuminated only one side of Bell's face. She could see uncertainty in his shaking eyes.

"I…I, um…"

He started to open his lips, body swaying side to side, but no words came out.

Seeing him flustered was the last straw. Thundering anger roared to life within the storm of emotions and it all rushed straight to Lilly's head. Teeth clenched, fists shaking, she felt her chestnut-colored eyes flash menacingly as she looked up at him.

Her head started to rise—and then a heartbeat later, all the built-up anger exploded.

"Lilly hates that you can never make up your mind!"

Her shriek rang inside the room, every word raining down on the boy in front of her like hammer strikes.

"That settles it! Lilly will meet the Braver!"

"You what?!"

"An offer of marriage from the Braver? Lilly will be the envy of not only other prums but every woman in the city!! He has it all—power, money, fame! Yes, it's the wealthy marriage Lilly has always dreamed of!"

"L-Lilly, don't you think you're sounding a little desperate…?"

"Lilly is not desperate!!"

They matched each other tit for tat, almost like a quarreling couple. More harsh words tumbled out as they continued to go back and forth.

Lilly's face turned red as her ranting intensified, which made Bell only more defensive.

"Finn Deimne is so, so, sooooooooo much better than some indecisive, womanizing blockhead who can't even understand emotional signals obvious to a child, like Mr. Bell! He's a class act, the perfect gentleman!!"

Lilly's last verbal blow had the same effect as a knockout punch. "Ge-hah?!" Bell staggered backward, bent over at the waist.

Being compared to Finn, not only as an adventurer but also as a person, shook Bell to his core with feelings of inferiority.

Lilly turned sharply on her heel, but Bell wasn't able to make a sound.

"‼"

Flinging open the door, she ran out of the room.

"Lilly!"

Bell stepped forward and yelled at the top of his lungs, but it wasn't enough to reach her. The girl was already out the back door.

Passing through the rear metal gate, she dashed into the city sparkling with streetlights.

Lilly let her emotions take over as she ran headlong into the city.

"—Riveria, I'll be away from home all day tomorrow as planned. Keep an eye on things for me."

The home of *Loki Familia*, Twilight Manor.

Their residence was composed of a group of several high towers, one of which contained the office of the general. Finn's room was decorated with a thick rug that was as colorful as a garden, a marble fireplace, and a tall grandfather clock. Every item in the chamber was high quality and fitting for someone of his rank. But the most striking feature inside the spacious room was, without a doubt, the tapestry on the wall—an image of a goddess wearing armor, with spear in hand.

Finn was sitting in a chair behind a black wooden desk that was covered in stacks of paperwork. He filled them out while talking about tomorrow's plan with his second-in-command, Riveria.

"...This is unexpected."

"What is?"

"I am well aware of your personal mission, as you've told me on many occasions since we met. It would be unreasonable for me to feel any different after all this time. However, you don't seem to be showing much interest in romance. Your extremely assertive approach...surprises me."

The elegant elf's long jade hair flowed down her back below a small ribbon that tied it back to the nape of her neck. She stood quietly, analyzing Finn's face from beside him.

Proposing marriage to someone of his own race was much more proactive than anything he had ever done.

At the same time, ignoring the fact that it was part of his mission, the prum hero appeared to be looking forward to it.

"...I've been far too busy to reach this stage, but now it feels like taking it into consideration might not be such a bad idea. That and...there might come a day when I lay down my life in service to this familia. Taking recent events into consideration, I can't help but feel that day draws near."

"..."

"Of course, my will is just as strong as ever."

Finn's feathered pen kept moving throughout their conversation. He stopped writing and looked up from the paperwork.

"I might be getting on in years," he said to Riveria with a strained smile.

Saying that his forwardness might be his own way of having insurance for the future, the small prum adventurer added one more thing.

"But above all...I was lucky enough to meet someone special. Seeing one of my own kind do what that girl did that day left quite an impression on my heart." Finn closed his eyes as if remembering the moment he first saw her. Leaning back in the chair with a smile on his face, he slowly looked out the window and up at the moon rising over the city.

"Now, will she come?"

The darkness of night faded, replaced by light appearing in the east. Morning had arrived.

Many adventurers were already on their way toward the Dungeon. Lilly trudged her way through the crowd on South Main Street.

"What am I doing…?"

Head low, she whispered to herself while looking at the stone pavement beneath her feet.

She went directly to the Gnome Trader after running out of her home last night. Of course Bom, the owner, was surprised to see her, but he didn't turn her down when she asked him to put her up for the night. She stayed there until morning…As for the out-of-breath white-haired boy who came looking for her, she asked the owner to tell him she wasn't there and to send him home.

It was all out of desperation. How shameful. Had she wanted Bell to feel anxious, worried…or perhaps jealous?

How shallow, Lilly scolded herself as an air of gloom enveloped her. She had run away to avoid hearing what she didn't want to hear, to turn a blind eye to what she didn't want to see.

"…"

It shouldn't be a big deal, but she didn't know how to face Bell now. What could she do? How could she apologize? Could she go home?

Her feet stopped in front of a certain building as she pondered these questions. It was the place described on Finn Deimne's note; the place where he was waiting for her.

She had walked a long way from the main street, passing through several alleyways to get here. Coming this far, she might as well see it through to the end. She had hit rock bottom and was perfectly fine with letting the cards fall where they may. *Why not?* she thought to herself as she stood on the front doorstep.

The building indicated on the note was surprisingly small. Located in the west-southwest area of the city, it was on the outer edge, close to the city wall. Almost no one frequented this area, so the café known as the Hidden Home of the Prums was very difficult to find among the other tall buildings on this narrow street.

It also happened to be a bar, by the look of it.

"So this kind of place can be found in Orario, too..."

Lilly passed by a big sign that said PRUMS ONLY! written in big Koine letters, before placing her hands on the wooden door and opening it with a soft creak.

Everything inside was built with prums in mind—in a word, small.

Not only were the ceilings lower, but the tables and chairs looked suitable for children of other races. Quite a few patrons were already inside despite it being before noon. The customers, the waiters on staff, and even the bartender behind the counter—every single one was a prum.

All of them fit right in with the size of the café, and no one felt out of place. However, if someone of a different race, like a human, saw what went on here, they would likely be quite shocked. After all, no one expected to see what looked like a bunch of children sitting at a bar, downing ale. Even Lilly, a prum herself, felt it strange to see prums sitting in chairs and their feet touching the floor.

Despite its location, the prum-only bar did some brisk business—maybe it was because many of the patrons felt a sense of pride coming here because of how exclusive it was. Lilly was standing just inside the front door, taking it all in, when one of the prum waiters came to greet her.

"Welcome. If you're by yourself, there's a spot at the counter—Wait." The rather discontented-seeming employee froze on the spot once he got a good look at her face.

The hood of Lilly's robe shifted as she tilted her head in confusion. But then—

"Ah!"

"Lilliluka Erde?! *Hestia Familia*?!"

"Might you be…Mr. Luan?"

Lilly recognized the man who had shouted as he pointed at her. With large, round eyes and brown hair, he looked like a child whom nobles would hire to take care of odd jobs.

Luan Espel.

An adventurer and former member of *Apollo Familia*, *Hestia Familia*'s opponent in the War Game.

Lilly and her friends had emerged victorious from that encounter and, as a result, exiled Apollo from Orario. Former members of *Apollo Familia* had been released and been given the chance to join another familia of their choice…Luan, it seemed, had taken a job as a waiter at this bar and café.

Luan's surprise quickly turned to anger. He glared at Lilly with seething hatred.

"I-it's all your familia's fault that I'm stuck here cleaning tables instead of down in the Dungeon as an adventurer! So, what are you going to do about it?!"

"Wasn't it your side that hunted Mr. Bell and declared the War Game to start with? There is no reason for Lilly to do anything…But yes, there were a few dirty tricks involved."

By the sound of it, Luan had been rejected by every other familia after the War Game.

Prums were already subjected to discrimination, and he was just a low-class adventurer who had never leveled up. He might have been a former member of the middle-class *Apollo Familia*, but unlike third-tier members like Daphne and Cassandra, no one came to him with an offer.

Even when he went to offer his services, all the talk turned to his apparent "betrayal" during the battle at Shreme Castle. The obstacle was too much to overcome, and he had been shown the door every time.

…His reputation as the "Trojan Horse" had spread throughout the city, when in fact it had been Lilly, disguised as Luan using her

Magic, Cinder Ella, who stabbed *Apollo Familia* in the back. The real Luan never made it to the battlefield and spent the entire time locked in a storage container somewhere in the city. Apparently, all the attention had been on the battle taking place outside the castle, and there were no witnesses to Lilly's big reveal, when she deactivated Cinder Ella. Therefore, the dramatic shift in the War Game was blamed on Luan...He couldn't escape the stigma.

Although it was common practice to devise strategies before the War Game to reduce an enemy's fighting strength before battle—Welf, Mikoto, and Lyu themselves had been hindered by a *mysterious robber* while in transit to the battlefield—Lilly still felt they had wronged Luan in their pursuit of victory.

"But Lilly has heard that Lord Miach offered you a place in his familia. Lilly also heard his offer was rejected...Why didn't you accept?"

"E-wh...I-I was a member of *Apollo Familia*, you know? Why the hell would I join such a weak familia that's drowning in debt?"

Lilly looked at him with her eyes narrowed in a pointed stare, clearly unswayed by the short adventurer's excuses.

It wasn't as though she didn't understand the stress that came with a loan...but more than that, she felt it was Luan's trivial pride that was stopping him. As proof, Daphne and Cassandra had chosen to join that "weak familia that's drowning in debt" of their own accord.

"Well then, how about joining Lilly's familia? Lilly will ask Lady Hestia herself," she suggested with a hint of sympathy in her voice.

"Like hell I would! You guys have even more debt than Lord Miach's lot!" He shot down the suggestion. He brought up the bombshell of her own familia's financial situation. Lilly could see there was no point in trying to help anymore and gave up.

"...Someone is waiting for Lilly, so Lilly's going inside."

"Whatever."

She brought the fruitless argument to an end. Luan turned his back, seething with anger.

A little put off by his rudeness, Lilly stepped past him and onto the dining floor.

She started looking for the one who invited her to this place—and found him immediately.

He was sitting at a table at the back of the bar, next to an open window. Illuminated by incoming sunlight, he was extremely easy to find due to all the excited whispers and people looking in his direction.

"—Oh, you decided to come."

Finn Deimne had been reading a small book, one sized for prums. Noticing Lilly's presence, he looked up from its pages as she approached.

Perhaps to hide his identity, or perhaps as a fashion statement, Finn was wearing glasses.

They gave him an air of intelligence and suited his combination of childish visage and mature aura, which was one of the main reasons he was so popular with female adventurers all over the city. Lilly could see that firsthand now.

He gave her a friendly smile, stirring onlookers into a small frenzy. No one would have guessed that Lilly was the person the famous top-tier adventurer, beloved by his people and proud holder of the title "Braver," was waiting for.

Lilly could feel the surprise in their collective gaze gathering around her. Even Luan, mouth open and glaring daggers at her, was frozen in disbelief. She felt like a fish out of water, unsure what to do next.

Finn, on the other hand, didn't seem to care about their audience and kept talking as if nothing was out of the ordinary.

"I honestly didn't think you would come here today. Perhaps a messenger, but never you in person."

"...If you were so uncertain, then why make the offer in the first place?" The situation with Bell still weighing on her heart, Lilly's response was heavily laced with irony.

Oh no! she thought as soon as the words were out of her mouth. She had just addressed a first-tier adventurer, someone who was unquestionably her superior, with such a rude tone. A thrill ran up her spine as she waited for his response, but he just quietly chuckled to himself.

His golden hair gently swished in the soft sunlight coming in through the window.

"How about taking a seat?"

"..."

His calm demeanor was unchanged as Lilly stayed quiet and did as she was told. She didn't take her eyes off his smile as she sat down in the chair on the opposite side of the table from Finn.

"Since this is the first time the two of us have had a chance to speak like this, I think self-introductions might be in order? I'm Finn Deimne. Thank you for coming today."

"...Lilliluka Erde."

Both of them knew each other's names, but Finn still gave her his name out of courtesy. Lilly followed suit. Their meeting to discuss the possibility of marriage was officially under way.

Finn set his glasses down next to a cup that was still mostly full. He ordered a drink for Lilly, and Luan brought it to the table. He set a glass in front of her, his expression a stew of complicated emotions. As soon as Luan stepped away, their conversation began.

"Is it safe to assume that you are open to my proposal, since you came here yourself?" Finn didn't try to make small talk or give any explanations. His voice was soft, and a gentle smile never left his face as he spoke. All Lilly could do was look at her lap.

—*It might be a good idea to accept his offer*, said a little voice inside her head. Her feelings for the boy would never lead to anything; that was painfully obvious now. Therefore, she couldn't shake the feeling that going along with the proposal of the man sitting in front of her was the best option. Finn was a prum like her, but the one everyone knew as the "Braver."

Bell had said that she would "live happily." That was likely true. Sitting face-to-face with him, she got a good sense of Finn's integrity as well as the strength of his character. Considering his social position and resources, whoever became Finn Deimne's partner would no doubt live in great comfort, without a worry in the world.

This kind of offer would never come her way again. It was a once-in-a-lifetime opportunity, her only chance. Without Hestia's permission, Lilly couldn't leave the familia, but if she chose to follow Finn, most likely she'd live an easy, privileged life for the rest of her days.

There might even come a day when Finn would displace the young white-haired boy in her heart.

"...Please answer one question." Lilly had posed many questions and answered them inside her own head up until that point. Her words came out as little more than whispers. She slowly lifted her head and her chestnut-colored eyes met his blue ones. "Why was Lilly selected?"

That was the most important question.

To be blunt, she hadn't had the best upbringing. A life of crime—her past was stained by her time as a thief.

Lilly thought that a person who had walked her path was unfit to be with someone like Finn. So she wanted to know how he truly felt.

"Did Bell Cranell not tell you? It was your courage that made an impression on me."

"Courage? Countless other prums have courage. What's more, there are many far stronger prums than Lilly."

"You may be right. But strength and courage don't always come together. You faced incredible danger and still had the will to overcome it while knowing your own weakness. I remember what you did on the eighteenth floor. You put your own life at risk to help others, much like the great Phiana. You are a shining example to prums everywhere."

Lilly blushed as Finn brought his innermost thoughts to light without any fanfare. Caught off guard by his honest praise for a moment, she shook her head as soon as she collected her thoughts.

"You give Lilly too much credit. Lilly is not some great angelic prum. As an adventurer, Mr. Finn surely has heard rumors of a prum with 'sticky fingers'? One who steals items and money from other adventurers?"

"That I have."

"Lilly is that prum. She lured adventurers into traps and stole everything valuable they carried. Yes, anyone Lilly didn't like met the same fate. So Lilly is the worst, a horrible—"

"The fact that rumors exist in the first place means the victims lived to tell their tale. I have looked into these incidents myself, since one of my subordinates was involved. Every single one of the victims is alive and well."

"..."

Even after Lilly confessed to her dark past, Finn was unfazed and calmly pointed out that she hadn't killed anyone.

Lilly looked back down into her lap.

She wanted to refute his words. She had committed so many crimes over the years, and there were a few times she'd seriously considered taking the lives of adventurers.

However, those adventurers had been so tenacious.

Despite losing everything, they clung to life with the persistence of cockroaches.

That was the reason she had stayed her hand—it wasn't worth it.

The best way to get revenge was to make them suffer as much as possible. Killing them quickly would have been too merciful and a waste, so she chose not to go through with taking their lives.

Lilly...had been naive.

"I've lived in Orario long enough to know that stealing possessions rather than taking lives is very tame...I'm no god. I have no right to judge you, nor am I interested in doing so."

His words were strong, piercing like a spear. But his expression was gentle. Finn smiled and said:

"All I see is who you are now."

"..."

"And who you are now possesses an important quality that our people have lost."

Finn's blue eyes blinked. He looked at Lilly with admiration.

"Lilly...hasn't come home."

I whisper to myself while standing in the living room.

I looked all around the city for Lilly last night, but there was no sign of her, so I came back to our home with my nonexistent tail between my legs.

The one shred of hope that I still had, that I repeated to myself over and over, was that she'd be back by morning...And now the sun is up, but no Lilly.

"Did she really...go to meet Finn...?"

She said she would. And today's the day.

Welf and Mikoto are making breakfast in the kitchen...I think about it long and hard, but I decide to go to the goddess for advice.

After climbing the stairs, I arrive at her third-floor room and knock on her door. "Come on in," comes her voice from the other side.

"Oh, it's you, Bell. I heard from Haruhime that our supporter is gone. You know anything about it?"

I...I don't know what to say.

She's getting ready to go to work at her part-time job at a Jyaga Maru Kun street stand when I step inside. She hits me with that question right off the bat. I avoid making eye contact, looking around the room for a few moments before I divulge everything that happened last night with what I'm sure is a pitiful look on my face.

I give her every detail, hoping for some tidbit of advice. She sighs.

A big one, too. I blink a few times.

"Bell. You—If you're trying to make her happy, you can't think so hard before you take action."

"!"

My head snaps up to look at my goddess.

It's true. Considering all that happened to Lilly while she was with *Soma Familia*, I don't want to say it's out of sympathy, but I want her to be happy.

And after Finn said that...Finn said that she would "be happy." And knowing who he is, I'm sure he would make her happy. She'd be happier with him, a top-tier adventurer much stronger than me.

Lilly said it herself. That the famous prum hero is much better than me, a class act, the perfect gentleman.

...No matter what I say or do, nothing will change.

"Just to let you know, should the supporter...Lilliluka...ask to leave my familia, I won't stop her."

"?!"

My goddess could see right into my mind—Is she actually reading my thoughts?!

A part of me deep down believed that, as our goddess, Lady Hestia would put an end to this whole thing if it came to that. Suffice to say, that confidence is gone now.

"That'd be one less rival to worry about..."

My mind is going in too many directions at once to comprehend what she just said under her breath. Then she raises her head.

"Bell. From the supporter's point of view, your inability to make a decision either way just feels like meddling in her business. I'm pretty sure she'd say it herself: that she'll decide how she wants to live, how she'll be happiest."

"Ah..."

"If I were in her shoes, and you were the one who came to me with that proposal, it would be a real shock."

She looks at me kindly and says something that sounds like criticism, but it also sounds like she's enjoying herself.

"Bell, our supporter will disappear if you don't do something. Is that what you want?"

"I...I..."

"You know, you should be more selfish."

She smiles at me with those pure blue eyes of hers. I stand still for a moment. My hands curl into fists a heartbeat later.

"—Please excuse me. I don't need breakfast!"

I turn away from Lady Hestia and run out of the room. I see her soft smile after taking one last look over my shoulder. Then I'm down the stairs and out of the manor in no time flat.

"…Haaah…Gods always have to suffer."

Hestia let out a long sigh as she watched Bell race through the front gate from her window, knowing full well she was helping her rival.

Despite what she had said, the smile hadn't disappeared from Hestia's lips.

"Hey! Hey, Aiz! Get a load'a this! Finn's gonna get hitched!"

Aiz turned her head to face the voice and received a hug from behind.

It was at *Loki Familia*'s home, in a narrow hallway of the residence. The Amazonian girl Tiona ran by many doors as she raced through the passageway toward Aiz. She had both her arms around the human girl's shoulders in an instant and was absolutely bubbling with energy.

"Finn is…?"

"Yep, yep! I heard him talking about it with Riveria in the hallway last night! Just happened to be at the right place at the right time!"

Aiz's golden eyes were wide open in a rare expression of surprise. At the same time, Tiona was vigorously nodding, barely able to contain her excitement.

"And get this! Finn was wearing glasses when he left this morning—saw it myself! He was going to meet his bride for sure! Ohhhhh, I wonder what kind of lady he's gonna bring home?"

Tiona verbalized every thought flying through her head, causing a ruckus in the hallway.

Aiz did her best to move with the elated Amazon who currently had her in a bear hug. "Hmm," she said quietly, raising her chin as she thought about it. It seemed strange to her that that prum, her general, would be discussing marriage. She was just about to mention that when—

"—Want to clarify what you're talking about?"

A voice as cold as ice.

""Ah.""

Aiz and Tiona froze in place. They knew who the female warrior standing behind them was without looking.

"I only received the grandiose title 'Braver' because I pressured Loki into it."

It was a corner in the Hidden Home of the Prums.

Finn and Lilly's conversation continued with the whispers of onlookers still swirling around them.

Finn explained how he had negotiated with Loki to push for his moniker to be "Braver" at his naming ceremony during a Denatus session. It was his way of denying himself an escape route from his mission. He was bound and determined to become the rallying flag of the prum race.

"I'm willing to do anything for the revival of our people. That goes for the prums yet to be born into this world as well. And to do that... I need an heir of my own."

Lilly sat, dumbfounded, and listened to Finn talk about the extent of his resolve and why a fitting partner was necessary for him.

Orphaned at an early age, Lilly had struggled just to stay alive. She had no time for faith in Phiana, nor did she know all that much about the goddess. However, she knew that Phiana was important to prums, which was just about how much other races knew about the prum goddess as well.

Despite that, Finn helped her understand the important role courage played in providing a beacon of hope in place of Phiana. As well as how much he devoted himself to it.

"…Mr. Finn, is there no woman who holds a special place in your heart?"

The question came out of Lilly's mouth before she knew it.

Everything she'd heard up to this point made her believe that Finn was sacrificing himself for the good of his people. She couldn't help but ask. Her question caught Finn by surprise, but he answered.

"…There is one obnoxious girl who is rather fond of me."

He paused for a moment then chuckled at himself.

"It's led to some embarrassing moments and quite a few head-aches…but it feels like something's missing when she's not around. Sometimes I wonder if there's something wrong with me."

His lips awkwardly turned up into a forced smile, but Lilly could see the kindness in it.

"—But I have no interest in just living a happy life. No, the moment a simply happy life grows on me, everything I've done, every obstacle I've overcome so far will have been for nothing."

A new wave of conviction passed over his face. Like a valiant knight renewing his vows, Finn's blue eyes sparkled in the sunlight.

It was all for his people. As a fellow prum, Lilly was moved by his awe-inspiring willingness to devote himself to that cause. She couldn't help it. She could never possess such strong conviction, such dedication to a lofty goal as he had to his people.

Ah—.

Seeing the way Finn lived his life inspired something within her heart.

No, made her *remember*. Her feelings for the boy.

That's right…

The one who had rescued her wasn't her fellow prum Finn Deimne, nor was it one of the gods.

It was Bell.

Everyone had always ignored the muddy prum at their feet. The first person to look her way, to really see her, was that white-haired boy.

Yes, that's right. Lilly is…

As unlikely as it was, even if Hestia ever turned away from him, Lilly would never abandon him. Even if the world labeled him a criminal, exiling him to some faraway place, it would be Lilly right by his side. She would continue to support him.

The boy was barreling forward at a breakneck pace, but even still, Lilly would travel that path with him for the rest of her life.

On that day he forgave, accepted, held, and laughed with her—she had made her decision.

"…"

What's this? Lilly laughed to herself.

All in all, she and Finn were one and the same. It was almost like looking in the mirror. She had something to devote her life to.

In that moment, a guaranteed happy life slipped through Lilly's fingers. The same emotions that had caused her so much pain over the past two days would probably strike again.

However, she had already decided: No matter what happened, she would never leave that boy's side. It was not completely out of atonement—she simply wanted to. Lilly would continue to support Bell.

She would devote her life to her family, much like the man in front of her was doing.

"It really…didn't matter…"

"?"

Lilly quietly whispered under her breath. Finn tilted his head.

In negative terms, Lilly was blind; to a more neutral perspective, she was loyal. But looking at it in the best possible way, it was unconditional love.

She, a very plain-looking girl, was competing with a goddess, among others. A tiny part of her felt that way. But whether Aiz Wallenstein was in the running or not, whether Bell had someone special to him or not, none of that had mattered from the beginning.

"…Sorry, Mr. Finn."

Lilly sat up straight and looked Finn directly in the eye.

"Lilly declines your offer."

She smiled softly and bowed her head.

"Can I hear the reason?"

Finn returned her smile and asked why.

"Just like you have devoted your life to our people, Lilly, too…has devoted her life to Bell. Lilly has made up her mind."

Lilly explained that the two of them were one and the same.

The scale of their commitments might be completely different, but their level of determination was identical. Lilly responded with gratitude to the man who had reminded her of something she nearly lost.

"I see," Finn said with a nod. "…Haaa…So it wasn't going to work out after all." Finn closed his eyes and sighed, a weak smile on his lips.

"I had an inkling going in that there wasn't much hope. Even my thumb told me this wouldn't work out…Call it my intuition."

"If that's so, why make the offer?"

Lilly was confused by his remarks. Finn, however, whose youthful expression matched his appearance, gave her a genuine smile.

"Didn't I tell you? It was your courage that caught my eye."

"Ah…"

"From one prum to another, your courage took my breath away," he said. "How could I not try to make a move?"

He placed his right hand over his chest, but he seemed truly happy. It was his standard as Braver.

Just as he was trying to inspire his people, he was looking for a partner who could inspire him.

"Well, looks like I'm back to square one."

Finn leaned back in his chair and cast his gaze thoughtfully toward the ceiling.

It wasn't *Loki Familia*'s general sitting across from Lilly at the table but Finn as he truly was as a person. Seeing that made Lilly smile.

"If Lilly meets anyone special, she'll introduce you right away."

"Please do. I don't think I'm cut out for this sort of thing. I've always been unlucky."

Finn grinned back at her.

Although she had turned down his proposal, the two were happy to at least find someone who shared their strong feelings of devotion to a cause, and they exchanged lighthearted smiles.

A calming air descended upon the table.

"Sir, sir! What are you doing?!"

"""?"""

That's when it happened.

The door was practically thrown off its hinges as every customer looked toward the front in a mix of surprise and confusion.

Lilly and Finn were among them. And what should greet their eyes but an extremely out-of-breath white-haired human boy.

"M-Mr. Bell?!"

Lilly reflexively jumped to her feet as the boy made a remarkably late entrance.

His eyes opened wide the moment her voice reached his ears. Breaking through the bar staff trying to block his path, Bell rushed over to their table.

The boy had made his way all the way to the Hidden Home of the Prums either by his vague memories of the map on Finn's note or by wandering around aimlessly until he found it, and he went straight to Finn. Lilly watched in dumbfounded silence.

"Mr. Finn! Please, please don't take Lilly away!"

"Huh?" was all Lilly could say.

Finn stayed seated with a blank look on his face.

But only for a moment. Instantly piecing together what was happening, he glanced over at Lilly and winked. A slightly evil smile appeared on his lips.

"How unfortunate—She's already accepted my offer, Bell Cranell."

Lilly was speechless. Shock was the only thing keeping her from jumping in and asking what he meant by that.

Just wait, the prum said with his eyes, stopping Lilly in her tracks. Her chance to get angry at him was gone.

At the same time, all the color had drained from Bell's face. But he didn't give up.

"I still—I still want to be with Lilly! I don't want to let her go!"

The strength behind Bell's scream caught Lilly by surprise, making her blush.

A glint appeared in Finn's eyes, as if he was enjoying himself. He started speaking again, the wicked smile still on his lips. "The two of us have already decided to unite as one. Are you really going to trample on that?"

"Yes!"

"Well, it sounds like you have a vested interest. So then, what is she to you?"

"She's part of my familia—my family!"

"Is that all? That's hardly enough."

"...She was my first ally and is a very, very important partner!"

Finn spurred Bell into yelling his true feelings for Lilly at the top of his lungs.

She listened to every word, her heart beating with every syllable. Heat built up inside her, to the point that her chest was aching.

That's when she figured out his plan. He was trying to show her exactly how much Lilly meant to the boy. It was unfair, almost dirty. Was there a way to stop this runaway train?

This human who had forced his way onto the dining floor was now exchanging words with Braver in the center of a crowd. Lilly was turning redder by the second, unable to do much more than look left and right between the two.

"At long last, I found the bride I've been searching for. I won't give up on this marriage that easily...Or will you try to take her by force? From me?"

Screech. Finn stood from the chair, looking up at Bell as he issued a challenge.

He was Level 6, a top-tier adventurer even stronger than *Ishtar Familia*'s Phryne Jamil. Bell cleared his throat but didn't back down.

It was his turn to be selfish, and he would see it through to the end no matter who stood in his way. Bell squared his shoulders and faced Finn directly.

"You've got spirit, and this could be interesting...The winner of our duel will decide her fate!"

Braver was getting caught up in the moment and having a bit too much fun. Forgetting his age, Finn pointed at the ruby-red-eyed boy, like he was a cocky teenager itching for a fight.

Luan had gone completely slack-jawed as he watched it all unfold. The rest of the prum staff and patrons gathered around the table, excited to see what would happen next.

As for Lilly, she couldn't be blushing any harder.

Wh…What is going oooooooon?!

Bell and Finn were about to fight over her?

One of them might've been just joking around, but the other one was completely serious. She could see it in the boy's eyes.

It was like a scene out of a fairy tale—two knights fighting for the right to marry a young maiden, or perhaps the queen. That was her part in the story, and it made her face burn with embarrassment.

I'm not fit for this role! I'm a servant of the castle, at the most! Or so she silently screamed inside her head.

Looking vaguely similar to a boiling apple, Lilly watched Bell muster up every bit of courage he possessed and Finn grin with the same twinkle in his eye.

Surrounded by the cheers of his kin, Finn declared:

"If by some chance you manage to land a hit, I will concede. However, should I win, she will be my bride."

"Get him!" came the jeering voices of the prum onlookers. Bell slowly nodded and took three steps back away from the corner of the dining floor before turning to face Finn once again.

This has gone too far, Lilly thought to herself, the shame taking its toll. She had to stop this, run in between them and—

"——General?"

A cold chill swept through the bar.

""""?!"""""

Lilly, Finn, Bell—all flipped around to face the terrifying, murderous aura emanating from the front.

On the other side of the panic-stricken crowd was an Amazon shrouded in a black miasma.

"T-Tione…How long have you been standing there?"

"General, what did you mean by that just now? Marriage…Your bride?"

Finn reeled backward. Tione hadn't been there long enough to hear the whole thing.

There was no light in the Amazon's dead, empty eyes. Her plump, heavily exposed breasts swayed with each heavy step she took in his direction. The floor under her feet groaned precariously.

Her very presence overwhelmed the bar's patrons. Unable to withstand the pressure of a top-tier adventurer, many collapsed to the floor like flies, staring at the ceiling with drool running down their chins.

"How did you know I was here…?"

"I followed your scent."

"What are you, some kind of animal person…?"

While it might have been in jest, she was the last person Finn wanted to hear say those words. Sweat was pouring down his face. At the same time, this Amazon who was head over heels for the general to a frightening extent swayed back and forth as she made her way through the tables and closer to the corner of the bar.

As soon as Tione got within three meders of Finn, her voice exploded:

"GENERAAAAAAAAAAAAAAAAAAAAAAAAAAAAALLL—!!"

"Get a hold of yourself, Tione!"

Finn darted away to get out of the charging Amazon's path. Pushing his small body to its limits, he stayed as close to the floor as possible and dashed away like a scared rabbit, hopping in leaps and bounds.

An ominous light came to life inside the Amazon's eyes. Going berserk, she spun around and chased the Braver out of the bar and into the streets at breakneck speed.

Thump, thump, thump, thump, thump! The last of their footsteps echoing through the bar, a strange stillness filled the air.

Lilly, Bell, and the still-conscious prums were stunned.

"…Um, Lilly."

"!"

At a time when no one knew what to say, Bell cautiously broke the silence.

The rest of the prums lost interest, returning to their seats and massaging their aching heads. Lilly's shoulders jumped up to her ears as she spun around to face the boy.

Bell threw his body into a deep bow right in front of her.

"I'm sorry! Sorry I couldn't make a decision, sorry that I wasn't clear…"

"N-no! This is a misunderstanding! That was all Mr. Finn's idea…! He was teasing you!"

"He…he was?"

"Yes! Lilly didn't accept his offer!"

Lilly desperately tried to explain what happened. Relief swelled within Bell's heart with each passing moment.

Hand over his chest, the tension started to disappear from Bell's shoulders. He still had a guilty look on his face, but he maintained eye contact with Lilly and spoke as clearly as he could.

"I'm sorry—for everything. But I just…I still want you to be here with me."

Bell bared his heart to her, his cheeks taking on a slightly scarlet hue.

Lilly was much the same way, wide-eyed and blushing. Her lips slowly spread into a smile.

"…Lilly is sorry, too. Suddenly getting angry, running away from home…"

"N-no, that was all because of me…"

"No, Mr. Bell. Lilly is at fault. She said in anger so many things she doesn't believe about you and put you in a bad situation."

The two stood there, exchanging apologies. They looked away at the same time, spouting even more explanations. Then they made eye contact again, blushing in embarrassment and feeling a little awkward.

"…Shall we go home?"

"Yes!"

Bell shrugged and smiled. Lilly enthusiastically smiled back as she answered.

Bell then went to apologize to the prum staff for all the trouble he caused, breaking into their bar, and did the same to the patrons soon after. Luan looked up from one of them who was still passed out on the floor and yelled, "Never show your face here again!" with all his anger. With that, Lilly and Bell left the Hidden Home of the Prums.

A clear blue sky above their heads, the two of them passed by crowds of demi-humans as they walked down the side streets.

"Um, also, how can I put this…?"

The two of them were almost home. They were in such a good mood that the events of last night didn't feel real anymore, and Bell felt comfortable enough to say what was on his mind.

Lilly looked up at him and saw him blush a little as he stumbled over his words.

"Lilly, you're like a little sister to me."

"Mhh…"

"I-I only ever had my grandfather. No brothers, no sisters…So I didn't want to lose one."

The boy shyly exposed the very deepest part of his heart to her. The corner of Lilly's mouth twitched. She knew that he thought of her as nothing more than a little sister, but hearing it still stung. She had decided to never leave his side no matter what happened, but this was something else entirely.

Cheeks trembling as anger started to take hold once again, Lilly suddenly thought of something and flashed a grin.

"Mr. Bell, oh Mr. Bell. Please lean in close."

"?"

Making a face fitting for an innocent little sister, she came to a stop and Bell did the same, albeit confused. The clueless white rabbit did as he was told and bent over at the waist so that the prum could whisper into his ear.

Lilly put her lips right next to it.

"——*I am older than you, Bell.*"

She spoke in the most adult, seductive way she knew how.

"?!"

A jolt ran down his spine as Bell stood up with a start. As he held his ear that Lilly had spoken into, the rest of his face hung limply. It wasn't long before he began to blush.

Lilly was looking back up at him, barely open eyes twinkling. Without warning, a grin appeared. The innocent-little-sister smile was back.

"Now let's get home, Mr. Bell."

"...Ho-hold on a second, Lilly! Are...are you serious?!"

"Who knows?"

She walked ahead at a brisk pace. Bell desperately tried to keep up.

Lilly's robe swished as she took a peek over her shoulder and saw that the boy was beet red and practically falling over his feet. It brought yet another smile to her face.

I see, I see.

So thinking of her as an older sister triggered a reaction like that.

It was worth remembering.

Lilly's cheeks turned a light shade of pink as she listened to the boy's rambling behind her and smiled happily.

Holding her hands behind her back, she had a bit more spring in her step as her footfalls echoed off the stone pavement.

The boy's pitiful voice echoed through the busy street.

The prum girl enjoyed the warmth of the sunlight, dimples forming in her cheeks as she savored the moment.

© Suzuhito Yasuda

CHAPTER 3

LOVE SONG TO A
GODDESS OF THE FORGE

© Suzuhito Yasuda

"Finally, everything is in order."

Light from a magic-stone lamp flickered in the darkness.

Two cloaked shadows stood facing each other in a small room and whispered quietly.

"Our soldiers have made it safely inside. Once we're done, they can deploy anytime."

"Is that right..."

One voice was that of a man filled to the brim with enthusiasm; the other, a stern, solemn voice of someone many years his elder. Their private conversation continued.

"We already know where he is. I'll make contact myself in a day or two."

"..."

The youth took a step closer to his silent companion.

"Don't tell me you're getting cold feet."

"..."

"It's too late to start wavering now. We have received an important task that leads directly to a promotion by our lord. This may be our last chance."

"I'm aware."

The elder nodded as the younger leaned toward him.

The man was most pleased by that response. Without missing a beat, he channeled into words the numerous emotions coursing through his veins.

"We must bring him back. That power belongs to us, and this place isn't worthy of it."

"..."

"Lost glory is once again within our grasp."

The elder figure stayed silent throughout his younger companion's impassioned speech.

Light from the lamp cast two long, flickering shadows high onto the wall.

Bright flames filled the inside of the forge.

Hephaistos intently watched the dark-red fire, the same color as her hair, rise and fall.

She was standing in a workshop where the large forge, an anvil, and other big tools sat ready for use in the corner.

Hephaistos, dressed in work clothes, came to a stop with a hammer in her hand. The shaft of a silver sword had already taken shape on top of the anvil beneath her, the metal still glowing with heat.

Flames from the forge illuminated half her face, including the prominent, bandage-like black eye patch.

The heavy blows of hammer on metal ceased, leaving behind only the crackle of the fire.

"Where'd your spine go?"

The front door of the forge creaked open and was closely followed by a new voice.

A rush of cold air came in from outside, making the flames flicker and ruining the perfect conditions inside the workshop. Hephaistos turned to face her visitor.

"Tsubaki."

"Now, I'd heard rumors you shut yourself up in this workshop. I came all this way to check on you, and you're not even swinging that hammer. So, what are you up to?"

The woman who entered the forge workshop had long black hair tied back behind her shoulders and wheat-colored skin.

Just as Hephaistos had an eye patch over her right eye, this woman had an eye patch over her left. Wearing a crimson pair of Far Eastern–style, skirtlike pants called *hakama*, Tsubaki rebuked Hephaistos for the lack of hammer work.

They were in *Hephaistos Familia*'s store, located on Northwest Main Street. Not far from Guild Headquarters on the road known as Adventurers Way, the store was equipped with a workshop on the first floor.

"Nothing much," Hephaistos responded to her follower.

"You've spent a lot more time in your head since Welfy boy left, now haven't you, My Ladyship? A bit lonely, are we?"

"…I'm always sad whenever a child leaves the nest. That goes for anyone, not just Welf."

Tsubaki, obviously put off by her goddess's condition, showed no restraint or fear in conveying her dissatisfaction. Hephaistos knew there was no point in trying to fool her and confirmed her suspicions without beating around the bush.

The woman watched as the goddess put the finishing touches on the weapon in a flash before starting to clean up the workspace.

"Well, then, any news?"

Releasing her crimson hair from its restraints and working her way out of her tight-fitting work clothes, Hephaistos addressed her follower. The woman nodded, her long black hair swishing behind her head.

"A message from the Guild and *Loki Familia*. Rakia has a plot afoot this time, by the sound of it."

The goddess narrowed her left eye while listening to Tsubaki explain the finer details.

"So, Hestia's children are to be the bait…" The goddess sounded deep in thought as the name of a friend rolled off her tongue. "All right then," she said with a nod. "Do exactly as the Guild says. Tsubaki, take command for me."

"Was planning on holing up in the shop for a bit, but this could be fun. You got it, I'll be takin' the helm."

With that, the woman left the workshop with a smirk on her face.

Hephaistos watched her leave, then returned her gaze to the corner of the workshop.

Flames still burned brightly inside the large forge.

Heat from another forge bit at the side of Welf's face.

The flames burned with an intensity on par with his own passion. The young man's face was covered in rolling sweat despite the towel wrapped around his forehead. With only the roar of the furnace at his side in the dim workshop, Welf repeatedly slammed his hammer into the red-hot metal on top of his anvil.

High-pitched, metallic echoes reverberated through the air. Showers of sparks scattered across the floor. It was a battle between him and his craft.

His gaze didn't move from what was directly beneath him. Completely focused on shaping the metal, nothing could distract him from the task at hand. Crimson hammer in hand, he simply guided it to the target with his gaze.

Every swing of his hammer left a thin, dark-red trail of light through the air, generated by his Advanced Ability, Forge. It allowed him to breathe a sublime power into each of his weapons and armor, making them stronger and sharper as they ascended to levels of awe-inspiring quality.

Slam! Slam! His ears had grown to love the sound of metal on metal. Each impact had a slightly different ring to it, and he could hear every detail.

It was as if the metal were talking to him, guiding the next hammer fall. A smile grew on his lips before he knew it.

—*Listen to the metal's words, lend your ears to its echoes, pour your heart into your hammer.*

Back in a long-forgotten corner of his memory, the voice of an old man from many years ago made its way past all the rust and into his thoughts again. He had heard the mantra in a workshop just as dim as this one. The smell of metal in his nostrils, Welf had been a young boy and nothing more than an assistant.

Brief images of those days flashed through his mind as Welf brought the melody of the forge to life. The hot metal bent to the will of his hammer, taking the shape of a sharp sword as his passion burned as hot as the flames burning at his side.

"Sorry for the wait. I finished your order, a katana."

Soft red light emerged from the open iron shutters of the workshop. A small stone structure built behind their home, the workshop was quiet under the evening sky.

The sun had almost set by the time Welf finished what he set out to complete. He'd gone to greet his allies, home from the Dungeon, in the main building while still wearing his sweat-soaked jacket.

Welf had stayed out of the Dungeon today in order to complete a few tasks. "Ooo!" came the collective voices of Lilly, Haruhime, and Mikoto, mouths open in surprise and excitement.

"I made sure the measurements match your old one as close as possible. It's a metal synthesized from a liger fang's tooth and noh steel mined from floor twenty-seven. Should be able to take a lot of punishment."

"Thank you so much, Sir Welf! It's gorgeous...!"

The curved, ninety-celch blade was both black and silver.

Mikoto took from him the blade forged from an adamantite drop item and an ore mined from the Deep Zone of the Dungeon, arms shaking with a mixture of elation and gratitude. It wasn't just the weapon's beauty that made her adventurer's heart fall in love with it at first sight. She could tell that a High Smith had forged the third-tier weapon by hand due to the blade's characteristics.

She had put off asking him to make this weapon in favor of the equipment she'd need—a spear and light armor—to fill her role in the middle of their formation. Feeling complete once again, Mikoto's cheeks glowed.

"It's so convenient to have a smith in the familia."

"Don't talk about people like they're some kind of magic-stone product, Li'l E."

Lilly looked at him out of the corner of her eye, commenting as if every household should have at least one person who could restore worn weapons back into shape and even create new ones when needed. Welf, however, wasn't going to take it lying down.

Making his rebuttal with half-lidded eyes, the young man then turned back to Mikoto. She was still holding her new katana, her mind somewhere around cloud nine. He was slightly intimidated by Chizan—the dagger securely fastened at her waist, a part-ing gift from Takemikazuchi that was one of a pair of extremely high-quality daggers forged by *Goibniu Familia*—because it was difficult to compete with. However, he was rather proud of how the katana had turned out.

Extremely satisfied with the blade and sheath, the latter deco-rated in a black and silver striped pattern, Welf took a step closer to Mikoto and tried to keep his pride under wraps while making a suggestion.

"Okay, now it needs a name...Iron Tiger, *Kotetsu*...No, Stripey, *Shimajirou*."

"Sir Welf, please waaaaaaaaait!"

Welf put his right hand to his chin, a grin on his lips. Mikoto vigor-ously voiced her objections. Breaking out in a nervous sweat, blood boiling in her veins, she made every effort to prevent that name from sticking.

"I-isn't it a wonderful name: Master Stripey. It's quite cute..."

"Do you mind?!"

"Its future hangs in the balance, Miss Haruhime, so please stay silent!"

Haruhime spoke like the sheltered girl she was, while Welf was overjoyed to find someone who could understand his tastes. Mikoto yelled at her childhood friend in desperation.

Their spirited discussion went through many twists and turns with an unamused Lilly watching from the sidelines. It ended with Mikoto, begging with her hands and knees on the floor and tears pouring out her eyes, finally winning the battle to give the new katana the name *Kotetsu*.

Welf scratched his red hair with a look of utter disappointment on his face while Mikoto clutched the weapon to her chest in relief after her hard-fought victory.

"...And these are for you two. For defense."

"Is this...a cloak?"

"Mr. Welf, could this be...?"

Welf handed Haruhime and Lilly each a black hooded robe.

He nodded at Lilly's surprise.

"That's right. Made it from the drop item we got from that Goliath. Bell and Lady Hestia gave it to me."

He was referring to the battle against the abnormally powerful monster, an Irregular, on the eighteenth floor: the Black Goliath.

Bell had received the drop item when all was said and done after the battle. Welf used half of it to make protective equipment for Lilly and Haruhime. The drop item, by the way, had to be recovered from the wreckage of Bell and Hestia's old room under the church because they hadn't had time to sell it.

That monster's hide was so strong that it had completely nullified the attacks of hundreds of upper-class adventurers without so much as a scratch.

Therefore, Welf had used its incredible defensive attribute to help the two supporters who were vulnerable to attack. He'd made a few personal choices in their design, but the cloaks were, without a doubt, top-tier defensive items.

"It's pretty heavy, isn't it…?"

"Yeah, but please try to overlook that. Remember how crazy strong the Goliath's skin was? No blade or spell is getting through these."

Lilly put the cloak over her shoulders right away and commented while looking down at it.

While Lilly had her Skill, Artel Assist, to help carry the load, Haruhime was on her own. "Ah, uwaah!" She struggled to stay on her feet under the weight of her cloak.

The Goliath's rampage depended on its brute force, so its hide had to be strong enough to repel both physical and magical attacks. The cloaks created from its drop item were no doubt strong enough to withstand attacks from monsters in the middle levels and the lower levels of the Dungeon without much trouble at all. Now it was Lilly's turn to feel grateful.

"But don't forget, this does nothing to soften the blow. One hard smack and it's all over."

Welf explained to Lilly that it was exactly the same as armor.

An iron plate could prevent the cut of a blade, but the flesh beneath would still feel the full impact. Lilly and Haruhime were both Level 1, meaning it didn't take much to launch them off their feet. Should they take the full force of the monster's attack, there was a real possibility they could die with the cloak in perfect condition around their bodies.

Meek expressions grew on Lilly's and Haruhime's faces after hearing Welf's warning.

"...But if this is so good, wouldn't it be better to give it to Mr. Bell on the front line?"

He would be exposed to far more ferocious attacks than Lilly.

The risk of taking damage would be greatly reduced if he was wearing this kind of defensive equipment.

Shouldn't Bell be wearing a Goliath robe rather than the style of armor he had been wearing from the very beginning? She made the suggestion very clear.

Welf looked away from them, his mouth a straight line on his face.

"...I take great pride in forging his armor with these hands. Giving him a drop item to wear into battle just won't cut it."

No matter how impressive the properties of the drop item were, his pride as a smith would take a serious blow if he were to just pass it off as is.

It was his job as Bell's personal smith to forge all his equipment by hand, and he wasn't about to change his mind.

The young man folded his arms and turned away from the girls. Lilly was a bit tired of his stubbornness, but Mikoto and Haruhime shared a giggle.

The last of the daylight coming in from outside the shutters cast Welf's face in a red hue.

"...That should cover it—now get out of here. I have to finish up."

"Mr. Welf—. Tomorrow's the day we go into the Dungeon with *Takemikazuchi Familia*, so don't forget to prepare your own equipment—"

"I know, now scram!"

Welf ushered the girls out of his workshop as a way to hide his embarrassment.

The three young women made their way across the garden, smiling among themselves with his loud voice echoing behind them.

Hestia Familia and *Takemikazuchi Familia* had decided two days prior to travel down to the seventeenth floor.

The two groups had worked together many times before, so no one was worried about their teamwork in combat. Now they were shifting their attention to long-term goals, specifically going even farther down into the Dungeon. Therefore, the best thing for them to do was to go on their very own mini-expedition as a practice run.

Going deeper into the Dungeon than they'd ever been, their next goal was to reach the twentieth floor, which meant there weren't enough hours in the day for them to return to their homes on the surface at night. Trying to do so would cut their time in the Dungeon drastically short and wasn't worth the trip.

The solution was to camp inside the Dungeon. The plan was simple. They would spend a full day in the Dungeon, and the two groups would take turns at guard duty when they needed to rest.

They might have dubbed it with the grandiose title of "mini-expedition," but as spending more time in the Dungeon was fast becoming a reality, this was their important first attempt at it.

Twenty-four hours. After packing sufficient food and blankets, they said their good-byes to a reluctant Hestia and a smiling Takemikazuchi, who told them to be careful. *Miach Familia*, whom they'd asked to look after their home while they were gone, saw them off along with the other deities as the large party departed Hearthstone Manor.

The group, numbering ten in all, spent half the day journeying deeper into the Dungeon until finally reaching the seventeenth floor, and then got ready for half a day of roaming.

—At least that was how it was supposed to happen.

"Aaaaaaaall you slackers on the shield wall! Flex those dirty rumps and hold your ground!"

An angry roar of a command managed to break through the pandemonium of relentless howls and clangs of battle.

A line of massive shields held side by side with absolutely no space between managed to absorb a giant fist, but the impact of the shock wave made arms go numb.

The dwarves and animal people who held the shields grimaced in pain as their heels were driven into the Dungeon floor. Cries for help and calls to charge swirled all around them. The voices of magic users in the middle of their incantations filled the air.

A large group of adventurers was fighting a giant monster that towered far over their heads.

"How did it come to this...?!"

"S-sorry, Lilly...!"

Yells of man and beast erupted from all over the battlefield. Lilly stood in the center of it all, shooting a stream of arrows from her bow gun as Bell finished off the hellhounds and liger fangs bearing down on them while apologizing mid-strike.

The joint battle party had been drawn into a large-scale skirmish taking place in a large cavern at the end of the seventeenth floor.

The mass of adventurers stood in front of the gateway to the safe point, the eighteenth floor.

Spread over a hundred meders right to left and front to back, the chaos of battle echoed far and wide with screams and roars colliding as much as steel and fangs. Under the looming vista of the Great Wall of Sorrows, by far the most prominent monster on the battlefield was a seven-meder-tall ash-colored giant.

"—OUUOOOOOOOOOOOOOOOOOOOOOOOOOOOOOOOO OOOOOOO!!"

The seventeenth floor's Monster Rex swung both its arms out wide, intimidating the adventurers below with a threatening howl. The ground shattered wherever one of its boulder-like fists came down, sending shock waves through the ground. Welf, Lilly, Mikoto, Haruhime, and all of *Takemikazuchi Familia* struggled to keep their balance.

It had all started when they arrived on the seventeenth floor and heard the sounds of battle echoing in the distance, followed by the unmistakable roar of the monster Goliath. The group had exchanged glances, decided to put their plan on hold, and taken the fastest route through the floor...only to find a massive battle between Goliath and a large party of adventurers waiting for them.

Both familias had done extensive research and preparation aboveground to make sure they chose the safest time to go on their mini-expedition—but the fact that the underground town of Rivira was planning to exterminate the floor boss on this day had eluded them. It just so happened the timing for their plans had coincided.

The Goliath was always reborn on a two-week interval, making it difficult for upper-class adventurers to pass through to the relatively peaceful eighteenth floor. That, in turn, had an effect on the profits of the business owners residing in the town built at the safe point, since there would be hardly anyone to swindle out of money. Therefore, it was in their best interests to form a temporary alliance and travel up to the seventeenth floor to exterminate the Goliath.

That's what Bell and his party had come across—the collective might of Rivira colliding with the ash-colored giant.

Welf and the others didn't have the stomach to ignore the screams of their fellow adventurers that echoed the constant vibration of the giant's footsteps. Most important, their white-haired leader couldn't abandon them after hearing "GEHHAAHHHHHH!!" echoing through the tunnels.

The group of slightly shady adventurers had come to his aid in the past, so Bell led the joint party into battle against the floor boss.

"UOAHHHHHHHHHHHH!! Little Rookie, HELP MEEEEEEEEE!!"

"Whoa!"

Third-tier adventurer Mord Latro was in the fray when the Great Wall stopped another one of the giant's attacks, when the magic users were finishing their spells, and when the attackers set out for another run at the giant's legs.

Mord had considered Bell to be an enemy from the moment they met, even though the boy didn't feel the same way. Mord had joined forces with some equally shoddy rogues and put him through an adventurer's baptism of fire, but he came to recognize Bell's true character through the events on the eighteenth floor. His opinion of the white-haired human had improved so much that seeing him brought a smile to his scarred face. Just like the other adventurers of Rivira, Mord had come to accept Bell as a fellow adventurer after seeing his exploits in battle against the Black Goliath.

The man had spent many years at Level 2, content to live out his life as a third-tier adventurer. But now he had started to push himself, to go on adventures once again, as his presence here in the extermination team showed. However, that adventurous resolve disappeared the moment he put his pride aside and called out for help at the top of his lungs.

A pack of large-category monsters, Minotaurs, had appeared from the main hallway that connected to the cavern. Bell charged past the panicking adventurer and engaged the monsters with the Hestia Knife and a shortsword newly forged by Welf.

"Since when did extermination teams run into this much trouble…?"

"There are so many more monsters this time around! There aren't enough people to attack the big guy!"

"Do they not understand how to work together…?"

Mikoto sliced through a charging monster and called out to the closest Rivira adventurer. He shouted a response back at her as Chigusa mumbled under her breath and skewered a hellhound with her spear.

Walls had been set up at various points around the gray giant to protect the attackers between sally attempts. The small arc of adventurers holding the shield wall was planted just in front of the gateway to the eighteenth floor.

Compared to the Black Goliath in Bell's memory—a much more powerful offshoot of the same species—this one was rather weak. However, the average Goliath was still classified as a Level 4 monster by the Guild. The beast had shiny black hair that reached all the way down to shoulders that looked to be carved out of solid stone. The ash-colored giant slammed its fists into one wall after another.

The brawny, masculine men behind the shields managed to keep their feet, but there were no attackers to take advantage of the window. The ones who should have been keeping the beast off balance and trying to bring it to the ground were too busy engaging the smaller monsters in combat. The same was true for the magic users. Some of them were forced to stop their incantations halfway, some lost their chance to cast their magic despite finishing because of the oncoming monsters, and others had no choice but to release the built-up magic energy without a target. The occasional fireball or rain of light arrows passed through the battlefield from time to time.

It all came down to this: The residents of the town of Rivira were not in the same familia. It was to be expected from a group of rogues. Teamwork was not in their vocabulary.

The newly leveled-up Level 2 Chigusa fought side by side with Mikoto, their movements blending together so well they looked like afterimages of each other. The teachings of Takemikazuchi, a god of martial arts, served them well as a pile of monster corpses built up at their feet. On the other hand, the other upper-class adventurers continued to fight as individuals in chaos.

"Don't know what else to expect from adventurers, but…!"

A line of battle developed between friend and foe. No one in the extermination team lent anyone a helping hand as they continued to fight their own battles.

Ouka had willingly joined the fray as one of the new arrivals, but one look at their ragtag parties made him sigh as he chopped a liger fang in two with the battle-ax in his hands. His efforts saved an Amazon in the group of attackers from certain death.

"—This beast's got a bit more pep than the usual ones!"

An adventurer yelled from the main battlefield after trying to engage the giant head-on.

Just as the many species of monsters that roamed the hallways of the Dungeon varied in strength among individuals, so did the Monster Rex. The Goliath spawned this time was definitely one of the stronger ones, or so claimed a blood-splattered animal person in the attacker group.

The joint battle party was disheartened by this frightening news. Even so, they bravely joined the extermination veterans from Rivira and charged out onto the battlefield over and over.

"Tsk! We need more…You there! Go back to town and get some help! You got ten minutes!"

"Like hell I can pull that off, Boris!"

The makeshift commander of this extermination force from Rivira barked the command, but the human on the other end yelled back his own complaint. He still turned to run toward the tunnel that connected the floors, but his send-off amounted to Boris shouting, "Shut up and do it!" behind him.

Including the extra members from Bell's battle party, there were forty adventurers fighting in the cavern.

Either they'd been reluctant to commit more people to the extermination party or they hadn't taken it seriously, but it was too late to do anything about it now.

There was also Rakia's invasion to take into consideration.

A great number of the upper-class adventurers who normally resided in Rivira had been called back to the surface to join the Alliance and were currently outside the city wall. The fact that none of the extermination team ranked above Level 4 was proof of that. Even the Level 3s could be counted on one hand. The second-tier adventurers were needed all over the battlefield in support. Bell was racing here and there like a speedy white rabbit and had no time to charge his Skill that could bring them back from the brink—even the powerful gravity magic that Mikoto had at her disposal wouldn't be much help because of the low ceiling and the number of her allies who would be caught up in it along with the monsters.

Their only hope lay in reinforcements coming up from the eighteenth floor. However, considering the distance they had to travel, as well as the time it took to equip armor and weapons, their saviors wouldn't arrive for some time.

Everyone could feel they were fighting a losing battle, and morale started to drain from the adventurers.

Without the help of a concentrated blast from the magic users, the adventurers manning the Wall took too much punishment. One sweeping kick from the giant's foot sent an entire group flying.

"GYAAHHHHHHHHHHHHHHHHHHHHH!"

"Dammit…!"

Many voices cried out in pain as shields and bodies flipped through the air. Welf swore to himself as he fended off a monster with his greatsword.

Next, his free hand reached behind his shoulder.

Another long weapon was strapped to his back, just underneath his greatsword's sheath. He had forged it just in case things went south during their mini-expedition—a Crozzo Magic Sword. Wrapping his fingers around its hilt, he pulled it free.

To be blunt, he didn't care if any of these nameless rogues lived or died. But at this rate, the giant's overwhelming power was putting his friends at risk. He would not compromise his allies for his pride.

"Dammit, dammit!" he spat through gritted teeth as he raised the sparkling dark-red blade high above his head.

This sword would be overkill, but he took aim at the Goliath and prepared to bring it down, when suddenly—

"———*Grow.*"

"‼"

An elegant singing voice reached his ears.

He turned toward the alluring sound and saw someone by herself in a corner of the cavern that was devoid of adventurers and monsters—the supporter Haruhime.

Mikoto and Lilly fought valiantly to protect the girl. The hood of her cloak was extremely low over her face as she continued casting.

"*Confine divine offerings within this body. This golden light bestowed from above. Into the hammer and into the ground, may it bestow good fortune upon you———Grow.*"

Welf near jumped out of his boots when he realized the gorgeous melody emanating from her was nearing completion. The name of the spell escaped her lips a heartbeat later.

"*Uchide no Kozuchi.*"

Mikoto, who had fallen back to protect the supporters, was engulfed in a pillar of light that took the shape of a hammer from above.

She was the target of Haruhime's Level Boost. The hammer of light disappeared, leaving behind a sparkling residue on her body.

Lilly was quick to remove her own black cloak—the Goliath robe—and throw it over the shoulders of the girl covered in the twinkling lights.

Mikoto pulled the hood over her face just as low as Haruhime had and wrapped her body in the dark fabric before racing off into the chaos.

"!!"

A black arrow shot through the battlefield, cutting through everything in its way.

The knife Chizan tore asunder the monsters unlucky enough to be in her path, their limbs and torsos flying left and right. She then zipped past the business owners of Rivira and Mord's band of rogues and made her way toward the giant that was still kicking its way through the walls.

In very similar fashion to traditional board games of the Far East, Mikoto had leveled up into a more powerful piece. Now on equal footing with the Level 3 adventurers, she wasted no time in coming to their aid.

Attackers moved in to cover the members of the newly destroyed wall. They drew the beast's attention as others got clear. Mikoto, however, was free to use that window to attack and quickly jumped into close range. Her sparkling arms thrust Chizan back into its sheath and drew Kotetsu in one swift motion.

"———HAAAAAAAAAAAAAAAAAAAAAAAAAAAAAAAA AAAAAAAA!!"

The katana emerged from its casing with blinding speed and cut into the Goliath's leg with a flash of light.

From there, the beast that had allowed Mikoto to get close so quickly took more hits all over its body.

"?!"

A stream of blood spurted from the giant's thick, stubby left leg.

The sturdy ash-gray hide had been pierced. The deep gash was pouring blood, a blow that signaled a change in the tide of battle.

Losing strength in its knee, the Goliath tumbled to the ground with a loud thud and accompanying shock wave.

The other second-tier adventurers, including Bell as well as the ones under Ouka's command, watched in amazement as the katana-wielding figure in the black robe deftly avoided the giant's fall and carved through another area of the battlefield like a black arrow shot from a bow.

"That's gotta be cheating…!"

Seeing Mikoto's incredible slash—no, the awe-inspiring power of Haruhime's Level Boost—left Welf speechless. The shock was so powerful that he forgot to be proud of the fact that one of his weapons had delivered the blow that had literally brought down the giant.

"Holy shit!" "Who does that guy belong to?!" Cheers and praise for the mysterious hooded adventurer erupted from the ranks of Rivira's adventurers as she performed a perfect hit-and-run maneuver. While managing to keep her identity a secret, Mikoto could feel all the eyes on her from beneath the Goliath robe. She turned around to make another attack run on the floor boss. It was the same technique that she'd seen with her own eyes used against the Black Goliath, movements that mirrored her vivid memories of the "Gale Wind."

Behind all the thrilled spectators, Welf, Lilly, and Haruhime quickly distanced themselves from Mikoto's starting point to avoid any unwanted attention.

"All you lazy attackers, forward! Cut it up! NOOOOOWWWWW!"

It was the chance they'd been waiting for. Spirits suddenly alight, a wave of adventurers charged forward while yelling at the top of their lungs.

There was one strategy for taking on large-category monsters and floor bosses: hit them low, bring them down.

The attackers were practically drooling as they saw their target writhing in pain on the ground.

Greatswords, war hammers, and battle-axes glinting menacingly in the dim light, the wave of adventurers reached the Goliath and raised their weapons.

Then...

"—Let me have a crack at it."

A shadow burst out of nowhere, crossing the battlefield in the blink of an eye and *severing the giant's right arm*.

"OOOOOOOOOOOOOOOOOOOOOOOOOOOOOOOOOOOO!"

"Wha...?"

Welf froze as soon as he got a good look at the person who had landed at the beast's side.

One thick katana, crimson *hakama*, and long black hair swishing from the momentum in her sudden stop. His lips moved on their own.

"Tsubaki..."

Almost as if she'd heard him, the newcomer turned to Welf and flashed a grin.

The Goliath's arm arced through the air and landed a short distance away, crushing all the monsters unfortunate enough to be beneath it. Bell, Mikoto, Ouka, and all other adventurers present spent the moment in stunned silence.

Wheat-colored skin and black hair tied back into a ponytail. Her minimalist armor was just gauntlets and a few other light plates around her body. With the large katana in her grasp and choice of clothing, she had the air of a swordswoman from an island nation in the Far East.

But the one feature that stood out above all else was the bandage covering her left eye.

"Cy...Cyclops..."

"...Level Five."

Several adventurers gulped as they beheld the warrior who bore so many similarities to the Goddess of the Forge, Hephaistos.

"W-WE WON, YA BASTAAAAAAAAAAARDS!!"

The arrival of the leader of the smith—part artisan, part top-tier adventurer Tsubaki—invigorated the adventurers even further, and they cheered in celebration.

That was the finishing blow.

Her presence on the battlefield skyrocketed morale to an all-time high, and the tide of battle completely tilted in their favor. Loud cheers caught the attention of other adventurers who were finishing off the last of the smaller monsters, and they came rushing in toward the fallen giant. Even the joint battle party joined in the charge once they got their bearings back.

The extermination party's mission was completed in a matter of moments with the help of the Level 5 smith. The large cavern fell silent soon after.

A scramble for the loot ensued soon after the floor boss was slain.

Everyone tried to lay claim to not only the larger-than-usual Monster Rex magic stone but the Goliath Fang that appeared in the ashes of the beast. The small mountain of magic stones from the smaller monsters was also up for grabs.

Those on the outside of the scrum—as extras who came in later, they weren't allowed to stake any claim—were either overwhelmed by the Rivira business owners trying to sell some of the smallest magic stones or standing in awe of the spectacle as a whole. "We're adventurers, what else is there to say?" Mord said with a forced smile as he and his rogues walked by with their share of the loot firmly in their meaty arms.

Since it didn't make any sense to see how the battle for the remaining valuables turned out, the joint battle party of *Hestia Familia* and *Takemikazuchi Familia* decided to go down to the eighteenth floor because they were so close anyway.

A safe point filled with lush greens and beautiful crystals where no monsters were born.

A mass of blue and white crystals, shaped like a mum flower, sat in the middle of the crystal blue "sky" over the floor known as the

Under Resort. Bell and the rest of the party finally had a chance to rest their tired bodies.

"Once again, we come to the eighteenth floor without planning on it..."

Lilly muttered as she shielded her eyes from the sparkling light of the flower crystal that shone far overhead like the midday sun.

The party members who were involved in the events that took place a month and a half ago reflected on their experience as the remaining members of *Takemikazuchi Familia* admired the scenery with a mixture of awe and wonder. Haruhime, who had only just recently gone through Conversion, eagerly swished her thick fox tail back and forth as she smiled alongside Mikoto and Chigusa. The three girls were each remembering the same thing: the scenery where they played together as children. "It's like we've stepped back in time," said Ouka with a forced smile as he watched their little group from afar. However, Bell and Welf could hear the excitement in his voice that his stoic expression wouldn't show.

Several rivers wound their way through the forest in the southern region of the eighteenth floor. A few of the tired adventurers kneeled at their banks and drank some of the clear water, while the others sprawled out on the grassy floor. The joint battle party was just starting to recover from the fight against the floor boss when the rest of Rivira's adventurers finally made their way through the connecting tunnel. "Why don'cha come up to the town?" shouted one of them as he waved. More spoke up, saying they were going to celebrate their victory, and invited them to join in.

Part of their motivation was guilt for keeping them out of the loot scrum. They were in a great mood and offered to treat them to a feast as an apology. Their offer was difficult to refuse. The joint battle party was just that tired.

So they joined the group of adventurers traveling west toward the rocky island in the middle of a lake. Crossing the log bridge to the island, it wasn't long before they arrived at the town on the cliff and passed through the wooden gate at its entrance.

"Oh wow...! Is this the town of Rivira?"

"Um, is this your first time here, Miss Haruhime?"

"Yes, it is. I participated in many ventures during my time with Lady Ishtar and have thus passed through this floor many times... but I was never allowed to enter the town."

Haruhime's Level Boost and her very existence had to be kept top secret, so she had been hidden from view as often as possible. Now she was walking among the various tents and ragtag shops, gazing at the crystals and blushing with joy. The renart's fox tail and ears moved back and forth excitedly as she couldn't decide where to look. Bell could feel the excitement emanating from her and blushed when the two made eye contact for a moment.

The town of Rivira had a great view of the lake directly below as well as the expansive forest to the south and east. There was also a great deal of black-market money being made inside the tents and shops that lined the town's streets. A bar had been built directly into the Dungeon terrain. Many happy and drunk voices echoed from the other side of the door in the cliff face.

The streets were much less crowded than the last time they were here, due to Rakia's attack. Even so, uplifting melodies from string and wind instruments filled the town. Everything was peaceful beneath the crystal sky underground.

"That was some nice work up there, Little Rookie! Would have been screwed without you!" said the "leader" of Rivira, Boris Elder.

Extremely muscular, the adventurer stood even taller than Ouka.

Most members of Bell's battle party had seen him many times during the large-scale fight against the Black Goliath and recognized him right away.

He wasn't someone easy to forget, with his intimidating build and gruff aura.

"You bein' here means *Hestia Familia*'s going for the Deep Zone, that right?"

"Uh, yeah...Eventually."

"Atta boy! We'll be your staging area for attack runs to the Deep Zone! I'll make sure everybody gives you a discount, fellow adventurer!"

Just like Mord, the leader of Rivira had seen what Bell did against the Irregular Black Goliath, and he was comparatively friendly with the white-haired human boy.

"Yes, keep coming back! Many times!" said the man who recognized Bell's power with a mighty grin; he wrapped his beefy arm around the boy's shoulders. Lilly, however, eyed him suspiciously as she walked behind them.

"...Oh yeah, Little Rookie. Somethin' I wanted to ask you about."

"A-and that is?"

Slightly intimidated by the fleshy tree trunk around his shoulders, Bell forced a shaky smile and looked up at the leader. The man tried his best to look docile and brought his voice down very low to ask.

"That magic-sword blacksmith is with you, ain't he? Can you introduce me?"

"——C'mon, please!! Make me a magic sword!"

Wrinkles appeared in the middle of Welf's brow.

It happened in the middle of the feast, free of charge as promised, when Bell had left the group to go talk to the leader and Welf had gone on his own to find a comfortable spot at the base of twin crystals, one blue and one white.

The greatsword and magic sword were still strapped to his back as a small horde of adventurers rushed up to him, shouting as loudly as they could.

"A powerful one, like those amazing magic swords I saw in the War Game!"

"You're one of the Crozzos, aren't you?"

"I heard they were cursed so they can't forge magic swords no more. All a lie, wasn't it? They pack one hell of a punch!"

"I'll pay anything, just name your price! So come on!"

They formed a ring around him, pushing and shoving their way to the front with exactly the same request:

"Make me a Crozzo Magic Sword!"

Most of Orario had witnessed the War Game through Divine Mirrors that had been placed all over the city. Word that the legendary magic swords—ones from the actual legend—were Welf's handi-work had made its way through the ranks of adventurers like wild-fire. Everyone wanted magic swords powerful enough to instantly turn thick castle walls into piles of rubble. It was easy for them to work out that the smith in question was a member of *Hestia Familia*.

"Bastards..."

He had many visitors after the War Game who made similar requests...but none were as insistent or aggressive as these today.

Hestia Familia had come to Rivira—the maker of *those* swords was here. The only residents of Rivira were adventurers, and all of them knew how to get information. Word spread, and practically everyone in town wanted to have a word with the magic-sword blacksmith.

Filled with greed, they came after Welf in droves, all begging him to make a magic sword for them. The young man had had enough.

"———Shut up, all of you!! I will never sell or give any magic swords away! Now tell your cronies and leave me the hell alone!"

He drove the adventurers away, roaring in anger.

The earnest requests and rude replies shot back and forth, but Welf wouldn't budge. Spitting in disgust and spewing complaints, the adventurers finally gave up when they realized his will was as strong as steel, and genuine fear of the weapons strapped to his back started setting in.

Haruhime and Chigusa also shrank back in fright. "Bastards..." he whispered again, chewing on the word as his bad mood contin-ued to get worse.

"..."

"...What's with that look, big guy?"

"Nothing...Want some of this honey cloud?"

"Why the hell would I?"

Ouka took pity on Welf and kindly offered a sweet fruit in an effort to cheer him up, but the red-haired man would have nothing of it. The girls were definitely scared now, which made him feel even worse, so Welf broke away from the group and set off to find a place to calm down.

His usual friendly big-brother personality had disappeared. Now he was the lone wolf, striking out on his own.

"Welf!"

"...Bell."

Bell found him once Welf had reached one of the most scenic points in all Rivira.

The smith had found a place isolated from the crowd. The boy walked up to him, looking apologetic and scratching his white hair.

"Sorry, Welf. Sounds like everyone in town came to find you... The leader asked me if he could talk to you, and I tried to turn him down, but..."

"...No, none of this is your fault. I knew this would happen long before we crossed that gate."

He had been ready for it the moment he chose to use a magic sword rather than let his friends' lives hang in the balance. Even so, his pride as a smith and his stubbornness had come to a head, leading to his livid reaction.

"Don't apologize," he said with a forced grin to the boy who still didn't know what to say. Then he closed his eyes and took a deep breath.

"But damn, do they know any other words besides 'magic sword'...? Do they have any shred of self-respect? The only things an adventurer needs is a reliable weapon in a strong arm, that's it."

"Ah-ha-ha-ha..."

Bell's face relaxed as soon as Welf recovered enough to string words together.

"Speaking of that—of swords, anyway—that shortsword I made do all right?"

"Pretty good. It's not that hard to use, and it helped out quite a bit in the battle earlier today."

Bell withdrew the shortsword from its sheath. The weapon in his left hand had a longer reach than the knives he carried, so it was great to pick off monsters from a safer distance. The blade sparkled in the light from the crystals overhead. "Glad to hear it," said Welf with a satisfied nod.

Just as a smile finally appeared on his face…a set of footsteps emerged from the shadows.

The two of them turned. Welf's eyes bulged in surprise.

"Ha-ha-ha, aren't you popular, Welfy boy."

They could see a crimson *hakama* and battle gear in the style of the Continent. One thick katana hung from the waist. A smith with long black hair tied into a ponytail. The leader of *Hephaistos Familia* and the one who had jumped in to save the extermination team, Tsubaki, walked closer.

"You—what do you want…?! Why are you even here?!"

"What's with you, Welfy boy? That how you greet a former boss and fellow smith? How disappointing. Didn't I take really good care of you until you left?"

"Just answer me, dammit!"

"Hmph. Fine, then, but I'm answerin' the second one first. I've wanted to stretch my legs in the Dungeon for far too long. As for the first…I came to make you squirm."

She grinned with a twinkle in her eye. "Go to hell!" Welf retorted, clenching his jaw at the memories flooding back into his mind.

Leader of *Hephaistos Familia*, Tsubaki Collbrande.

Standing 170 celch tall, she was often mistaken for human. Although her mother was indeed a human from the Far East, her father was a dwarf from the Continent, making her half dwarf. Her wheat-colored skin had a healthy luster, and her breasts were rather large despite being tied down beneath her battle cloth. She had all the physical qualities to be a very attractive woman, but her free spirit and desire to enjoy herself meant that she spent little time trying to act like a perfect lady. She always seemed to be around Welf from the day he entered the familia, but that was only because it was so much fun to tease him.

She still liked to poke fun at the young Crozzo smith, but back in those days she treated him more like a child, occasionally helping out and giving advice, but mostly using him as the butt of her jokes. It happened so often that Welf couldn't remember every single time.

However, he knew that other smiths in the familia referred to him as "Tsubaki's toy" behind his back.

Even the time when he, Bell, and Lilly had been forced to make the life-or-death decision to travel to the eighteenth floor not too long ago and *Loki Familia* had come to their aid, Tsubaki had been a part of *Loki Familia*'s expedition. Of course, she sought him out, asking if he was lonely without her in the workshop. There was absolutely no doubt that Welf was not very fond of her.

At the same time, Tsubaki was renowned in all of Orario, both as a smith and as a top-tier adventurer.

The fact that she had achieved the rank of Master Smith rubbed Welf the wrong way. Considering how she had treated him on a daily basis, the young man made every effort to avoid her.

Welf frowned and tried to hide his face as Tsubaki gave Bell a short greeting, since the two had crossed paths on the battlefield already. Then she turned back to him.

"Our goddess has been stuck in one hell of a rut since you left, Welfy boy. She's lonely."

"…That's a lie."

In truth, Welf was surprised to hear that. But he was quick to hide any reaction.

"Oh, but it's true," responded Tsubaki with a big-hearted nod. The twinkle was back in her eyes and another grin grew on her lips.

Bell watched their conversation, not really sure if he should step in as he spoke up.

"Huh? What's going on?"

"It ain't that hard to figure out. Those two have a special connection…or somethin' like that. At the very least, Welfy boy here has a thing for that goddess. Don't you?"

"Oi, cut it out! Why would I—?"

Tsubaki's grin widened the more frustrated Welf became. However, the young man's face flushed and voice trembled as he shouted at her not to make assumptions.

As for Bell, he had never seen this side of Welf. Never once had he suspected that the young man felt anything more than the usual reverence followers had for their deities. The sudden revelation blindsided him.

Welf, on the other hand, looked away from the boy, unable to withstand Bell's visible surprise. "Dammit..." he muttered with his hand over his cheek.

Then the young man said a few things like, "Cut it out already," and a few other saltier expressions. Tsubaki chuckled to herself, shoulders jumping up and down—then her aura suddenly changed completely.

"That's right, any old smith could fall for that blockhead of a goddess."

Her red right eye, opposite of the bandage, narrowed at Welf.

"As a deity, as a woman...and for her skill with a hammer."

Bell's and Welf's jaws dropped as Tsubaki continued.

"Welfy boy, why the hell didn't you use that magic sword from the get-go in the fight? Why'd you refuse to make them?"

"You—you were there the whole time...?!"

"I thought you were past spouting all that rubbish 'bout not wantin' to make magic swords?"

Knowing that Tsubaki had been watching him from the time they joined the battle's extermination team made Welf gnash his molars together. She ignored the anger appearing on his face and kept talking in a low, cool voice. Playtime was over.

The teasing ended and the interrogation was under way.

"Whether it's talent or blood, we as mortals can't come close to forgin' a supreme weapon without pourin' everything we have into our craft. The dimwit you've got the hots for is on a whole other level. You won't even reach her in your dreams this way."

The female smith's harsh words left Bell speechless. Welf, however, was fuming.

The goal that drove all smiths through their trials and tribulations, forging a supreme weapon...Hephaistos had shown him what the realm of the gods looked like, but he refused to take advantage of the blood in his veins to get there. Tsubaki touching that nerve was far worse than any insult and made him retaliate.

"Don't tell me what I can and can't do! I don't have a shred of interest in reaching the supreme realm by forging magic swords! I hate the things!"

"..."

"I *will* get there doing it my way, you'll see!"

Welf's declaration that he would reach that height on his own terms without relying on magic swords made Tsubaki's right eye squint to nothing more than a sliver.

Her glare then shifted to Bell—she was in point-blank range before he knew what was happening.

Tsubaki moved so fast that the flat-footed Welf couldn't even see her. Bell forgot to breathe.

All he saw was a blur, but that blur was her grasping the handle of her katana—with a flash of murderous intent in her eyes. The boy's body reacted on reflex, bringing the shortsword still in his left hand up to protect himself.

It was over in a flash. Tsubaki's katana came screaming out of its sheath and collided with the shortsword, breaking it in half.

"_____"

Snap! Time stood still for Welf, the high-pitched metallic tone ringing in his ears as he watched the blade he had forged come apart.

It didn't break; it *was split*.

A simple upward slash. There was no technique or anything fancy in her attack, just a simple impact of blade on blade. And in that moment the blades collided, his skill as a smith had lost.

The broken silver blade spun through the air in front of the two boys. Bell was speechless. Welf was in shock.

Now it was Tsubaki's turn to lash out as the piece of the sword hit the ground.

"Was that supposed to be a toothpick?"

A bright blue sky was above; the town of Rivira was at peace.

But all that might as well have been another world entirely. The woman who stood at the top of the smithing world maintained her cold tone even as her loud voice resounded across the floor.

"Your own way? Idiot, at that rate you'll die long before ever comin' close to the realm of the gods."

"...?!"

"Did becomin' a High Smith put a chip on your shoulder?"

The reality in her words pierced his very soul.

He had no intention of acting pompous. However, he couldn't deny that the feeling of accomplishment and the pride he felt in carrying the title of High Smith had made him lose a bit of his edge.

The woman's right eye was burning with an accusing glare.

"Smiths who make blades like that are a dime a dozen."

Tsubaki's voice lowered in anger as she delivered the final blow.

"Don't overestimate yourself, Welf Crozzo."

Beneath her anger, her words felt like a warning as well.

A heavy moment passed before she turned her back, ponytail whipping to the side.

Welf and Bell stood frozen in place as she took her first step away from them.

"You'll be gettin' payment for the broken weapon tomorrow."

Not bothering to look over her shoulder, Tsubaki left them behind.

Welf still hadn't budged. It was another several heavy heartbeats before he collapsed to the ground next to the ruined blade. He couldn't take his eyes off it.

"W-Welf..."

There was no way the boy's words could reach him now.

All the challenges and hardships he had overcome up until now paled in comparison to the shock he'd just received. Welf fell into the deepest, darkest pits of despair.

Light from the crystals above disappeared as "night" descended on the eighteenth floor.

The joint party had decided to spend the night in Rivira.

Their weapons were in rough shape, and they had used a great deal of their items during the fight against the Goliath—in truth, they were down to their last ones—so rather than camp in the forest where the threat of random monsters was real, they opted for the safety of the town. Deciding to have their mini-expedition another time, the group searched for a place to sleep.

Though they complained about how all their preparations had gone to waste, the group settled on an inn that was built into a natural cave.

Everything in the town of Rivira was expensive because the business owners knew exactly what adventurers would need and that they would pay extra to get it. Despite all that, this inn was remarkably reasonable. There were no obvious problems inside; quite the opposite. With liger-fang fur rugs on the floor, magic-stone chandeliers, and rooms complete with beds, everything looked to be in great shape. Considering the other options, this place was definitely one of the higher-quality inns in Rivira.

And yet, the price was much lower...

"...Word has it that this is the very inn where an adventurer's headless corpse was discovered..."

"A-are we absolutely sure staying here is the best idea?!"

"L-Lady Lilly, why not look into a different location...?"

"No, not possible. Every other place is too expensive. Lilly doesn't care what did or didn't happen here, price trumps all. It's not as if the slain adventurer haunts these halls...!"

—That gruesome incident was the reason that customers didn't come to this inn.

Haruhime, Mikoto, and Chigusa were visibly shaken as they raised their objections, but they failed to convince the frugal prum to reconsider. Lilly put on a brave face and went to check in at the front desk. The animal-man clerk nearly wept with joy at the sight of his first customers in a long time.

So overjoyed, in fact, that he treated them to light snacks and wine. Once they were done, everyone went their separate ways to get ready for bed. They had reserved two rooms, one for men and one for women. The girls huddled together in their room, doing their best to overcome the fear of what couldn't be seen by lying side by side on the floor and trying to get some sleep.

Lights faded in the tents and shops around the town.

Only the bars remained lit. Drunken, jubilant voices filled Rivira as night descended.

"…"

Welf left the inn by himself and returned to the same vantage point where everything had happened that "afternoon."

He could see the many sparkling crystals that dotted the town-scape on the other side of the railing, as well as the pristine scenery of the eighteenth floor even farther beyond. The soft glimmer of the crystals far above reflected off the lake surface beneath him like stars.

He hadn't exactly come back up here to take in the view, which was like nothing else aboveground, but he admired it for a few moments until he realized he had company and slowly turned around.

Bell had left the inn after realizing the young man had disappeared. Staying just out of sight, he had followed him all the way to the vantage point.

"What is it, Bell?"

Welf did his best to sound friendly.

"Welf…I, um…"

"…"

"I…Ever since then…Even now, I prefer your…"

The boy had difficulty speaking, his mouth opening and closing awkwardly as he desperately tried to convey how he felt.

But he just couldn't, after seeing the look in Welf's eyes. His own ruby-red eyes looked away and he fell silent.

Somehow, he understood how the smith was feeling, as though he had been through something like it before. He also knew that, in this state, no words would comfort him.

After looking left and right for a few moments, he walked up next to Welf.

The two stood side by side in silence, listening to the heavy voices wafting up from the bars and looking out over the town of Rivira.

They were in the same place that the blade Welf forged had broken so easily.

"...Hey, Bell. Can I have a look at Lady Hestia's knife for a moment?"

"Huh?"

"Please."

Welf spoke up after a few minutes, making a request.

The boy stood there for a moment before nodding and removing the jet-black knife from its sheath at his waist.

Welf took the Hestia Knife from his outstretched hand.

"Ahhh, damn...It really is a thing of beauty..."

His eyes followed the series of hieroglyphs that were carved into the blade surface as a mixture of admiration and pain swirled within him. A dreary expression took over his face.

The divine blade had nearly taken his breath away the first time he saw it.

The weapon itself seemed to dim the moment it left Bell's grasp. Welf had never been able to figure out why until he learned that it was Hephaistos herself who forged the blade.

That was its true worth. The skill of a god had gone into its creation. A skill that was in a realm of its own.

A fresh wave of admiration for the Goddess of the Forge rose within him as he held the weapon in his hand.

"...All smiths go through a rite of passage before joining *Hephaistos Familia*."

"...Like a ceremony?"

"Yeah. Every single one of us, no exceptions."

Returning the knife to its owner, Welf reflected on his own beginnings and explained how he had first met Hephaistos.

He had run away from his birthplace, the Kingdom of Rakia, and was looking for a new country to call home.

He had stumbled across a small town that specialized in metalwork and managed to get hired as an apprentice, when who should walk into his shop but Hephaistos herself. Not only that, but he caught her attention.

After he accepted her invitation, she brought him to a room at her familia's home and his rite of passage commenced.

"All of us are shown one sword. Then we decide whether to join or not."

Just the two of them, alone in the room. Hephaistos had told him: *"If you don't feel it, go someplace else."*

Then she'd opened the door to a back room. *It* was there.

A single sword on top of a pedestal.

The sight of that one weapon had sent chills down Welf's spine.

"—I was shaking. I could hardly believe that any human smith could ever make a weapon like that."

Remembering the sight of the blade forged by Hephaistos's hands still gave him goose bumps.

With her Arcanum power sealed and no other special Skills to speak of, the goddess had used pure, refined techniques to forge that blade.

It was the sword all swords were judged against, the original, forged by the equivalent of human hands. The absolute apex of what people of Gekai could achieve.

It was a divine work, a piece that truly belonged in the realm of the gods.

"It's the absolute. The best a human without any special Skill might hope to achieve."

Welf didn't look at Bell. Instead, his gaze was cast out over the town as his words reflected the passion still burning inside his heart.

He couldn't help but smile as memories of what he saw that day came shining through.

"I want to make a weapon that surpasses it."

Welf clenched his right fist just in front of his chest.

Anyone who saw that blade instantly felt a connection with Hephaistos, a kind of love for her to make them want to learn from her and eventually surpass her. Made them want to reach out to the awe-inspiring goddess. Made them want to see themselves reaching her realm and finding out what lay beyond.

It was a path far more difficult than anyone could ever imagine.

By comparison, his journey was far more strenuous and challenging than Bell's quests to catch up with Aiz Wallenstein.

The boy's goal was the Sword Princess—also known as the Kenki—a mortal who stood at the place where all adventurers wanted to be, among the best of the best. The place where Welf wanted to be was among the realm of the gods.

It was a height that required far more effort and devotion to reach.

Surprise started to appear on Bell's face as he began to understand the depth of Welf's ambition. The redheaded smith's gaze was locked on his clenched fist.

"…I want to make it…or at least I did."

Shadow covered his face as his head drooped.

—*"We as mortals can't come close to forgin' a supreme weapon without pourin' everything we have into our craft.*

—*"The dimwit you've got the hots for is on a whole other level. You won't even reach her in your dreams this way."*

The High Smith knew the limits of his ability.

She, who stood at the top of the smithing world, was a monster in her own right recognized as Hephaistos's leader.

She, who knew his goal lay even further beyond, understood.

But today, she'd driven that point home to a painful degree, as well as made it clear how much he wasn't needed.

After all, he was but one smith trying to challenge a god, dreaming a legendary dream. Was it absurd?

Was it as Tsubaki said, and he would never reach his goal without taking advantage of the detestable blood in his veins?

Without being a magic-sword blacksmith, would he ever be in the same realm as Hephaistos?

"I…"

Bell watched as Welf looked up at the dark blue sky of the labyrinth.

The next day.

Hestia Familia and *Takemikazuchi Familia* left the eighteenth floor.

After spending a little bit of time in the middle levels recouping their financial losses from the fight against the floor boss and spending the night in Rivira, the joint battle party made it back to the surface just before nightfall.

Some of them went to the Exchange; others went directly back to their gods to inform them about what had happened in the Dungeon. Everyone went their separate ways in Central Park. Welf went off on his own, walking through the city streets under the dark red sky.

The buildings on either side of the street were filled with boisterous voices and well lit by magic-stone lamps. Adventurers, just back from the Dungeon, shared their stories of bravery with other patrons, staff members, or anyone who would listen. Bards used an array of instruments to fill the bars with upbeat melodies as listeners sang with jugs of ale in their hands. Even the prettiest women working at the bars got in on the act by dancing along with the music. Everyone was smiling, laughing, and having a good time.

Welf passed through the lively crowd without saying a word. No one said hello to him as he passed by on the edge of the street. It was as though no one noticed he was there.

He hadn't seen Tsubaki since their heated conversation.

Her words, however, had never left. Still lingering in his ears, they dragged him into a whirlpool of anguish every time he let his guard down.

"Dammit," he groaned, and shook his head. He'd been asking himself the same questions over and over since last night but had yet to come to any conclusion.

Despite the fact that, in the end, there was only one answer.

Frustration on the rise as his spirits sank, Welf looked at his feet as he walked. His eyes did nothing more than trace the stone pattern of the pavement as it passed beneath him.

He drifted to the west, the last rays of sunlight illuminating his jacket, when suddenly...

"—Welf."

He heard a voice he couldn't believe.

"_____"

Welf froze on the spot. Eyes widening, he quickly turned his head toward the voice.

For a brief moment, he was sure something was wrong in his head, that he was hallucinating and it was just a figment of his imagination. But sure enough, he could see a faint outline in the shadows of an alleyway beside him.

The shadows swirled as if swishing a cape in front of the motionless Welf and moved farther into the alley. An invitation, no doubt.

Welf followed without any hesitation.

Oi, it can't be, why would—?

He made his way through the narrow alleyway.

More and more new questions filled his mind every moment, sending his thoughts into turmoil.

Why would he be here?

His pulse quickened. The thumping of his heart against his ribs was too loud to ignore. Anxiety threatened to overwhelm him as he pursued the cloaked figure even deeper into the winding alleyways of the city—until, finally, the shadow came to a stop.

They were somewhere in the backstreets. Litter scattered about the road; lively voices drifted from the bars off in the distance.

The cloaked figure turned to face Welf as he stood in a completely deserted and narrow path. Then it lowered its hood.

"It's been a long time, Welf."

The face of a middle-aged man who looked far older emerged from the hood. The unusually large number of wrinkles covering his face made his age difficult to determine. His brown hair, long for a man, was tied behind his head. His eyes spoke of years of hardship, trials, and tribulations. There was no luster, no strength in his gaze.

Welf couldn't believe what he was seeing as he looked upon the aged human who was a mirror of himself, showing what he would look like in a few decades. Then he spoke to him.

"Old man...?"

The person in front of him was none other than his real father. They had the same blood running through their veins.

Wil Crozzo.

Welf had severed all ties with him seven years ago. This man should be nothing but a part of his past.

A citizen of Rakia, he was the current head of the fallen family of blacksmith nobility, the Crozzos.

"Why are you here...? Why would *you* be *here*?!"

"Does that need an answer, foolish boy?"

Welf struggled to control his trembling voice. Wil cast his weary gaze on the young man.

He clenched his jaw.

Just as the man had said, the obvious answer was right outside the city wall. Thinking wasn't necessary.

Everyone knew about the 30,000 troops currently fighting with Orario's Alliance.

The man in front of him belonged to the army of the divine king who came from the West.

Welf's blood boiled as he pieced everything together. This man had snuck into the Labyrinth City as part of the Rakian invasion.

Don't tell me...?!

The reason that Wil came into the city, the reason that he'd sought him out, the reason that Rakia wanted to attack in the first place——.

The young man's father watched the expressions pass over his son's face and stated his purpose.

"Welf. *Forge magic swords for us.*"

"...!!"

"The Kingdom of Rakia, Lord Ares himself, has recognized the power of your magic swords. The ones that you forged for that pointless match between deities using our family's gift."

The match between deities—the War Game.

Just as his skill had attracted attention from the adventurers inside Orario, word of the incredible strength of Welf's magic swords had spread to the Kingdom of Rakia. And now Ares had launched an attack in an effort to secure Welf's powerful Crozzo Magic Swords for himself.

"The only reason this war drags on is because of you."

That harsh truth hit Welf like a punch to the gut, the shock traveling through his entire body and leaving him speechless.

Those magic swords had once elevated Rakia's army to invincibility, allowing them to obtain unimaginable levels of glory in the days of yore. Now they wanted to regain that legendary status by invading Orario to reclaim him.

Welf was floored by the level of Rakia's obsession with Crozzo Magic Swords.

"Of course, we'd been preparing to attack Orario for some time. However, once news of the War Game reached us, Lord Ares and our king decided to change our plans."

"…!"

"Then it became my role to retrieve you…Come with me, Welf. With you and Crozzo Magic Swords by our side once again, Rakia shall regain her former glory."

Their deity had a thirst for battle. Welf figured that he most likely wasn't Rakia's only objective.

However, the fact that the Kingdom of Rakia had raised an army of 30,000 and started an all-out war just for magic swords, and then sent this man to collect him, only added fuel to the fire burning in his heart. "Are you brain-dead?!" Welf practically spat the words from his mouth.

The Guild was very strict when it came to monitoring the flow of capable warriors, so luring an upper-class adventurer out of the city was next to impossible—and climbing over the large city wall was no easy feat. Even if Wil managed to make contact with Welf, the full, outrageous strength of Orario's adventurers would be there to bar his retreat.

The solution was to bring the 30,000 troops and draw out as many of the adventurers as possible. Most likely, the reason they were still fighting now was to buy enough time to get Welf out of Orario.

The Kingdom of Rakia was willing to go to such lengths to reclaim the lost power of Crozzo Magic Swords.

"Go to hell! Me, join you?! Dream on! I said good-bye to the family and Rakia a long time ago! There's no reason for me to play along with your batshit insane scheme!"

"Foolish boy, I was giving you a chance to come peacefully out of paternal mercy..."

Father and son, locked in an intense stare down.

The air was electric, but Welf wasn't intimidated by Wil's threatening words. Reaching for the swords strapped to his back, he curled his lips into a grin.

"So then you're going to kidnap me? Drag me away by force?"

Welf was now aware of the other figures trying to conceal themselves in the darkness.

He looked down to the alleyways, grinning as if itching for a fight.

"We might be out of the way here, but not so far that people won't hear a brawl. This is Orario—there'll be no escape once they know you're here."

Welf was Level 2. He was stronger than most of the people who lived outside the city, including the average member of Rakia's army. His opponents would have to employ other strategies. Although the young man was genuinely surprised that they had made it this far without being discovered by the Guild, that also meant there couldn't be many of them. It would take more than a few soldiers to overpower him.

Welf held the advantage, as well as the hilt of his greatsword. However, Wil's expression remained unchanged as he said to his son:

"If you refuse to come quietly, my comrades within the city will set it ablaze with magic swords. Authentic Crozzos, at that."

"_____"

The glint of the blade was a few celch out of its sheath when Welf's hand came to an abrupt halt.

His eyes trembled in shock as he yelled.

"Don't give me that shit! There can't be any more Crozzo Magic Swords left in Rakia!"

"Actually, yes, there are. Fifty of them were spared at the time of the fairy's curse."

He continued by adding that Welf hadn't been old enough to learn that family secret before Welf had left.

A smile appeared on Wil's face for the first time.

Back in the days of yore, when Crozzo Magic Swords paved the Kingdom of Rakia's advance with utter destruction, anything close to the battlefield—be it lakes or mountains or an elvish forest—became nothing more than piles of charred ash. That drew the anger of the elves and other fairies, who broke all the magic swords into useless fragments. Their last act was to place a curse on the family of blacksmiths who created them. Now, Welf was the only member of the family able to forge magic swords.

However, there was no uncertainty in Wil's voice when he claimed that several of the magic swords had survived the fairies' purge and the curse.

"The commanders were afraid of losing them, so they sat collecting dust all these years..."

The smile still plastered on his wrinkled face, Wil reached inside his cloak and withdrew a blade.

"This should be proof enough."

"———!"

The weapon firmly in his father's grasp was, without a doubt, a magic sword.

Welf knew in an instant what the red swirling energy inside its blade meant, and it left him speechless. The Crozzo blood in his veins knew how to recognize one of its own. This was no bluff.

"My compatriots each have one as well. If I give the signal or fail to return in due time, they'll unleash hellfire on Orario."

Should the Crozzo Magic Swords be used inside Orario's walls, the results would be cataclysmic.

Just like the elvish forest and the fairies' homes, this peaceful city would turn into a sea of flames, its buildings reduced to rubble. Countless civilian lives would be lost should that come to pass.

Wil could see that his son understood the situation and narrowed his eyes.

"You come with us and none of that happens. Nothing at all."

The elder Crozzo watched the fire disappear from his son's face, and his smirk turned into an ominous grin.

He then started speaking with unbridled joy, gradually breaking free from years of suppression with each word.

"Welf, the Kingdom of Rakia will rise once again upon your return! And we, the Crozzo family, can once again bask in the glory of the old days! Money, status, fame—all of it ours!"

"...!"

"Lord Ares has given his word that he'll restore our family to its rightful place if you agree to forge magic swords once again! Our family name will be heralded as it once was! The Crozzo family's utmost desires will become reality, and I will see it through!"

Wil let his emotions take over, a new light shining in his once-dead eyes as his long hair waved beneath the tie behind his head.

The vigor in his eyes was very close to the brink of insanity. They twinkled abnormally bright in the dim light.

Welf was overwhelmed by the devotion of a man trapped by his family's obsession.

The many wrinkles in Wil's face bent and curved as he smiled in his son's direction.

"Make your preparations to leave Orario tonight. Bring all the magic swords you have in your possession to the storage facilities located on the southwest edge of the city at midnight...I shouldn't have to remind you what will happen if you tell anyone, right?"

Wil finished giving orders to his son before slipping back into the shadows.

The other figures in the alleyways also retreated, but some stayed close enough that Welf could still feel their presence. He was being watched.

Welf stood there, staring after his father until he disappeared. His hands clenched into trembling fists.

After returning home, Welf made up an excuse to spend the night in his workshop to avoid talking with anyone.

He wasn't confident in his ability to keep a calm expression.

The last thing he wanted was for Hestia to figure out something was wrong.

Alone in the stone building in the rear garden of their home, the light of red flames illuminating his face, Welf stared into the heart of the fire in the forge. He sat on his bench, not moving a muscle.

His mind began to churn along with the subtle dance of the flames.

Each shift in the fire brought forth a slew of forgotten memories that had been awakened by the sudden reunion with his father.

——"*Listen to the metal's words, lend your ears to its echoes, put your heart into your hammer.*"

Before he knew it, there was a hammer in his hand and hot metal over the anvil. *Wham! Wham!*

A shower of sparks fell to the floor with each impact, echoes filling the workshop. His heart listened to the song of the metal, synchronizing with it to create a calm in the storm. Welf was finding his center.

Crackle, crackle. The sounds of the roaring forge rose into the deepening night.

He had completed the sword by the time he had to depart.

It wasn't a magic sword, but the light-silver weapon emanated a clear glow. A type of blade he'd never made before was in his grasp.

He spent several moments looking at his reflection on the mirrorlike surface of the off-white sword. Then he placed it gently on the anvil. Wrapping several other weapons in a piece of thick white cloth, he left his workshop.

Time had passed much faster than he'd anticipated.

The night sky was clear and filled with stars. No lights came from the windows of Hearthstone Manor.

Welf gazed at his home for some time before leaving through the back gate.

The appointed time drew near. Welf silently made his way through the streets toward the outskirts of the city.

When suddenly...

"What the...Bell?!"

He felt the presence of someone following him and moved to confront whoever it was, only to find the white-haired boy.

Bell stepped directly into the light of a magic-stone lamp and spent several seconds trying to figure out what to say. A few heavy heartbeats later, he said in a quiet voice:

"You looked upset...And I was worried."

Bell was the only one who had noticed something was off with the smith during their brief interaction back at home.

Welf was taken aback by the boy who had snuck out at night to follow him...But then he smiled.

It had happened again, just like on the eighteenth floor when Bell came hopping after him like some lonely rabbit. It made him feel warm inside.

He reached out with his right hand and ruffled the boy's hair.

Seeing the blank look on the boy's face broke down his last defenses, and Welf smiled in earnest.

Seeing that softer expression made Bell follow suit.

Welf had been dead set on solving this problem on his own, but now he felt as though he could share the load. He told the boy about everything that happened earlier that evening.

"R-Rakia?! Not only that, but your father...!"

"Yeah. That country really has a thing for Crozzo Magic Swords."

Bell was dumbfounded by the news as the two of them continued through the streets.

Welf could still feel the presence of his observers keeping their distance, but what could they do at this point? With Bell around, they wouldn't be able to sneak up on him and would be forced to let this transgression slide.

"...So, what are you going to do?"

Bell anxiously looked up, visibly shaken.

He was legitimately worried that the red-haired smith would give in to their demands. Welf laughed dryly, cracking a grin.

"I'm not gonna leave you—any of you—behind. So don't worry."

He told the boy to leave everything to him.

At the same time, Bell's concern helped Welf relax. The two

continued to walk under the night sky toward their date with destiny.

There was a way station among the storage facilities located on the southwestern edge of the city.

It served as an entrance for shipments coming into Orario by land and sea. Products from other regions and countries were brought here and stored until merchants distributed them across Orario. It also served as a marketplace, as many people came here to buy unusual items from foreign lands.

Bell and Welf made their way into a part of the facility that housed many large and small storage warehouses. Magic-stone lamps were few and far between and couldn't illuminate all the paths that spread out through the facility like a spiderweb. There were too many dark alleys and blind spots to count. The intimidating presence of the towering city wall was also nearby.

The two kept a close eye on their surroundings until finally one cloaked man appeared in an alleyway. He swished his cloak as an indication to follow him. *Gulp.* Welf heard Bell swallow hard as he followed the man, the white-haired boy at his side.

The alleyway was completely deserted except for the sound of three sets of footsteps. The cloaked man led them to an old rectangular warehouse that had seen better days.

"—I told you to come alone, Welf."

"I meant to, but he followed me here on his own. What was I supposed to do?"

Wil Crozzo stood in the middle of the old storage unit, illuminated by the moonlight coming through the glass windows at the top of its high walls.

The man's eyebrows sank in displeasure. Welf, however, reached out and ruffled Bell's hair with his right hand.

Wil watched the white-haired boy blush as his son teased him. "It doesn't matter," he said with a forced smile.

"Was nice meeting him, but this is where the two of you say good-bye."

Wil reached into his cloak and withdrew his magic sword. Almost on cue, other hooded figures emerged from the shadows of the old warehouse.

There were at least fifty of them, far more than Welf had expected.

Bell at his side, the young man braced himself in the face of overwhelming numbers.

"How the hell did all you get into Orario? Were the gatekeepers sleeping?"

"The Guild might be powerful, but Orario is no fortress. Merchants, familias...There are several ways of getting in and out."

Wil left his words open to interpretation, conjuring ideas of a mole inside Orario or that the Guild's surveillance was far from perfect. It served only to worsen Welf's state of mind.

Wil's allies started stepping into the moonlight—the soldiers of *Ares Familia* had concealed their identities with an assortment of hooded robes and capes, disguising themselves as travelers. Drawing knives and daggers from sheaths hidden at their waists, the warriors moved to surround Bell and Welf.

"Now, foolish boy. You're coming with us!"

Bell and Welf stood ready. Wil's voice crackled with a joyous laugh. But then...

Countless magic-stone lamps flickered to life, flooding the warehouse with bright light.

"?!"

Wil, his soldiers, Bell, and Welf were stunned.

A ring of demi-humans that outnumbered Rakia's soldiers had the entire group surrounded. The warehouse was under their control.

Welf squinted to protect his eyes from the sudden rush of light coming from their lamps. The first thing he saw when his eyes adjusted was the emblem engraved into the newcomers' armor.

Hammers overlapping in front of a volcano.

"He-Hephaistos Familia?!"

Bell's voice echoed through the warehouse at the same time the ring of demi-humans parted to allow a woman through.

"Well, looks like Finn hit the nail right on the head."

"Tsubaki?!"

Welf's jaw dropped at the sight of the female smith, her long black ponytail swishing back and forth and one eye hidden by an eye patch.

Leading a familia known the world over, Tsubaki appeared alongside the many High Smiths who composed one of Orario's most powerful groups of adventurers and artisans. Wil's voice shook as he yelled as loud as he could:

"Wh-why, how did you find us?!"

"Oh, we've known about this little ploy for a while now. So we've been keeping a close eye on your target."

Wil's face tensed in a mix of shock and disbelief. At the same time, Tsubaki's lips pulled back into a smug grin as she spoke.

Loki Familia, realizing that Rakia's army had been avoiding a decisive battle, had figured out their true objective. Working together with the Guild, they had ordered that *Hestia Familia*—especially Welf—be put under surveillance.

"So I was bait, was I...?"

Welf's anger was palpable as he yelled at Tsubaki when she finished explaining to his father and the Rakian soldiers. That was the reason why she had kept showing up—even at the Dungeon—over the past few days.

Tsubaki shrugged off Welf's fiery glare as a deity appeared next to her.

"My children have captured the reinforcements you had stationed outside the warehouse. Be grateful."

"G-Goddess Hephaistos...?!"

Wil recoiled at the appearance of the goddess who wore an eye patch similar to but on the opposite side of Tsubaki's.

Hephaistos's eye patch, beauty, crimson eye, and hair were instantly recognizable all over the world. Her sudden appearance stunned even Rakia's soldiers. Wil fired back with a tone that bordered on insanity.

"This isn't over! We still have our magic swords—the power of Crozzo is on our side!"

He lifted the sparkling red blade in his grasp—the Crozzo Magic

Sword—high into the air. An anxious chill ran through Bell and the members of *Hephaistos Familia*.

It was one of the last legendary magic swords said to be able to "burn away the sea." Tsubaki's expression became far more severe in the face of a weapon perfectly suited to take on superior numbers.

Hephaistos remained calm and composed. She cast her gaze onto the still silent Welf.

Rakia's soldiers were invigorated by Wil's call; each drew their own magic swords one by one.

"Welf, come with us if you don't want to see the city become an ocean of flames!"

Wil called out to his son, with eyes that had long ago lost their vigor now burning from ghastly desperation.

"Well, didn't plan for that. So, what to do…eh, Welfy boy?"

"All of you stay out of this."

"Welf!"

"You, too. Trust me."

Tsubaki called out to the red-haired man walking toward his father. But Welf didn't look up when he responded. When Bell also took a few steps toward him, Welf flashed a grin over his shoulder.

A look of relief washed across Wil's face as his son came closer.

"That's right, Welf! Now come, hand over all the magic swords you brought!"

Welf continued to walk toward his overjoyed father but came to a stop ten paces in front of him.

Everyone in the warehouse watched with bated breath as Welf reached into the roll of white cloth he carried over his shoulder.

The young man withdrew a single dark-crimson longsword from within the mass of blades contained inside the cloth. Then he raised it.

"This is all I got."

"What…?"

"Yeah. This is the only one I made."

He declared that at his home and workshop, this was the only Crozzo Magic Sword there was.

It was then that Wil realized that Welf had brought all the other weapons wrapped in the cloth to help him break away from their clutches. His face instantly changed from surprise to burning red with rage.

Welf simply said there was no way to forge a magic sword in less than half a day and shrugged.

"Already forgotten what I told you, foolish boy...? Orario will become a hellscape...!"

Welf interrupted his father's trailing protests.

"That sword in your hand is the only real Crozzo, isn't it?"

"_____"

Bell, Tsubaki, and all of *Hephaistos Familia* reflexively leaned closer to the two men in the center of the warehouse after hearing those words.

Only Hephaistos herself was unaffected as she watched the tense scene play out.

"Spending some time cooped up in my shop was just what I needed to cool off. Even if that many magic swords survived the purge, there's no way Rakia would let them all out at the same time."

Just like his family, Welf knew the Kingdom of Rakia pined for its glory days when Crozzo Magic Swords reigned supreme, and was therefore very attached to them. They wouldn't risk the few magic swords that remained on a plan that might or might not succeed. It was highly unlikely that this expeditionary force would be granted access to the remaining Crozzos in the first place.

He had reasoned that their original plan must have been to reunite with their allies outside the city wall, armed with all the new Crozzo Magic Swords he had supposedly forged, and then trap Alliance forces in a deadly pincer.

Welf had figured out that his return to Rakia was the bargaining chip, how his father had negotiated his way to acquiring one of their precious remaining magic swords.

Wil stood there in shocked silence, all but confirming Welf's suspicions. His allies did indeed all carry magic swords, but they were not Crozzo Magic Swords. Each of them exchanged nervous glances.

Welf stood tall, confident. Wil took a step back in the face of his son's sharp gaze.

"Gah——GRHAAAAAAAAAAAAAAAAAAAAAAAAAA!"

Wil's eyes suddenly flashed as he howled with rage.

"Stay back! Just one is enough to burn all of you into oblivion!"

Another wave of nervous energy shot through the warehouse as the man holding the sparkling red blade teetered on the verge of losing his mind.

Their fate would be determined by the flick of the wrist. Bell thrust out his right arm to unleash his own Magic at any moment. Tsubaki licked her lips, her hand nervously resting on the hilt of her thick katana, her right foot shifting closer to get the best jump possible.

Amid all this tension, Welf said:

"Do it."

His father froze. Welf's red hair flicked to the side as he jeered coldly at the man.

"Go ahead and try."

He grinned, flashing his teeth.

His father must have gone past the breaking point because he ignored his allies' calls to stop and took a step forward with the Crozzo Magic Sword held high above his head.

"Y-you FOOLISH BOOOOOOOOOOOOOOOOOOOOOOOOOY!!"

Then, before the red sword could fall—

Before Bell, the High Smiths, and even Tsubaki could react—

Welf's eyes flew open as he slashed the dark-crimson longsword in his grasp with all his might.

"—*Raging Inferno!!*"

An explosion of flames rushed forward.

At the same time, a wave of fire surged from Wil's red magic sword to meet it.

In front of all of Welf's current and former allies, in front of Hephaistos's intense one-eyed gaze, the young smith's crimson flames absorbed and overpowered the red—and wiped them out. A roaring fire and a small mountain of sparks filled the warehouse, the heat blasting in all directions.

Those who were caught in it were thrown off their feet; others dropped to all fours in a desperate effort to withstand the shock wave. Red *hakama* violently shifting around her legs, Tsubaki stood tall in front of her goddess to protect her.

Then, when everyone's eyes had recovered from the red glare enough to comprehend their surroundings...

Bell and the other observers slowly looked up...and saw Welf, standing tall on both feet, and Wil, firmly planted on his rear atop the charred floor of the warehouse.

Wil's face froze in disbelief, when suddenly—*CRACK!* The red magic sword in his grasp fell to pieces. Welf's dark-crimson longsword was not only still in one piece but sparkling with even more magic energy.

The difference between the power of the two blades, as well as their limits, was plain for all to see. There was no comparison.

The magic sword forged by the boy, who had coughed up blood working as hard as he could to improve his Status, was superior to the one forged by his forefathers, who relied on only their inborn talent. That was all it was.

"...Why?!"

Wil, absolutely dumbstruck as he stared at the remains of the magic sword, howled at his son.

Trembling from head to foot, the last of his self-control disappeared and every pent-up emotion came raging out of him at once.

"Why do you not forge magic swords when you have all that power?!"

"..."

"Why do you not use that power for your family—for your country?!"

Welf didn't respond to his father's howls.

With Bell, Hephaistos, and Tsubaki looking on, he tightened his grip on the magic sword in his hand.

"Why is it you who can forge magic swords?! If it were me, if I had been born with the gift, by now...! Damn you, you worthless boy!"

Wil climbed to his feet as he unloaded years of frustration onto Welf.

The man's eyes were bloodshot, not much different from a ferocious beast's, as his cloak rippled around his body. "Are you still spouting that bullshit, that you can't stand to see a weapon that'll break? Weapons are disposable! You can just make another one!"

That got Welf's attention. He glared daggers at his father. But Wil didn't notice and continued his rant. "'Make more blades, bask in never-ending honor'—have you forgotten the teachings of the blacksmith nobility who obtained glory with magic swords?"

With those words, Welf exploded. "*What* blacksmith nobility?! *What* honor?!"

The young man's voice cut through the air inside the blackened warehouse. Wil fell silent as Welf took several impassioned steps forward.

A moment later, Welf's clenched fist buried itself deep in his father's cheek.

"GEH!"

The Rakian soldiers watched their leader fall to the ground in disbelief. Several stepped forward, drawing their weapons, but...

"Stay right there!"

Welf's rage-filled warning made them freeze on the spot.

While the howl of the High Smith instilled fear in the soldiers, it was intended for Bell and Tsubaki as well.

"Stand up! On your feet!"

"...!"

Discarding his magic sword and white cloth full of weapons, Welf grabbed his father's collar with both hands.

Once Wil was back on his feet, lip split and bleeding, the red-haired young man delivered another blow.

"UGAH!"

"The 'pride of nobility'? Have all of you forgotten the need that drives all smiths?!"

The flurry of punches and verbal strikes drove Wil backward, but he raised his head, cheeks burning red with rage.

Wil channeled that anger into his fists and threw a punch the moment that Welf's face was exposed. It connected with the young man's jaw.

"Compared to honor, our futile desires are nothing more than trash!" Wil unleashed his mind and fist at the same time, making

Welf recoil. However, the young man was quick to strike back. The dull impacts of their punches sounded throughout the warehouse. Knuckles dug into cheeks.

Both men staggered, struggling to maintain balance as they exchanged powerful blows. Wil was clearly surprised by the strength of his son's punches. Welf launched another verbal tirade.

"The hell you callin' trash?! Can't hear you, you done-for old man!"

"You…you…YOU FOOLISH BOOOOOOOOOOOOOY!!"

Overcome with rage, Wil knocked his son's arms out of the way and jumped in close with his right fist held high.

However, every time his father's fist connected with his face, Welf was quick to counter with an elbow or a punch of his own.

The onlookers, including Bell, watched in stunned silence, their eyes intently following every move.

The current situation and their physical pain long forgotten, father and son continued to intensify their fighting. Nothing else mattered to them anymore.

"A weapon only needs to be strong! Pretty words don't change a thing!"

Brown hair and red hair whipped back and forth with each blow.

Both father's and son's faces were already a swollen mishmash of black and blue, with streaks of blood leaking from broken skin. Red droplets scattered every time another punch connected.

His father's fists continuously pummeled his face, but Welf held his ground. The young man refused to show any pain as he powered through the impacts and retaliated.

"GHA…!"

Wil lost his balance and staggered backward. Welf roughly wiped the blood off his face with his forearm.

"Right now, I'm no different from any other guy who swings a magic sword!"

"…!"

"Is that real power? Is it our fate to keep making these things?"

On one side, a Level 2 High Smith. On the other, a Level 1 descendant of fallen blacksmith nobility.

Despite the absurdity of it all, Welf put all his being into every punch, his spirit behind every blow.

"Of course it isn't! It can't be!"

His father's eyes went wide as Welf drove his fist directly into the man's jaw.

"A weapon is part of its wielder! A valued partner that stays by their side through thick and thin, carving a way forward! A piece of their soul!"

"That's...that's nonsense...!"

"As smiths, we have to take pride in providing that kind of weapon!"

Catching a glimpse of the white-haired boy out of the corner of his eye, Welf delivered three more blows.

He poured all his soul into his blood-splattered fists.

"...We'll have nowhere to go if we get run out of the kingdom! The name of Crozzo cannot survive without the glory of nobility! We will not survive...! Why can't you understand that?"

The bloodline had lost its noble status, its pride. The moment the family was exiled, it would lose the only way that Wil knew how to live and would die out before long.

The only way to save their family was with magic swords.

Wil insisted that the power lurking in their blood, the magic swords it could produce, was the only path to their salvation. His powerless punches barely connected, but his voice was still as passionate as ever.

"You're alive, aren't you? Your hands can still swing a hammer, grasp metal!"

"...!"

Welf grabbed his father's collar and pulled him in close.

He glared directly into the older man's eyes, his throat trembling as he shouted:

"A hammer, metal, and a burning desire! With those, you can forge a weapon anywhere! Nobility, kingdom—they don't mean shit!"

Wil bore the brunt of his son's rage as Welf tried desperately to make his father see the truth that was in plain sight.

Hephaistos watched as Welf repeated the words that were on the verge of being forgotten.

"—'Listen to the metal's words, lend your ears to its echoes, put your heart into your hammer'! You and Granddad taught me that, didn't you?"

A smelly workshop covered in soot.

His youth, when he worked alongside his father and grandfather, putting hammer to metal.

A time before the latent abilities in his blood awakened, when the disgraced family was determined to make a new name for itself without magic swords. A time when three generations of smiths came together to make that a reality.

Days that had once existed in their past.

Welf awakened those memories in his father. Wil's eyes quivered.

Flexing the powerful muscles in his arms and tightening his grip on his father's collar, Welf was nearing tears as his voice exploded once again.

"Where did *that* pride go?"

Those words hung in the air, echoing throughout the warehouse.

They lingered in the ears of Rakia's soldiers, the High Smiths, and Bell. No one moved.

His breathing ragged, Welf kept his grip on his father's cloak and broke off eye contact by looking at the floor.

Wil's face was an absolute mess. The older man's eyes widened, and he let his arms drop.

All focused on the two smiths. A thick stillness descended on the warehouse.

"Enough."

An old man's voice broke the heavy silence.

One figure stepped forward from the group of Rakian soldiers and pulled back his hood.

Welf's shoulders trembled the moment he saw the man's eagle-like eyes between his white hair and white beard.

"Granddad...?!"

"Father...!"

Welf continued to stare at his grandfather as Wil turned to face him.

Garon Crozzo.

Quite muscular despite his advanced age, the man stepped into the moonlight with his spine straight and head held high. He was even taller than Welf, over 170 celch. The former head of the Crozzo family, he and his son Wil were the ones who had given Welf his foundation as a smith.

It wouldn't be an exaggeration to say that Welf had learned what a smith should be by watching this man shape metal to his will.

The red-haired young man did his best to hide the shock of learning his grandfather had come to Orario as well.

"...Granddad, you came here for the same reason as..."

"I did. I, too, was called upon to ensure your return."

Welf stepped away from Wil, gaining some distance before turning to face his grandfather with his fists ready.

The eldest Crozzo, however, cast his gaze on Wil, who'd fallen to his knees.

"But, enough."

"...!"

"Your will is too strong, much like tempered steel."

The corners of Garon's lips curved upward, sending a jolt along Welf's spine.

Never once in all his life had Welf seen his grandfather smile.

"Back when you were still a youngster, I was never sure if forcing you to make magic swords was the right decision...Looking at you now, it's my greatest regret."

There was a great deal of remorse in his low voice.

When his talent was discovered seven years ago, and Wil was dead set on forcing him to forge one Crozzo Magic Sword after another, Welf had looked to him for help. Instead, the elder Crozzo had stared down at his grandson with an emotionless face and said, "Do it," in no uncertain terms.

For Welf at the time, Garon himself was the very essence of a smith. Receiving that direct order was an incredible shock and pushed him to the brink of despair. That event had become the main reason Welf ran away from home, from the Kingdom of Rakia, to start a new life.

Hearing his grandfather's true feelings caught Welf by surprise. But there was an edge to Garon's expression.

"However, the blood in your veins will never disappear. The curse of Crozzo will hound you for the rest of your days, endlessly drawing you back to the path of magic swords," Garon continued, eyes burning with a passion that time hadn't taken away. "Despite this fate, are you certain your will won't bend?"

His words had a great deal in common with Tsubaki's; their content was almost identical.

They both pointed to the makings of the blacksmith and whether or not he would access the power hidden in his blood.

He hadn't been able to say anything to Tsubaki. At that time, a feeling of powerlessness had shaken his will.

That was then—this was now.

Standing before his father and grandfather—his link to the Crozzo family—reminded him of a conviction he couldn't afford to bend.

"No way in hell!"

Welf responded to Garon without missing a beat.

He let his level of devotion be known, especially to Tsubaki, who was standing not too far away.

"I'll forge a weapon that puts magic swords to shame! Our bloodline means nothing, and I'll prove it! I'm not just a Crozzo—I'm my own man!"

He would make a weapon his way, something that wasn't a Crozzo Magic Sword.

He put words to the ambition that drove him to create something godlike.

"…Cheeky young'un."

Garon narrowed his eyes after Welf made his case.

Almost as if he was happy to see how much his grandson had grown.

"We won't pursue you any further."

"But, Father! If we don't…our place in the kingdom, it's as good as gone…!"

Wil looked up from his crouched position, voicing his objection to Garon's decision.

Every muscle in his wizened face strained under his bloody skin as he pleaded to the elder Crozzo. The old man responded calmly.

"We will start over. Not as blacksmith nobility but as smiths."

Wil couldn't say anything back. His gaze slowly dropped to the ground as he clenched his trembling hands into fists.

Then Garon made eye contact with his grandson.

"'With a hammer, metal, and a burning passion, a weapon can be forged anywhere'…was it? You couldn't be more correct."

Garon looked away from Welf and over to the goddess who had taught him this valuable lesson.

He narrowed his eyes down to a sliver, as if trying to peer straight through her, before going into a deep bow.

"We surrender, oh Goddess. The responsibility is mine and mine alone. Please have mercy on my companions."

"…Fine, then. I shall."

Hephaistos slowly nodded, accepting his declaration of defeat.

No one among the Rakian soldiers voiced any objection. Their defeat had been a foregone conclusion the moment that Wil's Crozzo Magic Sword shattered. Completely surrounded by High Smiths, they knew they were in no position to resist. Dropping to their knees and discarding their weapons, they held out their hands for the members of *Hephaistos Familia* to tie them up.

"Idiot."

"…"

Tsubaki busied herself with restraining the soldiers but still found time to get in a verbal jab even without looking at him.

Welf could hear the disappointment in her voice as she led the prisoners away, but he said nothing.

He stood in the center of the charred warehouse, battered and bruised as he watched Rakia's soldiers be escorted out the exit and toward Guild Headquarters.

His father, Wil, and grandfather, Garon, hands tied behind their backs, were among them.

At the last possible moment before leaving through the open doorway, Garon flashed him one more grin. Welf burned that image into his memory.

Even once his family members were gone, Welf continued to stare at the open door like a statue.

"Welf…"

Bell and Hephaistos had stayed behind.

They looked at the red-haired man, standing alone in the moonlight shining in from overhead.

The light of magic-stone lamps started to fade from the streets of Orario as night came to an end. The moon overhead became faint as the eastern sky took on a lighter hue.

Welf sat cross-legged beneath the last of the night sky as it steadily became brighter all around him.

He was on the roof of the warehouse. High above the ground and doing his best impression of a stone statue, he kept to himself without saying a word.

"…"

Bell stood a little ways behind him, unsure what to do.

The clash with the Crozzo family behind him, Welf wanted to be alone. So he had climbed up to the roof, taken a seat near the edge, and hadn't moved since. Bell understood the young man wanted some space and kept his distance.

He'd been outside in the chilly night air for several hours now and was very cold. However, the white-haired boy couldn't just leave the young man behind.

Unable to find the right words, he settled for staring at the man's back the whole time.

"So, the two of you were up here."

"Lady Hephaistos…"

The clanging of the goddess's boots against the steel roof announced the arrival of Hephaistos. Bell turned to face her as she walked up behind him.

She came to a stop shoulder to shoulder with the boy, squinting her left eye as she observed the young man beneath the sky that grew brighter by the moment.

"Bell Cranell. Can you leave this to me?" The deity asked if she could be alone with the smith.

Bell stood wide-eyed for a moment but responded with a short nod. He made a quick bow and left the situation to the goddess before climbing down off the roof.

Hephaistos walked up to the young man as the boy's footsteps grew fainter in the distance.

"The Rakian soldiers are now in Guild custody."

"..."

"Their path of entry has also been revealed. An informant let them inside on the promise that they would start a war. Their main objective was to acquire you, though whether or not there were others remains to be seen..."

Welf remained sitting with his legs crossed even as Hephaistos gave him a factual update on the current situation.

She wasn't looking at him, though. Instead, her eye was focused on the open skyline as she continued her report.

"The Guild will negotiate with Rakia to pay for their release. Even if talks fall through, they'll be released outside the city once things die down."

"...I see," whispered Welf after hearing the fate of his father and grandfather.

Daybreak had arrived. The two were side by side, watching the sunrise.

"...Am I out of my mind?"

Welf finally said something as sunbeams reached out to them from the eastern sky.

His decision to leave the blood in his veins in the past and find a different route to a higher realm occupied his thoughts.

The young man's gaze didn't leave his lap as he spoke to the goddess. "Maybe. Who knows?"

"..."

"Tsubaki is not wrong. Children like yourself are only allotted a brief window of time. In order to reach where we deities stand, you must commit everything you are toward accomplishing that goal." Hephaistos laid everything out plainly. "But," continued the goddess as Welf pushed his lips together, "you've made a commitment, have you not, Welf?"

"...I have."

"Then never doubt yourself. There's nothing more fragile than hollow steel."

Then the Goddess of the Forge turned to Welf and smiled.

"If there's one thing that we look for in children, it's a will powerful enough to make the impossible possible. We want to witness that moment when the children called heroes overcome incredible odds and fight when all hope is lost."

All deities wanted to look upon "children" who defied logic and reason. The goddess said in a soft, gentle voice that she knew of the potential those like Welf possessed.

"...I *will* catch up to you—my way."

Climbing to his feet, Welf reaffirmed his ambitions to the goddess.

There was no uncertainty left in his voice. He squared his shoulders and looked directly into Hephaistos's eye.

"Is only catching up enough?"

"...I'll surpass you."

The eye next to the black bandage squinted, as if the goddess was enjoying the moment. Welf also cracked a grin.

Hephaistos's expression was something similar to a mother taking pride in her child's growth. Then she reached out with her right hand.

She started to run her fingers through his hair, gently patting him on the head.

"—Wh-what do you think you're doing?!" Welf tensed, blushing bright pink as he swatted the goddess's hand away.

"Oh, you don't like this?"

"I-I'm not a kid anymore! Do that to someone Bell's age!"

"Hee-hee. It's really cute how you try to act like a big brother. I like that about you, actually."

"!!!!!!!!!!!"

Hephaistos enjoyed a lighthearted giggle as Welf's ears burned bright red.

Indeed, he put on the air of the eldest brother around his new familia, but he couldn't maintain it in front of this deity.

"Dammit," he swore under his breath, and hid part of his blushing face with his forearm. For a moment, seeing that smile from the fiery-colored deity nearly made him fall for her. He scolded himself for it.

But more than that, the fact that he couldn't say anything back reaffirmed the feelings that he had for her. It was just as Tsubaki had said: He admired Hephaistos as a goddess, as a smith—and as a woman.

It had started as an ambition to make something equal to or greater than the Goddess of the Forge. His goal was to show her that he could create something in her league or even something beyond it.

But that ambition changed little by little each time he stood in her presence.

He was the same as Bell, plain and simple. An immense respect and admiration had quickly become a longing for his idol. The weapons she created were what caught his attention, but he soon fell for the goddess who forged them.

He wasn't naive enough to call it infatuation, nor was he formal enough to call it love.

I'd prefer to call it...an occupational hazard.

He continued to look at the side of the goddess's face, with his smile and blushing cheek hidden by the palm of his hand.

"...Or so you say. But is it true?"

"?"

The sun had almost completely emerged on the eastern horizon. Welf, who'd been getting teased this entire time, folded his arms across his chest and said that something didn't add up. "I heard from that woman...from Tsubaki that you've been lonely since I left."

A blank look took over Hephaistos's face.

"Haaa..." A long sigh soon followed. "...My word, that child cannot keep a thing to herself."

She was neither flustered nor angry. She was just complaining about this slipup by one of her familia's most well-known members.

With Hephaistos admitting the truth right away, Welf had lost his only way to retaliate. But at the same time he was also a little sad... Finding out that she didn't see him that way sent a twinge of pain through his heart.

What's more, realizing that Tsubaki's choice of words had given him hope in the first place now made him want to curl up in a little hole and die.

"Well, yes, it's been much too quiet without you around. 'Haaa, another one of my children has left the nest.' That kind of empty feeling."

"Okay then..."

Welf was too embarrassed to make eye contact despite her gentle tone. Instead, he stretched out his shoulder and squeezed the muscles with his other hand.

"I would never say this to any of my followers...but you're no longer in my familia, so yes, I'll say it. I had my eye on you and couldn't wait to see what you would become."

Hearing his goddess's true thoughts once again threw Welf's feelings into chaos.

That was most likely the highest compliment she could give him as the Goddess of the Forge. As a smith, there was no greater honor. It made his body tremble.

Whether or not Hephaistos knew what was going through Welf's mind, she turned to face him with a twinkle in her eye and an evil grin on her lips.

"And I was going to reward you if you ever forged something that satisfied me...Too bad."

She glanced at him out of the corner of her left eye, obviously teasing. At the same time, a switch flicked on inside Welf's head as he looked at the crimson-haired, crimson-eyed goddess.

"Is that still on the table?"

"Is what still on the table?"

"If I bring you a weapon that makes your jaw drop, will you still reward me?"

Hephaistos, caught off guard for once, stuttered, "Y-yes. Yes, if you can," to the young man whose cheeks were now as red as his hair.

His rash attempt to secure a promise from another familia's goddess a success, Welf took it a step further by harnessing the passion once again burning within him.

"If I do...if I make a weapon that satisfies you, then I want you to be mine!"

He said it.

Welf overcame his reservations, as well as the roaring of his heart thumping in his ears, and watched Hephaistos carefully.

After hearing his once-in-a-lifetime confession, the stunned goddess...tried to hide a giggle behind her fingertips.

"I-I'm putting my neck out there and you...!"

"Hee-hee-hee-hee-hee...! S-sorry, but I just...can't help it...!"

With her free hand on her stomach, the goddess's body swayed as she laughed. In fact, her lungs were in pain because she couldn't breathe.

Finally calming down enough to wipe the tears flowing out of her left eye, Hephaistos smiled at him. "It's been so long since I've had those words said to me."

"Huh?" Welf froze on the spot. Hephaistos continued.

"Several of my followers a long time ago...Smiths confessed their love for me, just like you did."

Welf had become nothing more than a breathing statue. The Goddess of the Forge smiled at him with her left eye. "You're being outdone by your predecessors."

Now he really wanted to die.

This time, death sounded really, really good.

An urge to jump off the roof shot through his body.

Why are we all like this…?!

Stubborn to a fault, it seemed smiths could confess their feelings only to someone far superior. Welf grabbed his beet-red head and cursed every smith who ever lived, including himself.

Hephaistos continued to giggle to herself as the mortal experienced even more agony. However, her expression quickly became subdued.

"However, not a single one succeeded."

Welf's ears perked up. He raised his head from his hands.

There was a grin on the goddess's lips, the grin of someone issuing a challenge.

"Will you be the first?"

Welf forgot to breathe. He couldn't even blink as the crimson-haired goddess looked right through him. A confident smile appeared on his face a few heartbeats later. He looked her square in the eye. "You bet I will."

He would make a weapon that surpassed magic swords, belonged in the higher realm, and exceeded this goddess's expectations.

Now he had more goals to achieve.

The morning sun warming the side of his face, he exchanged glances with the goddess.

"Still…all this talk about me being yours aside, it's about time for you to find a partner of your own."

She must have been satisfied with Welf's mental recovery because she changed the subject as she stretched her arms in the early morning light.

At the same time…"Huh?" Welf tensed again, blindsided by her words.

"You're pretty stubborn, but I'm sure you can find yourself a great girl."

"H-hang on a sec! I'm not fooling around here…!"

"Welf, there's nothing to gain by pursuing an immortal like myself. A family will never happen."

Hephaistos forced a smile to try and stave off Welf's latest advance.

"Not to mention I don't meet the standards of a true woman."

There was no sense of belittlement or self-scorn in her voice. The words naturally came out of her mouth as she reached for her right eye—and ran her fingers down the black bandage.

"There's a face under here that's so hideous it'll make you cringe."

"…!"

"Strange, isn't it? A goddess like me. I've never been able to figure it out, no matter how much thought I put into it. I was ridiculed by the other deities in Tenkai, constantly laughed at."

Her fingers softly ran down the bandage as she did her best to smile.

The Goddess of the Forge, Hephaistos.

The one with power over fire and metalwork possessed a "hideous" face unbecoming of a deity.

Gods and goddesses were supposed to be the living embodiment of perfection. And yet, even with her divine powers of Arcanum, Hephaistos had been unable to do anything about the true face that made her the Goddess of the Forge.

She had avoided interacting with her own kind, been called "grotesque," and been laughed at throughout her entire existence.

"To this day, there's only been one goddess who didn't laugh or jeer at me after seeing my true face—Hestia."

Hephaistos's cheeks relaxed as she explained why there was a strong connection between her and the young goddess. Why Hestia was her one and only friend.

"Even the ones who sought me out on Gekai became afraid. So please, don't pursue this any further."

She flashed a meek grin before turning away from Welf.

The young man watched her take a few steps, her back getting smaller.

Welf stayed rooted to the spot for a moment before his eyes opened wide and he caught up with her in a few long strides.

Although he knew it was on the verge of blasphemy for him to do so, Welf reached out and grabbed Hephaistos's shoulder. Then he pulled her around to face him once again.

Face-to-face with the shocked goddess, he reached out toward the black bandage with his left hand.

"Wh-what are you doing?!"

Ignoring her startled voice, Welf pulled the bandage off her face, his fingers gliding against the fringe of the deity's crimson hair.

Hephaistos didn't budge. This was the first time for the young man to see both her eyes.

The true face of the Goddess of the Forge was revealed.

Standing slightly shorter than he, Hephaistos only stared up at him, crimson pupils trembling. As for Welf—his expression didn't change in the slightest. "Meh," he said with a shrug.

The corners of his lips pulled back into a grin. "Come on, Lady Hephaistos, that's nothing. Did you think I'd give up on you for something like this?"

He gently placed the bandage in the goddess's hands and gave her a resolute grin. "This is nowhere near enough to quell the fires you stoked in my heart."

The deity looked up at him for a few moments before slowly reattaching the black bandage that served as an eye patch.

With almost half her face now covered, she lightly shook her head, crimson hair waving in the morning light as she looked at her former follower.

"You certainly talk the talk."

"Now we're even."

"Haaah! Smiths. Every single one of them stubborn and hating to lose."

Hephaistos returned his grin and added her own verbal jab.

Welf knew he had finally taken a point back from the goddess. One look at her clear expression brought a shadow of pride to his face.

The two stood beneath the sunrise. Surrounded by cool morning air, the young man and the goddess exchanged smiles.

Later that day.

Only those directly involved with the small-scale Rakian invasion knew what had occurred. Even most Guild employees were kept in the dark.

Guild higher-ups thought that informing the public would do more harm than good, so they dealt with everything themselves. The captured enemy soldiers were held in chambers deep in the Pantheon, far out of sight.

Life in Orario continued as normal, the citizens unaware of what might have happened had events turned out differently.

Amid all that...

"And then Welf—you know what Welf did?"

In an office of the workshop, the voice of an exceptionally chipper goddess echoed off the walls.

"You've told me seven times, Ladyship..."

Hephaistos sat in a chair, cheeks in her hands and elbows on her desk. Tsubaki held a large stack of paperwork in her arms as she gave her goddess an annoyed glare.

Ever since their conversation, Hephaistos had been going on and on about the moment that Welf captured her heart. Plain and simple, she sounded like a teenager with a crush. Of course when she was in front of him, and in front of her followers, she maintained the dignified air of a goddess. However, that was not the case in her private quarters.

Softly blushing, Hephaistos began to recount her story with a giddy grin on her face. Tsubaki let out a long sigh and braced herself for the eighth time.

"Sure took you long enough to find your feminine side..." muttered Tsubaki through gritted teeth.

She was clearly frustrated that her high-spirited goddess hadn't done any work all day. "Now you've done it..." she whispered out the window at the smith who had finally found a way to get back at her.

Even later that day.

As with Tsubaki, Hephaistos was unable to keep her story secret and spread the news even further. Other gods and goddesses knew every detail about her interaction with the man before nightfall. The line that had stolen her heart became a punch line. """"Lame—!""""" Everyone had the same reaction, and the entertainment-starved deities had something to provide them with laughs for a long time to come.

The naming ceremony of Denatus was scheduled for the next day. With this story fresh in their minds, they decided the young man's title quickly and decisively.

Henceforth, Welf Crozzo would bear the title of…Ignis, the Ever-Burning.

And so it was that the young man was forced to endure a giggling Lilly and Hestia, a moved and inspired Mikoto and Haruhime, and Bell's forced smile whenever the origin of his title was mentioned.

He had to hide his blushing cheeks every single time.

© Suzuhito Yasuda

CHAPTER 4

BELOVED BODYGUARD

© Suzuhito Yasuda

"Welcome back, brave adventurers. How can we assist you today?"

Should adventurers ask for advice on how to improve the efficiency of their Dungeon prowling, the young women respond in bright and cheerful voices.

"Right away, good sirs. I will inform your adviser, so please wait in the consultation box."

The girls' eyes sparkle admiration every time an adventurer comes to report a Level Up.

"Congratulations. Level Two...Your advancement to third-tier adventurer is now official. Keep up the good work and may good fortune smile upon you."

Should the adventurer's true motive be to invite one of the lovely young ladies out for dinner that night, they smile from ear to ear while politely turning him down.

"If you don't have a pressing need, please allow others to the counter."

And whenever a newbie adventurer stands in front of the Dungeon entrance for the first time, the young women send them off with a smile.

"Welcome to the Labyrinth City Orario. We, the Guild, are here to assist you."

The Guild Headquarters receptionists.

Answering the needs of adventurers, they are the "flowers" of the Guild.

The Guild Headquarters was as busy as ever.

The white marble lobby was so crowded that at times it was hard to breathe. Adventurers came and went nonstop, wearing body armor and weapons of all kinds attached to their backs and waists, giving the air a distinct metallic smell. Elves carried staffs and bows; dwarves preferred axes and hammers. Demi-humans of all types were equipped with the weapons and armor that their race was best suited to wield.

The adventurers worked their way through the busy lobby to one of the many bulletin boards or toward the receptionists waiting patiently on the other side of the counter.

"Good morning, sir."

"Yes, concerning that issue————"

"The law clearly states that the one who finds valuable items in the Dungeon holds the rights to it. Therefore, it's highly unlikely it will be returned..."

Several lines formed in front of each receptionist. Each one of them listened intently to the problems of the adventurer in front of her window and worked to solve them.

Each of the young women, hailing from a wide variety of races, was extremely professional. Humans, chienthropes, cat people, and even a few elves populated their ranks. If the young ladies had one thing in common, it was that every one of them was stunningly beautiful.

The Guild receptionists were each a bombshell in her own right.

Adventurers who came to Guild Headquarters almost always went to the reception counter first, so saying that the receptionists were their first image of the Guild wouldn't be an overstatement. An adventurer's opinion of the Guild, whether good or bad, had a direct effect on their efficiency in the Dungeon—how many magic stones they brought back each day. So, while skills and personality were considered during the selection process, the Guild prioritized looks when hiring its receptionists.

This naturally created an environment where the many rugged, strong adventurers with a wild air about them could let their softer side show in front of the lineup of beautiful women and young ladies.

"The quest has been successfully completed. Thank you for your hard work. The Guild shall inform the client that their request has been fulfilled."

Eina, a half-elf, was one of the Guild's receptionists.

Her brown hair was just long enough to sit on her shoulders. Emerald-green eyes looked out at the world from behind a pair of glasses. Her pointed ears, shorter than an elf's but longer than a human's, were a direct result of the thin elvish blood running through her veins.

A female animal person had completed a quest that had been posted on the Guild's bulletin board. Eina presented her with the reward that the client had provided.

"Here is your reward. Please take it with you."

Eina smiled as the box of items changed hands, and she gave the adventurer a polite bow. She watched her turn to leave before going back to the counter to help the next person in line.

This was her fifth year of working at the Guild.

After graduating from the education district, circumstances at home had dictated that she find work immediately. She had chosen a career at the Guild, but even now she was surprised by how well this job suited her. Of course, it was not easy, and there were some trying times, but she felt it was worth it. She had always been a busybody, but now her workaholic nature was being put to use for the adventurers who journeyed into the Dungeon every day.

Today was another hectic day where she dealt with one adventurer's request after another.

"Eina! Hey, Eina. Let's go get some food!"

"Sure. Sounds good."

At long last, it was time for their lunch break.

The flood of adventurers had finally subsided, giving the sunlit lobby a moment of peace.

The girls, who had worked diligently to solve every issue brought to their attention in a timely manner, stood up from their chairs and stretched their hands high into the air. Eina let herself relax for a moment just as a human coworker stationed at the next window over called out to her.

Her full head of pink hair swished from side to side as the girl waved.

With a highly expressive face and cute features, she was rather charming.

Misha Frot, a friend of Eina's since their school days, couldn't wait to escape their workplace and quickly led the half-elf away from the counter.

"Sooo hungry. I swear, my stomach's going to eat me from the inside out!"

"Misha! Don't pull."

Eina informed her coworkers that the two of them were going out while the pink-haired human tugged on her arm.

"Enjoy your lunch!" said one of the other receptionists with a wave. The two girls left the station in their coworker's capable hands.

"You're in luck! I found a place the other day that has reaaally good food! It's in the West Block."

"Misha, are you sure we have time to eat and get back before our lunch break is over?"

"Hmmm, it's probably fine."

"You know…"

Misha's carefree lack of attention to detail made Eina cringe and smile at the same time.

The free-spirited Misha and the serious, straightforward Eina had been together for a long time. Now working side by side, the two were almost like a set.

They started chatting just like they had during their school days and left the Guild Headquarters through the rear exit. They came out on the side of the building opposite from the main street.

"E———Eina!"

"Ah…Is that you, Dormul?"

Eina's pointed ears twitched when a loud voice roared down the backstreet.

A young dwarf man was waiting for her when she turned around.

Misha felt very out of place as the dwarf jogged up to them, excitedly waving his meaty arms.

"Wh-what a surprise, seein' ye out 'ere. I was just on me way by..."
Eina immediately knew that was a lie and grimaced to herself.

As with most dwarves, Dormul was a stout, thick man. He did, however, stand taller than most of his kin at 170 celch. Both of his limbs looked like sturdy branches emerging from a solid tree trunk of a torso.

Unshaven, he smiled with his long, thin eyes. Dormul looked as though he would be more at home living out among Nature than in the big city, with an accent to match.

He nervously scratched his pronounced nose as he did his best to talk to Eina.

"Say, Eina, ye wouldn't be off ta lunch, would ye? I'm on me way ta grab a bite meself...W-would ye care ta come with? Oh, of course I'd be pickin' up the tab!"

"There's, um, no need for that...But, Dormul, today I'm with one of my coworkers, so..."

She'd lost count of how many times the dwarf had bumped into her "by chance" and invited her to lunch. At this point, Eina didn't know what to do about it anymore.

The bulging muscles beneath his valiant armor showed that Dormul was an adventurer. Currently Level 3, this upper-class adventurer who had made a name for himself for his strength in battle had once called Eina his adviser. The two had known each other for years.

Eina was aware that the man had taken a liking to her.

She didn't want to give the impression of being full of herself, but she also didn't want to hurt his feelings.

He's not a bad guy, but...

Being on the receiving end of an adventurer's advances was a daily occurrence for the Guild's receptionists.

But Dormul wasn't like the other adventurers hitting on the cute girls. He was always sincere, maybe too much so, in his attempts to ask her out, so Eina couldn't just shoot him down. She had always refused but made sure to choose her words carefully to avoid hurting him. However, Dormul still hadn't gotten the hint.

"…Eina, I can get lunch by myself if I'm in the way."

"W-wait, Misha…!"

"Dah! Da-ha-ha-ha! Just 'cause we're perfect fer each other, ye don' have ta go thinkin' ye're gettin' in the way, li'l missy!"

A conniving grin appeared on Misha's lips, and Eina quickly chided her. Dormul, on the other hand, took it as a sign of good things to come and couldn't contain his joyous laughter or the tears forming in his eyes.

Since the dwarf was also older than she, it was more difficult than ever for Eina to refuse his offer.

"Stop this at once, despicable dwarf. Can you not see that Eina is in distress?"

"Uhm?!"

A sharp voice cracked like a whip.

Dormul spun around to find a handsome elvish adventurer who embodied the very definition of the word *elegant* standing behind him.

Ears longer and pointier than Eina's stood out from beneath his long golden hair. Dressed in leather armor, he carried a longbow and had a quiver of arrows strapped to his back. The two men stood at about the same height, but their body types couldn't have been more different. The elf was as lean and sleek as the longbow attached to his shoulder.

The awkward atmosphere suddenly became hostile. "Step aside," said the elf as he roughly passed the dwarf's shoulder and came to a stop in front of Eina.

"L-Luvis…"

"Are you all right, Miss Eina? This man didn't try to touch you with his dirty hands, did he?"

"Wanna say that ta me face?"

The elf named Luvis huffed through his nose, brushing off the dwarf's thinly veiled threat.

Eina had once been the adviser of this Level 3 elf as well. It seemed that, just like with Dormul, he had developed feelings for Eina while under her tutelage.

In typical elf fashion, Luvis looked down his nose at Dormul before turning back to Eina. "Heh-hem." He cleared his throat, making a louder sound than necessary.

"I just happened across the most rare, beautiful bouquet at the boutique just down the road. I thought of you the moment I saw the flowers' ravishing hues and elegant form…Please accept it as a gift from yours truly."

"Y-you know I can't accept this, Luvis…"

The elf extended the bouquet in his arms out to her with both hands.

Eina's eyes were drawn to the vivid colors, but she did her best to graciously decline—when a thick hand suddenly snatched the bouquet away.

"What are you doing?!"

"Hmph. Ain't ye the one turnin' Eina inta a fish outta water? Pushin' these sissy li'l flowers on her in a back alley? How do ye think she's feelin'?"

"Apparently the aesthetics of a bouquet are beyond your comprehension, foul dwarf…! We elves are noble. Keep your distance!"

"Eina is only half! Don't be groupin' her with yer vile lot!"

It was uncommon for elves and dwarves to see eye to eye, and this was the perfect example.

Eina had seen this kind of thing play out far too many times. Giving up on solving the situation, she said a quick "Excuse me" and ducked her head. The two men were so caught up in their argument that they didn't even notice.

Giving Misha a gentle push in the back was her signal for the two of them to take their leave. They didn't linger.

"Is this okay?"

"Not okay, but…it'll only get worse as long as I'm there."

She chanced a peek over her shoulder and saw that Dormul and Luvis were in each other's faces, exchanging heated insults back and forth.

No, the two didn't get along.

Recognizing each other as rivals, perhaps, in the quest for her heart had only escalated their mutual dislike into their current relationship.

Actually, both had become much more aggressive in the past few days…That might be an overstatement, but the fact that they were being much more forward was undeniable.

The two adventurers had expressed interest in her in the past, but recently they'd been finding ways to talk to her after business hours, during her personal time. Dormul's actions this afternoon, waiting for her to come out the back door of the Guild and then moving in, were only the latest episode. What's worse, their strategies were becoming only more elaborate.

It was as though they were trying to outdo each other in finding new ways to approach Eina.

I know they're not bad people, but…

Dormul and Luvis's argument came to a sudden stop and both looked left and right.

A sudden chill ran down Eina's and Misha's backs as they stared at the two men before abruptly turning forward.

They could feel the gazes of the two adventurers on their backs as they continued on their way. Feeling a little disheartened, Eina adjusted her glasses as she walked.

Guild Headquarters, the archives.

Information about the city, the surrounding areas, monsters, and everything concerning the Dungeon was stored in this massive two-story room that was located behind the lobby on the other side of a restricted hallway. Rows of wooden shelving units standing just above the average human height turned this near library into a labyrinth in its own right.

The bookshelves, floors, and weight-bearing pillars were all painted in a low-key dark-brown finish. Several Guild employees in their trademark black suits silently read the books in their hands or passed through the long aisles.

"A-all done..."

"Good work. Now let me see..."

Her coworkers had come to the archives for many different reasons, but Eina had claimed several desks to create an island in the reading space. She sat in a chair at one end of the island, and on the other side of several open maps and books was a white-haired human boy. Bell handed her a sheet of paper.

She was in the process of delivering one of her occasional private lessons about the Dungeon.

Eina wanted to make absolutely sure Bell was ready to face anything in the Dungeon. Her method of choice was to hit the books.

That was the role of an adviser.

The Guild assigned every adventurer an adviser to provide them with support and prepare them for Dungeon prowling.

Adventurers could make a request as to the gender and race of their adviser. Since they met the receptionists most often, the beautiful girls were often selected to fill that role. There was about a 10 percent chance the Guild couldn't meet an adventurer's wishes—but in any case, Eina had served as an adviser for many adventurers.

However, her superiors had taken notice of the speed and quality of her work. Constantly faced with mountains of paperwork and given important assignments within the Guild, she had requested that her coworkers take over as advisers for most of her adventurers.

Right now, Bell was the only one she looked after.

"...Your recollection of the information about middle-level monsters is nearly perfect."

"Do...do you really think so?"

"Yes. So then———time for a pop quiz. Describe a combat strategy for every single monster. Draw maps of every floor, too. If I find any mistakes, you'll write each of them out until you can remember them in your sleep."

"...Okay."

Bell's expression clouded as Eina handed him another blank sheet. Clapping his jaw shut, the boy gave a firm nod.

Eina's emerald eyes watched the boy's pen move at a furious pace, elbow resting on the table and head in his hand. She was elated to see him work so hard.

Eina had a very particular stance when it came to advising adventurers.

In addition to the usual Dungeon-prowling advice and regular meetings, she would also summon her adventurers to private lessons, where she crammed as much Dungeon knowledge into their heads as possible.

Her beautiful face hid an extremely strict instructor who would have made the Spartans of the Ancient Times proud. It was to the point that she had gained a scary reputation among many adventurers. No one had lasted all the way to the end of her course, running away halfway through. Even Dormul and Luvis couldn't endure her teaching style.

Bell was barely keeping his head above water.

Tears threatened to leak out of his ruby-red eyes on more than one occasion. But even so, he stayed firmly seated at the desk.

His drive came from his idol.

The determination to reach that lofty goal was just slightly more powerful than his fear of Eina's harsh training.

Sometimes his brutal honesty and straightforward nature worked against him.

No matter how many times he fell in battle or in the classroom, he would always get back up and face the problem head-on.

Those were qualities that Eina rather liked about him.

At the very least, they were the reason that she wanted to support him, cheer him on.

Time's almost up...

Eina, whose gentle gaze had been centered on Bell's face, looked up at the clock on a nearby pillar.

The hour hand was pointing toward ten. Before starting their study session, Bell told her in person that *Hestia Familia* had had a busy few days. It would be cruel to keep him tied up much longer.

Night had already fallen and few other Guild employees were still walking around the archives. The only constant sound was the scratching of Bell's feathered pen moving across paper coming from the reading area located in the middle of the massive chamber.

A few more quiet minutes went by before an exhausted Bell turned in his quiz.

Eina immediately spotted a few mistakes, but she couldn't bring herself to follow through on her threat. She forced a smile and passed right over them.

They could be brought up at the next session.

"Good effort today, Bell. That will end today's lesson."

"…Th-thank you."

Bell lifted his face from the surface of the desk. There was a weak, lofty smile on his face.

Eina told him he could sit and wait, but the boy insisted on helping her clean up. Grabbing a few of the books and maps, he joined the half-elf in returning the materials to their proper places.

Bell had come here directly from the Dungeon. Re-equipping the armor that had been sitting next to the pillar, he followed her out of the archives and through the restricted hallway to the lobby.

Saying a quick good-bye, the boy staggered along the path through the garden in front of Guild Headquarters. Eina watched him go until he disappeared into the night.

"That was a long day, wasn't it, Eina?"

"Misha…And everyone, too."

Eina was surprised to be greeted by a group of her female coworkers after she returned to the office.

It was very rare for all the receptionists to still be at the Guild at this late hour.

"I don't know how you do it, working that closely with an adventurer. It won't change a thing on your paycheck."

"Ah-ha-ha…"

Eina grinned dryly at the senior receptionist's words as she handed her a ceramic cup filled with hot tea.

There were no men in the office, so the ladies each grabbed a chair and griped about work for a while.

"Oh, that reminds me, Tulle. An adventurer made another pass at you today?"

"...Misha."

"What was I supposed to do? How could you expect me to keep a story that juicy to myself?"

Eina glared at her friend who couldn't keep a secret to save her life. But soon she lightheartedly laughed it off. She couldn't stay mad at Misha for long.

Holding back the urge to sigh, she looked toward the eldest receptionist. Her coworker sat with her arms crossed, obviously not amused.

"Seriously, I'm right here, and yet you get all the attention... Adventurers need to have their eyes examined."

"But, Rose, you've sworn off adventurers, haven't you?"

"Every single one of them. Adventurers always break their promises."

Rose, a werewolf, fiddled with the ends of her long red hair as she continued her rant.

"Nothing good comes from being with someone with a death wish."

The atmosphere in the office suddenly changed.

The other receptionists looked at the floor, off to the side, or hid their faces behind their teacups as if they all could relate to her.

"They say 'I want you,' 'I love you,' anything that they think we want to hear. But when push comes to shove, they never come home. I guess adventurers are more interested in monsters than women."

There was a great deal of irony in her voice, sticking her tongue out at no one as her mood worsened. After a few moments, though, everyone could see it was just a brave face.

For the most part, the receptionists—no, all Guild employees— kept their distance from adventurers.

No one tried to cross the line drawn in the sand—although it might be better to say that the number who did was constantly decreasing.

Just as Rose had said, it was only a matter of time before the adventurers disappeared.

Forever lost in some deep, dark corner of the labyrinth beneath Orario.

It was almost a guarantee that more than one of the women present had loved one of them with all her heart, only to soak her pillow with tears. Eina herself had once collapsed to her knees in grief when one of the adventurers she was advising returned from the Dungeon as a corpse. The half-elf glanced to her side and saw that even Misha didn't have her usual pep.

When it came to adventurers, there was always a danger that they wouldn't be around to see tomorrow.

So the receptionists did their best to keep them at arm's length.

They might be smiling and using kind, gentle words in their daily interactions with adventurers, but that was all part of the job. The receptionists were being professionals.

"Tulle, I won't say anything about how you do your job at this point...but the more you try to be everyone's friend, the more regrets you'll have and the more complicated things will get."

"...I see."

Out of all the receptionists, Eina was the only one who tried to make personal connections with her adventurers.

She helped them try to reach their goals, provided them with valuable information, took the initiative to get them to study, and did it with a smile on her face.

All because she thought there was something she could do for them, provide a little extra push that would ensure their safe return from the Dungeon.

Eina didn't want to give up and believe that they would all just die off; she wouldn't let them.

She bore several invisible scars from the pain of past events. Even so, Eina joined adventurers in her own way.

"That goes for the rest of you, too. Never get too close to an adventurer. You'll just have to deal with the familia, and they won't leave anything behind, not even money. You always get the short end of the stick...And if you do end up with one, squeeze his pockets dry before he passes on!"

That last line got a dry laugh out of the other receptionists.

Even though there was a joking tone in her voice, the senior receptionist's message was a warning as well as advice.

Not just to Eina but to all her younger coworkers.

They were known as the "flowers" of the Guild. However, unless the young women managed to create a solid wall between work and their personal lives, it could become hell on earth.

The receptionists said their good-byes, and Eina set off to go home by herself.

Crossing Northwest Main Street, she continued north from the Guild Headquarters and into the northern district.

Many Guild employees chose to reside in the north district because of the high-quality housing and community. The Guild had also built a share house there for the receptionists. In fact, the Guild owned several buildings in the area and allotted them to its employees.

Everybody's friend... Well, I can't deny that.

It was already late at night, but Eina was surrounded by activity on either side of the street as she walked.

While it was nothing compared to the main streets, warm light and jubilant voices floated from the open windows of several bars in the area. The street was completely illuminated by magic-stone lamps, so much so that she could see down each of the alleyways.

The senior receptionist's words replayed in her head, making her feel a little depressed.

"...I'm not trying to be Miss Congeniality, but it must look that way."

Eina had no intention of fishing for compliments or going out of her way to receive praise. However, the extra time and effort she spent with adventurers might be misinterpreted by her coworkers.

Her desire to help adventurers was genuine. She wasn't about to change her way of interacting with them. But at the same time, a part of her knew that might complicate things.

In truth, there were more than a few adventurers who felt a connection with the always-friendly Eina. Dormul and Luvis were perfect examples.

More than likely, her coworkers' relative aloofness made her stand out even more.

Eina whispered to herself and sighed while readjusting the bag over her shoulder.

"...?"

Zip! A cold chill ran up her spine as she felt someone's gaze on her back. Eina looked over her shoulder.

There were several people outside, standing on top of the stone pavement. But no one was looking her way.

She didn't recognize any faces, either. Tilting her head to the side, she turned forward again.

Then, after taking just a few steps...

"...!"

She felt that mysterious gaze again.

Her heart beat so hard she couldn't breathe for a moment. Trying to act like she hadn't noticed, Eina walked casually for a few moments before spinning around as quickly as she could.

The side street's nightlife reflected in her emerald eyes. A straight road, no twists or turns.

She knew this area like the back of her hand, so the black shadow that jumped out of her line of sight stuck out like a sore thumb.

Whoever it was was wearing a black hooded robe. A few moments passed before it cautiously peeked around the corner of the building and kept staring at her.

Zip! Another jolt of the spine, and now a cold sweat.

"...!"

She started moving again, toward home, at a faster pace.

One thought after another racing through her mind, she drew near to the share house.

Almost no one was out on the street anymore. Sure, there were plenty of people in the bars, but her only defense was the light coming from the magic-stone lamps. She was uneasy, to say the least.

Still following me…?!

She could still feel the gaze plastered to her back. Whoever it was, they were persistently following her.

Leaving the high-class community behind, Eina emerged onto a quaint, classy-looking street. However, it was completely empty and lit by only the occasional magic-stone lamppost every few meders. Her pursuer must have sensed the change in circumstances because he felt closer than ever.

Eina was running; she didn't even notice. Holding her bag close to her chest, she dashed down the stone pavement as fast as her legs could carry her. Completing the last leg of her journey in what felt like an eternity, she finally arrived at the front gate of the share house.

Through the gate and up to the building. Eina put her hand on one of the outside pillars and tried to catch her breath as she looked around. All she saw was her neighborhood shrouded in night. No hooded figure, nothing out of place.

Clutching her ribs to get a handle on her racing heart, Eina didn't move from that spot.

"What?! You were stalked last night?!"

"M-Misha! Not so loud!"

It was morning in the lobby.

Adventurers were beginning to come through the front doors when Misha shrieked after hearing Eina's story.

Quickly covering her mouth with both of her small hands, she whispered a muffled "S-sorry!" to her friend.

"He didn't try anything fresh, did he? Did you see his face?"

"He didn't touch me, but I never got a good look at his face…There was a hood in the way."

Eina explained every detail of the previous night's events.

The two waited patiently for adventurers at the neighboring

counter windows. However, Misha's concern wouldn't let her stay silent, and she leaned closer.

"This is really bad, Eina! Talk with the bosses and see if you can't get a bodyguard! Some of *Ganesha Familia*'s best are still in the city—one of them could take you home tonight."

"D-don't you think that's going overboard? It might've just been my imagination."

Misha still spoke much louder than she needed to, and Eina shrank back away from her.

She thought that getting a familia involved, even one with close ties to the Guild, was going much too far. And yes, there was a real possibility it was all in her head.

But above all else, she didn't want to receive any special treatment.

"Overboard? How's that going overboard? It was a while ago, but I've heard stories about this kind of thing—young girls being targeted, followed, kidnapped, and taken outside the city!"

"I doubt that...This is Orario, after all. Gate security thoroughly inspects anyone leaving the city, and who would dare target a Guild employee...?"

"But, but, but...! There're so many rumors about girls being sold to brothels, and even some about a group of Rakian soldiers who found a way inside only recently...!"

Eina gave her friend a suspicious glare as the pink-haired girl started spouting baseless conspiracy theories.

Misha was fond of the rumor mill. She probably picked up a few stories around town and repeated them to anyone close by who would listen.

She was about to say something else when an adventurer appeared at her counter window. Misha reluctantly left it unsaid and went back to work. Eina soon did the same.

But...I'm sure I was being followed.

Just thinking about it sent shivers down her spine.

Trying to ignore the problem made her even more anxious. It wasn't going away.

She knew she shouldn't believe anything out of Misha's mouth, but…Goose bumps ran down her arms.

Her train of thought carried her to a place she didn't want to go, making her body tremble.

"Miss Eina?"

"!"

She knew that voice. Her eyes popped up right away.

Bell was standing in front of her, looking rather confused.

Apparently, he had lined up in front of her window, and it was now his turn.

————*Focus! I'm working!*

She quickly smiled after scolding herself.

"Sorry about that, Bell. I zoned out for a moment there. What can I help you with today?"

"I…I have a question about something in the Dungeon…"

That was all Eina needed to hear, and she stood up from her seat.

She left Misha and the other receptionists at the counter and met Bell in the consultation box as soon as she gathered some documents for the meeting.

"What? You've already conquered the seventeenth floor?"

"Yes, thanks to all the help we got from *Takemikazuchi Familia…* …So we'd like to make a serious attempt to prowl the nineteenth."

Both sat on opposite sides of the desk in chairs that were waiting for them in the soundproof room. Bell cut right to the chase and explained the situation.

The boy had just registered his second level-up less than a week ago.

Although she didn't show it, Eina was absolutely stunned by Bell's incredible pace. He was already Level 3.

He held the record for the fastest level-up. Pretty much everything the boy sitting in front of her did surprised her in one way or another.

"Um…Miss Eina."

"What is it, Bell?"

"Did, um, something happen?"

Eina's eyes shot open at the question.

"You just…don't seem like yourself today…"

Eina had thought she was pulling off a great acting job by pretending that today was business as usual. Apparently, her mask was showing some cracks.

Cracks big enough for the boy to notice, at least.

"I don't know if I can help or not…But if you want someone to listen, I could, um…"

Bell's words became muddled as his cheeks turned pink. He scratched the back of his head and said, "You always listen to my problems, Miss Eina."

Maybe it was because Eina was still rattled from last night, but seeing the bashful boy try to offer help gave her the slightest warm, fuzzy feeling inside.

Words left her mouth before she knew it. Forgetting her position for the time being, she accepted Bell's offer.

"Last night…"

She recounted everything that happened and watched the boy's expression change several times during her story. He was speechless when she reached the end. Smiling wanly at his reaction, Eina dimly looked to Bell from across the desk.

If…

If Bell was willing to walk her home…

If he was willing to become her bodyguard, just as Misha had suggested…

Her train of thought got that far before…*No, how stupid!* She frowned at herself.

How shameful it was to even consider that.

"Sorry. Please forget everything I've said, Bell."

"Huh…B-but—"

"This is my problem, and it's not that serious. I'll find a way to fix it myself."

Surely it would be a nuisance for him to be dragged into this, so she took back her words.

Back in Guild-employee mode, Eina repeated to Bell that she was fine and tried her best to smile.

However, Bell interrupted her before she could say anything else.

"Th-this probably is serious! Definitely serious! Rakia's trying to invade, and even inside the wall...!"

"B-Bell?"

The boy pressed forward as if he knew something. But one look at Eina and he realized his mistake. *Oops!* It was written all over his face. Rolling his shoulders and clamping his mouth shut, Bell somehow managed to keep the information from coming out. He scrambled to change the subject.

"If you think I can help, please ask! I'm not sure how much good I can do, but if you need a bodyguard or anything, just say the word!"

Bodyguard. He said bodyguard. Eina's eyes opened wide once again.

"You've helped me so much, Miss Eina...So please!"

"...Thank you, Bell. But this is my job. You don't owe me anything for my support."

Finally calm, Eina put together a solid argument.

The reason that she listened to Bell's problems and gave him advice was only because she was employed by the Guild.

She strengthened her position by saying that she was flattered Bell was willing to go out of his way to help her, but politely declined.

"—Th-the armor!"

"The what?"

Bell had found his counterargument.

"The vambrace! The one that you bought for me! Please consider this my way of paying you back!"

That was a long time ago.

Eina had suggested he needed new armor, and the two of them had gone to investigate options together.

On that day, Eina had bought him an arm-size shield, a vambrace, as a present.

He was right. That wasn't part of her job.

It was a decision she had made on her own, and the fact that she hadn't asked for any kind of reimbursement spoke volumes to the meaning behind it.

"...So persistent."

She could tell by the look in his eyes Bell wasn't going to back down. Eina accepted the defeat.

A long sigh escaped her lips, muscles in her face tightening. But even so, she smiled at the boy.

"If you insist, I'll take you up on it. I'm counting on you, Bell."

"I-I won't let you down!"

The sun sank behind the city wall as night began to show its face.

Eina was seated at the reception counter with her coworkers, as usual, when she spotted Bell, back from the Dungeon, making his way to the Exchange. The two nodded to each other, and she got up from her seat.

No one else noticed their brief communication.

"My apologies, but I must call it a day."

"Oh? Going home early? See you tomorrow."

She gathered her things between brief conversations with her coworkers. Misha looked up from her all-out battle with the paperwork taking over her desk with concern in her eyes. Eina waved her off, saying not to worry.

"Sorry to keep you waiting, Bell."

"It's, um, no big deal. Shall we…?"

"Yes, let's go. Just…until I get home. Counting on you."

"I-I'll do my best."

Eina, who had exited Guild Headquarters' rear door, found Bell waiting for her. The two set off together.

It was official: After their conversation, she had asked Bell to become her bodyguard.

The boy had left his allies to protect her during her commute home from work immediately after emerging from the Dungeon.

"Sorry about all this, Bell. You must be tired from Dungeon prowling."

"Not really. We came back early today, so I'm still in good shape. Nothing to worry about."

"…Thanks."

She traveled the same road as always, but this time there was another set of footsteps accompanying hers.

The streets were alive under the darkening red sky because, just like Bell, other adventurers were returning from the Dungeon. The bars were starting to fill up with demi-humans left and right, making it difficult to navigate the throngs.

Eina and Bell did their best to avoid bumping shoulders with other people as they weaved their way through the crowd.

…*This is a little nerve-racking.*

It was nothing too drastic, but she could feel how close they were.

They had yet to decide how long this would continue, but the thought of going home with Bell every day got her heart pumping. She hadn't forgotten about her mysterious pursuer by any means, but she couldn't overlook the boy next to her shoulder as they walked side by side.

Her eyes darted around as she wondered what the other pedestrians thought of them.

Bell had never been through this part of the city before and was taking it all in. Eina leaned forward, trying to sneak a peek at his face.

"_____!"

At that moment…

Bell's aura completely changed, catching Eina by surprise.

"B-Bell?"

"…We're being watched, probably."

"We are…?"

Unlike yesterday, she had no idea.

Eina might have been dumbstruck by his acute senses, but the serious, focused look on Bell's face stunned her even more.

His ruby-red eyes scanned the crowd and surrounding buildings, leaving no crevice unchecked.

Her heart skipped a beat.

While it felt strange to see Bell acting like an honest-to-goodness adventurer, her pulse quickened ever so slightly.

So he has this face, too...

She'd seen flashes of it while watching the War Game...but seeing him like this in person was making her a little excited.

She watched him carefully for several moments before the tension left his shoulders.

"I think...it's gone. Whoever it is might be hiding, though..."

"Y-you can sense that, Bell?"

"Yes. Something's pretty much always watching me, so I've gotten good at noticing..."

"Huh?"

"Um, it's nothing."

Bell's keen perception had been developed under the powerful gaze of a mysterious goddess. The results made Eina tilt her head.

And if it was true, that all but confirmed that she had a stalker. Last night wasn't a figment of her imagination after all. Someone was following her.

A cold chill worked its way under her skin, when suddenly—the flow of the crowd shifted without warning.

Eina was swallowed by a wave of humanity before the surprise could even set in. Bell's white head was about to disappear.

A hand burst from out of nowhere and took hold of her wrist.

"A-are you okay?"

"...F-fine."

Bell had somehow managed to find a crease in the mob. Eina's words sounded wispy when she responded.

Five strong fingers held her hand and weren't letting go.

Still connected, Eina couldn't help but blush.

"Ah...Oh! Sorry!"

Bell realized why she was redder than usual and immediately released his grip.

The lingering warmth of his hand felt like a glove around hers. But the moment she saw Bell get embarrassed, a nervous laugh escaped from her lips.

"Shall we go?"

"Um, yes."

A quick confirmation and they were off again.

It took everything the girl had to hide her nerves. A smile slowly appeared on her face as Eina once again looked at the boy next to her, protecting her. Her bodyguard.

When they left the Guild, the lack of space between them had made her nervous. Now it was reassuring to have him so close.

"Hey, Eina. You've been walking on air these past few days. What's up with that?"

"…What?"

Morning, two days later.

They were in the middle of work, but Misha's words gave Eina pause.

"You're grinning nonstop with a sparkle in your eye. It's like you're giggling to yourself or something."

"I-I am?"

"Very much so."

Every window at the reception counter came equipped with a mirror for receptionists to use. Eina took it out and had a look.

Indeed, her cheeks were dusted with pink beneath the rims of her glasses. Suddenly embarrassed, she kept her eyes on her reflection and fixed her bangs.

"Someone was stalking you just the other day. Did that work itself out?"

"Well, I wouldn't say it's exactly solved, but…"

"Okay, so what's the deal, then? Something good happen?"

No words would come out of Eina's mouth.

She didn't have an answer ready for Misha's question.

There was only one answer that made sense—the reason that she was in such a good mood was that she was looking forward to the time she spent with Bell.

Eina searched for the right words, but Misha cut off her train of thought with a sudden cry. "Ah! It's that dwarf from before. What was his name...Dodomel?"

"Really?"

Overlooking her friend's obvious mistake, Eina followed her line of sight. Sure enough, Dormul was standing at the other end of the lobby.

Mouth closed, staring in her direction, he quickly turned away the moment he realized she was watching him.

Usually he'd make up an excuse to talk to her...However, this time he went directly to the exit as Eina watched him with confusion.

"He left. Wait a minute, there was an elf here doing exactly the same thing not too long ago."

"Was it...Luvis?"

"Yep. He kept glancing at you."

Luvis always engaged Eina in conversation whenever he visited the Guild, just like Dormul. It shouldn't be all that strange for them not to say hello once or twice, but the thought of it puzzled Eina as she tilted her head.

Her friend had already restarted their previous conversation, but the half-elf kept watching the place where the dwarf had exited the building.

"The party was completely surrounded by Minotaurs before we knew it, so we had to book it out of there..."

"Hee-hee...Now that was dangerous."

That evening. Bell joined Eina for her walk home, just as he'd done the past couple of days.

It was already late at night. Returning from the Dungeon took longer than Bell had expected, and he told her everything that happened. Eina smiled and listened, interjecting her opinion every now and then.

The ominous shadow hadn't shown itself since Bell started accompanying her. Bell had said that he felt flashes of its gaze, and most likely whoever it was was biding their time.

This arrangement can't go on forever...I've got to find a solution.

It was her fault that Bell had been caught up in this, and she hated it. Reassuring herself that it was only temporary, Eina's mind was elsewhere as she talked with Bell.

...What is Bell to me?

All of a sudden, she realized that the thought of their time together coming to an end made her feel a little lonely. Remembering her conversation with Misha that morning, Eina decided to ask herself some questions.

To Eina...Bell was like a little brother. That was the best way to describe it.

Nothing more, nothing less. With that mind-set, there shouldn't be any space for thoughts of him as a *man* to enter her head.

But then again, she was attracted to men just like Bell.

—Eina blushed furiously and looked at the ground as soon as that thought came through loud and clear.

Idiot! She scolded herself over and over for wanting this time to keep repeating.

Bell was right next to her, trying desperately to figure out what was wrong with the bright-red half-elf.

"M-Miss Eina, we're here."

"...! Oh, thank you, Bell."

They had arrived at the gate in front of the Guild's share house in no time at all.

Still flustered, Eina looked up and said a quick thank-you. Only then did she notice the fatigue on the boy's face.

Of course, it made perfect sense. He had just finished an extremely difficult outing in the Dungeon and had come to take her home immediately after. He'd been doing that for days on end.

"Well, Miss Eina, I'm going home." Delivering her safely, Bell turned away from Eina.

She felt so bad for putting him through all this that the words formed on her lips before she knew what was happening.

"...Bell? Would you like to come up?"

"Huh?"

She realized what she had done after the words were already

hanging in the air. But she couldn't ignore how tired the boy looked and decided to keep going. "Well, you work so hard every day and still come to my aid...The least I can do is make you a cup of tea."

The nerves were back. She struggled to keep her voice from trembling. Her pointed ears were burning up.

Eina's kind offer caught Bell off guard for a moment. But soon his face relaxed, and he smiled over at her before refusing.

"Thank you very much, Miss Eina. But my familia's waiting for me, so...Good night," he said, and turned his back once again.

"...Haaa."

A disappointed sigh escaped under her breath.

But a smile grew on her lips soon after as she watched him go.

She stayed put until he was out of sight before going in.

The following day was the fourth in a row that Bell had served as Eina's bodyguard.

It was also the day that everything changed.

"B-Bell, what's wrong? You're sweating an awful lot..."

"The watcher...wants to kill..."

The two of them had met up behind the Guild Headquarters like usual in the late evening hours. It happened when they were halfway home.

Bell kept his head on a swivel, incessantly checking their surroundings.

"A-are you certain?"

"Yes...although the murderous intent seems to be aimed at me rather than at us."

Bell made no attempt to make a molehill out of a mountain. The expression on his face revealed just how strong the pressure was bearing down on him.

Understanding the severity of the situation, Eina took a quick look around herself before leaning in close to Bell's ear.

"Bell, turn in to that back alley."

"Huh?"

"We'll lure whoever it is away from other people. There's no doubt they'll follow."

Anyone who was emanating that powerful an aura probably wasn't thinking straight.

Considering the circumstances, their pursuer would follow them anywhere, especially if there were fewer people.

At the same time, the chances of a fight breaking out as soon as they encountered the stalker went up immensely.

Bell understood all this without Eina having to say a word. He knew the danger, but he made up his mind in the blink of an eye and gave an affirmative nod. The time had come for Bell to fulfill his role as her bodyguard.

The two left the busy street and entered the dark alley. After traveling a good ways in, they found an ideal place to lie in wait, well hidden by the shadows.

They heard hurried, powerful footsteps a few heartbeats later. Eina clung to Bell as the echoes thudded in her ears. She did her best to be as quiet as possible, breathing only when necessary.

Then it came—a black shadow passed over their hiding spot. It continued even farther down the alleyway toward a dead end. Bell jumped out from the shadows the moment their pursuer came to a stop.

"Eh?!—Dormul?!"

Eina stepped into the dim light behind Bell and gasped the moment she saw the man glaring at her bodyguard.

The dwarf wore a hooded robe that was just barely large enough for him. However, he must not have heard Eina's voice because his seething glare was locked solely on Bell, his entire face burning red.

"The hell ye think ye're doin', bringin' Eina ta a place like this, eh—?"

Dormul howled as he unhooked a war hammer from its sheath on his back.

He grasped it with both hands, lifted it high above his head, and charged before Bell could say a word.

"B-Bell! Dormul! Stop th—!"

The deafening impact of Dormul's hammer drowned out the last part of Eina's desperate scream.

Stone shards flew high into the air; a tremendous shock wave shot through the street. Bell knew at that moment he couldn't hold anything back against this opponent and quickly drew two knives.

Spinning out of the way, he moved to counterattack.

"White 'air, red eyes, human…I know ye, ye're the Little Rookie!"

"!"

"But ye don' stand a chance against me!"

Dormul easily blocked Bell's attack with his war hammer like it was child's play. He grinned as he swung the massive weapon.

Bell had no choice but to fall back. The dwarf's muscular arms guided the hammer's momentum into a series of powerful swings, turning the back alley into a stormfront as he began his offensive.

This isn't good, thought Eina.

Bell and Dormul were both second-tier adventurers. However, Bell had only just recently leveled up, whereas Dormul had reached Level 3 nearly three years ago. In terms of strength and skill, the dwarf was a true veteran. Therefore, he possessed a distinct advantage.

Eina feared the worst, instantly regretting her decision to put Bell in danger. But those fears were soon proven pointless.

"_____!!"

"WAHH!"

Bell was trapped in the dead end with nowhere to escape. Dormul raised his hammer to deliver the finishing blow, but a jet-black knife intercepted its path. Carving a violet arc through the air, it forced the war hammer to the side and into the ground.

A stunned Dormul watched with wide eyes as Bell picked up speed.

He…he's fast——!

Eina was equally surprised.

The boy was too fast for her to see. Jumping off the walls and through the air like a rabbit, Bell found his way into the dwarf's blind spots—and attacked from behind and from the sides. Just when Eina thought Dormul had a window to counterattack after blocking one of Bell's strikes, the boy was already gone. Her eyes spun, trying to keep up with his movements.

Eina's surprise came from the fact that Bell truly looked like a second-tier adventurer.

Even compared to the experienced Dormul, the crispness of his actions was in no way inferior. He wasn't relying on his Status's blunt power; instead, his form was conjuring images of a former teacher from the top-class adventurers.

Even when cornered at a complete stop, he moved his body extremely well and executed techniques that put him on equal footing with his opponent. This was close-quarters combat at its finest.

Eina couldn't help but be reminded of his exploits in the War Game. The white rabbit versus the enemy commander, the higher-level Hyacinthus—the underdog turning the tables against an overwhelming favorite with skills and techniques as sharp as a sword.

Seeing it with her own eyes, Eina could tell that the teacher who had drilled combat techniques into him was extraordinary.

"Stop…stop hoppin' around, DAMN IT!"

Dormul was losing his ability to keep up with Bell with each passing moment. Every swing hit nothing but empty air, and the boy was taking advantage of even more openings for counterattacks.

The white rabbit's hit-and-run tactics. Dormul's frustrated howls as he swayed to and fro.

Bell's Agility—his speed was on a different level.

Dwarves were known for their strength and power, but those were a horrible match for Bell.

"DAMN YE! Try dodgin' this, ye rodent!"

Dormul's frustration had hit its boiling point. He reached behind his shoulder and pulled out yet another giant hammer.

—A magic sword?!

Eina knew immediately that the glowing yellow energy enveloping the weapon wasn't just for show.

Magic swords came in all different shapes, but each had the ability to summon incredible magic power in the blink of an eye. Should one of these powerful weapons unleash its energy in this confined space, it would hit its target without fail. Dormul knew what he was doing.

Eina forgot to breathe. She had to stop this, but before she could try...

A wide-eyed Bell charged Dormul head-on.

Bell!

Judging by his angle of attack, Eina saw right away that he was drawing the attack away from her so she didn't get caught in the blast.

Dormul's lips pulled back into a grin as he watched his target come right at him. He brought the magical weapon down straight into the boy's path.

All Bell could see as he zipped across the stone pavement was the dwarf putting every muscle in his body into the swing.

"EAT THIIIS!!"

"—Hah!"

Bell brought the crimson knife in his left hand up to meet the hammer.

Leaving a trail of scarlet light in its wake, the knife blade went beneath the crackling hammerhead and sliced clean through *the handle.*

"_____"

The heavy part of the hammer-shaped magic weapon spun high into the air.

The rest of the weapon, the severed hilt in Dormul's hand, failed to connect with its target. The ace in the hole had failed.

Bell passed right by the dwarf and jumped in front of the shocked half-elf with blinding speed. He took a defensive stance with her at his back, protecting Eina like a bodyguard should.

Dormul froze in place, absolutely dumbfounded that his magic-sword attack had failed.

Recovering quickly, he picked up his war hammer once again and turned to face Bell, ready for more.

"This ain't over!"

However.

The rest of the beheaded hammer came tumbling down out of the sky right above him with a loud *whoosh!*

Eina and Bell watched in shock as the flat part of the hammer connected with Dormul's head.

"——GWAAAAAAAAAAAAAAAAAAAAAAAAAAAAAA!"

A thick lightning bolt struck the moment his scream echoed through the alley.

The yellow energy pulsing within the magic-sword hammer had been released in a mighty flash, bringing a pillar of electrical energy down on top of the dwarf.

Bell and Eina were blown off their feet. Colliding in midair, they fell to the ground in a heap.

"B-Bell! Are you hurt?"

"I-I'm all right…I'm more worried about him, to be honest."

Eina had landed on her back, Bell facedown on top of her. Propping herself up on her elbows, she could see that the boy's back was singed. Bell, on the other hand, pointed to the origin of the blast with a shaky hand.

A feeling of relief flooded through her veins as the two got to their feet. Then they went to check on Dormul.

"Ehh…"

Each of the walls that made up the dead end had taken considerable damage. The dwarf lay in the middle of piles of charred stone rubble, burned from head to toe.

Next to his smoldering body was the large hammerhead. Energy spent, it cracked and fell to pieces.

"I-is he alive…?"

"Yes…He's breathing."

Arriving at his side, the two checked for vital signs. Seeing that he was okay, the boy finally let his shoulders relax.

Eina, however, wore a cloudier expression.

She couldn't believe it. Dormul was her stalker? That couldn't be true.

She had encountered all kinds of adventurers in her years working as a receptionist at the Guild. She was pretty confident in her ability to see a person's true character. How could an awkward dwarf with a kind and gentle soul do something like this…?

Eina glanced away, a somber look in her eyes.

"…"

Bell stood next to her, looking around the dead end and at the walls surrounding them.

His inquisitive gaze fell on Dormul and then up into the night. He was unable to shake a funny feeling.

Bell helped move the unconscious Dormul to Guild Headquarters before the end of the night.

The dwarf would be given a chance to explain himself once he regained consciousness, but the blow from the magic sword had been so powerful that he hadn't come back to himself just yet.

Eina was still reeling from shock. She couldn't even focus on work.

"Eina, you feeling okay?"

"Yes, I'm fine. Sorry."

There was a lump in her heart all day. Time passed by, and night fell once again.

Eina forced a smile at Misha and her concerned coworkers before she left Guild Headquarters.

Of course, Bell wasn't waiting for her. The stalker incident had been resolved, so there was no reason to ask him to accompany her anymore.

The night sky overhead, Eina made her way down familiar streets on her way home.

"—Wha?"

There was no warning.

Eina just happened to glance over her shoulder, only to catch a glimpse of a figure she couldn't miss. Someone in a black hooded robe. It was the same garb her pursuer had been wearing on the first night.

All the blood drained from her face.

"!"

It can't be! She silently screamed and took off at a run. Another look over her shoulder confirmed the hooded figure was following her.

So it wasn't Dormul after all...?!

The true perpetrator was someone else; the kind dwarf had nothing to do with it, causing even more thoughts to race through Eina's mind. Dormul had just happened to be in the area and misunderstood. He must have honestly believed that Bell had forced her into that dark alley.

She ran out of the high-class community and onto the quaint street. No one else was in sight. The occasional weak light of a magic-stone lamp illuminated the side of her face as she ran by.

Her pursuer was quicker. There was no escape.

She could feel them getting closer, faster. Eina took in a deep breath in preparation to let out a scream that might or might not reach anyone else's ears.

"Firebolt!"

A streak of flaming lightning flashed before she could scream.

It came from behind her and her black-cloaked pursuer. The magic raced across the stone pavement and exploded so close to them that both Eina and the figure stopped to look.

Suddenly, the sound of footsteps echoed from overhead, from atop the houses that lined the street——a flash of white hair appeared from the shadows as someone jumped into the air.

The blur came down on top of the hooded figure, a foot slamming into its back.

"Uph!"

"!"

"B-Bell?!"

"S-sorry, something just didn't feel right...I-I should have come quicker."

Bell fought to get words out between his ragged breaths. Free from the grip of terror, Eina couldn't have been more relieved to see him and was suddenly filled with the urge to embrace the boy. Quickly wiping the tears building up in her emerald eyes, she asked him a question. "Wh-what do you mean, something didn't feel right?"

"I didn't want to scare you, so I didn't say anything, but...there were several pairs of eyes watching us every day when we went back to your place..."

Bell continued by saying that he had felt a few distant gazes focused on them even when he fought with Dormul.

Apparently, he had planned on taking her home again tonight because he couldn't convince himself he was just paranoid. Once he had heard from the Guild that the depressed receptionist had already left, he'd dashed out at full speed.

"———DORYAAAAAAAAAAAAAAAAAA!"

"""""!"""""

The situation changed yet again a heartbeat later.

A muscular dwarf burst onto the quaint side street like a vigorous tank breaking through enemy lines.

The three figures stayed still, unsure how to respond as the dwarf's massive fists went straight for the person wearing the black cloak.

The target spun out of his grasp.

"Ye all right, Eina?"

"Is that you, Dormul...? What are you doing here? How did you get out of the Guild?"

"Made me own door outta that puny wall!"

Eina slapped her hand against her forehead.

But Dormul didn't notice her reaction or the fact that Bell broke out in a nervous sweat. All his senses were focused entirely on the hooded figure, his gaze burning with fury.

"So ye're the one? The sicko who's been stalkin' Eina?"

Eina's eyes went wide in surprise that Dormul somehow knew about her situation.

At the same time, the trembling hooded figure placed his hands on the edges of the hood.

"You dare to address me by such an uncivilized title, foul dwarf?"

"L-Luvis?!"

Yet another surprise—Eina had lost count of how many—made her jaw drop.

Elegant golden hair exposed, the elf returned the dwarf's glare with his own beneath sculpted eyebrows.

"Prefer I call ye a pervert, two-timin' elf! How ye gonna explain this away?"

"Gh...I-I only wanted to express my true feelings for Eina..."

The area under the elf's eyes turned a light shade of pink as he cast his gaze in Eina's direction, before he switched gears and went on the offensive.

"In...in any case, I became fed up with following all the twists and turns of social convention. It's my nature to be more straightforward! You've made a grave misunderstanding!"

"Oh-ho! What misunderstandin' would that be?"

Bell had been completely left out of the conversation. He stood there, looking left and right as the two other men exchanged verbal blows. Eina watched with the inexplicable feeling that both parties were missing vital information.

She stepped between them and summoned forth every shred of professionalism she had developed while on the job. "Stop right there, both of you! Both sides of this argument need to be heard, so calm yourselves this instant!"

The crack of Eina's verbal whip made Dormul and Luvis fall silent, but the two were still glaring daggers at each other.

Now that things had settled down a little bit, Eina first turned to the elf.

"May we please hear your side of the story, Luvis? Every detail that led to this point."

"S-sure, I suppose…"

Luvis gulped down the air in his throat under the pressure of Eina's stare. Shifting uncomfortably in his robe, he finally nodded.

"A few days past, when I was present in the Guild lobby…I heard that you were being pursued by an unknown individual, and I took it upon myself to make sure no harm came to you."

Eina blinked a few times. The moment that her friend Misha had practically shouted behind the counter immediately replayed in her head. That put that question to rest.

Most likely, Dormul had also learned of her situation in a similar fashion.

"Huhhh? Quit yer lyin', we all know ye were the one from the start…!"

"Dormul, you will have a turn to speak, so please be quiet for now. As you were saying, Luvis?"

"Oh, yes…I consulted the god of my familia."

…*What?* Eina froze in place.

"He advised me that real men should protect from the shadows. So I concealed myself while making sure no harm came to you…"

"…I-I was told da same thing by me god. A man worthy o' the title protects from behind."

"Wh-what?"

…Something was very, very off.

"Basically, the both of you were worried…so you decided to secretly follow me around?"

"That 'bout sums it up."

"I guess, if you put it that way."

It was a bitter pill for Eina to swallow. The two adventurers had just admitted to behaving exactly like stalkers.

But there was more to the story. Their increasingly aggressive approaches were also due to their gods' advice. They both would do whatever it took to win her heart, and they had blindly followed their deities' instructions.

As for the boy who'd been pulled into the situation as a bodyguard, both adventurers saw him as an enemy at the very least. That one-sided rivalry had spiked to dangerous levels when they saw him holding her hand and generally being friendly with her.

So then that would mean—Eina felt that she was one step away from identifying the true culprit.

"Dormul also wore something like this, but...Luvis, could you explain the robe...?"

"Oh, this? My god says it's the latest 'trend,' or something along those lines..."

"Uh, um...Don't you think it would go the other way? That would scare her..."

"What?"

That was it exactly.

The white-haired boy cautiously raising his hand as he spoke was right. Wearing that kind of suspicious robe at night would only instill fear in her and make it more likely for Eina to misinterpret their intentions.

Dormul and Luvis clamped their mouths shut as though it had taken them this long to realize what had happened.

An awkward silence fell around the four—"Geh-hee-hee-hee!"

A crackling laughter filled the air from somewhere out of sight.

J-just as I thought...

The mortals immediately looked toward the rooftops. That's when they saw them: two deities holding their stomachs as they pointed and laughed at them.

—They'd been played, all of them.

They had danced in the palms of the hands of two bored gods.

That being the case, most likely the first black-hooded stalker had been one of the two deities. Their plan was to pit their two love-struck followers against each other as soon as both Luvis and Dormul came to them for advice.

All for "entertainment."

Deities typically had no problem treating the many children living on Gekai as nothing more than pieces on a board. They'd been unwittingly sucked into a divine prank.

"Awww, and I thought for sure Eina would reject them both once they made their move."

"I won the bet, fair and square."

Both of them shook with laughter beneath the light of the moon. Their followers, Dormul and Luvis, were shaking, too, but for much a different reason.

"Grrrrrr..." The dwarf growled, grinding his molars together. Even the proud elf's skin had turned a scalding red from head to toe.

Hands clenched into fists, they bore the humiliation.

"Luvis, Daddy just struck it rich gambling. I'll treat you to a grand feast once we get home tonight!"

"Dormuuuul. I'm a bit low on cash—could you lend me a few valis? Pretty please?"

""—GO TO HELLLLLLLLLLLLLLLLLLLLLLLLLLLLLLLLLLLLL!!""

A fusillade of bolts from the elf's short bow and any rocks the dwarf could reach bombarded the two deities.

However, the two slippery gods made their escape before any of the arrows or rocks could connect. Their laughter echoed off the buildings as the jolly pair disappeared into the moonlit night.

"..."

"...Umm."

Eina couldn't say a word, and Bell did his best to break the silence as he looked over at her.

Dormul and Luvis were furious, shoulders rising and falling as every insult imaginable came flooding out from between gritted teeth under their breaths. That is, until Luvis raised his head.

"No, no, no! I refuse to let it end this way! Eina, I am in love with you! Please become my eternal partner!!"

"I-I have a greater love for ye, Eina! Become me bride!"

"Eh...WHAT?!"

One more revelation had been waiting for her, and Eina shrieked in surpise. Luvis and Dormul were both blushing as they looked at her. She, too, turned bright red.

Plenty of men had confessed their love for her, but a marriage proposal? That had never happened in any of her nineteen years of life.

What's more, she could tell by the look in her suitors' eyes that both proposals were completely serious.

Bell, once again out of the loop, watched the events unfold with a slack jaw.

"Like 'ell I can entrust Eina to anyone like ye! Go hole up in the forest ye came from!"

"Stay your hand! A dwarf such as yourself could never produce offspring with a wonderful girl like her in the first place!"

"NGAH———! What ye plannin' ta do ta her, ye creep?"

"D-don't be a fool!! I'm not some closeted pervert!! I was simply bringing the difference in race to your attention…!"

Just when it looked as though another verbal sparring match between Luvis and Dormul was about to break out, both turned to Eina at the same moment.

She was speechless. Her shoulders jumped nervously.

"Please give me your answer, Eina!"

"I'm ready, whatever yer answer be!"

Panic flooded her veins as both pushed for a decision.

No matter who her answer was, it meant she would become engaged on the spot. Of course, she wasn't ready for that. And if she refused them without a viable reason, both would continue to hound her with even more determination than before.

Eina was on the verge of tears as she shifted her gaze.

There was Bell, just standing there. He shifted his weight from side to side, watching everything unfold without stepping in.

Say something already, anything…!

The boy's silence sparked anger for some reason.

Everything that had ever frustrated her about him started flashing through her mind as her wide eyes narrowed into a glare. "Huh?" Bell tilted his head to the side with a truly clueless look on his face.

Eina's cheeks had become an all-out inferno.

Whether it was because Bell was present, she didn't know.

Her usual calm demeanor long gone, Eina closed her eyes to hide the rage building behind them.

"—I'm unable to give either of you gentlemen an answer at this time."

Then she wrapped her arm around Bell's elbow and dragged him to her side.

"Because the two of us are in a relationship!"

""""WHHHHAAAAAAAAAT—?!"""""

Three shocked voices filled the night.

"Why are you so surprised?"

"S-sorry...!"

Luvis's ice-cold glare and Dormul's howling accusation immediately fell on the boy, who offered a terrified apology immediately.

Both adventurers took a few steps closer to Eina, despite the fact that Bell was still hooked to her side.

"S-say it ain't so, Eina!"

"This is a ruse, is it not?"

"No, we are seeing each other! He...he confessed to me!"

Eina squeezed her eyes shut and shouted as loudly as she could. Bell, however, had become somewhat of a rag doll, with a blank look in his eyes.

Eina's cheeks were red as apples. She released her grip on Bell's elbow, grabbed his shoulders, and brought his face directly in front of hers.

"Bell, of course you remember *that day*, when you came home safely from the fifth floor! You confessed to me, didn't you?"

"?!"

It felt like years ago. Attacked by a Minotaur but saved by Aiz, Bell had escaped with his life.

You said those words, Eina silently screamed through her eyes as she pulled the boy even closer.

Right now, right here, one more time—say them again.

All the energy in her body was channeling through her emerald pupils. Her nose was close enough to his that they'd touch with one sudden twitch. She wasn't blinking, only conveying the message with every fiber of her being.

The boy's lips started to open and close, yet no words came out.

"Tell them, Bell. Say it. *Say what you said on that day.*"

Bell's eyes started to spin in front of Eina's bright-red face and desperate plea.

Then his lips finally moved as it dawned on him.

"I...lo-ve...you..."

Cheeks burning bright red, the boy looked down at his feet.

"—There! There you have it! Hear—hear how he wants to protect me! And he—Bell is the right person for me!!"

The final blow.

BANG! Dormul and Luvis staggered backward as if they had been struck by lightning.

They couldn't see or hear any falsehood in Eina's words or demeanor. They drifted listlessly on the spot for a moment before their heads and shoulders sank. Then they took a few weak steps in different directions.

"..."

"..."

The dwarf and the elf left the quaint street. A chilly breeze swept past Bell and Eina.

The two of them were equally embarrassed, faces the same shade of red.

A few awkward heartbeats passed before Bell, tears beginning to leak out of his eyes, turned to Eina as if trying to make some sort of appeal.

However, Eina squared her shoulders in his direction, clapped her hands together, squeezed her eyes as tight as she could, and gave a deep bow.

"I'm so sorry...!"

She wrung a shameless apology out of her light-pink lips.

A bright blue sky in the morning hours.

Warm sunlight made its way through the glass windows. Guild Headquarters was busy again today.

Countless adventurers came and went. Many, as always, formed lines in front of the reception desk.

Eina, too, stood on the other side of the desk and took on the air of a perfect Guild receptionist, as she usually did.

It's going to be awkward if Bell comes in today...

The mere thought of what had happened last night made her face so hot she was sure her cheeks would catch fire.

She'd lost herself in the moment, even though she'd let her emotions get the better of her, even though she'd practically forgotten which way was up...

She regretted, more than anything before in her life, the fact that she'd pulled him into the center of her mess.

She was supposed to be the older one...Her heart sighed for what felt like the hundredth time that day.

""Ah...""

Bell appeared at the front of her line.

"..."

"..."

They exchanged silent stares.

Other adventurers watched from behind, frustrated by the time lost. The two started blushing before averting their eyes.

So embarrassing...What can I do? Eina's brain desperately searched for the right words to break the awkward stillness.

But it was Bell who broke the ice first, forcing a smile and shyly saying:

"Um, I need a little advice. Could you help me?"

It was a question just like any other day. Eina's eyes went wide.

Then, very slowly, a smile appeared on her lips.

"Of course...I'd be glad to."

The two made eye contact and came back to themselves in that moment.

Adviser and adventurer. Or perhaps older sister and younger brother.

They went to the consultation box to discuss the problem and sat on opposite sides of the desk. *This is good—this is enough,* she repeated to herself.

Eina was satisfied.

Their relationship was fine just like this.

"Sorry...Thank you, Bell."

"..."

"Saying that you loved me one more time...It made me happy."

"......"

Her voice was quiet, barely a whisper. Bell pretended not to hear even as he blushed and examined his lap.

Eina giggled to herself with a contented grin on her face.

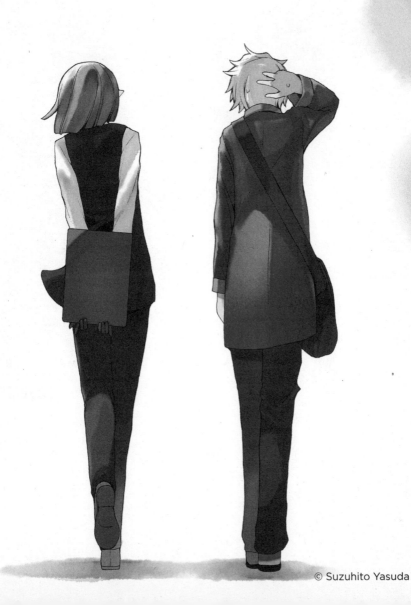

© Suzuhito Yasuda

CHAPTER 5
THE CITY GIRL'S SECRET

"—All done!"

Black smoke rose from the cramped kitchen.

Not only the various ingredients of the dish but many of the cooking tools themselves were either singed or charred. The culinary combat that had just taken place was extremely intense.

Apron tied around her waist, the silver-haired girl, Syr, emerged from the kitchen with a satisfied smile on her face.

Neither her coworkers nor the café owner was around.

Syr didn't even taste her creations—an oddly colored meat pie and several sandwiches that didn't smell like they should—before cramming them into containers. Then she piled all the containers into one large basket.

Humming a happy tune to herself, Syr changed clothes before leaving the café with the basket in her arms.

"I wonder if I'll get to see their smiles today."

A smile of her own on her lips, she went out into the city.

It's evening at Guild Headquarters.

Many adventurers, home from the Dungeon, are taking care of their own business inside the white lobby, which has fiery beams of sunlight from the west slanting in from the overhead windows.

"I'm going to go talk to Miss Eina."

"Understood. Lilly will take care of things at the Exchange."

"I'll just hang around."

I get in line to see my adviser, Eina. Lilly, carrying a backpack stuffed to capacity, Haruhime, her own tubular backpack bursting at the seams, and Mikoto walk over to the Exchange with the magic stones and drop items we brought up from the Dungeon today. Welf doesn't really have anyplace to go, so he decides to just kill some time. All of us go our separate ways in the lobby.

Just like all the adventurers around us, *Hestia Familia* has errands to attend to at Guild Headquarters.

Normally we just take care of our drop items and magic stones at the Exchange located in Babel Tower, but today we need to take care of the familia tax levied by the Guild. So, everyone decided to come here and take care of everything at once. I mean, we might as well get everything done at the same time as long as we're here.

Off on my own, it's really surprising to see the long lines in front of the reception counter. The Guild employees behind it are practically flying back and forth, trying to help everyone. Once it's my turn, I give Eina a simple update and leave it at that. I shouldn't waste her time with meaningless conversation, so I get in and out quickly.

But it looks like the girls aren't finished at the Exchange yet, so I've got a little time on my hands. It might be a good idea to head over to the bulletin board and see what's posted.

Guild Headquarters has loads of information about the Dungeon and many other things that are useful to adventurers, including the advice that advisers provide. There's no reason not to take advantage of everything the Guild has to offer.

I work my way into the crowd already gathered around the bulletin board and take a look at the many quests and mercantile familia advertisements for the latest posted items.

It's hard to believe we're under attack from Rakia…Everything seems so normal here.

I'm pretty sure the battle against the Kingdom of Rakia is still going on outside the city wall. But there's no difference between a day "at war" and a regular day at the Guild—all races of demi-humans are just bumping shoulders and talking among one another as far as I can see. The invasion has no impact on our day-to-day lives as adventurers.

I mean, I'm sure the top-tier adventurers are out there fighting for us, but not everyone in the middle of the pack and below has been called to the front. Probably the city of Orario—well, the Guild, since it's the governing power—is trying to maintain a constant incoming flow of magic stones to continue producing magic-stone products. Too many of us fighting on the front lines would have a direct impact on the economy, so the Guild probably wants as many adventurers in the Dungeon as possible.

At least, that's my theory as I stand here looking at all the adventurers fully equipped with different types of armor and weapons.

"What, seriously? Again?"

"Somethin's fishy here."

…?

While my brain was busy thinking about the Rakia invasion, my ears pick up a conversation just in front of me.

Actually, it's happening right in front of the billboard. Other people notice, too, standing on tiptoe and craning their necks to see what's going on.

I do the same, stretching up many times, trying to get a glimpse of the sheet posted on the billboard.

"Looks like there's a monster down there with a taste for armor and weapons."

"Ah, Welf."

Welf comes right up next to me.

He's a bit taller than me, so he can see over the crowd better than I can. He can read the posting, too, by the sound of it.

"…A 'taste for'? As in stealing?"

"That's right. Some of them take equipment off dead bodies, but this one likes to take equipment off adventurers in battle."

That's a real surprise.

Monsters stealing from adventurers?

When you think about it, it's not all that strange, considering monsters use landforms and other natural things in the Dungeon as weapons, but the thought of one of the beasts in armor is shocking. If it's true, I'm sure more than one adventurer wants to cry.

All of us work hard, shedding blood and tears to find a combination of equipment that suits us the best…If mine got stolen, I don't know what I'd do. Especially if one of the weapons I've gotten used to was suddenly gone.

A monster that steals an adventurer's weapons—the lifeblood we need to survive. It's frightening to think about.

—An image of a Minotaur wielding a greatsword suddenly flashes through my mind.

S-scary.

The memories I have of that day send shivers down my spine.

I shouldn't be scaring myself like this. Shaking the images out of my head, I turn to Welf.

"Wh-where was it spotted?"

"Deep Zone, mostly. From what I can see, the highest confirmed sighting happened on the twentieth floor."

Then he says that second-tier adventurers gathered all the information.

He seems to be getting a kick out of this, and he's not the only one. Quite a few people in the area are laughing it off like it's a funny rumor. They don't believe the reports.

In fact, a few of them are taking it as a joke.

"There's some more interesting info about that, though."

Welf grins as he looks over at me.

"This one's from a while back, but apparently a Black Minotaur wearing armor showed up in the Dungeon."

"Black…Minotaur…?"

"Yeah. Word spread around real quick but then disappeared just as fast. Now it's only a rumor I've heard."

Usually, Minotaurs are a rusty, reddish color.

I've never heard of a black one.

A subspecies…I ask him if it's a rare offshoot of monsters. Welf tells me not to take it seriously, grinning as he shrugs.

It makes me nervous whenever I hear the word *Minotaur*…I follow up with another question.

"When was that rumor going around, Welf?"

"About two months ago, maybe?"

Two months ago…That's about the time that I leveled up to Level 2.

Welf adds that that story was circulating at about the time he joined the battle party, so that's why it's stuck in his memory.

"..."

I look back at the board, the voices of countless adventurers around me.

There's an artist's rendering of a monster wearing armor and holding a sword. I stare at it until the girls come back from the Exchange.

"Um, is Syr taking the day off?"

The day after we paid our familia tax for the month, I decided to visit The Benevolent Mistress. As soft morning sunlight brightens the sky, I arrive at the front door.

"That she is, meow! Syr's playing hooky again, meow!"

The catgirl Ahnya is standing right in front of me, her long, thin tail twitching behind her. She looks irritated.

Even after I moved into *Hestia Familia*'s new home, I still swing by here to pick up a lunch from Syr before going to the Dungeon.

Now that my familia has more members, especially Mikoto with her great cooking skills, I didn't want to bother Syr. Making a lunch for me every day is just one more thing on her to-do list, but Lyu and a few of the other waitresses visited Hearthstone Manor directly and practically begged me to keep coming.

"Just because you've picked up a useless way to sense danger...!" "Think of the guinea pigs, think of their pain, meow...!" Runoa and Chloe pleaded with me as Lyu looked on with a blank look in her eyes. For some reason, all of them had been clutching at their stomachs.

Anyway, since then, I've kept coming here every day like usual... but I haven't gotten a lunch from Syr in a while.

I've been wondering what's going on, so I came here today to ask some of the other waitresses about it and found out that Syr was absent today as well.

"Syr has a way of going 'poof' and disappearing, like today."

"Hee-hee-hee, sounds like our young maiden has some secrets, meow...But she doesn't want us to work too hard and always comes back, meow! I don't know the first thing about accounting, meow!!"

Other waitresses—the human Runoa and another catgirl, Chloe—are on break and come to join Ahnya and me at the front door.

I remember them saying something about it when we stopped by to get the recipe for Mikoto's cake, but Syr's been absent ever since then...That had to be at least ten days ago.

"You must understand, Syr is not like us, in that she does not reside here. She has her reasons, so this situation is bound to occur occasionally."

The catgirls and Runoa keep talking among themselves as Lyu calmly explains the details over their voices.

The other waitresses are all excitedly grinning as they speak, but there's a centered composure in Lyu's sky-blue eyes.

"Um...Couldn't you just go to where she lives and ask her...?"

"..."

I question why they don't just go get a direct answer from Syr... but then Lyu and the others fall silent.

Well, that's weird. I tilt my head in confusion, but the waitresses look just as lost as I am.

"Now that you mention it, we...meow..."

"No one knows where Syr lives?"

"Well, that, and nothing about what she does in her free time, meow."

Ahnya, Runoa, and Chloe all speak in turn. I can't hide my surprise.

These girls work together at this café and bar, so the fact that no one here knows anything about Syr outside of work surprises me.

Lyu stays quiet for a moment as I look around in shock. Then she confirms what her coworkers had been saying.

"We have tried—we've asked her about her private life...She says it's a secret and quickly changes the subject every time."

Lyu looks slightly off to the side before explaining.

"Only one thing to do, meow—A quest, boy! Find Syr, trail her, and discover her secrets, meow!"

"Huh?!"

"Oh! Great idea! We might find out a few of her weaknesses at the same time! Two birds, one stone!"

W-weakness…?

Chloe and Runoa enthusiastically jump on board right away. I break out in a cold sweat at the prospect.

Lyu cocks an eyebrow. "Stop this at once. You are putting Mr. Cranell in a difficult spot." But that doesn't put an end to their excitement.

"As long as there's a reward, what's the problem, meow? What should it be, meow…I could sing you a song, meow!"

"Huh? Ahnya, are you a good singer?"

"The best! Why don't I give you a little taste, meow? My throat's feeling great today—"

"Stop that, tone-deaf kitty!"

"We told you, customers won't come if you sing, meow!"

Ahnya was all set, ready to start humming a few bars, when the other girls descended on her with a vengeance.

Two of them pinned the catgirl to the ground and held her mouth shut. "MpFHHH!" Another bead of sweat drips down my skin.

Just how bad a singer is she…?

"Mr. Cranell, please don't take them seriously."

"Ha-ha…Okay, I won't."

Lyu was very clear. I try to smile.

I decide not to stick around much longer and say a quick good-bye. I leave the bar and café behind.

"Now, what to do today…"

The sky is bright and blue over my head. I walk among the many demi-humans on West Main Street, taking in the sights and sounds.

We aren't going into the Dungeon today.

To be honest, the goddess and Welf insisted. "You've gone in every day for a while now, so take a rest," they said, and practically forbade me from going anywhere near the Dungeon entrance.

Welf spends a lot of time in the forge, and the girls are very careful not to work too hard and spend a lot of time away from the battle party. I guess that my going to the Dungeon every day without fail must've really made an impression.

But *she's* so far ahead of me. Catching up to her is going to take everything I've got…

"…Still, a day or two like this won't hurt."

I shield my eyes from the sparkling early summer sun and try to smile.

Everyone's looking out for me, and they do have a point. I won't be able to accomplish anything in the Dungeon without being well rested. Even Eina told me days off are just as important as days in the Dungeon.

Time to spread my wings. I should try something new and walk around the city for a change. It might do me some good.

I live here, but it's amazing how much of the city I don't know…

The small, family-run shops that have lined the backstreets for generations, the flower stores that are run by animal women who aren't affiliated with any familia, the random Jyaga Maru Kun street stands in the most out-of-the-way places…There are hardly any adventurers here because they're in the Dungeon. Everything I see as I look all around is new, and it's painfully apparent that I don't know the first thing about Orario aboveground.

The Labyrinth City is huge.

There are many different neighborhoods in the city, from the Industrial District to the Shopping District, and the one I recently became too familiar with, the Pleasure Quarter.

I've lived here for over three months now, but there's still so much I haven't seen yet. It seems like there's a new discovery around every corner. Then again, I'm sure the fact that I'm always in the Dungeon has something to do with it.

The sky is bright blue and clear overhead. I'm in a great mood as I pass through the main streets and back alleys.

I see people I've never met and places I've never been to, and I catch new smells at every turn.

I'm really starting to enjoy this. Today's my break from the Dungeon, and it finally feels like I'm taking advantage of it.

Why not splurge? I happen to come across a place selling meat skewers at the edge of one of the side streets and decide to buy one. The animal man behind the counter is about to ring me up when he says, "Hey, aren't you the Little Rookie?" He's so happy that he gives me another skewer for free.

Honestly, I don't know if I should be embarrassed, but it's an amazing feeling to be recognized. I enjoy the warm happiness settling in my chest while walking down the street with a stick of meat in each hand.

"Whew…"

The last of the meat juices drips down my chin as I finish satisfying my hunger, so I find a bench in Central Park and have a seat.

Amid all the trees and water features built into the city's center, amid all the people coming and going, I look up at Babel Tower in all its glory. The white tower of the gods stretches all the way into the blue sky, practically into the heavens. I can't believe I forgot how awesome it is.

I see it every day, so I should be used to it. It's just…it looks different somehow today.

"Huh…?"

I've been enjoying the sun's warmth on my face for a little while.

I'm looking off in the distance at nothing in particular, watching the ebb and flow of many demi-humans passing through Central Park, when I catch a glimpse of a girl.

I recognize the silver hair waving back and forth and immediately sit up.

"Isn't that Syr?"

The conversation at The Benevolent Mistress was only a few hours ago. I shift to the edge of the bench.

She's wearing a clean white dress with a straw hat.

I usually see her dressed for work, so this cool, early summer look takes my breath away. She's pretty cute.

Syr comes from the southwest, walking north into Central Park. But she doesn't pass through the center, instead skirting around the edge toward East Main. I see her starting to disappear into the crowd from my bench on the northern rim of Central Park and get to my feet.

The voices of Ahnya, Chloe, Runoa, and Lyu are running through my head. Everything said this morning is on replay.

I think about it, but curiosity gets the best of me and I follow her into the crowd.

Not sleepy anymore, I go through the entrance to East Main Street. "Where is Syr going…?"

I avoid the path of the horse-drawn taxis and stay close behind the fluttering silver hair and white dress.

The Guild controls many of the buildings and facilities located in the East District. The massive Coliseum stands out among all the fancy red-brick hotels that spread out as far as I can see. I have a strong feeling that this area is for hosting events as well as tourists and travelers when they visit the city.

Syr has something in her hands—a large basket, maybe? There's a pretty big lid on it, too.

She must be taking something somewhere…I come up with few guesses as to what it might be, when she suddenly veers off the main road and onto a side street.

I follow her southeast, making sure to stay close enough to see her but far enough away not to be noticed, meaning I need to dash to catch up with her every time she disappears around a corner.

Wait a second, I know this street…

I've seen this narrow alleyway before. Even so, I follow her farther in.

A few more turns down other paths and my suspicions are confirmed. "Daedalus Street…?"

The whole place spreads out in front of me after I come out of the last alleyway, and my eyes widen.

Daedalus Street. Built by an architect said to have gone insane and remodeled the neighborhood many times over, it's a residential area with absolutely no sense of order or direction. With its stone buildings and stairwells and winding roads going up and down with no rhyme or reason, it's easy to understand why this place has been called Orario's "second Dungeon."

I stop to catch my breath and watch as Syr casually makes her way through the entrance.

I've already come this far...can't exactly turn back now.

Memories of bad experiences in this place hold me back for a moment, but my mind is already made up.

Passing through the gates to Daedalus Street myself, I double-check to make sure I can feel the Divine Knife snugly tucked into my belt.

For starters, this place is a slum where the poorest citizens in Orario live, and a lot has happened to me here, so having a weapon ready is reassuring. Keeping my guard up, I make my way into the maze of blackened brick and stone.

What would Syr be doing in here...?

I climb to the top of some stairs, only to have my path blocked by a room jutting out of a stone house. I turn around, looking for the way forward, only to see a dark, narrow street where the sun can't reach. The only light is coming from a worn-out magic-stone lamp. There are people here, but I don't think they've had a bath in a while; they're doing laundry next to the well or enjoying a game of chess by the side of the road. I make my way past and onto even more complicated roads.

I can still see Syr, but the way she moves through here without any hesitation is bringing up more questions than answers. Down-on-their-luck and less-than-respectable adventurers are known to hide in this slum; this area's crime rate was the highest in Orario. A girl without the Blessing of a deity shouldn't be walking around alone in here. That's just asking for trouble...

But such concerns seem to be nothing to her because she's carrying that basket and moving forward without a care in the world.

I got completely lost in here during Monsterphilia and during my escape from the Pleasure Quarter. Honestly, I doubt I can get out of here by myself. There are red arrows—called ariadne—on street corners that should lead the way, and I try my best to memorize them. Unfortunately, I lose sight of Syr in those precious moments and take off at a sprint in the last direction I saw her in a desperate attempt to catch up.

Up and down, left and right, and forward through so many streets. Flashes of Syr's white dress guide me to the front of a building.

—*A church?*

Indeed, this building hidden at the heart of the city's labyrinth reminds me a lot of the place Lady Hestia and I used to call home.

It's built out of wood, and it's really big. There's an open courtyard in front of it with a broken fountain that doesn't spray water anymore. The buildings around the church encompass it on the remaining sides. I cautiously stick my head around the corner of the side street that led me here and see Syr open the church's front door with a loud creak. She disappears inside.

"..."

There's a church in this place, too...? Many questions fill my mind as I look up at the old structure.

There are several broken glass windows at the top of the outside walls. Moments pass as I stare at them, trying to decide whether or not to go forward. I have to see this through. I go to the front door and place my palms on the door handle.

"Anyone here...?" I say softly as I pull the old wooden door aside and go in.

"This place is massive!"

Sure, it looks big from the front, but the real surprise is how deep it goes.

The main chamber has got to be at least ten meders across, and the walls to my left and right are lined with doors that lead to other rooms. There's an altar all the way at the back. The tile under my feet has so many cracks that wild grass is threatening to reclaim the floor. The ceiling is high, too. The architect Daedalus himself would be right at home.

Several long wooden pews are stacked on top of one another nearby.

"That seems like..."

A fort that kids would make.

The back-and-forth pattern of the pile of pews makes it look like a small castle. I think to myself, as I pass it and search for clues as to where Syr went, that…I'm not alone.

Adventurers who've spent any time in the Dungeon have sharpened this sense to the point where we can pick *it* up very quickly. My body reacts to the feeling of being watched before any noises reach my ears. I look in that direction, ready.

I'm almost to the altar when I feel it coming from my right. Sure enough, a small face is poking out from behind one of the doors.

"…Who are you?"

I see a child, a blond elf with a vacant expression.

"I…um, I'm not a bad guy or anything. I-I'm just looking for someone…"

"Someone…?"

I kind of broke in here, didn't I? Flustered, I try to explain myself to the child. The elf stares at me and emerges from behind the door.

Dirty-blond hair and plump pointed ears.

Maybe not an elf; half-elf?

The kid keeps his eyes on me as he walks closer without any concern whatsoever.

A little boy…or maybe a girl? I seriously can't tell, but the kid comes right up to me.

I have no idea how to react to his continuous stare. But maybe he knows something about Syr. I decide to ask him and open my mouth, but before any sound can come out…

"Yo, Ruu, Big Sis Syr's going to have a fit if she sees—You. Who are you?"

"What's going on, Lai?"

The voices of two more kids cut through the air.

I look up and see them burst from the door and grab hold of the half-elf child, shield him from me. One is a human boy with brown hair, the other is a chienthrope girl with her tail tucked against her body.

Both are glaring at me like I'm some monster fresh out of the Dungeon, but they also have an extremely nervous light in their eyes. This isn't good. I have to convince them that I'm not a threat, explain my situation, and fast.

"Sorry! I didn't mean to startle you and I'm not going to do anything! I'm just here looking for…Wait a second, didn't you say 'Syr' just now?"

"…What if I did?"

"That's who I'm looking for! Do you know where she is?"

The boy and girl glance at each other, apparently startled, the moment I bring up her name.

They don't move, but the half-elf they're protecting pushes them away, swatting at their hands.

"Lai, Fina…This one is…not bad."

We've never met before, but he sounds so sure of himself.

The human and the animal girl let their shoulders relax after hearing that, but they're still very much on alert.

"…So, do you know Big Sis Syr?"

"Ah, yes. I'm really sorry for scaring you. Can I ask who you are? And about this church, too…"

I bend down to their height, a little bit shorter than the goddess. I'd say they're about as tall as Lilly.

That's also when I catch a glimpse of several more little faces poking out the door behind them. They aren't saying anything, only watching.

The chienthrope girl is closest to me when I ask my question, but it's the half-elf child who answers instead.

"Lai, Fina, and me, Ruu…We live here, in Mother Maria's house."

The child points to everyone in turn and then talks about the church. Mother Maria…I wonder what he means by "house."

Well, that didn't tell me very much.

"Okay, um…What were you doing?"

"…Running away from Big Sis's lunch box."

The little girl, Fina, answers this time, but I can tell she's still on edge. "Huh?" I respond, not sure how to process what she said.

I take a moment to think it over—when the boy, who'd been watching me with suspicious eyes this whole time, suddenly flinches. His arm flings forward, finger pointed directly at my face.

"White hair and red eyes—you're Bell Cranell, second-tier adventurer!"

"Little Rookie?!"

"From the War Game?!"

The door bursts open the moment Lai yells, children toppling over one another as they rush out into the main chamber.

My eyes go wide as the wave of children consumes me.

"Holy cow, it's really him!"

"He's no hume bunny, but he looks just like a rabbit!"

"Can I see your knife?"

The initial hit knocks me off balance. That would've been fine, but more and more kids jump onto my legs, some of the larger ones trying to tackle me. "Ouph!" *Was that a headbutt just now?!* Their high-pitched screams and laughter fill my ears as I try desperately to keep my feet.

It's a tidal wave of youthful humanity, with the boy named Lai at the helm. Even the chienthrope girl has gotten excited and joined the ring forming around me. The half-elf, looking aloof as ever, is outside the ring, quietly watching us.

Completely surrounded with many sets of hands on me from all angles, I grab hold of my knife to protect it. But what can I do? I can't just throw them off me by force, and at this rate—.

"Wait, wa——WAAHHHHHHHHHHHHHHHHH!"

I fall flat on my back in the middle of the floor.

"Wh-what's going on out here?!"

"Children!"

My pitiful scream and all the children's laughter draw two women out of the room directly behind the altar.

One is an elderly human, and the other is…Syr.

She looks down at me in surprise. Must be quite a sight, me cradling the Divine Knife in both hands while underneath a pile of excited children.

All I can do is laugh dryly as I look back up at her, while trying my best to ignore all the small hands pulling at my hair and cheeks.

"So then, you followed me out here?"

"Y-yeah…I'm really sorry."

We're in the cafeteria at the back of the church.

I'm sitting in a chair next to a large round table, getting scolded by Syr and apologizing to the best of my ability.

After I was unearthed from a mountain of kids, everyone came inside the cafeteria.

Sure, the walls and pillars are showing their age. There are cracks all over the place. But the use of magic-stone lamps and half-melted candlesticks is proof that there are people living here. There are at least twenty children around Syr and me, watching and listening to us with great interest.

"Um, so, this church is…?"

"Exactly as you're thinking, Mr. Cranell. This is an orphanage."

The elderly woman is facing us…I've only just been introduced to Mother Maria, but she's smiling at me like an old friend. The half-elf from before, Ruu, and another child are standing at her sides with a tight grip on her arms.

She told me that she's been living with all the children here inside this old abandoned church for quite a while now. This isn't part of some organized program, but the elderly woman explained that they're living happily here. Poor, but finding a way to make it day to day. What's more, she said everything with a smile.

She has long black hair, but it's tied up on top of her head. She's on the thin side, so her facial features are a little more pronounced. Even so, she has a calming air about her. All the children here call her "Mother," and after being on the receiving end of her kind gaze, I understand why.

She must love kids.

"But…if this is an orphanage, that means…"

"Bell, this kind of place isn't all that uncommon on Daedalus Street."

I started a question, unsure about how to ask. Syr speaks up from the chair next to me and offers an explanation.

She says it's impossible to know how many children have been born among the adventurers residing in Orario, but there are a lot of them. And it's not a guarantee that they have parents who have sworn to spend their lives together and work toward a common future. In fact, many babies are the product of single nights of passion or the result of working in the Pleasure Quarter...Anyway, there are many reasons a woman might have to give up her child.

After all, this is Orario. Many adventurers lose their lives in the Dungeon, leaving widows and children behind.

The ones unlucky enough not to be allowed into a deceased adventurer's former familia, as well as the parents who can't handle the responsibility, often resort to abandoning their offspring in this slum, Daedalus Street.

"At first, it was out of pity. I just couldn't bring myself to ignore a child who'd been abandoned by their parents...so I claimed this abandoned church as my own and decided to help these children in my own way."

Maria explains this sad truth all while patting the children on the head.

I hear that she once was one of the women left behind by an adventurer and had never joined a familia. She wasn't fortunate enough to have a child with the man she loved but instead took in a child—abandoned during a rainstorm in the middle of the night—she had found in this slum. She couldn't bring herself to think of the situation as someone else's problem and raised the child as her own.

That sequence of events repeated itself several times, and that's how this place came to be.

"..."

Mother Maria's story still in my ears, I take a look at the children seated around the table.

Every single one of them abandoned by their parents...That's another side of Orario I didn't know about. I can feel the muscles in my face tightening, my heart sinking.

"What's that face for, Little Rookie? We're happy here with Mother, so we don't need your pity."

"S-sorry."

The human boy, Lai, glares at me, the many half-healed scratches on his face bending with his frown.

"Watch your mouth!" Mother Maria scolds him, but I still apologize right away.

He's right…I don't need to feel sorry for them. These children are smiling, laughing every day with a loving mother. I doubt any of them feels like life gave them the short end of the stick.

"Can I, um, ask another question? Do you have enough money…?"

"Yes, enough to manage. We're lucky that several compassionate goddesses lend their assistance."

It'd be impossible to take care of this many kids without a healthy bank account. Mother Maria lightly smiles when I bring it up and lays my fears to rest. She also explains that other than this one, "Maria's Orphanage," there are even more places like this on Daedalus Street. They're all funded by a group of familias, providing them with enough money to keep their heads above water.

One woman would certainly have her hands full taking care of these kids, so I'm sure she's grateful for any help she gets in keeping them fed. She still has that gentle smile on her face.

Maybe I could talk to the goddess, see if we can help, too.

Then again, we don't exactly have much money to spare…

My train of thought takes off when, out of the corner of my eye, I see Syr chuckling to herself as if she's reading my mind.

"Syr has been gracious enough to come by and play with the children ever since we met. She does so much to help while she's here, I don't know what I'd do without her."

"Oh, so that's what's been going on…"

"Hee-hee-hee. Have you solved the case, Detective Bell?"

"I-I guess so…" My cheeks get hot as Syr starts teasing me.

So then, Syr comes out here whenever she has any free time.

Which means that she's playing with these kids when she's not working at The Benevolent Mistress.

"Big Sis Syr brings us delicious food from her restaurant."

"She's been here every day recently..."

The chienthrope girl, Fina, chimes in with a smile on her face, and the half-elf boy (?) Ruu tells me even more in his spacey voice.

Judging from all the excited, happy grins, they want to play with Syr just as much as she wants to be here. That explains where she's been for the better part of these past two weeks while playing hooky from her job at the bar and café.

"This is a secret from everyone, including Lyu, okay?" Syr warned me once I figured out the truth.

It sounds like she thinks they'll be angry with her if they find out she's been playing with kids.

Hmm, I really don't think there'd be a problem if she explained the situation...

But...

Why is she coming here in the first place?

Going back a bit further, how did she meet Mother Maria?

It's going to bother me if I don't ask about it. I turn to do just that, when suddenly...

"Hey hey, enough about that stuff. What's the Dungeon like?"

Lai's champing at the bit. He's even halfway out of his chair.

That gets the other kids going, too. More and more of them jump out of their seats, asking me to tell them stories about being an adventurer.

I look around, trying to figure out if I should. "Please, go ahead." Syr smiles at me from her chair at my side.

While I'm a little surprised by this turn of events, I start talking. Thinking back on my time as an adventurer, I give them a few highlights, jumping around a bit.

Of course, I leave out the battle against the strange Black Goliath because the gag order from the Guild is still in effect. But the kids seem to enjoy hearing about the beautiful quartz in the Dungeon pantry and the time the Goliath chased me on the seventeenth floor.

Seeing that twinkle in their eyes makes me really happy, and I start giving even more details...But then I see the look on Mother Maria's face.

Her eyes are cloudy, almost depressed. "Oh, I'm sorry." She apologizes when she sees me looking at her.

"Many of the children I've raised became adventurers..."

Her eyebrows sink as she smiles sadly.

"A great deal of them joined a familia, went into the Dungeon, and shared their earnings with this church...That is, until they didn't come back."

"Oh..."

"I don't want these little ones to suffer the same fate...That's all."

Being an adventurer is a high-risk, high-reward occupation where your life is always on the line.

There's no better job to have if you want to make money quickly, but at the same time, death is always one wrong step away. And many of the children who were lovingly raised by Mother Maria didn't listen to her pleas, choosing to help the orphanage by going into the Dungeon. They became just like the adventurers who left their families behind...

I should've known. The children might have goaded me into it, but it was careless of me to fill their heads with ideas that glorified the work of an adventurer. Now they probably want to go into the Dungeon more than ever, and history will repeat itself.

What can I say to Mother Maria now? She's so worried about their futures, and I just...Lai suddenly jumps to his feet.

"You don't have to worry about me, Mother! I'm going to the Education District!"

The oldest of the children declares this with a beaming smile on his face.

"I'll study so hard and learn so much and get so strong that I can make lots of money!"

"Well...Of course I won't stop you from going to the Education District..."

"Money's not a problem! There's this thing called a 'scholarship,' isn't there? The Education District is coming back to Orario this year, so everything should work out perfectly!"

"You might be too old to start, Lai…"

The boy grins ear to ear, his brown hair swishing around his head as he excitedly explains his plan. Maria can only force a smile. Fina and the other children start piping up, "I'm going, too!" "And me!" Many hands shoot into the air, following Lai's lead. The large round table comes alive.

Syr watches them, a burgeoning smile on her lips. I seem to be the only one who's confused.

"Education District…?"

"Don't you know?"

"Seriously, Little Rookie? Some adventurer you are!"

Fina and Lai start an avalanche of childish retorts and teasing remarks all aimed at me because I'm clueless. Blushing again, I try my best to laugh it off.

"Hey, have some respect for your elders! And he's not 'Little Rookie'! His name is Bell, yes?"

Syr stands up and comes to my defense.

They quiet down right away, but several of the kids, including Lai, have evil grins on their lips even as they say, "Oka—y."

Well, this is different.

Syr's being an older sister.

I've never heard her raise her voice like that before, and it catches me off guard.

I stare at the side of her face, dumbfounded until…*DING! DONG!*

Bells start ringing on the eastern side of the city. It's noon.

"Oh, it's lunchtime. Well then, let's eat."

With that, Syr puts the large basket onto the table. It's the one that I saw her carrying on the way here.

Flipping open the lid, she takes out one container of food after another. Grilled meat, sandwiches, you name it…There's a little of everything.

So then, the basket she was carrying was filled with food for these impoverished kids.

I missed my chance to learn more about this "Education District," but I can just ask Eina next time I see her.

Happy with that conclusion, I look around the room and...all the children are completely silent.

"Ah...huh? What's wrong?"

"Big Sis's...lunch box..."

Fina's close by, so I ask her what the problem is. The expression on her face is so glum it would make a grown man cry. The other kids, too. Even the ever-distant Ruu has his lips clamped shut.

Wait a minute, didn't they say something about running away from Syr's lunch when I first walked in...? Huh?

Maria smiles wryly as I take a step back.

"Now everyone, dig in!" says Syr, arms open wide and beaming like a goddess as she faces the table.

After the children recover from the mental trauma of seeing Syr's cooking placed in front of them, they slowly but surely extend their hands toward the precious food that will delay starvation for another day.

"Ugh, uhhh."

"Today, again, like last time..."

"Have to eat it...or the food'll...go to waste...!"

Moans and groans fill the room as the kids force the food down their throats.

Starting with Fina, Ruu, and Lai, every face around the table darkens with the first bite of meat or vegetables. Only their love for Mother Maria and the orphanage they call home gives them the will to clean their plates.

...Sure, Syr's cooking always has some unique flavors to it, but...

The contrast between her happy smile and the suffering of the kids around the table is astounding. It can't be that bad, can it? I reach out and take one of the sandwiches to see for myself—*Snatch!*

Syr takes it right out of my hand.

"These aren't for you, Bell."

"Eh? But..."

"I said no."

"O-okay."

I've never felt so much pressure from a smiling face. Giving up now without a fuss is the best option.

Holding the sandwich in her hands, Syr tells me, "I made these lunches today for the children, so it wouldn't be fair to them for you to eat one, Bell." Now I'm just embarrassed. She says she'll go make some tea and takes the empty basket with her into the back of the kitchen.

"Did you see that? Big Sis was acting so girlie…"

"There's someone who she wants to compliment her cooking, for sure…"

Whispering voices start flying everywhere with Syr out of the room. A bead of cold sweat runs down my neck as many little eyes focus on me.

"It's your fault that Syr started making lunches…!"

"She used to bring delicious food from the café every time…!"

"We're guinea pigs…"

Lai glares at me with tears in his eyes, the same as Fina. Ruu is looking blankly off into space, muttering to himself.

It takes me a while, but I think I understand what's going on here.

These children are being sacrificed to protect my stomach.

The tragedy unfolding in front of my eyes is all for me, but I'm too scared to say anything.

I chance a glance at Mother Maria…and she looks away.

"No, no, the food is *edible*, and we are very…grateful…"

All the muscles in my face tense up. I'm at a loss.

"Ughhhh…" Another child's moan echoes off the wall before fading into the air.

"If you have time, would you play with the children?"

As soon as everyone is finished massaging their stomachs, Maria gives me the invitation.

"They seem to have taken a liking to you, Mr. Cranell…"

She smiles at me again, and I have no reason to refuse. So I smile and accept.

I hunch over as the children grab my arms and pull me out of the room to join Syr and the others out in the main chamber.

"Big Sis, story time, story time!"

"Bell, adventurers and monsters!"

Syr joins the girls in the corner, telling nursery rhymes and singing songs.

The boys corral me into the open space in the middle of the chamber. I'm the "monster" in their game before I know it.

Afternoon sunlight pours into the chamber through the broken windows. The children run around on the grass-sprouting tile floor, smiling and laughing.

They drag Syr and me all over the place.

"So, um, little Lai…"

"Lai, just Lai. You're an adventurer, aren't you? Why the heck do you speak like that? Feels weird. Just call everyone by their name!"

I talk with some of the kids amid the playful chaos and laughter.

The human boy, Lai—"just Lai"—has lived here the longest. He'll turn eleven this year.

His skin is covered in small cuts, like he plays outside all the time. There's a bit of a wild air to him, kind of like Welf, in a way. He keeps asking me about the Dungeon even after everything Maria said. I'm sure this boy wants to be an adventurer.

"Hey, Bell, are you Syr's lover?"

"Nothing like that!"

"Why not? Big Sis Syr's really cute. Not much of a cook, but, yeah… She's thinner than she looks. And her boobs are pretty big, too—"

"Don't say any more, please…!"

The chienthrope, Fina, is a blossoming young lady.

She and Lai are the oldest of the kids, and the leaders. Her long cream-colored hair is surprisingly straight. It looks a lot like mine, if my hair were longer and straighter. With her bright eyes and small nose, she'll be a beautiful young woman in a few years or so. She was really nervous when we first met, but she's warmed up to me quite a bit. Warmed up so much that…she's started to say things that shouldn't be said.

"Um, Ruu? Are you a boy or…?"

"…Sleepy."

"I, um, I see…"

The half-elf Ruu is a year younger than Lai, and a strange child.

Thanks to the elvish blood in his veins, the little boy—I think—is probably the handsomest of all the children here. Since Ruu doesn't say much at all and has short dirty-blond hair, I seriously can't tell if this kid is a boy or girl. His mind is always somewhere else, and there aren't any other clues to help me out.

Actually, there are many mixed children at the orphanage, along with humans, animal people, prums, and even a timid Amazon. But every one of them is bubbling over with curiosity and has a ton of energy.

"Big Sis Syr! Let's play!"

"Aww, I wanna play, too!"

"Sure. Everyone will have a turn, so don't fight, okay?"

Syr continues her rounds through the main chamber of the church, playing games with all the kids. I overhear her talking with a few and catch a glimpse of her being pulled in a different direction. Not just the girls, the boys want to play with her, too.

Just like before…This is strange.

I know Syr only as a bar waitress, so seeing her laugh like this, playing games with the kids, giving them hugs and whatnot…it feels so different.

The kids absolutely adore her; I can see it in their eyes. I watch her playing with the kids for a little while, entranced until she peers over her shoulder. She must've noticed my gaze because she's giggling at me.

Cute and beautiful at the same time…My cheeks are getting hot again.

"…?"

Children are on both sides of her, laughing and exchanging smiles. But Lai is sneaking up behind her with an evil grin on his face.

She hasn't noticed him. Lai's eyes flash as if he's spotted a once-in-a-lifetime opportunity to attack a defenseless target from behind——"Gotcha!" He grabs her skirt and flings it up in the blink of an eye.

"!"

"EEK!"

The ruffled white fabric goes up past her belly button. I see it all happen in slow motion, my eyes open wide.

So…so this is…what Gramps was always talking about! The legendary——The hell am I thinking?!

I get a full view of panties the same color as her dress. Now my skin is roughly the same color as an apple, my face burning red.

Her cute little squeal fills the chamber as she quickly pushes the fabric back down and turns to face me before freezing in place. Syr looks me right in the eye.

Her cheeks the color of an overripe peach, she storms up to me.

"Did you see?"

"No, not really, well, I…!"

"You saw, didn't you?"

"Y-yes, but…!"

"You're horrible, Bell!!"

"How was that my fault?!"

Her eyes filled with fire and the tip of her nose bright red, Syr lets the accusations fly. I blush even more and desperately try to stand my ground.

"A boy…A boy saw my panties…Bell, as punishment, you have to do whatever I say!"

"I—What?!"

"If you don't…I'll tell Lyu and the others you peeked up my skirt!"

"That's not fair!!"

I'll be dead by morning if she does that! She's blackmailing me with false charges! I yell back at the red-faced Syr, desperate tears beginning to leak from my eyes.

"…It worked…For the first time ever, I got to flip Big Sis's skirt…"

"You always catch him…No way. Big Sis, was that on purpose?"

"Skill and technique…"

Lai, Fina, and Ruu have gathered around our argument, their eyes wide as they mumble to one another.

I think that's fear in their eyes as they look at her. As for me, on the other hand, they seem to be enjoying my embarrassment...I give in, in the end.

My punishment for seeing under Syr's skirt becomes performing one task—anything she wants me to do.

"Okay, Bell...Take a nap with your head in my lap."

"?!"

"That girl, the Sword Princess, Aiz Wallenstein, has done that for you before, hasn't she?"

Why would she want that?

Wait a minute...How does she know that Aiz...?

"As you know, Bell, *Loki Familia* are regulars at the bar where I work. Their goddess, Loki, seems to like us...and she's quite the talker when drunk, so imagine my surprise when they started talking about the famous Sword Princess..."

"I'll do it, okay! You don't have to say anything else!!"

Sure, it was a while ago, but I remember what was said all too well. My skin flares pink yet again as I yell at the top of my lungs at Syr's extremely calculated verbal strikes.

I knew she was a witch!

"Good. Now, then..."

She happily crouches down, bends her knees, and sits on the floor. Every child in the orphanage is watching her, but she doesn't care. Getting comfortable, she sticks out her knees in my direction.

Skin still bright red, I hesitate for a second. She's looking at me, enjoying the moment and excited about what comes next—but then a light seems to go on in her head.

She's thought of something new, but the grin on her lips gives it away. It's easy to see the gears turning behind those eyes.

"...Bell, has the Sword Princess ever slept in *your* lap, by any chance...?"

"N-no, she hasn't."

Like that would ever happen! I practically choke on the words as they come out.

She locks eyes with me after my answer, and I swear I see a little twinkle.

A few minutes later…

"Wha-ha-ha…"

"…"

It has come to pass: me sitting on the ground, Syr sprawled out on her back, using my thigh as a pillow.

Her cheeks a bright shade of pink, she nuzzles her nose into my leg.

"Um, are we done yet…?"

"No, not yet."

I can't stand all these kids staring at us—it's like they're waiting for something to happen. My only way out of this shame has her head in my lap. I try to bring an end to the humiliation, but my plea is rejected.

This is a punishment from hell. I serve as Syr's pillow until my leg goes completely numb.

We play in that church for hours.

Either they run out of energy, or seeing Syr so comfortable with her head in my lap makes the kids drowsy.

The oldest kids, Lai's group, decide it's time for a nap. They lead the rest of the kids up to one of the rooms on the second floor of the church, yawning all the way.

"How about that, out like a light…"

"Out cold…"

The bedroom on the second floor is just as large as the cafeteria beneath it. The floor is completely covered with blankets.

Building blocks and old picture books are scattered all over the place. It's a kid's playroom in every sense of the word. I thought that some of the kids might need a bedtime story to get to sleep, but all of them are off to dreamland at the drop of a hat.

Cuddled up next to one another like a bunch of sardines in a can, the only sound in the room is their soft breathing.

"…"

"Zzhh…" Syr lightly pats Ruu's head.

She's only a little bit older than me, but watching her kneel next to the kids and smile affectionately makes her look more like a mother. If I didn't know it was Syr, I'd say she was a saint or even a goddess.

Her silver hair gently brushes across the nape of her neck.

"Shall I put you down for a nap, too, Bell?"

"I'll, um, pass."

I blush just as hard as during the "lap nap" incident downstairs, so I hunch over to try and hide my face as I look away and politely decline. She's laughing at me again.

"Mr. Cranell, Syr. Both of you must be tired, yes? Leave the children to me and get some rest."

Maria slowly opens the door and steps inside.

We take her up on the offer. She thanks us again for playing with the kids and sees us off with a short bow. We quietly close the door behind us and leave the room behind.

"Bell, how about a walk?"

Why would I refuse her invitation? I nod my head.

I follow her through the orphanage's main chamber and out to the small yard behind the church.

"A garden…?"

"Mother Maria and the children are growing their own vegetables."

There's a well and a small fenced-in area behind the building. There's not much sunlight back here, so the plants aren't very big, but I can tell that they're well taken care of.

Looking up, I see the back garden is surrounded by layer upon layer of square buildings in an almost random combination. However, there is a patch of blue sky above the labyrinth just overhead.

"Syr…how did you meet Mother Maria and these kids?"

"It was just…a happy accident. I just strolled onto Daedalus Street one day, and…"

There's a path among the buildings that surround the church's backyard. We follow it all the way to a wide road.

Well, a wider road, anyway. It still feels like a back alley would in a different part of the city, except here there are stairs going up and down in every direction. At the same time, there is quite a bit of rubble strewn about, as well as the last remaining walls of collapsed buildings jutting into the air.

Maybe it's because of the bright blue sky, but seeing this isn't all that depressing. I can't see or hear anyone else around, so walking through here with Syr is kind of calming. Even time seems to be passing at a leisurely pace.

We come to a massive building, probably community housing. The wall facing us is thick and tall, almost like the side of a distorted castle. Even so, we gradually make our way past while navigating through the rubble.

"The truth is…I grew up in this slum."

"!?"

"I don't have a mother or father…so maybe that's why I can't leave those children to their fates."

I turn toward her; she's looking off into the distance in front of us. I can see only half her face. The eye in my line of sight is almost completely closed, yet, somehow, twinkling.

Syr grew up dirt poor, as an orphan in this slum—.

This secret I've learned shocks me to my core.

She takes a quick glance at me before going into more detail, explaining she comes to Daedalus Street for the same reasons that Maria chose to open the orphanage.

Once she knew it was there, it had become her routine to visit and interact with the children.

Parents…

I have no memory of my mother and father. I don't even know what their faces looked like.

What I do know is that they both passed away soon after I was born.

But I don't think I was ever lonely. All thanks to Gramps...His happiness, his energy always kept up my spirits.

But...the desire to meet my parents, to hear their voices...I can relate to that feeling.

I'm not all that different from those orphans. They have Maria and Syr to bring light into their lives, just like Gramps did for me.

"But I——I didn't want you to know, Bell."

"Oh?"

Step, step, step. I look back in her direction and see her ascending a flight of stairs that leads to the top of only another pile of rubble.

There's no path through there; she's walking on top of the rubble on purpose. "That's dangerous!" I call up to her. But she just keeps walking, the hem of her white dress dancing around her legs as she goes. It's no use trying to convince her to come down, so I climb up after her.

"What didn't you want me to know?"

"What I do on days like today. Putting a lot of effort into making lunches, running around with a bunch of children...It's embarrassing."

I step carefully on top of the stone slabs as I follow her. She doesn't look back when she answers my question. All I see is her silver hair swaying in the light breeze.

Syr nearly loses her balance when one of the rocks beneath her feet shifts unexpectedly, but she catches herself in time and keeps walking forward.

"I don't really care about that..."

"Well, it was embarrassing for me...Although it never was before today."

Her voice trails off into a whisper. "What did you say?" I call out, asking her to repeat that second part, when...

"Eeek!"

Her foot falls into a crack in the sea of rubble, and she stumbles forward.

I warned her! There's no time to yell at her, though—I have to help!

Dashing forward across the stone slabs, I grab hold of her hand and pull her to my chest.

"…"

"…"

"Whew…" Even before her sigh of relief is over…

Her body is pressed against mine, her eyes raised toward me. Our faces are so close that I can feel her breath.

I can see my white hair and red eyes reflected in her silver ones.

Heat—my skin is heating up all over my body. I can feel her every curve against mine. My cheeks are boiling. Oh, she's blushing, too.

This is a side of her I didn't see at the church—a little flustered. Her true face.

"I…didn't mean to do that."

"Of course you didn't mean to!"

What is this girl saying?

Who in the world would fall like that on purpose?

"S-so embarrassing…"

She steps away from me, hiding her red face in her hands.

Seeing her reaction makes me realize something very important, albeit a bit late.

The reason she came up here, and probably the reason for the lap nap, was because she was ashamed and wanted to hide her "embarrassment."

The straight face was all an act. She had to go out of her way to do embarrassing things on purpose just to put up with her own shame.

"…"

She's older than me, but this is the first time I've seen her act like a girl. It really is strange.

I've always seen her as someone who's got every base covered, always on the ball, as well as polite and friendly.

But after everything I've witnessed and learned today, I don't think I can see her the same way again.

There are some butterflies in my stomach.

My cheeks flush as I look at her shyness; I'm drawn in by that look on her face.

"…Maybe this is a good thing."

"?"

A few heavy heartbeats pass in silence on top of the rubble. Syr looks up from her feet.

There's a carefree smile on her face, cheeks a rosy pink.

"Maybe it was good that you…found out after all.——Because it became a happy memory," she says.

She said that last part without hesitating, even though I can tell she still feels a little awkward.

Now it's my turn to blush. She puts her fingers to her lips and smiles from ear to ear. That's real happiness in her eyes.

I can only open and close my mouth a few times as I look at her beneath the beautiful blue sky.

"_____?"

Suddenly…

We're being watched.

I've recently gotten really good at sensing pairs of eyes focused on me. Reflexes taking over, I spin and look up.

The upper floors of the "castle" community housing.

A balcony is sticking out of a tower overlooking us. And on it is a black and gray catman.

That guy…I've seen him before.

For some reason, his thin frame triggers my memory.

I can't put my finger on it, but I'm sure we've crossed paths somewhere before.

"Bell?"

"!"

I'm facing away from her, and she calls out to me.

"What's wrong?" She tilts her head to the side. I look back up to the top of the building, but the catman has disappeared.

"Was somebody there?"

"Yes…I'm pretty sure."

My voice wavers as I look back and forth between her and the balcony.

Almost as if it was a midday mirage, there's no trace of the cat-man. The only thing left on the balcony is the bright sunshine from overhead.

The sun is starting to go down.

Syr and I were assaulted by a barrage of questions from all the children the moment we got back to Maria's Orphanage.

"Where did you go all by yourselves?" Fina led the charge as one kid after another upped the ante with every question. The two of us somehow manage to hold our own against the avalanche when I hear, "Would you like to stay for dinner?" Maria invites me to join them.

I don't want to make the goddess and the others worry…but I can't ignore the pleading looks on all the kids' faces, and there's Syr's request to consider. So I decide to grab a quick bite and then get home as soon as possible.

I never thought that I'd spend my day off playing with a bunch of friendly kids in an orphanage.

I can't help but grin once I see how happy they are after I agree to stay for dinner. Looks like I've got a bit of time on my hands before it's ready, though.

"…Hey."

"?"

Maria and some of the kids have gone into the kitchen to start preparing the food when I feel a pull on the back of my shirt.

I turn around and see the half-elf Ruu looking up at me with the same blank stare while holding on to the hem of his shirt.

"What's up?"

"Here…"

I bend down to his height as he holds out his hand…with three metal coins in his palm.

"O-oi! Ruu."

"Are you really going to ask?"

"Both of you said you're worried about it…"

Lai and Fina see us talking and dash over to Ruu's side.

Ruu's flat and level tone seems to have answered their questions. Falling silent, they look up at me.

"Um, what's this…?"

"It's our…secret stash."

S-secret stash…?

These three metal coins? A bead of cold sweat runs down the back of my neck as I look at the three valis in the palm of his hand.

"It's a reward…Sorry it's not more."

Okay, now I'm confused. The androgynous half-elf isn't done, though.

"Please accept our quest…"

A darkening sky is far overhead.

What's left of the sun casts us in a dark-red glow as I follow the three children outside and through the back garden.

"Out here?"

"Yes…Not far."

The quest they asked me to complete—well, more like a favor— involves the road filled with rubble that Syr and I walked through earlier this afternoon.

The all-important mission of said quest is to investigate a "mysterious voice" coming from somewhere around here.

"We keep hearing this weird 'uwaa…uwaa' back here!"

"I was sure it was a dog or something like that…but there's nothing here."

Lai and Fina tell me about how they walked through here in the middle of the night recently as a test of courage and heard it firsthand.

Ever since then, they've been avoiding this place yet still hear it from time to time. Apparently it's an unnerving moan of some kind, and they want to know what's making it.

I follow their line of sight out over the sea of rubble.

It's quiet out among the piles of stone and wood, no animals, no nothing...

"......wu...wuaa..."

...I hear it. It's real.

That has to be this mysterious voice the kids are talking about.

They immediately run to hide behind me even as I strain my ears to try and get a better idea of what's out there.

My Status also enhances my senses. Thanks to my sharp ears, it doesn't take me long to find the spot where the voice is coming from under the rubble. It's hard to describe, almost like a cry. I come to a stop directly on top of it, nerves starting to kick in.

It's the ruins of an old building, but...there's no mistake. The voice is coming from directly *below my feet*.

"One, two, three...!"

Grabbing hold of the top piece of stone, I start moving rubble out of the way.

The kids sound really impressed. My Level 3 strength allows me to move even the largest stone slabs and wooden logs out of the way to make a path.

A few minutes later, I take a step back to look at the exposed stone pavement. It matches the rest of the roads perfectly.

...*Wait, isn't that...?*

There's a stone slab sticking out just above the pavement that looks oddly familiar.

A few days ago, during my escape from the Pleasure Quarter—Lady Ishtar's home—Haruhime led me through a series of hidden underground passages. The exits were all hidden by wooden doors and stone caps that looked exactly like this one.

Sure enough, there's just enough space between the stone slab and the rest of the road to grab hold. What's more, the mysterious voice is definitely coming through it.

Slipping my fingers through the crack, I pull the "door" up off the ground.

"Whoa! That's awesome...!"

"Is...is this a secret tunnel?"

"You're amazing, mister…"

I swat the rising dust cloud away from my face as the kids run through the sea of rubble to have a look for themselves.

Hearing the excitement, curiosity, and admiration in their voices sets my train of thought in motion.

More than likely, this tunnel connects directly to the Pleasure Quarter. And, more important, there's something in there at this very moment.

My muscles tense as I silently prepare myself.

It's the same feeling I get before going into the Dungeon. I control my breathing to center my focus.

For the first time today, I feel like an adventurer.

"You three, and Bell, too! My word, what're you doing all the way out here?"

Syr's voice and footsteps sound from the street that leads back to the orphanage.

As bluish darkness covers the sky in the east, she approaches and waves a portable magic-stone lamp at us.

She's probably angry because we left through the back exit without telling anyone. But her silver eyes go wide the moment she sees the open doorway at our feet.

"What is that…?"

"I think it's an entrance to an underground tunnel. Syr, please keep an eye on them while I check it out."

I explain the series of events that led us here before letting her know my plan.

Of course, none of us knows what's down there, so I should investigate by myself first…or at least that was the plan.

"I'm coming, too!" "And me…" "It's…it's a bit scary, but I…"

The kids want to come with me.

What am I supposed to do? Maybe Syr can help.

"After seeing this, you understand how hard it would be for me to just wait here, don't you? I'll be joining you as well."

She said it all with a smile.

Well, it'd be a lie to say I *don't* understand that feeling…I look back at her, eyes half closed in an empty gaze, and fight back the urge to sigh. There's no refusing her at this point.

I agree to let them come along as long as they don't go off on their own and they promise to stay close to my side. "We promise!" come three excited voices on top of Syr's. This is starting to feel like a field trip.

But no, I have to focus. Taking the portable lamp from Syr, I start down the staircase that leads underground.

"Whoa…It looks like the Dungeon down here…"

"It's…very dark…"

"Dusty, too…"

The light from the lamp in my hand cuts through the overwhelming darkness engulfing the stairs.

Stone stairwell, stone walls, stone ceiling…I knew it. This passage looks almost the same as the one I traveled through with Haruhime. Then it's almost a sure thing that that estranged architect designed these tunnels.

Lai is excited, Fina is a little frightened, and Ruu is the same as always. Their voices echo off the walls as we go farther and farther down. Proceeding as carefully as possible, I catch a glimpse of something embedded in the stone wall—a lamp. Syr sees it, too. She reaches up and—*bzzt!* The lamp comes to life, making a small hum and lighting the tunnel enough for our eyes to adjust.

There are more lamps spaced out at intervals farther down the tunnel. With every step I take, I'm more and more certain that this is connected to the same path that I took when I ran away from the Pleasure Quarter.

Then, as the kids' curiosity is starting to reach its peak…the mysterious cry sounds from deeper in, louder than ever before. All of us pause to catch our breath.

"Stay quiet."

With whatever it is making that sound close by, I whisper to the kids to make sure they don't draw unwanted attention.

My serious tone must've caught them off guard, because all three freeze like statues, their mouths shut tight. Syr, looking as composed as ever, gives me a quick nod, and I leave the kids to her.

I have allies with me when I go into the Dungeon. Just having them there gives me strength but...I'm the only one who can fight right now. No matter what happens, I have to protect them.

The Divine Knife is still tucked snugly against my waist. Of course, I don't have any armor on. My item pouch...has only the three metal coins I received for accepting this quest. I'm completely unprepared for a fight.

A sense of the unknown overtakes me. I can't get this feeling in the Dungeon because it has been explored by a countless number of my predecessors. Now I'm the one making headway. Fully aware of my surroundings, I scout ahead to the bottom of the staircase.

"Uwaa...uh...Uhhaa."

A dark, open space. All I can tell is that I'm in a decently wide chamber and that the noise is coming from the opposite corner, completely shrouded in black shadows.

—No human or animal makes that sound.

All the muscles in my face tighten as I tell Syr and the kids to wait in the stairwell and shine my light into the dark corner.

It illuminates the owner of the sound that was neither a howl nor a cry.

"———Uhooo."

Emerging from the darkness are two curled horns, dark skin, flaming red hair, and a towering body frame.

The light from my lamp reflects off its golden eyes, making them flash like jewels in the darkness. Suddenly, I can't breathe.

Two legs and two arms, just like a Minotaur. This thing making noises—this *monster* is of the large-category variety. It springs to its feet with a powerful jump from where it was kneeling on the floor.

"Cover your ears!"

The monster unleashes a wall of sound at the same moment I shout the warning over my shoulder.

"UHWOOOOOOOOOOOOOOOOOOOOOOOOOOOOOOOOOOO OOOOOOOOO!"

Goose bumps cover my skin as the monster's fierce howl passes over me.

I have to protect myself. It's too strong for me to worry about taking care of anyone else.

What the hell is something like this doing underneath the slum? Its bright eyes flash, blood pumping through its veins and itching for a fight—it charges, the howl's echoes still shaking the chamber behind it.

I thrust my right arm out in front of the oncoming creature.

"Firebolt!!"

Flaming scarlet bolts blast their way out of my hand and connect with the creature's torso.

It howls in pain, completely blindsided by my Swift-Strike Magic. It staggers backward amid the scarlet flames. *Now!* I draw the Divine Knife and go on the offensive.

I drop the magic-stone lamp at the entrance and use the window created by my magic to get close to the monster, which is burning like a torch in the middle of the chamber.

"OHU, WHOOOOOOOOOOOOOOOOOOOOOOOOOOOOOOOOO OOOOOOOOOOOOO!"

"!"

Its pupil-less eyes flash with murderous intent as it swings a mighty fist directly into my path. Surprised by its quick reflexes and incredible strength, I duck out of the way and bring my knife to bear. A dark-purple arc carves through the air.

But it pulls back just in time, my knife cutting through empty air by the slimmest of margins. I see a look of shock on its face—shock that I somehow managed to dodge its attack. But that disbelief quickly turns to anger, and it throws another punch. I move once again to engage.

This monster—it's a barbarian! These things belong in the Deep Zone!

Thanks to the flames of Firebolt, I can finally see its whole body. What I do see delivers yet another shock to my system.

Standing over two meders tall, it's a large-category monster—a barbarian.

First spotted on the thirty-seventh floor, the Guild classifies them as Level 3—or even 4!

So what's it doing here?

Don't tell me—it's a leftover from Monsterphilia!

As much as I don't want to remember, flashes of the time when a Silverback chased me around this labyrinth fill my mind.

This beast that has managed to elude both adventurers and Guild extermination teams, this unidentified monster has been lurking underground all this time?

It continues to unleash powerful punches even as my brain endures more surprise and anguish.

Every time one of those massive limbs comes careening toward my head, I dive out of the way and slice with my jet-black knife. However, its unpredictable movements, coupled with the strength of a second-tier adventurer—possibly stronger than that—prevent me from getting into point-blank range. What's worse, my counter-attacks aren't hitting.

This monster is really, really strong. Every time I think I've got a window to strike, the creature either knocks my knife out of the way or steps out of its path before coming back for more.

It's like trying to fight a storm. But wait a minute, what's all that? *It's covered in blood?*

I certainly didn't inflict those wounds.

The light of its still-burning skin reveals several closed gashes surrounded by streaks of dried blood. Why would that be?

The barbarian's glowing yellow eyes become bloodshot. It's looking at me like I pose the biggest threat that it's ever seen. It's terrified—and it's trying to kill me with everything it's got.

It recognizes me as an enemy and continues to dodge my attacks while setting up its own counters. It knows how to fight using strategy and techniques!

I know this feeling—

I feel like I'm fighting another adventurer—no, not quite.

It's more like…that one-horned Minotaur.

Rather than relying on instinct and brute strength in battle, this beast is fighting with a sense of self—

My eyes tremble as I see flashes of that phantom of my past. I shake the images out of my mind, plant my foot, and charge straight in.

One of its massive fists swings right at me, but I jump over it just in time. With its arm out of the way, I've got an open shot at its lower back! I swing my knife as hard as I can.

"_____!"

A stream of blood flies as the barbarian's howl echoes.

"Nice one!"

The effects of the howl must've worn off because Lai and the others are poking their heads into the chamber.

"_____"

Their excited voices in the background, I stand tall in front of the wounded monster as it clutches its latest injury.

My ears are still ringing from that last roar.

Most of it was just like a regular beast's howl, but there was also anger, pain, and a hint of sadness to it.

I've never heard a beast's lamentation before. Words have left me. *What is this monster...?*

Anguish in a monster's howl? And I'm feeling sorry for it?

While I stand there contemplating these strange new emotions, the injured barbarian's eyes flash yet again. Its long jaws open as its tongue lashes out.

"Gah!"

It catches me flat-footed, its tongue nailing me right in the chest.

I tried to jump out of the way, but there wasn't enough time. Since I don't have any armor, the blow knocks me off my feet, and I tumble across the cold stone floor.

A long slash of burning pain sears its way across my chest. *Focus!* I scream at myself for having left myself that wide open to attack. I finally come to a stop at the opposite end of the chamber, away from the stairwell entrance. Ignoring the pain all over my body, I climb to my feet.

"Don't hurt my friend!"

Then I see him.

Lai, inside the chamber, throws a rock at the monster to draw his attention away from me.

"_____UHOO."

The rock hits its target, and the barbarian turns around to face him.

The child freezes in the face of the ferocious monster——It sees Lai as another enemy and charges him.

"NO——!"

"OHWOOOOOOOOOOOOOOOOOOOOOOOOOOOOOOOO OOOOOOOOO!!"

I launch my body at the monster, putting everything I have into stopping the beast, but I won't make it in time.

Syr rushes into the chamber and embraces the terrified boy, using her body as a shield.

I thrust my right arm forward, willing the instinct to run away out of my mind, and take a deep breath to scream at the top of my lungs.

"——UGAA!"

But my flaming lightning never thunders.

Instead, a single silver javelin tears through the air like a comet and punctures a hole straight through the barbarian's chest.

"——Ah."

It doesn't even have time to let out a dying breath. The monster's magic stone, along with most of its rib cage, is gone, leaving a gaping hole. It falls and dissolves into ash.

*Whoosh...*Thick stillness descends on the chamber that makes everything before feel like an illusion. The only proof that our battle ever took place is the fact that the drop item Barbarian Skin in the middle of the pile of ash is charred. Smoke wafts into the air.

Syr and Lai, still planted on the chamber floor, slowly, cautiously, look over their shoulders toward the entrance. But I can see directly behind them. The figure standing there is clear as day to me in the dim light. His presence is overwhelming.

Black and gray fur. A short, lithe body line.

He's the catman I saw earlier this evening.

"...Uh...umm!"

He jumps over Syr and Lai with nary a sound, landing softly in front of the pile of ash, and retrieves his javelin. I try to say something as I run up to him.

I have to thank him for saving us—all of us.

"Can't even protect women and children, worthless rodent."

The pressure coming from his glaring eyes silences me on the spot.

"I...I'm sorry."

"..."

He's right. There's nothing I can say, only apologize as I look at my feet.

If he hadn't been here, something horrible might've happened to Syr and these children that I'd never have been able to undo. An adventurer has failed the moment he allows average citizens to be exposed to danger.

The catman ignores me, turning his back as I fall into a vicious spiral of powerlessness and piercing shame.

He doesn't say anything as he walks back to the chamber entrance.

"Vana Freya...A top-tier adventurer?!"

Lai silently watches the man walking past and suddenly yells with the most excitement I've heard in his voice all day.

Vana Freya—as in the guy from *Freya Familia*?

Ishtar Familia collapsed not all that long ago. I was right in the thick of things when it happened, and this man was one of the adventurers who wiped out that once-powerful familia. He's awe-inspiring and intimidating at the same time.

But wait, that reminds me.

His voice...That night after training with *Loki Familia*'s captain, Aiz Wallenstein, on the city wall, a cat person attacked her in the middle of the street. The attacker had the same voice.

"..."

He comes to a stop in front of Syr as I gawk at him from behind.

He says nothing, only slightly bows his head before exiting the chamber for good.

Syr stays put but watches him go as a small smile appears on her face.

"S-Syr, are you okay?"

"Bell."

I still haven't recovered from the shock, but I rush over to her side to make sure that she and the children are all in one piece.

I apologize over and over for putting them in this life-threatening situation, even though she smiles and waves me off, saying it's fine.

"What's this, Little Rookie? You need Vana Freya to save you!" Lai doesn't seem the least bit sorry for his actions. Those words strike me like a bolt of lightning, send me deeper into that vicious spiral. That is, until Syr unleashes a tirade of a lecture, her words turning into whips that leave even Fina and Ruu in tears. I break out in a cold sweat almost immediately.

"Um, Vana Freya...Do you know him?"

"Yes. He's an adventurer who drops by the bar from time to time." We stare at the pile of ash for a few moments before I break the silence. She happily tells me about one of The Benevolent Mistress's regular customers. It sounds like they've become acquaintances.

"Isn't he...a little scary...? It was hard to be so close to him. Syr, you're amazing..."

"Oh, I don't think so. Actually, he has a really sensitive tongue. Whenever there's a hot drink in front of him, he curls up with the mug in his hands and blows on it until the steam goes away. It's really cute when he does that."

The words flow from her mouth easily; she giggles to herself as if she's remembering that image.

She just used the word *cute* to describe a top-tier adventurer...Is Syr secretly a powerhouse or just plain naive?

I force a smile.

"Does this mean the quest is over...?"

"Ah, yeah, I think so. Nothing else seems out of place..."

"I've never been so scared."

Ruu tugs at my arm. The two of us take a quick look around the chamber, checking every dark corner.

Fina lets her shoulders relax, a deep breath slowly flowing out of her lungs.

Just to be sure, I grab the magic-stone lamp and do a lap around the chamber, thoroughly checking every nook and cranny. I discover a connecting tunnel at the other end, but it's caved in. The only other exit to the chamber is the stairwell that we uncovered, so probably the monster didn't have anywhere else to go. So the cries we heard were because it was trapped, or maybe…

It might be a good idea not to get carried away. I'll let the Guild know the next time I'm there and let them worry about it.

After making sure the children promise never to come back this way—Syr's silent smile is scaring Lai and the other two half to death, so I'm sure they won't—we go back up the stairs, place the stone slab back over the entrance, and stamp it down tight.

It's already nighttime, the starry night here to greet us now that we're all back on the surface.

I'm sure that Maria is worried about us by now…

Wait, isn't…?

The children run circles around us, recounting their first adventure as we walk back to the orphanage. Syr's at my side as something important comes into my head.

Vana Freya…Isn't *Freya Familia* fighting outside the city walls right now?

I take a look at the moon overhead, wondering if something has happened.

"How fares the battle?"

A silver-haired goddess asked as she walked around inside a tent illuminated by magic-stone lamps.

Thirty kirlos due east from Orario, a beautiful starry night spread out over *Freya Familia*'s forward base.

The few followers accompanying her huddled around a boiling pot, ladling soup into their bowls. Meanwhile, Freya removed her robe and gave it to a human girl inside the largest tent in the facility. "Thank you, Helen," said the goddess as her follower gave a deep bow before leaving the tent.

The goddess took a seat upon her throne and looked up at an exceptionally large boaz, Ottar. He opened his mouth to speak.

"Enemy formations are in pieces. Hedin, Grale, and our most

powerful fighters are pursuing their broken ranks individually. Signal flares have been spotted, so one can only assume they have captured their targets."

"We should have done this from the start."

Driving Rakia's forces away from the city had been only a waste of time. Freya said she regretted not rounding them up all at once as she leaned back into the ornate chair.

Having a tremendous penalty levied against her by the Guild, she couldn't ignore their orders to remain on the battlefield at all times during the invasion. To the Goddess of Beauty, it was one big hassle.

"This might be one minor detail, but the enemy soldiers seem to be shaken, restless. Perhaps something has happened?"

"It's the work of *Loki Familia*, after they left us to do the dirty work. They must've succeeded."

The goddess wasted no time in responding to Ottar's observation.

Freya picked up a glass of wine from the round table next to her chair and brought it to her lips. At that moment, a catman appeared at the entrance of the large tent.

"Pardon the intrusion."

"Welcome back, Allen. I do hope your time away from the battlefield has been restful."

Allen Fromel—whose gods-assigned title was Vana Freya—made a polite bow as Freya showed her appreciation for his return.

He came to a stop next to Ottar directly in front of his goddess, answering politely yet retaining a sharp tone to his voice.

"That it was. However, that girl of yours left the bar…and I lost the better part of two days keeping an eye on her."

Allen's voice was laced with agitation as he continued speaking to Freya.

"If your Ladyship would issue a direct order, one telling her not to wander off on her own…it would be greatly appreciated."

Freya set her wine back on the table, a grin on her lips.

"Hee-hee, surely Syr is grateful for your actions?"

"…"

"Didn't she smile at you?"

Allen closed his mouth and fell silent. There was nothing he could say to that.

However, his usual cold, emotionless expression was lined with a very faint shade of pink. The long tail emerging from his waist twitched side to side.

In very much the same way a teenager would deny interest in the opposite gender, the young man endured the embarrassment.

The boaz said nothing as he watched his ally put up with the light teasing.

"Got a staring problem, Ottar?"

"..."

"I'm nobody's clown! Scram, would you?"

Allen's face flushed red as he told off the giant man. Ottar, however, didn't even flinch.

Standing over two meders tall, *Freya Familia*'s commander listened to his subordinate's wishes and stepped outside the tent.

The catman gritted his teeth as he watched Ottar's boulder-like shoulders slip through the cloth door.

"Hee-hee-hee..." Freya covered her mouth with her fingertips, enjoying the spectacle of her two followers' one-sided argument. Allen blushed even darker as he hunched over and turned to face his goddess once again.

Once her laughter had dissipated, Freya picked up her wineglass and took another sip.

"I'd love to return to Orario as soon as possible. On the other hand, I rarely leave the city anymore. This might be a great chance to just go and see what there is to see."

"...For you, My Lady, I would gladly become your chariot. Tell me where you would like to go and I shall take you there."

"My my, so dependable."

Freya made an offhanded remark about traveling, since they were already outside the city, but Allen took it as more than the musings of a goddess and swore to become her legs if need be.

The unquestioning loyalty of her follower brought a smile to Freya's lips.

"Allen. Have you seen Ahnya?"

"I've already severed all ties with that simpleton."

"No, we can't have that. She's the only sibling, the only family you've got, yes? I didn't separate you from her just to be cruel."

"……Fine, then."

The catman let a few moments pass before responding, and even then, he didn't appear enthusiastic about the idea as he nodded to her.

"Such a problem child," said Freya with a grin before drinking the last of her wine.

Her eyes shone like the moon in the night sky far overhead.

"Ah! She's back, meow!"

The first thing she heard through the door was Ahnya's excited voice.

The sunlight was just beginning to warm the streets of the city. Syr, in her waitress uniform, watched as all the other staff members came to greet her with smiles on their faces.

"I'm back, everyone."

"Meow, there's so much work to do because you've been gone so long, meow! We're going to work your fingers to the bone to teach you a lesson, meow!"

"Chloe, the work yet to be completed only remains because you missed your shift. That punishment should be yours."

"I was getting so worried because you'd been gone so long. So, where'd you go?"

"Sorry, Runoa, but it's a secret."

Syr turned to Runoa to respond, holding a finger up to her lips, as Chloe and Lyu broke into an argument next to them.

The happy smile on the city girl's face made Runoa moan. "Still…?"

"…Meow? Something happened with the boy?"

"What?"

"Mee-hee-hee, with that good mood, you look like a love-struck young lady, meow."

There was no fooling Chloe's eyes and instincts. The young catgirl giddily swished her tail side to side and stepped closer.

Syr cupped her burning cheeks with her hands, unable to keep the grin off her face.

The staff members all smiled in unison with twinkles in their eyes, as if they'd discovered something juicy, when the owner of the bar, a dwarf named Mia, appeared on the other side of the counter.

"Ya sure ya're ready ta come back?"

"Yes…I'm fine, now."

Mia took a look at the silver eyes staring up at her and said, "Then stop yer dillydallyin' an' get ta work." She huffed through her nose and turned her back.

"Same goes fer the lot o' ya!" With that, the rest of the staff members quickly returned to what they should be doing to get The Benevolent Mistress ready for business.

Syr still had the same smile on her face as she went to hang the OPEN sign on the front door to start the day.

"—Thank you for coming to The Benevolent Mistress. Welcome."

The city girl smiled to greet the day's first customers as they walked to the front door.

© Suzuhito Yasuda

CHAPTER 6
A CERTAIN GODDESS'S LOVE SONG

"The hell's going on out there?!"

Wham! A fist slammed onto a table set up in the middle of a cloth tent.

The clenched fist belonged to a male deity. The followers of Ares cowered in fear of their leader's infuriated howls as his golden mane sparkled in the dim light.

"Just as I said, our warriors are being captured by Orario's forces. Out of our original thirty thousand troops, at least ten thousand are now in the hands of the enemy."

"I know that! What I'm asking you is why! Why, Marius?"

"Because Orario's adventurers are stronger than the monsters in our worst nightmares, that's why."

The human the god had called Marius remained surprisingly calm in the face of Ares's rage. Every one of his simple, straightforward answers was accompanied by a long sigh.

They were in *Ares Familia*'s main base.

Far from the battles taking place against Orario's Alliance, near the Deep Forest Seoro, a meeting attended by Rakia's top generals was taking place.

However, it had deteriorated into a useless, one-sided shouting match the moment that Ares had learned of the horrid state of their forces.

"Considering the injured and our captured allies, there is no hope for the front lines to stand their ground, let alone press forward. To make matters worse, merchants have been draining our war funds left and right…"

"Those bastards…DAMN YOU ORARIOOOOOOOOOOOOOO!"

Ares reared back his head and roared at the ceiling of the tent. Marius, on the other hand, let out another long sigh. The rest of the generals were so scared of their god that only Marius, the highest-ranking mortal present, was able to utter negative comments.

The human's honey-colored hair was a far cry from the god's brilliant lion's mane. However, he stood 180 celch tall and had a decently muscular build that wasn't too thick or too thin. He certainly looked like he belonged among royalty. Still only twenty years old, if he weren't tired and at his wits' end, his handsome features matched with a full suit of armor would make this military commander a dignified knight on the battlefield.

His pride as their commander had been entirely crushed by repeated failures in the battle against the Alliance—his grudge against their god was threatening to come to light, mood worsening by the second. Willing himself to remain calm, he sighed yet again.

"I'm sure you're aware, but we can't continue this war, now can we? Let's go home, Lord Ares. If you've learned your lesson, please stop this pointless invasion of Orario."

"GRAH…! Marius, you insolent coward! And your father, Martinus, always obeyed my every command without question!"

"—That's what earned him the nickname 'Moronic King'—by trying to make your every whim a reality, dammit!"

"H-how dare you speak to me that way?! I'm this close to revoking your rank and exiling you from the kingdom!"

"You won't have to. I'll surrender this position right now! That way you won't care if I leave the country and fulfill my dream of becoming an adventurer in Orario, right?"

"I refuse. You will do no such thing!"

"So which is it?"

"My prince!" "My prince!" The other generals sensed their red-faced young commander was about to lash out and quickly moved to restrain him.

The crown prince of Rakia had been brought along for this invasion to provide him with valuable experience on the battlefield. The young second-in-command of *Ares Familia* frowned, a face the envy of every man in his kingdom twisting in an expression of anger as the argument between him and their god, practically a daily ritual at this point, continued to escalate.

With a spirit so strong that it called the fidelity of the queen into question, the prince unloaded all his frustration and anger onto the warmongering god.

"Wake up…! No matter what we do, Garon's attempt to bring Welf Crozzo back into the fold has failed. In fact, the Guild is demanding money to secure the release of Garon and his men. Our safety net is gone. Dragging out this war is pointless."

"GRAHHHH…!"

Marius had finally cooled off to the point that he could look Ares in the eye and state the facts. The deity roared back.

It was true. The strategy to obtain Crozzo Magic Swords, their trump cards, was no longer on the table. The war had lost its meaning. Ares's vision of using Welf's power to revive their magic-sword battalion and trap the Alliance forces in a pincer attack was now nothing more than a dream beyond a dream.

Marius had never believed that plan would succeed from the start. He wanted nothing more than to retreat as he locked eyes with the God of War…However, the only emotion in the deity's glaring red eyes was an intense desire to not lose.

"All right, fine, then—I will go into Orario myself!"

"WHAT?!"

"If you worthless excuses for soldiers can't get the job done, I will personally acquire those swords with my own hands! With them at our side, the glory days of the past will once again be in our grasp…!"

"Don't tell me you're planning to kidnap Welf Crozzo? He's Level Two! Raising a hand against him would be suicide! Instant death, I tell you!"

"Enough of that instant-death talk! The target is not the Crozzo boy, it's his goddess—Hestia!"

Apart from Marius, every general in the tent stood wide-eyed and slack-jawed at Ares's plan to kidnap a deity.

"It's just one tiny goddess. I'm sure you maggots can take her from one place to another, right? So, I lead a strike force, we capture her, and we demand Welf Crozzo in a hostage exchange with Orario! Ah-ha-ha-ha-ha! It's so perfect, I even surprise myself sometimes!"

"That is the worst, most underhanded ploy imaginable, and it came from your mouth! How the hell do you plan on getting inside the wall in the first place—?"

"How could I have been so blind; this should have been the plan from the start! If the king—no, the god—doesn't lead his men, they cannot follow! Marius, prepare my horse! We leave under cover of darkness, before that dreadful Freya and her lot know what's coming!"

"That fool, that divine imbecile…!"

It was impossible to sway the divine king's mind once he made a decision. The other generals quickly jumped to their feet and began preparations. Their youthful commander frowned as he followed the golden-haired god out of the tent at a run.

And so it was that the army of Rakia launched its last gambit at the behest of its god.

The final battle to decide the outcome of this war was at hand. Orario's patrols, few and far between and practically sleeping on the job, were completely unprepared for an attack so reckless, so crazy that no one could predict its descent on the city.

Today is just as peaceful as any other day inside the city walls.

The sun is shining brightly overhead on a morning when, unlike usual, the army of Rakia is fighting outside the city wall. Word is that they're trying to draw out the war.

I make my way quickly through the hallways of my home, listening to the birds singing outside the windows, when I spot someone just up ahead and call out to her.

"Miss Haruhime."

Her golden, fluffy fox tail is wagging back and forth beneath the skirt of her maid outfit.

She's holding a large basket in both arms, pressing it up against her chest as she looks over her shoulder at me.

"Master Bell. Good morning to you."

A beautiful smile appears on her cute face as the fox ears on top of her head bow to me because she can't bend over with the basket in her arms.

It's still early, before breakfast. The smells wafting up from the kitchen are making me hungry, while Haruhime attends to the housework before we go into the Dungeon. The basket is filled with the freshly washed laundry for everyone in the familia. She's on her way outside to hang it all up to dry.

I say good morning and walk right up next to her.

"Do you need any help? I'd be glad to lend a hand."

"It—It's quite all right, Master Bell. This duty has been assigned to me; I don't want it to take up any of your time…"

"It's no problem. Please let me help."

I quickly take the top half of the mountain of laundry in the basket off the pile. Haruhime's hands are literally full, so she can't stop me.

She might have a Status, but carrying that many wet clothes must be a real challenge. She looks back at me with timid eyes, insisting that she could do it by herself. But I just smile at her and carry my half of the pile outside to help her hang everything up.

Everything is set up in the inner courtyard next to the hallway. I help Haruhime tie a clothesline from one wall to another in the place where the afternoon sun will be strongest and start pinning clothes to it.

I leave all the laundry for the goddess, Lilly, Mikoto, and Haruhime to the fox girl while I take care of Welf's and my own stuff. I know it can't be helped, since both boys and girls of different races are living here together under one roof, but I do everything I can to avoid looking at the girls' clothes on the other side of the line. Haruhime is blushing, too. I doubt she'll hang any underwear out here.

My cheeks are feeling a bit hot as well. Maybe talking with her will help make this a little less awkward.

"Um, Haruhime? Are you getting used to living here?"

"Yes, I am. All thanks to Lady Hestia's, Lady Lilly's, Sir Welf's, and Miss Mikoto's assistance."

She adds that of course I've been a great help as well and smiles with all her heart.

It's not that empty, hollow smile she used to make while living in the Pleasure Quarter. It's a gentle smile, so warm that it feels like the morning sun is shining on me.

I smile back, my eyes almost closing at the same time. I'm glad I got to see her real smile again today.

"Unfortunately…my inefficiency is always causing trouble for everyone…just like Master Bell right now."

Suddenly that shining smile is replaced by clouds.

"Miss Haruhime, this is nothing…and no one feels that way."

"No, this is the only way for me to be useful. I must work harder; I must improve…"

She doesn't seem to believe me. Looking away, her apologetic gaze falls onto the courtyard lawn between us. She rubs her hands up and down the sleeves of her maid outfit, tail listlessly drifting around her ankles.

Despite what she's saying, I know that she's working really hard. Probably a little too hard.

Laundry, cooking, and cleaning, all on top of the Dungeon prowling. Not only is she a big help around our home, she's also a dual supporter and sorcerer in the Dungeon. She's not used to looking out for herself in the labyrinth, so I'm sure being in that position in the back of our formation is incredibly stressful for her.

The last of the laundry on the line, I turn to face her. Scratching the back of my neck, I string some words together.

"Um, Miss Haruhime…I think you shouldn't push yourself so hard."

"Eh?"

"I remember back when I first joined the familia, I was determined to do as much as I could around our home, cooking and cleaning, so that the goddess didn't have to bother with it…"

Back when *Hestia Familia* was first formed, it was just the goddess and me.

I made money in the Dungeon and did the housework, just like what Haruhime is doing right now. In the end, I was trying too hard and got sick, which ended up causing more problems for the goddess.

The circumstances might be a bit different now, but there are times the body can't keep up with what the mind wants to do. Having a Status doesn't change that. I explain all this to Haruhime. She listens with a surprised look on her face.

"So, what I'm trying to say...How do I put this?"

I'm sure that speeches like this roll off Ouka's and Finn's tongues with no problem. Compared to the other familia leaders, this is pathetic...Even so, I put my thoughts into words.

"...Rather than push yourself, I'd be happier seeing you...asking for help."

I smile, my face burning again.

I wish I could wrap this up with some kind of inspiring speech, but it's not coming. I scratch my cheek.

She looks at me with quivering eyes, her hands together over the feminine curves in the top part of her maid outfit.

Her eyes start to water, almost as if her spirit has been washed clean by what I said...Her cheeks have taken on a light-pink hue.

"W-well, then...May I ask for Master Bell's help right now?"

She's looking up at me through her lashes, almost like she's shy. Even her voice sounds a bit slow, spacey.

She's taking my advice! This is great, I'm so happy! Suddenly, she holds out her right arm.

"Would it be all right if you...held my hand...?"

"Huh?"

I blink a few times. Where did that request come from?

I freeze in place, but I'm very aware of the heat pulsing in my cheeks. Sweat running down my face, I try to find the right words to politely decline...Even so, she doesn't take her hand back, waiting and blushing even darker.

Looking at her fox ears and tail twitching like that, I kinda feel sorry for her. What should I do? I really have no idea, but even so, I extend one trembling hand and take hold of her thin fingers.

"Ah..."

They're cold.

Not just cold, Haruhime's fingers are freezing.

It's already summer, too...Probably doing everyone's laundry this morning chilled her to the bone.

I move my fingers to encompass her entire hand out of reflex, and I see her shoulders rise. Her whole body is quivering, right down to her tail.

"W-would asking you...to use both hands...be acceptable...?"

"Um, sure..."

I grant her request right away.

I bring up my left hand and hold her cold right hand against both of my palms. Then she puts her left hand outside of my right, our hands overlapping like a double handshake.

...What...is this?

Her trembling has stopped. She closes her eyes and squeezes my hands as if to absorb every bit of their warmth. Her cheeks—and mine—are bright red.

My heart rate picks up, but my mind starts slowing down, drifting.

"—What do you think you're doing, Haruhime?"

"Gasp!"

I've been holding her hands for about a minute.

Suddenly, a frighteningly low voice calls out her name from nearby. She almost jumps out of her skin.

It catches me by surprise, too. I look over and there's the goddess, standing with her legs shoulder width apart, arms at her sides, and glaring right at us.

"HIYAA!" She jumps forward, twin black ponytails whipping behind her like ocean waves as she delivers a knife-hand strike to our hands.

Ouch!!

Haruhime and I break apart immediately.

"Bell might have brought that on himself, but you're quite the troublemaker, Haruhime. I'm going to have to keep an eye on you whether I like it or not, aren't I?"

"L-Lady Hestia! This is a misunderstanding! There's no deeper meaning…!"

"No deeper meaning? That burning-red face of yours says otherwise!"

Haruhime might have grown up with a silver spoon in her mouth and not know much about the real world, but that innocence seems to have gotten under the goddess's skin. I can feel the anger emanating from her.

Her blue eyes glaze over in a flash of fury directed at the renart, forgetting all about me for the moment. But those thrashing ponytails…I can't move—part of it could be that she saw my pathetic attempt at being the leader. It's so embarrassing! My silence triggers Haruhime into a series of gestures, desperately trying to explain the situation.

Once she gets to the part about my telling her to ask for help, the goddess's blue gaze shifts in my direction. Surprisingly, Lady Hestia makes a gentle face and crosses her arms as soon as Haruhime finishes.

"Oh, I see. Well, nothing we can do about that—."

"Th-then you're willing to overlook this…!"

"—Is what you thought I was going to say, HUHHHHHHHHH?"

"M-m-m-my deepest apologies!"

Lady Hestia is halfway through an exaggerated, bighearted nod when she suddenly thrusts both fists high into the air in a feint of epic proportions. Haruhime recoils in fright, shrinking back with her hands covering her head. The goddess is waving her fists in the air, her breasts, even bigger than Haruhime's, jumping about in sync with her flailing.

Something seems missing in this interaction between a former member of the nobility and the furious goddess.

"Haruhime...I forgot to mention this before, but there are rules in my familia. Of course impure relationships between boys and girls are off limits, but that includes holding hands!"

"Ehhhh?"

The goddess's words hit Haruhime like a brick wall.

But, um, this is the first time I've heard that rule...

I've got a feeling that not being allowed to take hold of each other's hands might cause problems in the Dungeon...

"I was one of the top three virgin goddesses of Tenkai! Morals are important and will be protected!" the goddess declares. Haruhime doesn't know what to do; she just keeps glancing between Lady Hestia and me until her head droops.

"I have no excuse, Lady Hestia...I shall be more careful in the future."

"Good. As long as you understand, that's fine."

Haruhime looks really depressed as the goddess solemnly nods above her.

She makes herself as small as possible, saying that she will obey the rules of the familia and turns her back to me———Wait, what's that?

A flash of gold coming from below her waist. Her tail zips toward me.

It wraps itself around my wrist like it has a mind of its own.

"   "
...

"   "
...

"   "
...

Her soft tail squeezes my wrist a few times, while the goddess and I stand there completely silent.

Haruhime's body language is so downtrodden and compliant, but the fox ears on top of her head are flicking around in all directions.

"HIYAA!"

"EEEEEK!"

The goddess's second knife-hand strike knocks Haruhime's tail to the floor.

The renart girl lets out a cry.

Lady Hestia descends on her like a raging inferno. Haruhime's on her hands and knees, bowing over and over while apologizing with all her might. I take in the spectacle, sweating under the early summer morning sky.

"Is everyone listening? I won't tell you not to form relationships, but morals must be respected."

The goddess has gathered everyone together after breakfast and makes an announcement.

We're in the manor's spacious living room. All of us were summoned to the main table before going into the Dungeon.

Today is the goddess's first day off from her part-time job in a while. She makes eye contact with each of us, one by one.

"So that's why opposite genders are forbidden to physically touch each other. Hand-holding is a definite no-no."

"That's tyranny!"

The goddess's eyes were closed as the words rolled off her tongue. However, Lilly is quick to object.

Haruhime, the one who caused this meeting, looks really sorry. Still dressed in her maid outfit, she served tea to everyone before quietly taking a seat in her chair, trying to stay as unnoticed as possible.

Well, all familias have rules that are decided by their gods and goddesses, and this seems to be one of them…but I think that forbidding physical contact between boys and girls is going a bit too far…

"In that case, Lady Hestia is also subject to this rule, yes? Lady Hestia must never touch Mr. Bell or Mr. Welf for any reason!"

"I-I'm a goddess!"

"That doesn't matter! How can a goddess expect her followers to obey a rule that she won't obey herself?"

She's right—my Status will never be updated! Other objections flow in from around the table, asking her not to make such strange rules out of the blue as Lilly and the goddess's argument spreads like wildfire.

Mikoto is just as riled up as I am; I can see the sweat rolling down her cheek. Welf sighs to himself.

"A-anyway, all unnecessary contact is forbidden. That includes relationships with members of other familias!"

"Huh?!"

That last bit got my attention real quick.

"What's with your surprise, Bell? That should be common sense. Does this mean there's someone you like in a different familia? And even if so, there's no way you'd want to be in a relationship with her, right?"

"No, well, that's…that's not what I meant…"

Wow, her words were sharp. How can I respond to that?

Getting involved with someone in a non-friendly familia, basically having a forbidden love, only puts the familia in danger. What she's saying is absolutely right, it is common sense. It's obvious, but even so…

I look around the table, and surprisingly Lilly's gone quiet. She was so adamant before, too. Haruhime is glancing uncomfortably between the goddess and me while Welf's rubbing the back of his neck. "Here we go again…" he says under his breath.

Well, he's not wrong…

I look down at the table and give up trying to object to the goddess's rule.

"If I may, does this precedent also apply to deities?…As in, is it wrong to harbor feelings for one of them?"

Mikoto slowly raises her trembling hand.

Her cheeks have gone red, too. All of us, the goddess included, are caught off guard by her question.

"Oh, that's right. You have a thing for Také…"

"I-I'm not asking just about Lord Takemikazuchi! I-I just…!"

"I'm not one to get in the way of that! Actually—that's it!"

A light flicks on in her eyes. She must've thought of something. Even her twin black ponytails flip into the air.

"That should be encouraged! Deities and children forming couples sounds great to me! Of course, there are a few deities who should be avoided at all costs, but nice ones like Také, I see no problem with that at all!"

"C-couple...?"

I shrink back in my chair as the goddess's voice goes up an octave, the words spewing out of her mouth.

Haruhime still isn't used to the goddess's vocabulary and tilts her head in confusion. Lady Hestia turns to me, her eyes sparkling.

"It's just like those stories from before we came down to Gekai! Many romances happened between fairies and children! Isn't that right, Bell? Don't you think having that dream sounds wonderful?"

"Um, s-sure..."

All I can do is nod with all the attention suddenly on me.

Romances between fairies and humans or demi-humans are a common thread in stories dating back to the Ancient Times.

Unfortunately, most of those fairy tales and stories of heroes end in tragedy.

I pause for a moment to collect my thoughts, but Lilly jumps out of her chair with something important to say.

"Don't be fooled, Mr. Bell! Being with a deity is a recipe for disaster! Age is a foreign concept to immortals, and their love is intense! Death will become the only escape from a clingy relationship that will last until the end of your days!"

"Hey! What do you think we are?"

Lilly passionately refused to even consider talking about a romance involving the gods of Deusdia. Once her rant comes to an end, Lady Hestia looks at Welf.

"Any thoughts?"

"I think...what you're saying is right, Lady Hestia."

"Seriously, Mr. Welf?"

"There's no need to call it a 'forbidden love' or anything like that. Deities take care of us, show their affection their own ways. If they want to change the nature of the relationship, then it's not all that weird. At the very least, that's what I'd like to have happen."

Lilly's jaw drops. Even I'm surprised by Welf's confession.

"Huh? I didn't know you had a thing for goddesses, Welf..."

"I only have eyes for Lady Hephaistos."

"Oh-oh-oh! Yes, children with that kind of straightforward mind-set are so rare these days! Welf, I'm rooting for you!"

"Th…anks?"

I remember hearing something about that on the eighteenth floor when he was talking with Tsubaki…This is quite a shock. Hestia is beaming at him, enthusiastically patting him on the shoulder, since Welf is sitting right next to her.

He's so much taller than she, and yet he just sits there, watching with confusion as the goddess shows no signs of slowing down.

"Did you hear that, Bell? The power of love can break down barriers between races *and* gods!"

She's beside herself with joy as I sink into my chair as far as possible.

When did this meeting become about mortals having relationships with gods?

The ones agreeing with the goddess are the calm, cool, and collected Welf and the blushing Mikoto.

Of course the still-standing Lilly, as vocal as ever, is against it. I can't get a good read on Haruhime. She's saying nothing either way, but judging by the look on her face, I'd say she doesn't agree with the goddess.

The familia is split into two camps, and the goddess is looking at me with expectation in her eyes.

"So, Bell, what do you think?"

"M-me…?"

"Y-yes…Like, say if I were a different familia's goddess and—Oh, no no no no no no!"

Her face turns beet red, her hands waving back and forth. "A-hem!" She clears her throat.

Then she directs her unblinking gaze onto me.

"If another goddess offered you her love…what would you do?"

The living room goes silent, the goddess's question hanging in the air.

Everyone is waiting for my answer. Lilly gulps and leans forward in her seat. Welf and Mikoto appear interested as Haruhime looks on, her restless tail twitching behind her.

Just like Lilly, the goddess waits with bated breath, her mysterious blue eyes locked on me.

I have to say something before the atmosphere gets too heavy to breathe.

"I'd, um, turn her down..."

There was nothing to think about. It was just a matter of getting the words out.

The goddess flinches.

Lilly's and Haruhime's eyes fly open. Welf and Mikoto look genuinely surprised, too.

Something about everyone's reactions feels...strange. I try to explain my answer as the mood gets increasingly uncomfortable.

"I just don't think about goddesses that way...I'd be happy, sure, but it doesn't make any sense. It'd be too overwhelming."

A relationship with a deusdea? They're not like us—they're gods.

Welf and Mikoto seem to have a different opinion on the matter, shockingly so...But, yeah.

They're special beings who should be revered, worshipped, and respected.

I'm more than happy to interact with them as part of a familia, as a "child" of Gekai, and as a member of their family, but...I believe there's a line that shouldn't be crossed.

"B-Bell..."

The goddess's body language changes so quickly I can practically hear the *slam* of her mood hitting rock bottom.

Her face is down; her entire body is shaking...She rockets to her feet.

"Bell, you moron—!"

"G-Goddess—?"

She dashes toward the living room door at full speed, her voice still echoing around the living room.

She covers her eyes with her forearm, and I watch her run out into the hall, leaving the door open behind her. She just keeps going, all the way up to the front entrance and through the gate.

I'm halfway out of my chair, ears still ringing.

"Bell…you're denser than I thought."

"Huh? B-but…goddesses are goddesses…!"

From the living room window, I catch a glimpse of her running down the street. Welf comes over to me as I'm trying to decide if I should give chase or not.

Even I can hear the confusion in my voice as Lilly and the girls come to join us.

"You make a valid point, Sir Bell. There are people who respect deities, but…"

"Yes, but the same is true of many devout followers…"

Mikoto sounds like she's having difficulty choosing her words, and Haruhime looks just as confused. Even Welf is glaring at me—"Why'd you have to go that far?"—as if all of them seem to think my opinion of deities isn't normal.

They're not criticizing me, but I feel like the odd man out here.

"If, just if…Just as an example."

A few moments of heavy silence pass. Then Lilly looks up at me.

"Just on the off chance that perhaps Lady Hestia secretly has feelings for a human here on Earth…Mr. Bell's choice of words might have hurt her feelings."

It took her a while to get to the point. I watch her eyebrows sink on her face as my eyes get wider with every word.

"…Hey, Bell."

Welf was watching me from the side and speaks up.

"What are you so afraid of?"

"…!"

I can't breathe.

Welf's question cuts right through me. My hands clench into fists before I know it.

After a few more heartbeats pass, I still don't have an answer for him. I look away from everyone.

"…I'll go find her."

I leave the living room like a prisoner escaping from jail.

I feel their eyes on me, but no one says anything as I race out the door.

"Li'l E, you sure that was a good idea? Sayin' that."

After Bell had left the room, the remaining four members of *Hestia Familia* stared at the open door for a few moments before Welf turned to face Lilly.

"…Lilly doesn't care. Lady Hestia is our goddess as well. Things will never settle down without straightening this out…and she's always sticking her nose into Lilly's business, like the other week."

Welf wanted to make sure that she was okay with helping her rival. Although she whispered the last part under her breath, she turned to answer him right away.

Mikoto and Haruhime knew immediately Lilly wasn't being completely honest and grinned wryly. However, their slight grins were on the verge of bursting into laughter.

Welf couldn't hold back a smile, either.

"Well, I guess this means Dungeon prowling ain't happening today."

"I believe so, too."

Mikoto nodded after Welf's proposal. There weren't any objections.

The boy and the goddess would make amends soon enough, and they wanted to be at home to welcome them back.

I go into the city to look for the goddess.

Lots of adventurers are already on their way to the Dungeon, making the streets lively and crowded. Even everyday citizens are busy setting up their shops, and the horse-drawn taxis are starting to flow in and out of the main routes throughout the city.

The sky above Orario is clear again today. However, there is a cluster of gray clouds gathering to the north. *The mountains up there might get some rain today,* I think to myself as I weave my way in and out of traffic at a slow run.

There aren't any clues as to where the goddess went after leaving home. I can't exactly comb the city until I find her; it's much too big for that.

I can't get the look she had on her face out of my head. Lilly's words are replaying over and over. Ignoring the sharp pain in my chest, I ask storeowners and passersby if they've seen a young-looking goddess come through this way.

"Oh…? Well, if it isn't Bell."

"That's him all right. Hey, Bell!"

"Ah…Lord Miach and Lord Hermes?"

I come across the two gods by coincidence when I'm halfway through the Western Block.

Lord Miach is pushing a four-wheeled cart full of potions and other items while Lord Hermes is wearing his usual wide-brimmed feathered hat. He must've snuck away from Asfi because I can't see her anywhere. She usually shadows him like a bodyguard.

One deity with long navy-blue hair, the other one with shorter, vibrant orange hair, and both so handsome that I wouldn't be surprised if an artist had carved their faces out of stone. I say good morning to them but can't help thinking this is an unusual pairing.

"May I ask what you're doing this far out on a side street?"

"Well, I've just been offered a part in a scheme. This man here would like to use my familia's wares to make an easy valis or two, and I was trying to find a way to turn him down."

"Oi, oi! Miach! Why do you have to say something like that? I'm not scheming at anything!"

Lord Miach says it all with a grin on his face, but he's holding back a laugh. There's no hint of seriousness in his voice. Lord Hermes is laughing, too, so it was probably just a joke. I've heard that *Hermes Familia* is like a jack-of-all-trades. Whether it's Dungeon prowling, a delivery service, or economic ventures, they'll try anything to turn a profit. He probably wanted to ask Lord Miach some business questions.

I feel a smile growing on my lips when suddenly I remember why I'm here. So I ask the two of them.

"Hestia? Hmmm, sorry, Bell. I haven't seen her."

"Same here. Sorry I'm not much help."

"I-it's not a problem. Thanks for listening, but I should get going…"

I stutter an apology and bow my head. I'm about to turn my back and leave when, at that moment—

"Bell."

Lord Miach gets my attention, his calm gaze looking right through me.

"If you're not in a rush, we'll listen."

"Huh…?"

"We'll offer you some advice, Bell. There's something on your mind, isn't there?"

Lord Miach smiles as I look back at him in shock. Lord Hermes is grinning with his eyes.

…They read me like an open book; they can see into my heavy heart. Then again, maybe I'm not that hard to figure out.

The two gods look down at me like fathers watching over their child. I hesitate for a few heartbeats. In the end, I avoid telling them what happened at the manor but go straight to the question at hand.

Are deities capable of love? More specifically, how do they feel about us mortals?

"Lord Miach, Lord Hermes…Do you—do gods fall in love with people? As in, do you become more than friends, something like lifelong partners…?"

My eyes trace the patterns in the stone pavement beneath my feet while I speak. I see the two gods share a glance out of the corner of my eye.

Their expressions brighten, as if that was all they needed to figure out what was going on. They start talking.

"It happens, for sure. We're surprisingly vulnerable to it, to tell the truth."

"I agree. I'm sure you remember Apollo, Bell? Look no further. For him, love had no bounds."

Lord Apollo...The god we fought in the War Game.

Often called Phoebus, he once offered Hestia his hand in marriage. Apollo is a god who loves too much.

"Once a child captures Apollo's interest, he loves them fully and deeply until the end."

"Just like Miach was saying, that guy treasures everything through and through...And whenever one of his children dies, he goes a bit overboard, even for us."

This is all a big surprise for me.

"Over...board...?"

"For sure. Crying day in and day out for months on end. If said child wore some kind of trinket, Apollo would wear it day and night. If a tree started growing from where the child was buried, he would treat it like a holy site."

"I-I'm sure he didn't go that far..."

"Oh, he did."

I voice my doubt, but Lord Hermes laughs it off.

"But Takemikazuchi, on the other hand, he'd take a more fatherly role. Even if a mortal girl loved him with all her heart, pursued his love to the ends of the earth, I'm positive he would draw a line in the sand. He's not the type who can make a woman truly happy."

"Hephaistos is a bit more complicated. For her, watching the growth in her followers as smiths brings her the most happiness, kind of like a master artisan watching her students come into their own. I don't know if she'd be able to take a step beyond that. Her interactions with children are probably a mixture of warmheartedness as a god and her feelings as a woman."

Lord Miach offers Lord Takemikazuchi as another example, and Lord Hermes talks about Lady Hephaistos with a grin on his face.

They tell me about all the forms gods' love can take, whether it be an inability to produce an offspring, a stubborn sense of paternal obligation, or the guidance of a fellow artisan.

"Affection, simply paying attention, watching them come into their own like a parent...Each of us has their own way of loving our children. There are some of us who treasure their memories with children like you for all eternity and others who forget right away——and completely on the other side of the spectrum, there is a Goddess of Beauty who's known to chase the souls of her departed children all the way to the other side so she can keep them as her own."

Lord Hermes narrows his eyes, his gaze passing over me.

"Our way of loving might seem a bit warped, for lack of a better word. Especially from your point of view, Bell."

"I-I wouldn't say that."

Lord Miach's grinning in my direction, but I quickly disagree with his statement.

I disagree, but I can't flat-out reject it, either.

"...What about you, Lord Miach? Lord Hermes?"

The crowd swells for a moment, making it too hard to hear them.

I look at each of them in turn and ask as soon as the crowd moves on.

"Let me think...Takemikazuchi and I have a lot in common. I'd like to watch my child find a partner, start a family, and be by their side...as a god, until they move on to the next realm *because* I have feelings for them." Lord Miach looks up at the blue sky as he speaks.

"Oi, oi, no need to put that much thought into it! You and Takemikazuchi both? I keep all the ladies I like at my beck and call! Isn't that right, Bell? A harem is a man's romance!"

As for Lord Hermes, I can't tell how serious he is with that twinkle in his eye and joking tone in his voice.

"Are you still spouting that nonsense...?" Lord Miach casts his gaze on the other deity, raising an eyebrow. I smile weakly at the fact that Lord Hermes was expecting me to agree.

"—Bell. Our love lasts but a moment."

Then.

Lord Miach speaks to me with a gentle smile on his lips.

"Time has no meaning for us. Existing as long as we have, the feeling of falling in love and maintaining that connection is over in the blink of an eye. Many of us fall in love with children at first sight."

"For us, the whole thing is over in a flash. But for you mortals, it can last your whole lifetime."

My eyes open wide as Lord Miach and Lord Hermes bring their thoughts to a conclusion. They're immortal, and their time with us is very limited...Basically, we're gone in a matter of seconds to them. It's one of the saddest things I've ever heard, so why do both of them look so content?

"I won't say you have to, but...please accept a deity's feelings for you."

Lord Miach closes his eyes.

"Bell, you have a partner in mind, do you not?"

"I-I, um..."

"There is no need to apologize or grovel for being led in circles by a deity's wishes. Follow your heart—that's enough."

My body starts trembling, when suddenly Lord Miach reaches out and—*Pat.*

He lightly pats my head.

"Just...have faith. That's all you need."

He continues speaking and ruffling my hair at the same time.

"I'm sure that many gods will be satisfied with that."

"..."

He adds one more thing: "Please don't run away from a deity's love."

I can decline it, I can accept it, but I *must not be afraid of it.* That look in his eyes, the tone of his voice, it's like he can see right through me.

He stands a bit taller than me. So I look up into his gaze, my eyes quivering.

But no words come out, and I look at my feet.

Lord Miach doesn't say anything to put the blame on me or make me feel guilty. He just silently stands there, gently patting my head. My eyes trace the pattern of the stones again, my heart riding an emotional roller coaster.

Lord Hermes watches us with a smile. Neither of them pushes for any answer, and I gladly accept their kindness. The three of us stand in silence.

"Damn that thick skull of his!"

Hestia held her tearful eyes high as she walked through the streets of Orario at a brisk pace.

Passing through Central Park, she made her way onto North Main Street. Careful to avoid the fully armored adventurers on their way to the Dungeon, she'd traveled a great distance since storming out of the manor that morning.

"It's all because Bell has too much respect for deities. I mean, sure, it's great being revered and all, but…!"

Her rambling voice was loud enough for anyone passing by to hear. Oblivious to the fact that she was quickly becoming the center of attention, Hestia voiced her grievances about Bell without slowing down.

"It's not like we're all that great! Slacking off the first chance we get, cooping up in our rooms eating Jyaga Maru Kun…We get tired of keeping up the godly image!"

No, that's just you. All the humans and demi-humans in earshot had the same thought and the same expression as the youthful goddess passed by.

"'Other gods are so easily entertained, laughing at the simplest things! But they're deities, so they must be revered!' That's exactly what you'd say, isn't it?"

"I-I would…?"

Hestia howled at an animal person, a complete stranger who was unfortunate enough to be in her line of sight.

"He would, he would," the young goddess grumbled to herself, eyes closed as she nodded. The citizens of Orario were used to the crazy ramblings of gods and goddesses and went about their business without a second thought.

"You can open up to me, Bell! Don't apologize so much!...Have a spine, would you?"

The words exploded out of her mouth before she whispered the last ones.

However, all her ramblings blended into the everyday noise of the busy street.

"Stubborn, blockheaded rabbit head." Complaints and random words continued to pour out of her mouth as Hestia stomped her way through the main street.

"Oh! Hestia! Perfect timing!"

"Hnnh...? Boss lady?"

Sighing with every step, Hestia suddenly came to a halt when she heard someone call her name.

Looking up, she saw a rather pudgy animal woman waving her arms by the entrance to one of the side streets.

It was one of the women who worked at the same Jyaga Maru Kun street stand as she did.

"Is something wrong?"

"Well, you see, the owner sent me out to pick up a shipment of herbs that we use to make the potato puffs. It's outside the wall right now..."

"Herbs? Can't you just buy them at the market?"

"No, it's too expensive. And we're shorthanded as it is..."

The woman gave Hestia an apologetic bow as the goddess scratched her cheek.

*Today was supposed to be my day off, too...*she thought to herself, but also knew that there was nothing to do at home even if she did go back. She arrived at the conclusion that she might as well help out.

Agreeing to help brought a smile to her coworker's face as she bowed again a few more times.

"But you know, lady, I'm also the head of a familia, so I can't pass through the city gate."

"Ah, forgot about that..."

Hestia remarked as the two of them pushed the cart full of boxes and other tools straight north through the looming city wall and the gate built into it.

It was difficult for the adventurers of Orario, or anyone belonging to a familia, including the head god or goddess, to leave the city.

That was because it would have a direct effect on Orario's battle strength as a whole. Many problems would arise if, for some reason, high-level adventurers who had honed their skills in the Dungeon—adventurers belonging to *Loki Familia*, for example— were to leave the city and ally themselves with a rival faction.

The main reason Orario was called the "Center of the World" was because the world's most powerful individuals protected it. The Guild was extremely alert to the constant threats to the city and the threat of losing the protection provided by top-class adventurers to any of the surrounding countries. Therefore, anyone belonging to one of the city's various familias—especially high-ranking ones—had to go through a rigorous screening process and mountains of red tape in order to pass through the gate. They were particularly strict with deities. Even if their followers should leave the city, a hostage situation would surely follow if enemy forces captured a god. With the one glaring exception of *Hermes Familia*, it would be safe to say that no one could freely pass through the gate whenever they wished.

Entering the city was simple; exiting was far more difficult.

It was one of Orario's unwritten rules that everyone who lived inside its walls accepted.

"I'll go as far as the wall, but I can't help much after that..."

Hestia Familia was on the up and up and already recognized as a middle-ranking familia by the Guild. As the head of said familia, Hestia doubted that she would be able to pass through the gate right away. The two of them arrived at an open staging area where countless merchants and horse-drawn taxis lined up in front of the gate as Hestia explained her situation.

In front of the imposing north gate, Guild employees, adventurers belonging to familias that worked closely with them, and two gatekeepers were busy inspecting the people attempting to pass through the barrier separating outside from in. Should anyone try to go through the gate without a valid pass issued by the Guild, they would be arrested and restrained on the spot.

Hestia and the woman she worked with joined a group of five more of their coworkers waiting in line. It was still a small group for such a big job. Each of them had their gate passes ready. However, the news that Hestia wouldn't be much help made the animal woman put her hand to her cheek in contemplation. This could be a problem.

—All of a sudden, the staging area came alive with cheers and applause.

"Huh?" muttered a surprised Hestia as she turned to have a look.

"It is I! I am Ganesha!"

"Oh, it's just Ganesha."

The god was unmistakable. His rich, masculine voice, combined with his overwhelming presence, made him impossible to miss as he came in from outside the gate.

His dark skin, long black hair, and perfectly toned muscles were one thing, but the elephant mask hiding his face from view caught the most attention.

The god in command of the largest familia in Orario, its membership including many upper-class adventurers, appeared on the scene. The citizens and merchants present to witness his entrance welcomed him with smiles and applause. Even Hestia's coworkers waited happily as the deity approached.

"Do I spy with my own eyes—Hestia?!"

"You don't have to announce your every thought to the world, Ganesha. But why are you here? Wasn't your familia called out into battle?"

Ganesha's group approached Hestia, and he struck a bizarre pose.

"Dismount!" he yelled from his seat on top of a horse being led by two of his followers, and hopped down to the stone pavement.

"It would take a long time to explain, but the war is coming to an end. So I have returned."

"That didn't take long at all."

"I also brought the captured Rakian soldiers with me. There are so many that we couldn't keep them all in the forward camps."

"Oh? But are you sure it's okay to be back here? Your familia is huge, the backbone of the Alliance forces, isn't it?"

"There is no need to worry about the tide of battle! My strongest followers, my ultimate fighters, are still holding the line! They deemed me to be a nuisance and asked me to come back early!"

"Is that the way your children treat you?"

"Well, I *am* Ganesha!"

Ganesha's masculine voice thundered around the square as he struck yet another unusual pose. Hestia was losing patience fast.

Hestia had been on good terms with many deities while in Tenkai and was familiar with the mask-wearing god. It might be better to say that she couldn't ignore his overwhelming presence and did her best to tolerate it.

She wasn't the only one. Ganesha's two bodyguards massaged their temples as they endured their god's quirks. This time, Ganesha was the one to ask a question.

"So then, Hestia, what brings you out this way?"

"Well, this and that and a few other things."

She gave him a quick summary. Ganesha smiled, his pearly white teeth flashing in the sunlight.

"If that is the problem, I grant you permission myself! Go, Hestia, you may pass!"

"Wait, Lord Ganesha!"

His bodyguards immediately turned to their god, objecting on the spot as Hestia watched in surprise.

"What are you saying? We can't issue permission for something like this behind the Guild's back...!"

"I am the God of the Masses, Ganesha! Jyaga Maru Kun are bundles of joy that bring tears of happiness to the eyes of the people! Should they be unable to eat a single one, tears of sadness will be shed this night! I cannot allow such a travesty to befall the children!"

"Have you gone insane?" yelled one of his bodyguards as the two of them tried desperately to reason with him, but Ganesha showed no signs of conceding.

Ganesha was definitely one of the most bizarre deities in Orario, but as the cheers and applause erupting from the crowd around him proved, he was also one of the most trusted. Faith in him ran deep.

As his title "God of the Masses" showed, the people of Gekai were rather fond of Ganesha. His familia allied with the Guild, they were known for assisting in many events around Orario, as well as providing security and maintaining the peace. Even one of the guards standing at the north gate belonged to *Ganesha Familia*, although he was trying to hide that fact at the moment.

Ganesha's voice was easily heard over the din in the staging area, meaning the guards heard every word. Their faces went blank.

"If the Guild finds out, they won't let this slide with a warning!"

"Then they don't have to know, Follower A!"

"They already know! How many of their employees do you think are here right now? And my name is Modak!"

Quite a few sparks flew between the god and his bodyguards, but they were unable to convince him to back down. The two gave up, their heads drooping in silence.

Ganesha turned to Hestia and stuck his right thumb high into the air.

"Are you sure this is okay, Ganesha?"

"Of course. You are not a goddess with a taste for disorder but one who brings cheer to the children of Gekai! Now, go!"

A beaming smile appeared beneath his elephant mask. Hestia blushed awkwardly and gave him a thumbs-up in return.

Ganesha's bodyguards smiled tiredly as the frowning Guild employees allowed Hestia to pass through the gate along with her coworkers.

"Lord Ganesha is one weird fellow, but I must say he's a great god!"

"Yeah, I guess. Hard on the ears, but a good guy."

Hestia chatted with the animal woman as they joined the line of merchants and travelers heading through the colossal gate structure. Her coworkers were still talking about the "unique" god in the elephant mask who had captured the hearts of so many citizens when the group took its first step outside the city.

A vast green plain opened up in front of them on either side of the road leading off into the distance. Mountains lined the distant horizon. A lush green forest could be seen at their base.

It might rain soon, thought Hestia as she looked up at the clouds gathering in the northern sky.

"I still can't believe you actually went through with this. What if we're discovered…?"

"I'm restraining my divine aura. No one will be able to tell that I'm a god!"

"Keep your voice down! Trying to get inside during broad daylight with this much security? Are you out of your mind…?"

A heated argument drifted into their ears.

Turning their heads, the group saw a line of people on the opposite side of the gate waiting to go inside. At the front of the long, snaking line were two tall men wearing hooded robes. Their faces were well hidden. Looking like travelers, they blended in very well with the many people who wore the same style robe behind them in line. For some reason, both voices were crackling with nervous energy.

Merchants in line behind the two men gave one another confused looks as they listened to the conversation. "I suppose those types of people are everywhere in the world…" remarked the animal woman next to Hestia. The goddess, however, couldn't help but feel a little suspicious.

Then, when Hestia's group was about to walk past the hooded travelers…

""Huh?""

Her eyes met those of one of the men in the middle of the argument.

Strands of golden hair like a lion's mane were sticking out of his hood, and she knew she'd seen red eyes like that somewhere before.

The power in his gaze made her come to a halt. He, too, fell silent with his mouth half open.

Three seconds passed.

"—Ares?!"

"—Hestia?!"

The god and the goddess pointed at each other, yelling at the same time.

Hestia was stunned that she was face-to-face with the god who was trying his damnedest to invade the Labyrinth City, and Ares couldn't believe his luck that the target of his last-ditch plan had literally come to him.

Ares's red eyes flashed during Hestia's bout with disbelief.

He kicked off the ground, charging forward.

"Gotcha———!"

"GuWAHHH!"

Ares lunged and tackled Hestia.

Eyes going wide, she was knocked out of the line of her coworkers by the god's perfectly timed strike.

The two tumbled across the grass until Ares regained his footing and lifted Hestia over his shoulder.

"BWAH-HA-HA-HA-HA-HA! Did you see that, Marius? Objective complete!"

"N-no way...!"

Ares removed his hood as he called out to the human, Marius.

"Uwhhh..." The young goddess was barely conscious, her eyes spinning as she lay bent over his shoulder. He roughly adjusted her position and looked back at his followers.

"All forces, full retreat!"

With that, the "travelers" in the snaking line pushed their way out and took off at full speed.

It was pandemonium. Of course, the guards came rushing to the scene right away, but Marius led a counterstrike against them with sword in hand. The guards were vastly outnumbered.

Screams erupted from the crowd.

"Mission complete! Fall back, fall back!"

Ares took one look at the battle before running away with Hestia firmly in his grasp.

His allies—the soldiers of Rakia—broke off their attack and followed their god.

"Oh, no! Hestia!"

Her coworkers screamed at the top of their lungs as they saw Ares mount a horse like a valiant knight and race off into the distance.

"Where have you been, Lord Hermes?"

A woman with short aqua-blue hair roars at Lord Hermes. He's walking right next to me, so seeing her storm up to us makes me jump back in surprise.

After talking for a little while, I thought it might be a good idea to keep looking for the goddess. Lord Miach and Lord Hermes kindly offered their assistance. I feel kind of guilty for dragging them into this, but there was no reason to refuse their offer. So we'd been walking together for a little while when Asfi, a member of *Hermes Familia*, shows up out of breath and angry as hell.

Lord Hermes looks very uncomfortable as Asfi holds her glasses on her face with one hand to keep them from falling off while she unleashes her tirade.

"You said to follow you, but then disappeared to who knows where…!"

"Well, um, you see, I heard something interesting and just…"

"Just what?"

"Ah, never mind. Sorry!"

Overwhelmed by his follower's fury, Hermes offers a flat apology, his face glistening with sweat.

Only after gaining a moral victory over her god does Asfi notice we are here, too. "My apologies for that unsightly display…" She bows to us as Lord Miach and I smile weakly.

Straightening up, she adjusts her glasses over her blue eyes.

"If you don't mind my asking, what were you doing with this more-trouble-than-he's-worth deity of mine?"

"Ehh, um…Well…"

An excessive amount of sweat rolls down my back as I start to explain the situation, when suddenly…

The echoes of many hurried footsteps reach my ears.

"—What's that?"

What I see when I turn leaves me speechless.

There's a group of demi-humans in full armor and weapons, metallic clanks echoing with every move.

What's more, there's a blond-haired, golden-eyed female knight among them.

"M-Miss Aiz?!"

"It's you…"

Aiz, saber in hand, responds to my startled cry.

She stops for a moment, and I get a clear view of her silver breastplate and gauntlets. She's even equipped with shoulder armor. There's no doubt she's dressed for battle. So are the other members of *Loki Familia* running with her.

I've never seen a group of battle-ready adventurers running through the city streets in formation. The same must be true for Lord Miach, Lord Hermes, and Asfi, because the tension in the air strikes all of us dumb.

Aiz looks directly at me, and I see her lips move.

"All of you, come with us."

"Itty-Bitty's been snatched!"

Orario, north gate.

Loki's voice echoed through the staging area in front of the gate on the north edge of the city wall.

She was not alone. The general of her familia, the prum Finn, along with several more of her followers and even a few gods, had gathered.

"That's right! Some strange god carried Hestia away…!"

"A group of Rakia's soldiers was mixed in with the travelers! They all scattered as soon as Hestia was taken!"

The pudgy animal person and a Guild employee were on the verge of panic as they explained the situation.

Everything had happened about ten minutes ago. Guild employees had been dispatched to deliver the news all over Orario right away. It went without saying Guild Headquarters was informed, but the messengers also visited the homes of powerful familias. From there, word spread to the gods and down the ranks to lower-class adventurers. However, due to the fact that not much time had passed, only Loki and Finn's small group had arrived on the scene.

Merchants and travelers trying to exit or enter the city excitedly talked among themselves when Loki arrived. "Dahh..." The goddess pinched the bridge of her nose in an attempt to stave off a headache as she looked up at the sky.

"Finn."

"Sorry. I can't predict what gods will do..."

Loki glanced at Finn, clearly wanting to say something. The prum man wiped the side of his face with his hand.

The actions of Hestia and Ares were impossible for mere mortals to comprehend. Being forced to come along for the ride had taken its toll on "Braver," his face showing signs of stress.

"So tell me...What genius let Itty-Bitty through the gate in the first place? Oh, was it you, Ganesha?"

"...I-I am Ganesha?"

"Hey, where's yer usual spunk?"

Loki's bad mood was apparent in her glare. Ganesha shrank back, striking a meek pose.

The usually energetically loud deity was barely audible as he explained the sequence of events that led up to Hestia's capture.

"So then, you bein' an idiot, you let her through the gate?"

"Uh, yes."

"That mask stranglin' yer brain? It looks stupid enough, ya don't hafta go actin' the part, ya mondo moron!"

"...Because I...I am Ganesha!"

"I wasn't askin'!"

"Guild, y'all take 'im away!" Loki yelled at the uniformed gate guards.

"Noooo!" wailed Ganesha, his head in his hands. Meanwhile, his bodyguards and members of his familia working with the Guild glared at him with *"We told you so"* written all over their faces.

"Jyaga Boobies, why you gotta go an' make things harder than they gotta be...?"

After taking a look around at the injured gate guards lying on the ground, Loki looked up into the sky and spat her own dissatisfaction into the air.

"Rakia kidnapped Itty-Bitty...meanin' they're after the Crozzo Magic Swords again?"

"Looks like it. Most likely, they'll demand magic swords or Welf Crozzo himself in exchange for her release...No matter what we do, a rift will divide Orario."

The City of Orario wasn't a united fortress. Even if the Guild were to use all the resources at its disposal to drive Rakia away, the deities closest to Hestia—especially the powerful and influential *Hephaistos Familia*—would object to how the situation was handled, and the city would be split into two different camps. If worse came to worst, these divisions would expose them to threats from other countries and cities.

"Losing our advantage in such a stupid manner could really hurt our reputation..." mumbled Finn under his breath.

"We must retrieve Goddess Hestia before the enemy forces reach their own territory. Failure to do so could be catastrophic."

"Dahh, damn! Why do I gotta be the one to clean up Itty-Bitty's mess?"

Finn frowned as he started to explain what could happen while Loki tugged at her hair next to him.

More adventurers and gods were arriving at the scene, their reactions to the grave situation ranging from concern to the interested glee of the deities. A strategic meeting got under way immediately.

"Loki, Finn."

"Hey, Aiz, you're here. What about Riveria and the twins?"

"I'm the only one. And…"

Loki Familia's other top-class adventurers hadn't been at home when the messenger explained the news, meaning that Aiz was the first one to arrive. She had brought a group of her lower-ranking allies with her, along with Hermes, Asfi, Miach, and lastly, Bell.

As if pulled forward by Aiz's sweeping gaze, Bell rushed up to Loki and Finn with fire in his veins.

"Is…is it true? Lady Hestia's been kidnapped…?"

"…I'll give you the short version. Bell Cranell, listen up."

Aiz had partially brought the boy up to speed but had been missing several details. Finn concisely filled in the blanks. Bell was white as a sheet by the time Finn's explanation was complete.

"Where is she now?"

"We don't know. To make matters worse, Rakia's forces dispersed into three groups going north, west, and east respectively. No one has been dispatched to hunt them down as of yet."

Bell leaned forward, his eyes begging for more information. Finn's calm demeanor didn't falter as he answered.

"There's one other obstacle that I hate to admit," said Finn as he led into the next piece of information.

Since Orario's familias were largely forbidden to exit the city wall, Rakia's forces in the middle of executing their sixth invasion were much more familiar with the geography surrounding the city.

"They might know the best roads, passages through the mountains, and secret shortcuts that will allow them to reenter their territory as quickly as possible. Catching up with their main army will be extremely difficult," he continued.

Color drained from Bell's face with each passing word. Hermes was listening, too, and nudged Miach with his shoulder.

"It might be a good idea to tell Lilly and the other kiddos," he quietly whispered into the other deity's ear. Miach gave a quick nod and turned in the direction of Hearthstone Manor.

"—Loki, Finn. I'll go."

Aiz could see the beginnings of panic appearing on Bell's face, and she stepped in front of him.

The Sword Princess was known for her aloof nature. Stepping forward like this not only caught her god and allies by surprise, but even the surrounding adventurers donned shocked expressions.

"Hold up, Aizuu. Ya don't need to go outta yer way to bail out Itty-Bitty. The search is gonna be one hell of a pain in the ass, combing the forest and whatnot as it is…"

"But someone must go."

"Ughh…"

"And the fastest one here is me."

Loki flinched with every point Aiz made. The blond girl's eyes were serious and focused as she made an unrefutable argument.

Even if pitted head to head against her general, Finn, Aiz would win in a foot race. No one was able to object to this suggestion from one of Orario's best top-class adventurers.

As for Bell…

Despite not having much involvement with Hestia, the resoluteness in Aiz's expression stirred something within him. Even his heart was trembling.

Setting all his fears and reservations aside, Bell stepped forward, even with Aiz's shoulder.

"I-I'll go, too! I will…I will bring my goddess back!"

Bell took another step forward, closer to Loki than Aiz.

The goddess hadn't said anything to Bell, quietly observing the boy since his arrival. Now she turned to address him directly.

"Weren't ya listenin', boy? Aiz already said she'd go. Ya fixin' to hold her back?"

"…!"

"Think! What's yer Level? Ya know how far ya are behind. Hold yer tongue."

One at Level 3, the other at Level 6.

There was quite a gap between Bell and Aiz, with the latter being many times stronger. It was as simple as that.

It was the truth, but Loki's cool tone hit Bell like a smack in the face. Sensing that the up-and-coming "Rookie" had a connection with one of her own, she opened her vermilion eyes slightly more than usual as she watched the gears turning in the boy's head.

Her words sent Bell reeling, unable to respond—but his hands clenched into fists.

Bracing his shoulders, he roared with a might that even a goddess had to acknowledge.

"I'm going! The goddess—Lady Hestia is part of my family!"

Bell's ruby-red eyes flashed, burning with sheer willpower. All he saw was the task at hand; nothing else mattered. He channeled that determination into his voice.

"I won't hold her back! I swear I will keep up with her every step! So please...LET ME DO THIS!"

His voice went hoarse with desperation. The many other conversations occurring at the staging area were overpowered by his plea as it hung in the air.

The few deities present, as well as the other adventurers, all craned their necks to see what was going on. Despite Bell's display of willpower and conviction, Loki didn't grant her permission.

Nor did she refuse.

"———Do whatever ya want. You'll only just hold her back anyway. Aiz, feel free to ditch 'im anytime."

"...Understood."

A few heartbeats passed before Aiz responded to her goddess. Bell, who couldn't believe that the goddess had allowed him to accompany Aiz in the pursuit of Hestia, threw his body into a deep bow and yelled, "Thank you so much!"

Standing up again, the boy made eye contact with Aiz. Both shared a nod and exchanged mutual gazes of encouragement. With that settled, the strategy meeting picked up speed.

The other adventurers went to the Guild employees to ask them to look the other way just this once and allow large groups through the gate without passes. There was no time to wait for Guild Headquarters to fill out the necessary paperwork, and the Guild employees present understood that—or rather, they were forced to understand and nodded.

"I am Ganesha!" The god's loud voice led the confused merchants and citizens away from the staging area as the adventurers quickly gathered information about the possible routes Rakia's army might be using to retreat.

"There aren't enough people here to send out other search parties after Aiz and Bell. Unfortunately, there's no time to wait for Bete or the twins. We'll lose sight of the target."

"Trackin' down all the factions is gonna make everyone dead on their feet. Like I said before, we're gonna hafta comb the forest…"

One god overheard Finn and Loki's conversation as they tried to come up with the most efficient way to track down Hestia. He stepped forward.

"Could you leave that detail to me?"

Lifting his feathered hat off his orange hair and tipping it in her direction, Hermes flashed his charming smile.

"God Hermes…"

"Asfi here can find Hestia's location without much trouble."

"——What?!"

Keeping his gaze on Finn, Hermes reached around and grabbed Asfi by the shoulder, dragging her forward with a grin on his lips. His follower had no idea what was going on, but Hermes said it with the utmost confidence.

"That right? So, Dandy Man, what gives ya that idea…?"

"Come now, Loki. Asfi is Perseus—*the* Perseus. She has a few tricks up her sleeve that can find our wayward goddess. All you have to do is ask."

Loki cocked an eyebrow in suspicion as Hermes put extra emphasis on Asfi's title.

The head of *Hermes Familia* and possessor of the Advanced Ability "Enigma" looked at Finn and the group gathered around them, sighing as if the deepest part of her soul had grown tired of this.

Then Asfi straightened her spine, making her short blue hair and white scarf flutter as she adjusted her glasses.

"…If I have thirty minutes, I most likely can."

Finn looked at her with a scrutinizing eye and licked the base of his right thumb. "All right." He decided to put his faith in her. Loki intertwined her fingers behind her head, smiling as if interested in seeing what Asfi could do.

Spare armor and equipment were being brought into the staging area left and right. Bell hastily armed himself while listening to their conversation. Hermes noticed the surprise on the boy's face and went to his side.

"This isn't much, but I'll do what I can to help. Bell, Kenki, bring Hestia back safe and sound."

He said he didn't want this to be the way he had to say good-bye to her.

Bell was moved by Hermes's gesture to help a friend in need. He and Aiz next to him both nodded right away.

"I will!"

"Understood."

As if it had been waiting for the adventurers to depart, the colossal gate opened once again to beckon them forth.

"Lady Hestia was…?!"

The members of *Hestia Familia* were shocked to hear the news once Miach arrived at their doorstep.

They were standing on the front lawn, the main door wide open. Mikoto cried out, but it didn't take Welf ten seconds to figure out the reason why his goddess had been abducted. It left him speechless.

Fists trembling, the words "You bastards…!" hissed from between clenched teeth.

Now the goddess had been drawn into his family problem. Haruhime watched him in silence, a look of concern on her face as the young man's blood boiled. Meanwhile, Lilly rushed up to Miach with a sense of urgency.

Looking up at the tall god, she asked:

"Where is Mr. Bell right now?"

"At the city's north gate, awaiting Hestia's——No."

Miach stopped midsentence and took back his words. He then turned to look north.

Narrowing his eyes as he stared off into the distance, the look on the boy's face before he left fresh in his memory, he amended his statement.

"He's left the north gate to go find Hestia himself by now."

Whistling wind and running feet.

Two adventurers, one with long blond hair and the other with short white hair, navigated a steep mountain road at a speed that average people could never dream of achieving.

Directly north from Orario was the Beor Mountain Range.

It was known for steep drop-offs and incredibly dangerous paths. Clearing one mountain peak only brought several more peaks into view. For that reason, it had been dubbed the "Mountain Castle." Since it was located so close to the Dungeon entrance, monsters that had come to the surface during the Ancient Times had taken up residence among its countless peaks, resulting in the area being referred to as evil. That reputation and the rugged terrain meant that adventurers hardly came out this way, even during the modern age.

The mountains themselves bore almost no vegetation, their ash-colored rocky surfaces completely exposed. However, the areas between the sharp cliffs in the deep valleys were filled with green. One look toward the horizon showed many stark mountaintops separated by grand cliff sides and brilliant forests.

Bell and Aiz ran through the unforgiving terrain of the Beor Mountain Range underneath a gray sky.

It went without saying that wild animals and even the occasional threatening monster were quick to get out of their path.

One large-class monster, a bug bear, recklessly charged them but was dispatched by the girl's saber, sliced in half in the blink of an eye.

Monsters on the surface were much weaker than their brethren within the Dungeon. Even so, the only sound Bell could hear as he ran by the carcass still spewing blood into the air was the incessant pounding of his own heart.

"!"

As he gasped for breath, sweat flying off his pumping arms, his legs were a blur beneath him.

Bell pushed his body to the limit, yet the female knight at the edge of his vision was putting even more distance between them.

——*So fast!*

The moment they left Orario, Aiz had blazed forward with the strength of a gale wind, nearly knocking him off his feet.

The difference in their physical abilities was plain. The stark gap between them was even more evident by the time they had entered the mountain range.

She never once lost her balance on the rising and falling slopes, had enough leg strength to shatter the rock face with each step, and possessed a seemingly limitless amount of endurance and power. The truly scary thing about this display was that not a single droplet of sweat had been shed despite her vigorous pace.

The distance between Bell and the top-class adventurer continued to increase. He had been confident in his Agility, but by this point it had been shattered and ground into dust. No matter how hard he pushed, her back kept getting smaller in the distance.

"HaAH…HAaa…haaa…gah…haah…!"

No matter how much of the cool, crisp mountain air he tried to pull into his lungs, it was no use.

Leg muscles pushed to their upper limit, arms pumping with all his might, eyes bone dry from the wind howling past his face, he cried out. Even squeezing every bit of strength out of his body couldn't prevent the girl from going farther and farther into the distance. It was brutal.

Kenki, Aiz Wallenstein. Bell's goal, his idol. A flower blooming on the top of a mountain far above.

He could clearly see the distance, the canyon that separated them.

A difference in pure strength that he never even tasted during training sessions with her on top of the city wall.

His current standing, as well as hers, was a visual demonstration of how far above him she actually was.

Thinking he was closing the gap seemed like nothing more than a joke at this point. He wasn't any closer to that higher plane where she resided; he simply had a better view of it. The path to that summit in front of him was high, extremely steep.

His conviction to save Hestia compelled him to try to stay at her pace, but his body was already screaming in protest. It couldn't hold out much longer.

Lungs and throat burning with pain more intense than he'd ever felt before, Bell could tell that his legs were about to give out—when suddenly…

Aiz looked back at him.

"_____"

The side of her face barely peeked over her shoulder.

She didn't bother slowing down to check on him.

She watched the boy's shoulders pitifully heave up and down as he gasped for breath for a few moments, before increasing her pace.

—She was holding back.

"!!"

Seeing that lit a new fire within Bell, his whole body flaring up.

Shame and a desire not to lose provided the spark. His pride as a man served as the fuel.

An intense desire to not look like a pathetic fool fanned the flames in his heart into a thundering roar. Legs on the verge of giving up were suddenly revitalized. Bell kicked the ground with enough power to crack the rocks in his path, determined to catch up with her.

Expecting a battle, other adventurers had graciously provided him with armor—a breastplate, with shoulder and back armor. He tore them all from his body and tossed them away. The pieces of metal tumbled down the mountainside in his wake.

Feeling a bit lighter than before, Bell pushed himself to the brink yet again and managed to gain some ground.

"..."

Aiz silently watched the surges of emotion on the boy's face as he desperately tried to keep pace with her footsteps.

The female knight's delicate, doll-like expression didn't change as she turned forward again. Placing her faith in the boy, she increased her speed.

After a moment of stunned shock, the boy followed suit, zipping through the mountainscape like a deft white rabbit in a frantic dash to keep up.

Bell following behind her, Aiz raced up the rugged terrain and happened to cast her gaze toward the sky.

Drip. A single droplet of moisture ran down her face. Thick gray clouds blocked out the sun overhead.

The mountainside became dotted with the first sprinkles of rain. Aiz couldn't have cared less, but her golden eyes spotted something else and focused.

A white shadow was circling in the sky, its wings open wide.

"BAH-HA-HA-HA-HA! At last, Orario will get what's coming to them!"

Deep in the Beor Mountain Range, Ares's triumphant howl echoed through a mountain road overlooking a beautiful green valley.

The battalion of about thirty soldiers was all dressed to look like travelers. Rakia's main strike force accompanied their god through the twisting mountain roads and had already put a great deal of distance between themselves and the City of Orario. Every so often, a monster would jump out from behind a boulder or from inside a cave, but the Level 2 captains and the Level 3 generals demonstrated why they were the pride of Rakia and quickly dispatched it.

Ares watched these battles from atop his horse, in extremely high spirits as his followers protected him.

"Hey! Ares! What's the big idea? Put me down right now! There are boundaries to what you can and can't do, even if we've known each other since Tenkai!"

"Shut your powerless mouth, puny goddess! You are nothing more than a hostage to be exchanged for the Crozzo boy! Consider it an honor to have a role to play in my grand design!"

"Who you calling puny, you jerk?!"

Hestia, tied to the back plate of Ares's armor, furiously swung her arms and legs about in every direction.

Tying the ropes himself, Ares had forced her to come with them. The young goddess lacked the strength to loosen the tight ropes, let alone break free. The most she could do was squirm, kick, and punch, but…"Sit still!!" roared Ares as he drove his heavily armored elbow into her ribs.

"UGHFF!" She groaned in anguish. "So I'm a hostage, am I…?"

Hestia had been almost knocked unconscious when she was captured, but now that she could tell left from right, she understood her situation.

Knowing that pitching in at her part-time job had led to this was a hard pill to swallow, and it filled her with regret. Orario was probably descending into chaos at this very moment.

"Don't go thinking you'll get away with this! Bell—all the adventurers of Orario will catch up to you in no time!"

"Will they, now? Our strike forces split into three battalions, all of us executing several maneuvers to cover our tracks. Can they find the right one?"

"Ugh…"

"Take a look around, this is the Beor Mountains! We're so far in that victory was almost assured the moment we made it through the last pass."

They had divided their forces in an effort to confuse their pursuers. It was highly unlikely that their location would be discovered overnight. Ares pushed his point even further by saying that the treacherous terrain would bar search parties, thereby increasing the amount of time it would take to thoroughly search the mountains. She had no chance of being rescued.

"Uga-ga-gahh…! Then at least carry me like the prize that I am! Your armor keeps poking me! It really hurts, you know?"

"It's not my fault that I can't trust my cowardly, worthless soldiers after a series of unthinkable blunders! I get no pleasure from having a useless goddess like you strapped to my back! You'll contaminate me!"

Hestia continued yelling at the top of her lungs without denying Ares's claim. But the god didn't back down, saying they should share the discomfort.

Her back strapped to his and the ropes pulling every joint, she was in considerable pain. Eyes filled with tears, she howled, "What do you take me for?"

Although they knew each other from their time in Tenkai, Ares had been fond of causing disorder, while Hestia was known for keeping to herself and finding her own entertainment. Being so different, these two would never see eye to eye.

Marius walked next to the two crude divine beings, who were having an argument for the ages. "Haaah…" He let out a long sigh.

"…Looks like rain."

Drip. A raindrop ran down the bridge of his nose, prompting Marius to look up to the sky.

He was right. The gray clouds overhead started to open, and sheets of rain descended from the heavens. Within moments, a light drizzle had escalated to a downpour. Travelers' cloaks and warriors' armor soaked through in a matter of moments.

The same was true for Hestia and Ares. "Ak-choo!" The young goddess's entire body spasmed as a sneeze came screaming out of her nostrils.

"Prince Marius, it would be wise to halt our advance and seek shelter from the rain…I worry for Lord Ares's health."

"No…I'd like to proceed to the northern border. Don't forget that our enemy is Orario. We mustn't leave anything to chance. Also, that boneheaded deity won't catch a cold. There are more important things to worry about."

Marius rejected the advice of a nearby soldier, adding that he didn't want to run the risk of being surrounded by monsters at the same time. He pressed on, knowing that every one of the soldiers under his command carried Ares's Falna, his Blessing. This amount of rain wasn't enough to make anyone sick.

Then, out of the corner of his eye...

A strange shadow passed overhead, just close enough to get his attention.

"...A bird?"

The line of fully armored knights looked up into the sky as the falling rain peppered them.

A white shadow was circling just above them, with something that resembled flapping wings stretching out from its body. A creeping feeling of uneasiness went up Marius's spine.

The wind was starting to pick up, yet this bird showed no signs of taking cover. Not only that, there were times when it hovered in one spot. The prince racked his mind, trying to find an explanation, but a heartbeat later...

"K-KENKIIIIIIIIIIIIIIIIIIIIIIIIIIIIIIIIIIIIIIIIIIIIIIIIIIIIIIIIIII!"

A man screamed as if he had seen the oncoming apocalypse. His voice was loud enough to make Marius flinch.

"Wha—?"

While he didn't completely believe the soldier, he hastily turned to face the rear ranks.

They were halfway up the side of a mountain, the road overlooking a cliff. Sure enough, there was a human figure ascending the steep path at blinding speed.

Wet blond hair stood out like a beacon amid the rocks and rain. Golden eyes locked onto him as water droplets bounced off the female knight. Marius screamed.

"Holy! Aiz Wallenstein, the Sword Princess!"

"We—WE'RE UNDER ATTAAAAAAAAAAAAACK!"

The blond-haired, golden-eyed knight attacked with a vigor that would have given Tiona, "Amazon the Slasher," a run for her money. Her thin saber whistled through the air as she ran headlong into the rear of their formation. Screams echoed to the mountains, causing Ares and the forward generals to stop and turn their mounts around to have a look. Marius, however, cast his gaze back to the sky.

As hard as it was for him to believe, his eyes identified golden wings, a white scarf, and the forelimbs of a person.

That was no bird—but an *adventurer.*

"Since when did Orario obtain the power to conquer the skies…?"

An "eye in the sky" had nullified the dangerous terrain and spotted them from a distance.

A girl with aqua-blue hair was still circling over their heads, signaling their location. Marius frowned as the famed Perseus put the immense power of the magic item Talaria, her winged sandals, on display.

A new scream echoed through the mountain range the moment Marius fully comprehended what was going on.

"GAAHHHHHHHHHHHHHHHHHHHHHHHHHHHHHHHH!"

A whirlpool of slashes thrashed soldier after soldier.

One swing of Aiz's saber sent several of them to the ground or hurtling through the air at once.

The War Princess's path was paved with shrieks of pain and fear as she bulldozed a trail into the middle of their formation, where the mounted deity resided with a goddess tied to his back.

"Wall-Wallensomething…?!"

Hestia's eyes went wide. Ares, on the other hand, donned a ferocious grin.

He thrust out his heavily armored right hand in an attempt to raise the morale of his followers.

"Stand your ground, my soldiers! While this turn of events was unexpected, there is only one enemy, and we have the mightiest general of the Rakian army on our side! Go, Garyu! Trample that feeble girl into dust!"

"Lord Ares, Garyu and his battalion have fallen!"

"HE WHAT?!"

It was over in the blink of an eye.

A group of bearded, muscular soldiers literally trembled in their boots in the face of the blond-haired, golden-eyed knight before collapsing in her wake.

Ares ground his teeth together the moment he spotted his once-proud generals facedown on the ground.

"Damn you! So…so it's come to this…!"

"Uphh!"

Ares cut the rope that bound Hestia to his back and jumped off his horse.

Hestia fell to the ground in a heap as Ares, free from the unwanted cargo, drew a longsword from a sheath hanging from the horse's saddle.

"Come at me, Kenki!! I'll deal with you myself!"

"…"

"UWAOOOOOOOOOOOOOOOOOOOOOOOOOO!!"

Ares roared as he charged. Aiz was silent as she kept slashing her way through Rakian soldiers.

Shing! A dull metallic echo rang out. The deity's longsword had been sliced in half.

"N-not bad…!"

"The hell are you doing?"

Ares paused for a moment, shocked that his weapon had been broken on first contact. Marius witnessed everything unfold and dove into the fray to protect him.

His moronic god had just attacked a top-class adventurer on impulse. Marius was quickly joined by every other soldier in the vicinity, forming a wall of muscle and steel in front of Ares. The spot descended into chaos, swords clashing amid even more shrieks of pain.

"——Goddess!!"

"Ah…Bell!"

A boy charged his way into the mountainside battle.

Following the path that Aiz had cleared, he arrived one step behind her. All the soldiers were busy contending with the blond knight, and he seized this chance to reach Hestia.

The sight of her follower brought a smile to Hestia's face. She stood up to greet him but—.

She tripped over the legs of one of the soldiers desperately trying to defend Ares.

"——"

Pushed backward by the sudden impact, she stumbled toward the cliff that led to the valley below.

Her twin black ponytails seemed to float in midair for a split second before she fell over the side.

Making brief eye contact with Bell, the goddess plunged straight into the gorge overlooking the rough river rapids below.

"———!!"

Bell kicked off the ground.

Hestia in his sights, he cut through the rain and flew off the edge of the cliff in pursuit.

As the stone face of the mountain whizzed by, her hand reached out. Hestia's eyes trembled as she saw Bell hurtling like an arrow toward her and reached up for him.

The moment Bell felt her hand in his, he pulled her against his body and embraced the goddess.

From there, the boy held her tiny body against his chest and plunged straight into the river.

"!!"

Aiz was taking down one soldier after another, but she could still hear the faint sound of a splash from far below.

She broke away from the battle without a moment's hesitation and dove over the cliff in pursuit of the boy and his goddess.

It was a deep gorge, and the mountainside was steep. However, Aiz was close enough to the side to kick off the rock, and she practically ran down the mountain at breakneck speed.

"Bell Cranell, Aiz Wallenstein...!"

———Asfi watched it all unfold from her vantage point in the sky.

She couldn't hide her surprise at this unforeseen turn of events in their mission to rescue the goddess. She'd been sent here to mark the location of Rakia's army using Talaria. She had to go after them but hesitated for a moment.

Unfortunately, that moment cost her.

"!"

"Forget that goddess! Shoot down the spy in the sky!"

Asfi had drifted close enough to the ledge that she was in range of the chain Marius swiftly threw into the air. It wrapped around her arm and locked in place.

Hot pain tore through her muscles. Taking her eyes off the gorge and looking at the ledge, she saw Marius clutching the other end of the chain.

"A mythril chain…!"

"Without her, Orario's forces have no chance of finding us! We can't let her escape!"

Marius urgently called out to the few soldiers still able to move after their encounter with Aiz. Wrapping the immensely sturdy chain around his own arm, Marius was determined not to let Asfi get away.

"What is the meaning of this?!" roared Ares as several soldiers held him back. However, the second-in-command had adjusted to the changing circumstances and ordered the rest to eliminate Asfi.

"Marius Victrix Rakia—I had heard you were the son of the Moronic King, but you seem to have a decent head on your shoulders…!"

"I've heard interesting things, too, Perseus! Like how a god stole you, a beautiful young princess, from an island nation, and how you fell through the ranks of society to become an adventurer! Not as if that nation would ever admit it!"

The two sides of the tug-of-war antagonized each other.

It was a test of strength between him and an upper-class adventurer. Asfi, on the other hand, gently smiled at the prince of Rakia, who had displayed superior decision-making ability in battle, and complimented him. Marius shouted back at the top of his lungs, his expression far less relaxed as he glared at his airborne opponent. He channeled every ounce of strength into his arms and grip.

"It appears we have much in common—I sense that you have the same rotten luck that I do."

"—Those eyes! Enough with the sympathy! Don't look at me as if you know my pain!"

They were both at the mercy of their gods' whim, often pulled along for a ride they couldn't control. Asfi looked down at the man with an empathizing look on her face. It made Marius writhe in agony.

"My prince!" "My prince!" Exhausted soldiers wailed as they surrounded their vice commander, desperately calling out to him as they moved into position.

Her movement restrained by the rigid chain, Asfi came under fire of countless arrows and magic spells. Her white scarf torn to shreds and skin covered in burns, Perseus grimaced in pain.

She could feel her hair plastered to her cheeks by the pouring rain. Bell and Aiz were already out of sight, so she prioritized her own escape from this battle. Dodging another wave of arrows, she withdrew a vial of blast oil from her holster.

An explosion echoed through the mountain range and drowned out the sounds of battle, until it faded into the pounding of rain and the river rapids from far below.

The rain's not letting up.

Waves of water come rushing down the side of the mountain faster and faster, and the storm shows no signs of lifting whatsoever.

Trapped in a deafening tunnel of sound, swept up by a raging river through the gorge between mountains, I make my way to the riverbank and manage to lift the goddess up and out of the water. I climb out next to her in time to see that Aiz has followed us.

I get to my feet, swing the goddess over my back, and we race off along the riverbank.

"How is she?"

"Her body is getting colder and colder! She's not answering me, either…!"

Even I can hear how close I am to tears, yelling like this.

"Haah…haah…" Her chin is resting on my shoulder, so I can hear the weak breaths coming in and out of her mouth.

We're losing body heat. The same is true for Aiz, her soaking-wet armor slick and shiny. But the goddess and I are much worse off, having actually fallen into the river.

For Aiz and me, this amount of rain is no big deal. Our leveled-up Statuses make our bodies hardy enough to withstand it. Unfortunately, that's not true for the goddess. While she survived the plunge into the river, I can't feel any heat on my back, and her limbs are limp.

The gods and goddesses came to this world to enjoy a "game," and therefore they had to follow a set of rules.

The most important one is that no one can use their divine power, Arcanum. Without those all-powerful abilities, the deities are physically the same as people without a Blessing, or perhaps even weaker. Sure, they never age and never die, staying more or less the same for all eternity, but they're not immune to the common cold or getting really sick.

I hear it's all an "adjustment" to enjoy everything that Earth has to offer, or perhaps they're being flexible.

"If we don't find shelter soon...!"

The goddess won't last long like this. I've never heard of Arcanum being activated and the deity abruptly being sent back to Tenkai because of an illness, but that does nothing to ease her pain.

The current took us pretty far downriver, so I have no idea where we are right now. Aiz being here isn't much help as long as we're stuck out in the rain.

"I could break open the cliff face and make a cave..."

Heat is what I want, not shelter. Every minute the goddess stays this cold puts her in even more danger.

Making fire isn't the issue; Firebolt can take care of that instantly. The problem is *keeping* the fire going. We have to find dry kindling and a protected spot away from the river and out of the rain where we can rest and recover. There has to be a place like that farther along, I'm sure of it...!

Muscles in my face tense as I listen to Aiz speak and look up at the top of the unbelievably deep gorge. There's nothing to obstruct my view of the dark-gray sky as it continues to mercilessly drop an endless stream of rain on top of us.

"——KIYAWWWWWWWWWWWWWWWWWWWWWW
WWWWWWWW!!"

"ı"

A high-pitched squawk reaches my ears as we continue to race through the gorge.

Countless shadows descend on us from above and into the path ahead, the sound of flapping feathered wings accompanying them.

"Harpies!"

The descendants of the original monsters that emerged from the Dungeon millennia ago and settled here in the Beor Mountain Range are swarming in to attack us!

Harpies: half-human/half-bird, bizarrely female-looking monsters.

They look like women from the waist up, even have breasts. But both forearms are much larger than a human's, forming wings the size of shields. Everything from the waist down is covered in dirty feathers. Just like a hawk or eagle, both legs end with sharp sets of talons.

As for their faces—it would be easy to say they look like a woman's, but they're actually quite different from humanity as a whole.

First off, their mouths are full of sharp fangs, and their skin is riddled with wrinkles. To be blunt, they're horrifying. If I have to describe it, I'd say they look like overly obsessed old women. But no, a wizened old lady is much more beautiful than these things.

Their bodies may be close to what we're familiar with, but they're far more revolting than the normal monsters in the Dungeon. That's probably because of the putrid smell emanating from their bodies. It makes me want to rip my nose off my face.

Why now...?

They're swarming in like birds of prey, stark golden eyes flashing menacingly. I glare back at them and thrust my right hand forward, taking aim at the middle of the flock of harpies. I'm one breath away from unleashing my magic when I hear:

"Keep running."

Wind whistles by my ears.

I hear the unmistakable sound of a sword being removed from its sheath, and my eyes catch a flash of blond hair. The next thing I know, every harpy in our path falls to the ground in pieces.

Shrill squawks and fountains of blood fill the air. Aiz has sparked confusion among the harpies, and her eyes sharpen into a glare just as acute as her blade.

"————————————————————————KAAWWW!"

The air is suddenly flooded with countless black feathers falling to the ground like the rain.

The blond-haired, golden-eyed knight is running up the side of the gorge, dashing through the air, and slicing her way to the other side so fast I can't keep up with her. The birds of prey surrounding us on all sides let out high-pitched squawks as her blade carves them into cold cuts. I do exactly as she tells me and keep running with the goddess on my back. Meanwhile, there are constant streaks of gold and silver light going up, down, and all around us like a dome that shreds any monster that gets too close.

It's like her saber is creating a barrier of protection around us.

I know I'm being protected and all, but seeing her pull this off so easily, it's impressive and awe-inspiring at the same time. I'm running as fast as I can, but I can't help straining my eyes trying to watch her in action.

—She's very, very strong. Too strong.

Pa-loosh! Pa-loosh! While I was busy gawking, several de-winged monsters fall into the raging river and get swallowed up by the waves. I'm dodging carcasses one after another, and there's no telling how many hundreds of them are behind me along the riverbank.

The rain washes away the blood splattered against the mountain face.

"…What's that?"

Then, when the last squawk of the final harpy rings out…

Aiz lands on a boulder not too far in front of me and turns forward, as though she's noticed something out of place.

I look in that direction—there's a light wavering in the distance, a magic-stone lamp. What's more, it's coming this way.

"Hello out there! Anybody here?"

A human voice rises over the crashing waves of the rapids.

Aiz and I exchange glances and nods before rushing off in that direction.

Crackle, crackle. Sounds from the fireplace fill the room.

Everything here is cast in an orange light and flooded with warmth. The heat washes over me, embracing my cold body in a warm hug. My eyelids get heavy, but I shake my head every time sleep threatens to overtake me.

The goddess is lying in the bed in front of me, sleeping peacefully. I sit quietly, holding her right hand with both of mine.

"How is the goddess doing?"

"Ah, Mr. Kam…She's all right. Fell asleep a little while ago."

I hear a knock at the door, look up to see an elderly gentleman named Kam, and stand to greet him. A human girl a little older than me is at his side. "I'm glad," he says with a smile of relief.

—We came to this place, Edas Village, after we were fortunate enough to run into someone in the gorge.

Edas Village is located deep in the Beor Mountain Range. Surrounded by steep cliffs, it's a well-hidden small town in one of the valleys. Aiz and I were extremely surprised that a place like this existed when we came to it. Who would've thought people lived way out here?

After we explained the situation to the young men who came to check on the river, they brought us here, and the villagers immediately offered to help. The village elder, Kam, opened his home to us. Not only is the goddess resting in one of his guest rooms, but he gave me a change of clothes as well.

Words can't express how grateful I am for his help. I bow to the elder once again.

"I can't thank you enough. You saved my goddess…"

"Raise your head, young Bell. This is the least I can——*cough,*

cough!" He couldn't finish a sentence before breaking into a coughing fit.

The girl at his side supports him with both hands as the old man bends over, trying to catch his breath between coughs. The girl, maybe his daughter, urges him to go back to his room, with a concerned look on her face.

Kam slowly raises his hand, telling her he's all right, and gradually stands up straight.

"Um, please don't push yourself…!"

"No, it's all right…Bell, please make yourself at home. If you need anything at all, my daughter will be happy to help. I pray for your goddess's recovery."

I take a step toward him, unsure what to do. Even though he's not healthy, Kam says he's fine, but he keeps his eyes on the goddess, still lying in bed.

He has a thin beard and wrinkled face, but there's something about his eyes. I can tell they've seen a lot, and there's a mix of complicated emotions running through him right now. He then makes a small bow to her and says, "May the both of you stay in good health…" before exiting our room with the help of his daughter.

"I wonder if he's sick…"

We only just met, but he immediately pulled out all the stops to help us the moment he saw me carrying the goddess. It's almost overkill, but I'm extremely grateful for everything he's done. He's been so good to us throughout our time here that the lack of color in his face worries me.

I make my way back to the goddess's side and catch a glimpse of someone outside the window.

I watch the hooded figure approach for a few moments, trying to make them out in the rain. Once I realize who it is, I leave the goddess in Kam's daughter's care and rush out of the room and to the entrance of the house.

"Welcome back, Miss Aiz. And, um, thanks for going back out."

"It's no problem, and thanks…How is she?"

Aiz takes off the soaking-wet hooded robe in the front hallway, revealing her battle cloth and armor beneath. I hand her a towel as she asks about the goddess and tell her that she's in stable condition.

"So, what did you find?"

"Asfi wasn't there and neither were Rakia's soldiers…Just the broken weapons and charred aftermath of battle."

Aiz went back out to check on what was happening with Rakia's soldiers as soon as the goddess was safely inside Edas Village.

She says that she followed the overflowing river upstream to the point where we fell in. The storm had gotten worse, so she reasoned that Rakia's soldiers and Asfi had taken shelter somewhere. Whether the enemy soldiers were biding time to come after the goddess again or had completely given up and gone home, she didn't know.

Not only had she been pulled into this mess, but she also protected me the entire time. I apologize for causing her so much trouble, but she kindly shakes her head and tells me it's okay.

"We have no way to contact Orario…I don't think we should hope for rescue."

Going back to the city would require at least the rest of the night, and to make matters worse, the weather isn't cooperating. Getting lost in rugged mountainous terrain is a very real danger, separating her from us—and Lord Ares's troops are still out there. They're strong and numerous enough that she didn't want to engage them in battle under these conditions. So Aiz decided to come back to the village for the time being.

Asfi is an upper-class adventurer, so I'm sure she's returned to the city and explained what happened by now…but I highly doubt she knows about a village this far into the mountains, and that we safely arrived here.

"So then we stay here until the goddess recovers…?"

"Yes, I think that's best."

Aiz wipes down her wet hair and neck with the towel as she nods. Her soaked clothing is plastered to her skin, making it very difficult for me to figure out where to look as I agree with her plan.

The three of us will stay together and move as one. We'll have

to impose on the people of the village until the goddess is healthy
enough to make the journey back to Orario.

I feel bad for making Lilly and the others worry…but it can't be
helped.

Feeling a little guilty about it, I make a plan with Aiz for the next
few days.

The goddess opened her eyes the day after we arrived. I was so happy
I could cry, but I knew she wasn't out of the woods yet. She stayed in
bed the rest of that day, as well as all of the next.

Then, on our third morning in Edas Village…

"Sorry…Bell."

"You've already apologized many times, Goddess. I told you, it's
all right."

I've lost count of how many times she's said sorry while she lies
in bed. I'm in my usual spot next to her, tension leaving my face
as I smile. Her color is better this morning. She looks up at me but
avoids making eye contact, as though she's ashamed of something.

"This is…a nice village, isn't it?"

"Yes. Everyone is so warm and friendly."

Edas Village was originally an elf settlement, if you went back far
enough in time. Back to the Ancient Times, from what I've heard.

Elves generally don't like to mingle with other races, so a place
like this was perfect for their isolationist views. But apparently, the
way they saw the world began to change about 1,000 years ago. The
arrival of the gods and goddesses on Earth spurred the elvish youth
to leave their homeland and explore the world, while the older elves
began to accept people of other races into their village.

People unable to face their own reality, people escaping danger,
and young couples eloping from families who couldn't accept their
love all found their way here.

And, of course, exiled adventurers from Orario who wandered
into the mountains with the intention of dying out here ended up

settling in the village as well. As a result, the villagers are exceptionally friendly and open to new arrivals. More than half the people living here are the descendants of these wayward travelers. I have a feeling that's the reason they were so quick to assist lost people like us.

A hidden village not on any map, for people who had lost their way. This…is another world I didn't know about.

Deities must be a rare sight in the village because two demi-human children, a boy and a girl, keep peeking in through the window. Lady Hestia notices and smiles at them, gently waving her hand. The kids blush and smile back.

"How are you feeling today? If you need something, please let me know."

"Oh, Miss Rina. Thank you for everything."

Kam's daughter, Rina, steps into the room and asks how the goddess is coming along. I tell her the goddess is doing well and bow my head.

She's probably two or three years older than me and very friendly. She and several of Kam's adult sons have been taking care of everything for us these past few days. My gratitude for what all of them have done to help the goddess knows no bounds.

But there is one thing that feels odd. I don't want to sound rude, but Kam is pretty old. There's such a gap between him and his children, it'd be easier to think of them as grandchildren. Whenever I see them in the room or around the house, I can't help but be a little confused. What's more, I've never seen anyone the right age to be their mother during my time here.

Strange as it may be, I'm not about to ask. Instead, I bring up something else that's been on my mind.

"Um, is there something going on today? There've been a lot of people outside the window since yesterday…"

"There is. Today is our annual fertility festival. We were concerned because the rain wasn't letting up, but it stopped just in time… Everyone's getting excited."

There's a blue sky outside my window, and I can hear many people talking outside. She explains what's going on, her tied black hair swishing behind her head. I nod in understanding.

The small village where I grew up had festivals, too.

"Bell...go help with the festival preparations."

"Huh?"

Both Rina and I turn to face the goddess, surprised by what she said.

"B-but, Goddess..."

"After all they've done for us, with us not doing anything in return, I'd make goddesses look bad...Please, Bell."

She's much better now than she was, but leaving her side still makes me uncomfortable. She laughs at my worry and says she wants me to go.

...I want to do something to pay back the people who have helped us, too.

Going home without repaying the debt seems cold, and I'm sure I'd regret it.

With that in mind, I return the goddess's smile and agree to do what she asks.

Standing up from the side of the bed, I tell Rina that I'll help. My offer makes her happy.

Leaving the goddess in her care, I exit the room.

"Ah, Miss Aiz."

"Morning..."

I bump into Aiz halfway down the hallway.

She returns my greeting, but it's her outfit that gets my attention—so much so that my cheeks start heating up.

"Um, those...those clothes look cute on you..."

I always see her dressed in battle cloth and armor, but today she looks nothing like an adventurer.

She's wearing a long red skirt with vivid embroidery, with a loose white blouse underneath a patterned vest buttoned in the front. It makes her blond hair stand out even more than usual. She looks like a country girl.

She's beautiful, as always, but…I've never seen this cute side of Aiz before. My face turns red as butterflies run rampant in my stomach.

"These were recommended to me…Do I look weird?"

"N-no, no! You look great!"

She looks down at her outfit as I vigorously shake my head.

Just like me, she borrowed clothes from Kam's daughter to wear because the rain had soaked through her equipment and battle cloth. Apparently, Rina got excited choosing an outfit for Aiz because of her goddess-like beauty, and she wanted Aiz to look the part.

Aiz looks slightly off to the side when I compliment her, her cheeks turning pink…and shyly blushes.

—Jolt! Every move she makes sends a shock up my spine. I'm the one who complimented her, but it's my chest that's getting tighter every second. As fire in my veins turns my skin bright red, she looks at me with puzzlement while I turn into a pitiful wreck.

"Are you heading somewhere?"

"Oh, yes. There's a festival in the village today, so I'm going to help them get ready."

She tilts her head when she figures out I was going outside alone.

Over the past three days, I've hardly left that room. As for Aiz, in order to keep us safe—or perhaps because she's had nothing else to do—she's been on guard outside the guest room or patrolling the house. The rain didn't let up until last night, so there was no point in going outside.

However, she gave Kam's sons, and me, quite a scare by arming herself with her saber while dressed as a cute country girl…She's a knight through and through, no matter what she's wearing.

She nods while I explain what's going on and then says, "I'll come, too."

"Huh? Are you sure?"

"Yes. They provided clothing and more than enough food…I want to help."

Her expression is just as distant as usual, but her desire to help makes me happy.

The two of us exit Kam's house.

"It was dark when we arrived, and it was raining so hard that I couldn't tell but...this village is pretty big."

"Yes, it is..."

The puddles on the ground reflect the blue sky above. The villagers outside come up to greet us, and we offer our assistance for the festival preparations.

Being an old elf dwelling, Edas Village is surrounded by trees on all sides and much bigger than it looks. Add in the tall mountains of the Beor Mountain Range, and the term *hidden village* seems to describe this place extremely well. It would be really hard to find this place without knowing where it was first.

The fact that we're here must've spread around the village by now, so when we emerge from Kam's house, we get a lot of attention. Or, I should say, Aiz does. Looking around, I see the men of the village are gathering left and right to catch a glimpse of her in this outfit. Quite a few have their mouths open, gawking. At the same time, the ones who are already married are getting reprimanded by their wives. A slap or two rings out from the crowd. A smile grows on my lips as I watch the men shrink in front of the angry women and excited children next to them.

There are many houses built around a central square in the middle of the village. Many tables have already been set out in the open area, and several people are busy building a bonfire. Things are already getting under way. A group of muscular middle-aged men, probably the ones in charge of the event, are directing traffic. So Aiz and I listen to their instructions, go our separate ways, and get to work.

"Um...I hate to bother you, but what is that?"

Working among the many races of people living in the village, we made a great deal of progress. The afternoon was over before I knew it, and dusk arrived.

I was in charge of preparing firewood and carrying decorations from place to place, so I had a chance to see several peculiar objects scattered about the village.

They look like large, shiny obsidian rocks, but there's a strange aura hanging over them.

Each one is about the size of my chest. They form a ring around the village, creating a line between where the village ends and the forest begins.

I ask a nearby elderly animal lady about the black things that seem to be protecting the village. She smiles and answers right away.

"Oh, this? It's…one of the Black Dragon's scales."

"——It's what?"

I can't believe my ears.

Beneath an evening sky so red it might as well be bleeding, I'm sure I misheard her and ask for clarification as I step closer.

"The Black Dragon…As in the one in the legends? *That* Black Dragon…?"

"Yes, that's the one. Long ago, after heroes drove him from Orario, the Black Dragon fled north. These scales fell from his body as he passed over this valley."

The lady tells me the story has been passed down through generations of long-living elves.

So, many years ago, a legendary beast flew over that sky while scales dropped into the forest below…?

"Didn't you find it strange that a village situated in the middle of a forest filled with so many monsters never comes under attack?"

"W-well, yeah, but…"

Aiz and I were swarmed by harpies on our way here. But I haven't seen a single one since we came inside the village. Sure, I thought it was weird, but…

"It's all thanks to these scales. Monsters are so afraid of them that they stay far away. It's thanks to the Black Dragon that we can live in peace."

The strange aura coming from these things is the presence of the King of Dragons, or perhaps his power.

The monsters are afraid of the isolated pieces of the legendary beast, so they don't come close to them. That's why Edas Village doesn't worry about monster attacks.

Her story leaves me speechless. At the same time, she closes her eyes and brings her hands together as she takes a knee in front of the black scale.

"...I'm sure you find it peculiar that we worship a monster. The reason we are alive today is not due to the protection of adventurers or deities...but these scales."

——That, and they are afraid.

Afraid of the day when the legendary beast will return and destroy the world.

The villagers living in Edas both revere the monster as well as live in fear of it every day. They, who are more aware of the dragon's power than anyone, fear the day that it will be unleashed on the world. To the point that they can't help but worship it.

...A village built on faith in a dragon.

No, not quite. A village that prays to a dragon so that tomorrow will continue to come peacefully, and to hold back the calamity that is its power.

I'm stunned by this side of Edas Village, a place so far separated from the world I know.

The story of the calamities that Lord Hermes told me about feels so much more real.

The Black Dragon...I wonder if there's more evidence left behind by the one-eyed dragon in other parts of the world.

"But of course, should there come a day when Lord Dragon is gone from this world, we'll have no need to keep doing this, now will we..."

The lady, eyes still closed and hands still together, says this to me with a grimace. Suddenly, it all clicks.

The meaning of the Three Great Quests that have been entrusted to Orario.

The wish for salvation that the world still holds to this day.

"Well, this heart-to-heart chat got a bit serious. We're almost done getting ready, so why don't you run along and pitch in?"

"Ah...Y-yes, sure."

She looks up at me with a gentle smile. I manage to convince my head to nod. I've been carrying a few logs over my shoulder this whole time, so I start moving my feet toward my original destination.

After leaving the nice lady behind and delivering the wood, I pause for a minute and survey the village.

The black scales dot the landscape. With the preparations nearly complete, this place looks a little bit different from before.

"Ah..."

I spot Aiz while I walk through groups of villagers who've already finished what they had to do.

Still dressed like a country girl, she has her back to me. She's standing in front of a stone hut.

"Miss Aiz?"

"..."

She keeps her eyes on the stone structure, not reacting at all as I walk up next to her.

One of those black scales is inside the hut. Up on a pedestal, several plates of food and other offerings are lined up in front of it... This must be an altar. That would mean that this stone hut is a place where the people of the village come to pray to the thing that protects their home.

Aiz stares quietly at the scale. Like me, she probably heard from the villagers about the history of this place and the black scales.

"It's almost like a god, don't you think?"

Their fear of this piece of the dragon has led them to present it with offerings. The similarities with actual gods are uncanny. I casually voice my observations.

However...

"This *thing* is no god."

Her sharp words cut through the air, slicing through my off-handed comment.

"_____"

She's still looking away from me. All I heard was a low, stone-cold rejection.

Was that really Aiz just now? I've never heard her put so much emotion into her voice. Words are stuck in my throat.

My heart is trembling.

That voice genuinely scared me.

What did her face look like when she said it? Time comes to a halt without an answer.

"Let's go back."

"...S-sure."

Aiz turns to face me after a few seconds that feel like an eternity.

She's wearing the same aloof expression that I've seen many times before. It's the Aiz I know. Even her voice sounds like it always does. She walks away from the stone hut.

But I don't move. She stops and looks over her shoulder after a few steps. My legs finally wake up, and I scurry after her.

Now walking side by side, I chance a glance at her face. Cast in a red glow by the setting sun, nothing has changed. Absolutely nothing at all. Was what I heard moments ago just my imagination? Those words are still haunting my ears, but did they really ever happen?

I never work up the courage to ask.

Still a little bit shaken by what happened with Aiz, I finish what I was assigned to do and head back to check on the goddess.

There are many wooden houses built around the center of the village. I make my way all the way to the back to Kam's place, open the front door, and go inside. A quick walk down the hallway and I'm at the guest room that he's so graciously let us use.

"Huh?...Mr. Kam?"

I open the door and go inside, only to find Kam standing at the foot of the bed in front of the goddess.

She's asleep. *Zzz, zzz.* The breaths of the young goddess fill the room as the elderly man silently watches her.

Standing with the help of a cane, he slowly looks up at me.

"Don't be afraid. I haven't done anything to her."

"Eh, um, I'm not worried about that…I-is something wrong?"

I venture a question, unable to hide my surprise. I see him turn to face me almost as if he's moving in slow motion.

"I was waiting for you."

After yet another surprise, the elderly gentleman continues.

"Bell, can you spare a moment of your time on this old man?"

He leads me farther into the house, all the way to his room.

There's a bed, desk, and a chair in here. Not much else at all.

There's a small pile of papers and a feathered pen on his desk, but that's to be expected. He is the village elder, after all, but I don't think he's used the pen in quite a while. Even the top sheet of paper has a thin layer of dust on it.

"*Cah-ough…!*"

"A-are you okay?"

A loud cough comes out of nowhere.

I rush over to help him and offer to call his daughter, but Kam puts out his hand and waves me off.

"Please don't concern yourself. I understand what's going on with me better than anyone."

I'm not sure how to take that. It must've shown on my face because he tells me one more time not to worry.

The elderly man is thin but still stands a little bit taller than me. The grayish white hair on top of his head shifts as he smiles at me. I'm still worried about him, but I'll listen to what he has to say.

As golden-red evening light streams in through the window, Kam makes his way to the desk and opens the top drawer. Pulling something out, he sets it on top of the desk.

Whatever it is, it's very old. I lean in for a closer look, but the details are so worn that it's hard to see…Is that a fire? An emblem?

"Is that…a familia's emblem?"

"Yes, indeed. A long time ago, I pledged myself to a certain goddess."

My ears perk up. Kam begins to tell me about his life.

"I fell for her, and she had feelings for me as well. We were in love with each other."

"You were...?"

He fell in love with a goddess.

This is shocking news to me. Kam takes his eyes off me for a moment. Is he blushing?

"Unfortunately, I was unable to protect her. I was her only follower, and I had sworn to defend her with my life. But she was felled by a monster's claw..."

"...!"

"Her sacrifice saved my life...and consequently, she returned to Tenkai."

Kam casts his gaze up and out the window, as if remembering the events that happened more than fifty years ago.

They were attacked by a swarm of monsters while traveling. Kam lost his goddess on that day. She pushed him off the edge of a cliff and into the sea, saving his life at the cost of her existence on Earth. At the same time, he plunged into the deepest depths of despair.

His reason for living gone, Kam decided to throw his life away by wandering aimlessly into the Beor Mountain Range, but...

"...I found my way to this village. I was unable to cast away the life that she had saved."

After he met several others who had walked a similar path, they took him in with open arms. Crying tears of joy, he decided that he would one day be buried here. The Status on his back had been sealed due to the fact that his goddess was no longer in this realm—and he left it alone as the only remnant of the bond they once shared. He committed himself to the village that took him in and eventually attained the rank of village elder.

"...In that case, Rina and the others are...?"

"Adopted. Some of them lost their parents to the plague, others were abandoned...I took in every child who didn't have a place to go."

He admitted that he wasn't related to any of his "sons and daughters" by blood.

Kam, who had sworn his love to a goddess but had been unable to protect her, couldn't have a normal life, get married, and have kids of his own.

"Bell...please, please protect your goddess."

He doesn't need to ask me to do that because I fully intend to, but Kam does anyway.

"*Cough!*" He covers his mouth, and I take a worried step closer, but he just smiles at me.

"You must not live life with the regrets that I have."

Now I finally understand why he was so protective of the goddess, so quick to welcome us into his home.

He saw his younger self in us when we arrived, and he helped us so that I wouldn't go through the same loss he did.

That smile and his words make their way into my heart. They'll stay there for a long time.

"...Blah..."

Hestia lay in bed, staring at the ceiling and bored out of her mind.

"I can't sleep anymore..."

The day was practically over. The last of the red sunlight in the sky was fading. Only dim light came in from the window, night descending on the view outside.

Hestia used her elbows to prop up her top half and sat up.

"Still no energy...But I'm better, probably."

She looked down at herself, convinced that her drowsiness was the result of sleeping on and off for the past three days.

She wasn't sick, and her appetite was alive and well. Hestia felt that the worst was behind her, and she didn't have to take it easy anymore.

"Uph." She started pulling up her sweaty shirt—a hand-me-down from Kam's daughter that was tight across the chest. Her twin black ponytails, still messy from three days' worth of bed head, swayed to and fro as she adjusted herself.

There came a knock at the door.

"Please excuse me…"

"Wall-Wallensomething…?"

Aiz stepped inside the room, holding a tray in her arms.

Hestia watched her approach with unblinking eyes. The blond girl set the tray on the table next to the bed, steam rising from a bowl of soup on top of it.

"Have you recovered…?"

"I-I'm fine, but…wh-where's Bell?"

"Talking with the village elder, I think…"

The goddess asked why it was her and not Bell who came to check on her, and Aiz responded in a quiet voice.

Kam's daughter had made the soup, but she was summoned to help with something outside. So she had asked Aiz to deliver it to Hestia in her place.

Hestia had been so surprised to see Aiz that only now did she notice what the girl was wearing. She practically gasped.

"Wall-Wallensomething, what's with those clothes?"

"Rina lent them to me…"

"You trying to tempt Bell or something…?"

Hestia's body shook, a vein bulging in her forehead. Aiz, on the other hand, tilted her head in confusion.

Hestia knew. She knew that the boy liked the simple charming appeal of the girl-next-door type.

One look at the female knight standing in front of her, dressed like this——*Bell blushed more times today than he does in a year, no doubt about it!*

"Grrrr…" Hestia growled under her breath, on the verge of divulging her thoughts on the matter when it was neither the time nor the place to do so. But then she realized this was her chance and changed her mind. There was something she wanted to find out once and for all.

"Have a seat, Wallensomething."

"?"

Seeing the goddess flick her wrist toward a chair next to the bed, Aiz did as she was told.

"For starters...Thank you for saving me. Sorry you had to get mixed up in this."

"It's noth—"

"—But, and this is important, what do you think of my Bell?"

"What do I think...?"

"You know, it's that, um...! How do you see him? What's your impression?"

Hestia couldn't ask her directly if she had feelings for the boy. She tried but ended up blushing too hard and tripping over her own words.

No matter how doll-like Aiz's aloof expression was, it was impossible to lie to a deity.

Hestia cast her divine gaze onto the human girl, determined to find out what emotion was lurking inside her heart.

Under the goddess's intense gaze, Aiz casually looked up at the ceiling and gave the question some thought. She answered after a few moments of heavy silence.

"...A rabbit?"

Hestia closed her eyes and nodded decisively upon hearing her answer.

"I always believed in you."

"...?"

Thump, thump. Hestia reached out and petted Aiz a few times on the shoulder.

Although the answer was a little bit out there, she now had proof that Aiz didn't see Bell as a *man*—that is, a member of the opposite gender. Her spirits lifted immeasurably.

"But be warned, don't be too nice to him. While I agree that rabbits are very cute, if you're too nice to him, it'll go to his head. That'll be nothing but trouble."

"Under...stood...?"

Aiz once again tilted her head, not comprehending what the deity was telling her even as Hestia continued to enthusiastically pat her shoulder.

"Oh, My Lady, are you feeling well?"

That's when Kam's daughter appeared at the doorway. "Very much so, thanks to you," said Hestia with a genuine smile to the girl who came to see how she was doing.

"You seem to be sweating. Shall I prepare a change of clothes for you?"

"Hmm, that might be a good idea…"

Rina handed Hestia a towel and a glass of water as the goddess considered taking her up on the offer. She stopped in her tracks.

One quick glance at Aiz's outfit, and her eyes flashed with the spark of an idea.

"Sorry, but may I make one more selfish request?"

"The festival has already started…"

Kam and I talked for a long time, much longer than I thought we would. I take a look out the closest window when I finally leave his room, and my jaw drops at what I see.

It looks like the dead of night outside, and all the villagers have gathered in the main square. Everyone's talking, having a good time as logs are being assembled to make a bonfire.

My muscles relax as memories of the festivals in my home village come to the surface. Feeling nostalgic, I start walking to the guest room where the goddess is resting.

"Bell!"

"What, Goddess—eh?"

She's in the hallway, right in front of me, and wearing something that takes my breath away.

It's almost the same outfit that Aiz is wearing. But instead of the red colors that made her stand out, the goddess is wearing a more calm blue—although it looks like she forced herself into that blouse. I can almost hear those buttons in front of her chest screaming…

Standing next to Aiz like this, the two of them might as well be sisters.

"Hee-hee, so? How do I look?"

"You look great, but...are you sure it's okay to be out of bed?"

Yes, she looks really cute, and the butterflies are back, but my concern for her well-being is a little bit stronger right now. "Yep, I'm sure!" she says with a grin. Apparently, she made a special request, and Rina went out of her way to help.

Kam's daughter is standing by her shoulder opposite to Aiz, smiling just as wide.

"Since you are once again in good health, My Lady, why don't you come watch the festivities?"

The goddess immediately accepts her invitation.

Maybe it's because she's been in bed for so long, but she seems excited about the idea and yells, "I'd love to come!" I'm still worried about her, though. She should be getting some rest, but in the end I join her and Aiz as Rina leads the three of us out of the house.

"Um, are you sure this is a good idea, Goddess? You shouldn't push yourself just yet..."

"I'm fine! After spending so much time so close to you, I'd be worried if I didn't get better!"

She claims that staying in that room would make her feel worse. Seeing her giddy like this is making me only more concerned.

She looks fine, but...maybe I'm being overprotective after hearing Kam's story. I'm still thinking it over as we arrive in the village square.

"...!"

"Now, this is nice!"

"...Gorgeous."

The bonfire is already burning bright as all three of us voice our reactions in turn. The tables surrounding the bonfire are covered with a wide variety of food. The villagers see us coming and wave while holding their drinks in the other hand.

The goddess and Aiz bask in the warmth of the festival sprawled out in front of us. This energy is infectious; even I'm getting drawn in.

"Ah! My Lady!"

"Are you feeling well enough to be outside?"

Several villagers gather around us.

The goddess has been bedridden for days, and everyone is worried about her. At first, Hestia is overwhelmed by all the men and women voicing their concerns, but it doesn't take her long to start thanking them and smiling.

News of her recovery rapidly makes its way through the square as the festival starts to feel more like a celebration. Aiz and I get swept up in it, along with the goddess.

"So, My Lady, why did you come this far into the Beor Mountains?"

"Word is you got lost. Is it true?"

The villagers start pressing for details.

The three of us do our best to answer them as the villagers form a ring around us. I almost forgot; we're supposed to be in hiding. What if all this noise and the bonfire give away our position to the Rakian soldiers? This village might be hidden deep in a valley surrounded by mountains, but this bonfire would be easy to find...I glance at Aiz. She notices me and lightly shakes her head, as though she's thinking the same thing. A bead of cold sweat runs down my neck.

Orario's Alliance would have found them by now, and even if they haven't, I doubt that the Rakian army would stay in the mountains for three days in the first place...

"The truth is, an idiotic god took us for a wild ride. Then again, this whole mess started because I ran away from home—."

The goddess says that much before freezing on the spot. "Ah." The sound comes out of my mouth as I remember, too.

That's right, Hestia and I were fighting—well, not really, but something close to it.

The goddess slowly turns my way, craning her neck. A jolt runs through my body, and I quickly look away.

The villagers and Aiz stare at us with bewilderment.

N-not good! I have to apologize, and quickly...!

An apology might not solve the problem, but it certainly won't hurt. *Glance, glance.* The goddess is looking around, waiting for me to make a move.

I scramble to come up with the right words, to make an apology here and now, when…

"Oh…?"

People are singing.

It's an upbeat melody, and others are clapping along to the beat. I look past the people surrounding us toward the bonfire and see pairs of men and women starting to dance in the crackling light.

"Is that this village's traditional dance? Most of the dancers seem young…"

"Ahhh, you see…"

The goddess notices, too, and has a look. Just as she said, the villagers dancing around the fire right now are a mix of humans, elves, dwarves, and animal people, but the one thing they have in common is youth. Well, that and their shy smiles.

An older gentleman answers the goddess's question for us with a dry grin on his face.

"It's not a law of our village by any means…but it's said that when an unmarried man invites a woman to dance during the festival, it's the same as a confession of love. Should she accept, the two shall be blessed with a lifetime of happiness as lovers. Or at least that's how the story goes…"

"O-oh?"

His explanation fascinates me. For some reason, the goddess starts fidgeting.

"Please dance with us, Goddess! Today is our fertility festival, after all!"

"Please bestow us with a bounty of blessings!"

Several villagers use the start of the dance as an excuse to approach the goddess and say their wishes.

I don't think Lady Hestia has any power over fertility, but…this might be the first time they've seen a deity in person, so they're probably all the same to the locals. In any case, they ask her for good fortune.

Surrounded by villagers, the goddess closes her eyes and, "Ah-hem," clears her throat.

Step, step, step. She slides over to me with shifty feet.

"Oh—Bell? It looks like there's an urgent need for me to fulfill my role as a goddess, you know…So, eh, yeah."

Her face is turning red, redder than the warm light coming from the bonfire on her face. Actually, I'd say she seems nervous.

"If you'll dance with me…I'll consider *that incident* to be water under the bridge."

I blink a few times.

Almost as if on cue, the villagers surrounding us start happily whispering to one another.

My shoulders jump the moment I realize their excitement means it will be extremely difficult for me to turn her down. Well, if she's willing to let the problem slide if I dance with her, then yes, that's what I want…And also, I might enjoy dancing with the goddess.

Fulfilling her role as a goddess will help these people, too, so I fight back my nerves—and put up with the burning sensation in my cheeks. Then I nod to the goddess.

"All right…I'll dance with you, Goddess."

But for some reason, her cheeks are pulling back into a smug grin. This is what she wanted, isn't it? Why does she look annoyed?

"If you're going to invite me to dance, do it right, Bell. Like you did with Wallensomething at Apollo's Banquet, when you invited her to dance."

I freeze, my eyes wide. Aiz, standing right next to me, does the same.

The burning feeling in my cheeks grows to an inferno. My body jerks toward Aiz. She's still got that puzzlement in her eyes, tilting her head to the side.

W-well, it *is* true that I danced with her during Apollo's Banquet of the Gods, but…!

"There's a line you have to say at times like this, isn't there, Bell?" says the goddess, looking at me through half-open eyes. Meanwhile, I'm shrinking away from her, my skin pulsing red.

"But…but, Goddess…!"

"It's your job to start things off right by setting the mood. Isn't that right, everyone?"

She seals off my only hope of escape by appealing to the villagers surrounding us.

I can't go against the wishes of people who want her to be happy. All of them are nodding, urging me to take the first step.

I glance over at Aiz with sweat rolling down my face…She's staring back at me. It's almost like she's waiting to hear my answer.

I feel like I'm surrounded on all sides, trapped in a pincer of monumental proportions…but in the end, I can't go against the goddess.

"…W-would…would you dance with me, Goddess?"

I bring my hands together in front of my red face. The goddess looks back up at me with a satisfied smile that stretches all the way across her face.

"Whoa!"

Her thin, soft fingers wrap around my wrist.

She leads me by the hand, almost like a child, toward the bonfire.

The villagers give us an energetic send-off—I can't see Aiz's face, though—and we join the ring of young men and women.

Holding each other's hands, we start to mimic the movements of the folk dance already in progress.

"Th-this is pretty hard."

"Ah, aha-ha-ha-ha…"

"Bell, would you take the lead so I can focus on building up my divine energy?"

I'm trying to pick up the dance without staring at the couples around us, but it's not as easy as it looks. The two of us awkwardly drift around the bonfire with the rest of the dancers. I feel like a fish out of water, but the goddess seems so happy, dancing away with her hands in mine.

The light of the bonfire illuminating half her beautiful face, the skin beneath her villager's clothing is bright red. We spin around in time with the beat, and I feel the heat of the flames on my cheeks. However, I don't think that's the real reason my body feels so hot.

She smiles at me, so genuinely happy. I can't help but do the same. Sparks from the bonfire dance high into the air. Our shadows drift across the trees and nearby mountainsides. I feel her warmth through my hands.

The older villagers are watching us, singing and clapping along as we continue to dance.

"Whew..."

My dance with the goddess around the bonfire doesn't conclude until after many, many more verses.

Finally satisfied, the goddess releases me and goes to join a group of kids trying to learn the steps to the folk dance.

I start to ask her not to push herself...but one look at the kids' excitement and I hold my tongue.

A smile grows on my lips as I watch the goddess teach a little girl, probably of mixed descent, the dance. The joy on that kid's face... She's having the time of her life.

"Wait a minute, where's Aiz...?"

The festival really came to life the moment Lady Hestia decided to participate. Everyone looks like they're having a great time as I search the crowd to find Aiz...There she is. Standing next to a nearby house like a wallflower—well, maybe not a wallflower, but pretty close.

I jog over to her.

"Um, Miss Aiz."

"...Yes?"

She's watching the dance from a distance, almost like she's trying not to be seen. It takes her a moment to respond. Even her posture makes her as small as possible.

"Everyone looks like they're having a great time..."

A little human girl is dancing with her father; an animal mother is scolding her son as the giddy little boy runs circles around her.

Aiz squints, as if all of the villagers' smiles are bright lights flashing around her.

"...Your dance was very good."

"Eh...Th-thank you."

"…You're…a great dancer."

"I-if you say so…"

" …"

" …"

An unexpected compliment brings an abrupt end to the conversation.

Aiz hasn't stopped looking at the bonfire. She's not trying to make eye contact with me. That's normal for her, but still…

"Ah, um…Are you going to dance?"

"Everyone's having a good time…I don't want to ruin their fun."

"You won't!"

"And…I have no one to dance with."

Her words were no louder than a whisper, but they blasted their way into my head. I come to a conclusion after a few moments of getting my thoughts together.

Cheeks flaring again, I work up the courage to speak.

"If…If you consider me worthy…"

With those words, Aiz finally looks in my direction with her eyes open wide.

"…You'll…dance with me?"

"Ah, yes, but that's only if you're okay with it…?"

She watches with unblinking eyes as I turn even redder.

A few heartbeats pass and I slowly extend my hand——

"—Boom!!"

"Ah."

"Uphh!"

The goddess's tackle blindsides me, nailing me in the ribs.

"What's this, Wallensomething? You have no one to dance with? I'd be happy to dance with you right now!"

"…Thank you?"

Ignoring my stumble to the side, the goddess grabs Aiz's hand and doesn't take no for an answer.

Aiz blinks several times in confusion as Lady Hestia guides her toward the bonfire.

Then they start to dance.

One, a cute youthful goddess; the other, a beautiful young girl with a mysterious air about her.

Twin black ponytails and long blond hair sway with the two figures, gleaming in the light of the bonfire. Wearing the same style of clothing, they look like close sisters.

The dance shared by the dazzling young goddess and the elegant young girl receives the loudest applause of the night.

Men and women, the elderly and the children—everyone in the village claps their hands and smiles at the two beautiful girls.

My grin widens every moment that I watch them, to the point I have to open my mouth to contain it on my face.

Surrounded by so many happy faces, the two are surprised when they first notice…but then smile back with just as much joy.

The gladness continues long into the night. The festival maintains its celebratory atmosphere, the goddess happily beaming along with everyone else until the bonfire goes out.

The festival is winding down.

The goddess, Aiz, and I are resting in a corner of Edas Village.

"Uwahh, that's enough running around for one day…I'm so tired."

"Th-that's why I told you to take it easy…"

The goddess listlessly takes a seat on the ground. She ended up spending the entire night dancing with those kids, so I'm not surprised. She wasn't even at full strength to begin with, and she pushed too hard. I remind her of that in a quiet voice.

Aiz, silently standing next to us, watches our short conversation with the tiniest of grins on her lips.

"Okay, then, what's our plan from here…?"

Plenty of men are still in the village square. They should be cleaning up, but most are drunk and still laughing among themselves. Letting them do their thing, I pose a question. The goddess, who had been massaging her shoulder while absentmindedly staring at the boulder-like black scales that mark the boundary between the village and the forest, looks up at me.

"Oh, I'm good to go. Took a bit longer than I hoped, but I can walk just fine now."

Aiz doesn't say anything at first. The top-class adventurer does, however, make eye contact with us and nod.

"We leave the village…tomorrow morning."

We'll make sure everything is ready tonight and then wait for the sun to rise before making a return to Orario.

Neither the goddess nor I object to Aiz's plan.

The three of us look around the village that we will soon be leaving, taking in the mountain scenery one last time.

"——My Lady!"

That's when it happens.

A shrill voice erupts from the back of the village at the same time a woman comes rushing toward us.

It's Kam's daughter, Rina. She comes up to us, and I can tell immediately something's wrong. She can barely breathe.

A monster's roar echoes off in the distance. Hearing the beast's ominous howl and seeing the tears threatening to fall from her eyes make my heart sink.

She places a hand on her chest as a tear breaks free. Her voice sounds forced and shaky when she finally gets the words out.

"Would you see my father off…on his journey to heaven?"

Aiz, the goddess, and I file into the room. Kam is in his bed, surrounded by all his adopted sons.

His face is a ghastly color, his eyes closed.

I stop cold. All traces of life are gone from him.

"…Father wanted to see you one last time."

One of his sons invites us to come forward. I'm speechless.

How can this be? I mean, I was talking to him like any other day just before the festival started—

"I understand what's going on with me better than anyone."

Is this what he meant…when he said that?

I still haven't moved. Aiz has her mouth clamped shut, and the goddess is holding her breath.

That's when Kam slowly opens his eyes.

"…Ohh, Goddess. Thank you so much…for coming…"

"…No need to be a stranger, Kam. You've done so much to help me that I would come running at your call."

Kam's weak gaze falls on the goddess first, and he smiles.

The goddess forces a bubbly grin and walks to the side of the bed.

"When I first met you, memories of my beloved goddess, Brigit, came back to me…"

The goddess's eyes fly open in surprise upon hearing the name of Kam's former goddess.

"Did you say Brigit? Blond hair, deep-red eyes—that Brigit?"

"Do you…know of her…?"

"You bet I do! Brigit's a good friend of mine! We used to play together all the time up in Tenkai; argued, too!"

A hint of surprise fills Kam's gaze. What a coincidence, to have a connection through our goddesses. "Is that right…" he says with a weak smile.

"She was ever so kind…Treating everyone fairly and loving a lowly human like myself."

"Say what? She did? Kam, you've been duped! She resorts to calling me 'Tiny' and all sorts of other names the moment she loses the upper hand in an argument. And she's barely a smidgen taller than me! I bet she just wanted to look good in front of you and made sure you didn't see how she really is."

"Ha-ha-ha…Really? I never knew."

I can tell Lady Hestia is trying to lift his spirits. Kam tries to laugh but fails.

Actually, just saying that much looks painful, like he's wracking every word out of his body.

The small smile he made completely disappears after a few moments, leaving his face blank and emotionless.

"Goddess, please tell me…Will I see her, once I arrive in heaven…?"

"…Brigit will find you, I'm sure of it. She's rather insistent about getting what she wants."

Kam hears those words.

Then speaks again, barely above a whisper…like he's talking to himself.

"I'm scared…Scared I won't meet her, scared to see her…So scared."

The light in his eyes wilts like the last petals of a flower as he gazes up at nothing in particular.

His last moments drawing near, Kam's one and only daughter bites her lip to keep from crying out.

"Lady Brigit, please forgive me…I couldn't protect you, please forgive…"

Kam weakly lifts his trembling right hand into the air. But only just, like he's using the last of his strength to reach out to heaven.

His sons must be unable to see their father burdened by intense guilt in this weak state, because they look away with their mouths clamped shut. Aiz and I avert our eyes and stare at the floor.

Then Lady Hestia steps forward.

She slowly wraps both hands around Kam's.

"Thank you, Kam. Thank you for your love."

The goddess's voice is completely different.

"_____"

Kam opens his eyes as wide as they'll go.

Aiz, I, and everyone in the room suddenly focus on Lady Hestia.

That's not her voice. The tone, the words, even the rhythm has changed.

It's like someone else is using her body, looking down on one child with a loving, affectionate gaze and speaking.

She must be using her knowledge of Kam's goddess to speak and act like she thought her acquaintance would.

"Even now…and forevermore, I shall always love you."

The goddess's voice is so rhythmic and smooth that she sounds like a loving mother putting her child to sleep.

A goddess's sonnet of love.

Tears fall from Kam's eyes.

"Hhhhha…!"

Eyes that should have been withered and dry are now glistening under the magic-stone lamps.

His lips tremble, like he's seeing something on the other side of his aimless gaze.

"Lady Brigit, I…I, too."

Love you.

Those were Kam's last words.

The last of the strength in the hand in Lady Hestia's fades away, and it goes limp in her grasp.

The tears of his adopted children start falling to the floor. His daughter hides her face in her hands, collapsing on the spot.

I'm crying, too.

The tears aren't stopping.

My vision blurs to the point that I can't really see the man whose spirit has just left us. I try to wipe the tears away with my arm.

Even Aiz is covering her face.

Lady Hestia squeezes his hand before gently placing it across his chest.

The countenance of the man who devoted his love to a goddess is by far the calmest, most at-peace expression I've ever seen in my life.

The moon's light is shining through the trees.

The howls of distant monsters are gone, leaving the forest eerily silent.

I found a small clearing among the trees and took a seat at the base of the closest one and leaned back against it. Haven't moved since.

"So this is where you've been, Bell."

The sound of leaves underfoot reaches my ears as I sit cross-legged, my head drooping. That voice…it's the goddess's.

We're north of the village, a ways into the forest.

After Kam died, I came to this spot by myself.

News of his passing traveled through Edas Village very quickly. Villagers who would normally be asleep gathered at his home right away. Everyone who saw him lying in that bed was devastated and shed more than their share of tears.

I…I couldn't take hearing all the sobbing and grieving voices…I needed to get away, to escape.

"…"

"…"

The goddess sits down next to me.

We sit in silence under the dark-blue night sky. My head still drooping, I try to speak.

"Goddess…"

"What is it?"

"Will Kam be able to reunite with Lady Brigit on the other side?"

The fate of the spirit that has left Gekai and returned to Tenkai.

I want to know if Kam really has a chance of seeing the goddess who was sent back before him all those years ago.

"…That might be…difficult. There are some of us, like Freya, who are special, but the fate of the children's spirits is the responsibility of the gods who control death. It's not like anyone can pick and choose which spirits they judge."

The spirits that travel to Tenkai get purified—returned to a pure "blank" state before being reborn into another life on Gekai.

The goddess explains the process to me, but I tighten my grip on my legs with every word.

Silence once again descends on the forest.

"—So then, children shouldn't fall in love with gods after all. Is that what you're thinking?"

"!"

My shoulders quiver.

Lifting my head, the goddess's smile is right there to greet my eyes.

"After what happened at the manor, I thought you were just too stubborn for your own good…but that's not it."

She looks at me with those blue eyes as if she can see through everything. They're only half open, a kind gaze.

"I forgot something very important about you. You can see pain that you've felt in others…and you're afraid to inflict that pain on anyone. Am I right?"

My head droops again.

She…She saw right through me.

"Is it the pain from your grandfather's death that's holding you down?"

It is.

With Gramps gone, leaving me alone, there was no warmth to be felt. I remember it all too well. I remember my heart feeling empty, all the pain I endured when he passed on.

I know the pain of those who are left behind.

I know how Kam felt. He was suffering all the way up until the moment he was saved by the goddess.

—However, the end will always come for mortals like us.

Through our own death and rebirth, we can forget the pain of our previous life.

—What about gods and goddesses?

They live forever, so there is no forgetting. There's no way for them to soothe the scars left on their hearts after we leave this realm.

From friend to family, family to lover, and lover to partner—the deeper the bond gets, the more special it becomes, the deeper the scar that will be left behind. Is there any way for deities to escape the torment of loss?

Gods and goddesses can't grow old with us.

They will be left behind without question.

So, falling in love with them will only make them suffer.

Is pain—agony worse than what I felt after losing my family—promised to the deities who develop those strong feelings for mortals?

Causing that much pain is scary. I'm afraid of the sadness, the anguish.

It's not the same as with two people—it's an emptiness that can be felt by only deities, who cannot die.

"—Bell. *Our love lasts but a moment.*"

That's what Lord Miach said. Lord Hermes said the same thing.

A deity's love is over in a flash. And an eternity of emptiness is waiting for them after that one second of love.

The price of one moment of bliss: everlasting pain and sadness.

That's terrifying.

The loss that I felt after Gramps passed away, possibly even worse, will continue for hundreds, thousands, millions of years.

Absolutely horrifying.

"…Bell. Please don't think too hard about this. We—"

Not possible.

I close my eyes.

I don't even try to listen to her words, staying quiet like a kid and letting her voice drift into background noise.

The scale of "forever" is impossible for me to comprehend. I just can't do it.

And if I were in their shoes—I couldn't deal with it.

Carry the burden of loss, even more painful than the one I felt, for the rest of eternity?

To make a deity carry that burden of loss?

If that's the price, it's better not to love at all.

It's the same as the romances between fairies and heroes. A romance between gods and mortals will never have a happy ending.

Us and them—we can't live the same life.

"…You know, Bell, gods and children might not be able to live out the same lives."

As if she had read my thoughts like a book, she hits the nail right on the head.

I keep my gaze down, but I feel her left hand on top of my right.

"But I will always be by your side."

"Huh?"

My drooping head is lifted by her kind words.

"No matter how old you get, even if you become a bald, wrinkly old man, I will always be with you. You think I would ever leave?"

She looks back at me, eyes overflowing with affection.

"And even if death forces us to separate…I *will* find you."

A smile grows on her face.

"No matter how many hundreds, thousands, millions of years it takes, I will find you after your rebirth…Even after you're no longer you, I'll still be at your side."

"_____"

Words have left me, but the goddess continues.

"When I find you, I'll say, 'Would you join my familia?'"

The day when we first met, she asked me the very same thing.

"——ah."

I think I'm going to cry.

My jaw clenches.

Body trembling, I look up at her and try desperately to keep the tears back.

She wraps both her arms around me and gently embraces my shoulders.

"Gekai and Tenkai are just places—they don't mean a thing. We're just like Brigit and Kam. I will come find you again."

Her arms softly wrap around my head.

And like a kid—no, even more pitiful than a kid—I sniffle in a last-ditch effort not to cry.

"I'm not the only one. Other gods' and goddesses' bonds with children like you can last forever."

She quietly whispers into my ear.

"After all, we are gods. We live forever, you know."

She pats my head, gently running her fingers through my hair.

"So please, Bell. Don't be afraid of our love."

—*Please don't run away from a deity's love.*

I can decline, I can accept, but *I must not be afraid*—that's what Lord Miach told me.

The dam breaks. Tears pour down my face. The fear that had been weighing so heavily on my heart is melting away.

Family, lovers, partners, love—I don't know what these feelings are. Love for a deity, even less so.

I don't know, but I try to put words to it.

"Goddess…I want to always, always be with you…!"

"Yes…"

She's holding me.

All I can do is cry, but she doesn't break away from the embrace.

"I will always be here, Bell."

Moonlight shines through the trees. In a forest under a dark-blue sky, I cry and cry into a goddess's chest.

"…"

She could hear the boy's trembling voice, his crying.

Aiz stayed close to him even after leading Hestia to his hiding place. She stood still, leaning against the other side of the same tree.

"Always…together…"

The goddess's words and the boy's emotions resonated in her ears.

She looked up through the thin branches and foliage toward the golden moon high in the sky.

"Mother…"

The word that tumbled from her lips faded into the night.

The air is thick with fog.

The sun is rising in the east, turning the night sky into day as Aiz, the goddess, and I depart from Edas Village.

We ended up staying one extra day for Kam's funeral, helping out with whatever we could.

On the fifth morning after we came here as refugees lost in the Beor Mountain Range, we say our last good-byes to the villagers and set a course for Orario.

The oldest of the villagers showed us a route that he always took, one of the black scales in hand, when we left the village. We were out of the forest in no time and quickly made our way down the steep cliffs to an even path that ran along the river, arriving just in time to see the morning sun peek over the mountains and inundate the scenery with light.

"That was a nice place…"

"Wouldn't it be great to visit them again?"

"…If you go, I want to come with…"

"Huh? Are…are you sure that's okay?"

"Yes."

"Hey, hold on a second there, Wallensomething! Don't make promises out of the blue! If you want to go, go with your own familia!"

The three of us walk side by side, talking.

Something sad happened, but even so, all of us are in good spirits. The goddess makes a ruckus, I try to calm her down, and Aiz watches us with the same aloof gaze. And a few smiles, too. The crisp mountain air fills our lungs as we make our way up the next mountain road.

The morning fog is starting to clear.

"—There you are."

"Whoa! Miss Asfi?!"

Whoosh! She pops out of the sky, lands in front of us with her white scarf in tow, and nearly scares the crap out of me.

The golden wings on her sandals contract as a look of relief spreads across her face.

"I've been searching for you. I never feared for your lives, knowing the Kenki was with you, but…"

"You've been out here since then…?"

"No, only since last night, Goddess Hestia. Rakia's army had to be dealt with."

She adjusts her glasses and tells us what happened after we got separated.

Apparently, Asfi managed to escape the battle with the soldiers and return to the city. She passed along the information she gathered to Finn, who then organized the gods and goddesses of Orario into a strike force that prioritized capturing Lord Ares. Rakia's army sustained a great deal of damage and couldn't move at full speed due to the sheer number of soldiers who couldn't walk on their own. Asfi tells us that top-class adventurers caught up to them with ease.

The soldiers who didn't enter the mountains managed to escape, but the Alliance succeeded in capturing their leader, Lord Ares, yesterday. The outcome of the war was determined the moment their god was officially a prisoner inside Orario's walls. With that out of the way, the Alliance changed its focus to finding us. However, quite a few of the deities lost interest at that point and pulled their followers from the search-and-rescue mission.

Asfi was under orders from Lord Hermes himself to continue the search and is now smiling as if a great deal of weight has been lifted from her shoulders.

"I can carry all of you one by one using Talaria, if you so desire. What say you?"

"Hmm—…Well, this is a good chance to stretch my legs. It's not every day I get to be outside the city, so I feel like walking."

The goddess politely declines Asfi's offer. Aiz and I feel the same way.

"As you wish. I'll go on ahead and deliver the news. There are many in Orario who are concerned about your well-being, and I wouldn't want to keep them waiting."

She says this with a grin and takes a black helmet out of the pouch strapped to her waist. She puts it over her head and suddenly, she disappears.

The goddess and I are floored—Aiz looks fine, like she already knew about this—as the sound of flapping wings fills the air around us. Even that sound is gone moments later.

I suppose that's Perseus…With a combination of magic items like those, it's no surprise that very few people in Orario know about her ability to fly.

But wait, going invisible…haven't I been on the short end of the stick of an item like that before…?

Memories of a certain rogue threatening to come to the surface send a wave of cold sweat down my back. The goddess then speaks up in a cheerful voice.

"Now, I think it's about time we went home to Orario! I know a few children who have been worried for far too long!"

"Yes!"

"…Wallensomething, um, thanks. I'm, well, grateful."

"No problem…"

Aiz and I smile at the goddess as she says thank you.

The moment lasts a bit too long for the goddess, so she takes a few steps ahead of us to escape.

Aiz and I walk right behind her.

The goddess nearly trips, and the two of us barely manage to catch her. We walk through the mountain roads illuminated by the morning glow and finally down the last steep cliff to where the Labyrinth City is waiting for us on the other side of the open plain.

EPILOGUE **BIRTHDAY**

After Bell, Hestia, and Aiz safely returned to Orario, the war with Rakia came to a swift conclusion.

The battalion of soldiers that came too close to Orario sustained heavy losses in the battle against the Kenki. Without his escort, Ares was cornered and captured as soon as Orario's reinforcements arrived, thanks to Asfi's intel.

The deity became separated from his second-in-command, Marius, during the ensuing chaos. With that, the one known as God of War was taken all the way to the Guild's front lawn.

"Usually, this kinda thing would call fer sending ya back to Tenkai. But, like always, we'll spare ya. There's a lot of kids in Rakia who'd be in one heck of a pinch without ya. So in exchange, you're gonna release the Statuses of all the kids we caught from yer army."

"Wh-what is the meaning of this, Loki?"

"Plain as day. I'm not lettin' ya take all the excelia yer kids got from fightin' mine back across that border willy-nilly."

Thanks entirely to the kindness of Orario's adventurers—with the one exception of the battalion deployed by the warmongering familia—the Rakian army suffered very few casualties. Orario's staunch demand as this "play war" came to an end was that Rakia's soldiers didn't receive for free the benefits of the excelia gained during battle.

The Statuses of nearly 10,000 soldiers were to be released—and subsequently sealed by the gods and goddesses of Orario after Conversion. It went without saying that Ares fiercely rejected these terms, however. "Want a one-way ticket back up top?" Loki's threat sent tears of sorrow down his cheeks and he gave in to their demand. He spent the entirety of the next day releasing one Status after another outside the city wall. Ares wasn't allowed to sleep or even take a break until he finished. The God of War struggled to breathe, his hand shaking as he completed the required rituals to release his followers.

Rakia paid for this war and Ares's release with the Statuses of 10,000 soldiers, a substantial loss on any scale.

Their god, ranking higher than any general, was being held hostage by Orario. No matter what the city demanded, they had to accept and deliver.

Rakia had gone to war against Orario many times before, but the capture of their god resulted in the heaviest losses in the history of their country. A fed-up Marius came out to meet them during their march of shame back to their homeland.

The curtain fell on the Sixth Orario Invasion in a complete and total loss for Rakia.

It was peaceful inside Orario's city walls from start to finish.

"We're finally home..."

After separating from Aiz and passing through the north gate, Hestia sighed to herself but smiled as well.

Walking side by side with Bell, she took in the cityscape with relaxed, half-open eyes.

"...Bell."

"Yes."

"Always together, yes?"

"—Always!"

Bell's voice resounded with confidence as he made eye contact with the goddess looking up at him and smiled.

Taking her outstretched hand, the boy and his goddess emerged from the inside of the gate.

They were immediately greeted by the jubilant tears of their family members, divine friends, and comrades who had shared in the adventure. The two of them waved at the group of people rushing to meet them.

A blue sky spread out over the Labyrinth City again today.

Deep underground.

In the middle of the labyrinth that spread out in all directions through many twisting and turning paths, there was a wooden maze that resembled the interior of a giant tree.

Bluish green moss covered the walls and ceiling, making the area look like a hidden world yet to be explored.

Ominous howls echoed from somewhere off in the distance, sending a tremor through the intricate pathways of the labyrinth.

Out of nowhere—*crack!*

A wall fissured in a corner of the maze. A new monster was about to be born.

Crack, crack. A web of lines worked its way through the mossy wall. A light blue–skinned arm was first to emerge.

Soon a shoulder of the same color, then a neck and head followed. An upper and lower body then fell out of the wall and tumbled to the ground below.

Its body was similar to that of a human girl: four limbs and a smooth body. Its shoulders, waist, and a few other areas were covered in countless scales.

Long, bluish silver hair flowed down from its head, swinging from side to side as the creature slowly got up from its facedown landing spot.

The strikingly beautiful monster had dark-red eyes that sparkled like gems in the dim light. It shifted its distant gaze up toward the ceiling, which was blocked by the leaves of many trees.

Its slender, delicate throat vibrated.

"…Where is…this?"

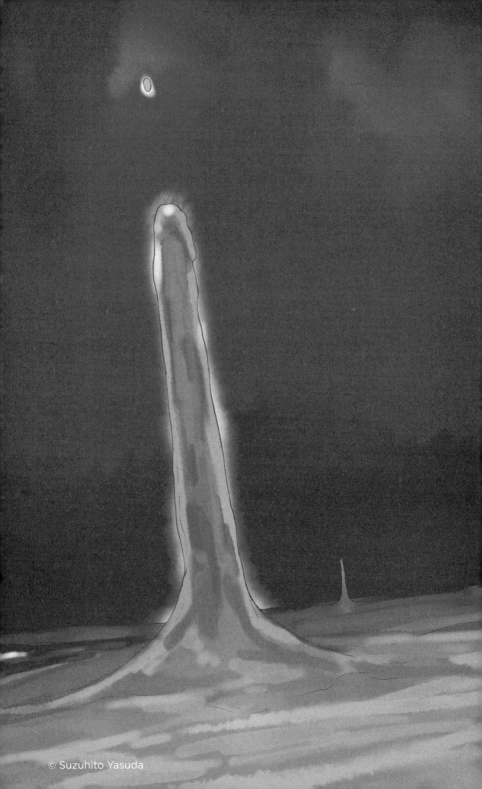

【BELL ✦ CRANELL】

BELONGS TO: *HESTIA FAMILIA*
RACE: HUMAN
JOB: ADVENTURER
DUNGEON RANGE: EIGHTEENTH FLOOR
WEAPON: HESTIA KNIFE
CURRENT WORTH: 301,000 VALIS

STATUS

Lv. **3**

STRENGTH: E 433   DEFENSE: E 423   DEXTERITY: E 437
AGILITY: C 647   MAGIC: F 391   LUCK: H   IMMUNITY: I

《MAGIC》

【FIREBOLT】
- SWIFT-STRIKE MAGIC

《SKILL》

【LIARIS FREESE】
- RAPID GROWTH
- CONTINUED DESIRE RESULTS IN CONTINUED GROWTH
- STRONGER DESIRE RESULTS IN STRONGER GROWTH

【ARGONAUT】
- CHARGES AUTOMATICALLY WITH ACTIVE ACTION

《PYONKICHI・MK-V》

- FORGED BY WELF, FIFTH IN THE SERIES.
- TIRED OF SEEING THE ARMORS HE FORGED CONSTANTLY DESTROYED, HE HAS TAKEN MANY STEPS TO IMPROVE HIS FORGING TECHNIQUES AND IMPROVE HIS FUTURE WORKS.
- WHAT LITTLE SAVINGS HE HAD WENT INTO THE PURCHASE OF "METAL RABBIT PELT." THAT WAS COMBINED WITH "DIR ADAMANTITE" TO CREATE THIS NEW ARMOR.
- THE INCREDIBLY DURABLE MATERIAL WAS ARTIFICIALLY ALTERED TO REDUCE ITS WEIGHT WHILE ALSO IMPROVING ITS DEFENSE ATTRIBUTES.

Afterword

Even while claiming this would be a collection of everyday stories, the eighth installment of the series went over 500 pages. To all my readers, I sincerely apologize.

My original idea was to write individual romantic stories involving mortals and gods.

However, once I put pen to paper, ideas flowed out of my head in droves.

To be completely honest, thoughts on how to add to already-published volumes also came to me one after another. No battle scenes, no traveling through the Dungeon...It amazes me that I couldn't adhere to these rules, and it became painfully obvious how much more I have to learn. At the end of the previous installment, I wrote that I would take my time and do some "light, everyday stories" so I could take it easy. Unfortunately, writing this volume didn't allow me to get any rest.

Romantic comedies are deep. I sincerely believe that.

The depth of each character's emotions and the intricate layers of conflict don't translate into words very well at all. There are times when even I can't fully wrap my mind around what the male and female characters are thinking, resulting in extremely detailed expressions and long explanations that required extra pages to express. I got caught in that spiral and was never truly able to escape.

On the other hand, there are many good things that came out of writing this volume.

One handsome deity said, "Our love lasts but a moment," through the power of my pen.

There were many things I was unsure of when creating love stories between mortals and gods, such as what was truly important. But I like how it turned out. Thanks to that, I believe it rounds out the story very well. Also, I never had much of a chance to write about the everyday life of the citizens of Orario. It was fun to get that opportunity.

Now the time has come for me to express my gratitude.

To my supervisor, Mr. Kotaki; to my illustrator, Suzuhito Yasuda; and to everyone involved, I must first apologize for delaying the deadlines as much as I did. It's thanks to all your hard work that it came together so well in the end. Thank you so much. Also, I must thank you, the reader, for picking up such a thick book and reading all the way to the end.

The second arc of the story is now complete.

I will go the extra distance to make sure that the next book, the start of the third arc, is just as exciting and enjoyable as the previous installments, if not more so. Please come along for the ride.

With one final thank-you, I'll take my leave.

Fujino Omori